Shores of Thunder Lake

By

M.K. Ernst

a

PO ET

First edition January 2019
Revision April 2019

Table of Contents

Acknowledgement

There are many people who participated in bringing this story to life. To Bill, who instigated this crazy idea of buying a resort in 1995. That experience became the backbone for this novel. To our dear friends who partnered with us those first years, we couldn't have done it without you and your help. Thank you to those who helped with editing and revising, and Josh, for the wonderful book cover. Becky Ann, who edited this for punctuation errors--wow, what a job you bravely took on--a very special debt of gratitude. All these contributions to my effort in publishing this book are much appreciated.

*To my family and friends
who wanted me to get back into painting again;
This is my latest painting,
created not with brush strokes but with words.*

This lake is so huge it's been likened to a freshwater inland sea. The surface of the lake changes from rolling waves to solid ice. The colors change from storm's steely grey to winter's blinding white; from summer's sky reflecting its ultramarine blue to being set afire as it mirrors the sinking sun.

Though weather and nature affect Thunder Lake, the greatest force this mighty lake reckons with is people. The people who call her shores home are varied and unique; native Ojibwe, sports fishermen, the wealthy and the poor, business owners and tourists. All rub shoulders as they live, work and play on the shores of Thunder Lake.

Chapter One

The Winter of 1996

The winter of 1996 broke numerous records throughout January and February. Tower, Minnesota, embarrassed Embarrass, Minnesota, with its record-shattering temperature of −60 degrees.

At a farm in northwestern Minnesota

It was a brisk morning in February 1996. Inside a small farm shed, a litter of plump, content Labrador pups slept in a heap next to their mother. One round yellow pup nuzzled against the fat, warm little bodies that surrounded her. They intertwined together—a black paw rested on top of her head, a brown scrunched face burrowed into her side. She opened her eyes, blinked a few times, and then something above caught her attention. Her tiny blue eyes followed dust particles as they floated suspended on beams of sunlight streaming through a window above her pen. The aroma in the shed filled her twitching nostrils. She stretched her muzzle out of the heap and smelled the cold morning air. The small shed was filled with the earthy scent of bird and rodent droppings, dusty dry straw, and old burlap sacks. With her head stretched above her furry cocoon, the only yellow pup of the litter was startled by the icy morning air. She burrowed her head into the furry heap again; the new day's adventures could wait a little longer.

****

On this same day, ninety miles to the east, Jed Porter climbed out of bed and walked to the kitchen window to look out at the great white expanse of Thunder Lake. Jed was a handsome man in his late 30s. He wore his full beard well. With his broad shoulders and

10

back, he was built like a French explorer. He could have passed for Kevin Costner if someone saw him in L.A. where one might expect to see Kevin Costner. But, it was Jed Porter who was stuck in this frozen northern Minnesota wilderness. Jed gave an involuntary shudder as he noticed the outside thermometer attached to the window frame. It read –56 degrees. He stared out in disbelief and concern. Jed and his wife Carmen were resort partners with their good friends, Will and Libby Edwards. The two couples had been friends for years prior to buying the resort, though this crazy venture they had gotten into was straining their close friendship.

The four friends had taken the adventurous step of walking away from their varied careers and buying Safe Harbor Resort together a little over a year ago. This hare-brained idea sprouted from a weekend at the cabin the two couples owned together in Wisconsin. Will and Libby announced one evening around a campfire that they had decided it was time for them to leave the Twin Cities' rat race. They had been living and working in the Minneapolis/St. Paul area for eighteen years, their two kids were grown, and they wanted to start a new life up in northern Minnesota. As they shared their adventurous plans with the Porters, who lived near Chicago, the whole idea took on a life of its own. Maybe it was the champagne they had consumed by the fire, maybe it was the disillusionment that they all felt about their careers…whatever it was, it started a midlife adventure for the two couples.

They had muddled through their first season of resort ownership. When they first opened the lodge store, none of them had run a cash register in twenty years. The lodge business and scheduling was still done with pencil in a three-ring binder. Will, the most computer savvy, eventually got them set up with a program of sorts on the computer for handling cabin rental, rates, and invoices for the guests' weekly stay. Carmen and Libby struggled through the back-breaking work of learning the skill of cleaning sixteen cabins in six hours. They couldn't have done it without experienced cleaners who stayed on at the resort after they bought the business. Jed and Will learned more than they ever wanted to know about septic systems, docks, bait tanks, plumbing, fish guts, and road maintenance. They barely made it through those first seven months: getting the resort ready for the season and then the running of the business from mid-May to mid-October. Then began the long winter up in the northern Minnesota wilderness. There was plenty to enjoy: silent snow falls, cross country skiing, snowmobiling and ice fishing. The downside was winter snows began in October and sometimes lasted until May. Entertaining yourself with outdoor activities, watching the birds flock to your feeders, reading books, and watching TV kept you occupied for only so many days. Eventually severe cabin fever set in and you started to question your sanity.

This was their first winter since purchasing the resort the previous April. While the Edwards had gotten away for a month, visiting family in California and Nevada, Jed and Carmen endured this record-breaking winter without escape. They had been concerned about spending money on travel when the business finances seemed uncertain at best. They also feared leaving sixteen cabins and two homes unattended. They felt better watching over the place and taking reservations they hoped would come in the month of January. The Porters watched with dismay as the snow continued to pile up on the sixteen cabins and two house roofs until it measured three feet in places that first month of 1996. Eventually, they decided, grudgingly, they needed to shovel the deep snow off all eighteen roofs, one by one, and then they cleared the six, already leaning, sheet metal boat slip covers in the harbor. It was a good thing they stayed home as the temperature plummeted to dangerous lows that month. They checked the heat in both homes often and the propane in the huge cylinder tanks to the homes. In such frigid temperatures as minus forty or lower, the propane could actually freeze, cutting off fuel to their homes. There had been lots to keep them busy while Will and Libby enjoyed the sunny southwest.

*****

But now it was the end of February and Will and Libby were back in their home down the hill from Jed and Carmen. The Porters were relieved that the responsibilities of the resort would be shared again.

Jed turned from the frosty window, and started the coffee. Then he walked out to the chilly entry where an old wood burning stove sat. He used a poker to stir the embers then filled the box with wood and closed the heavy door with a thud, swinging the handle around to lock the door tight. He knew Carmen would not want to get up until she felt the heat from the wood-burner creep its way back to their bedroom.

It was true, Carmen was finding it hard to toss back the warm down comforter and leave the comfort of their bed. She knew Jed was up, but she didn't want to face another day of northern Minnesota's frigid brutality. She struggled with the same question every morning during this cold winter: *Why had they come up to this frozen wilderness? Why had they quit their secure government jobs for a rundown, sixteen-cabin resort that only promised years of scrubbing, painting, repairing and uncertain financial security? What were they thinking?*

She pulled the covers over her face and tried to dream of better, or at least warmer, days. *"Maybe she'd call her mom once Jed had the fire roaring and she could smell the coffee. Talking to her always made Carmen feel a little less isolated."*

Carmen finally roused from under the covers. She visited the bathroom, grimacing as she sat on the cold toilet seat. She inspected herself in the mirror and, after a cursory running of her comb through her thick brown hair, she walked out to find Jed in the kitchen. He was pouring himself a cup of steaming coffee. Jed placed his coffee mug back on the counter and put his arms around his lovely wife. Carmen was still that beautiful, sparkly-eyed woman he had met eight-years-ago when they worked for the State of Wisconsin. At work she was all business and by-the-book, but the more he got to know her, it was plain to see she was as warm and caring a woman as you could hope to find. Carmen had two children from a previous marriage who Jed soon loved as his own. They married after a few years.

******

Carmen kissed Jed's kind, bearded face. "Mornin' baby," she tried saying with as much exuberance as she could muster.

Jed knew her cheery countenance was for his benefit. He feared living in this ice-box was driving her into a depression--or worse, might just drive her crazy. He remembered a year ago when the two couples walked the grounds of the old resort. It was in mid-January, and he thought the resort's north woods setting was awe-inspiring, and the monstrous 100,000-acre lake was breathtaking even in its frozen state. But the more they walked the grounds the more panic he felt roiling up from his gut. Where was that panic coming from? He didn't understand at the time. He remembered feeling like Jack Nicholson in the "Shining," --that he would go insane up here in this wild territory. Maybe it had been a premonition of Carmen's going insane. Now, as he hugged his wife tighter, he pleaded in his heart, *Spring has to come early this year. Please.*

******

Down the sunlit hill, crisp and white with new fallen-snow, lived Will and Libby Edwards. They sat, drinking their morning coffee at their dining room table. Their large windows looked out on a wintry February wonderland. The old resort was a sight to behold. Safe Harbor Resort had a beautiful northern Minnesota setting. Gentle rolling hills supported giant white pine, towering 100 feet or more. Tall majestic stands of birch trees filled the woods with vertical white trunks while four-foot deep jewel-encrusted snow blanketed the grounds. Beyond the old resort harbor lay an immense two-foot thick sheet of ice that held Thunder Lake captive until May.

Will took a bite of his toast as he watched the morning news. Then his attention was drawn to the snowy scene outside their window. Libby's attention was averted too. A squirrel scampering on a high, snowy branch loosened a clump of snow causing a small avalanche to fall to the ground. Will was amused by how often he and Libby did things at the same time. Like reaching for his cup of coffee and seeing Libby reach for hers. He would tease her by putting his cup down without taking a sip. She would notice what he did and give him her knowing smirk. They spoke the same words simultaneously and finished each other's sentences. Will, a strong, intelligent, hardworking man in his forties, had spent twenty years of his life in front of a computer monitor and twenty-three years married to Libby.

Will, Libby and Carmen had known each other since tenth grade. They had all been good friends throughout high school, but Will realized by his senior year that there was more to his feelings for Libby than just being her friend. Libby enjoyed Will's quick wit and heart-melting good looks, but most of all she was comfortable in their friendship. When Will professed his true feelings for her back in high school, Libby soon realized she felt more than friendship for him. From then on they were inseparable. They married at nineteen, and had two children by the time they were twenty-three. They managed somehow to survive, being children themselves, raising two children, and staying in love with each other.

Their two children were grown. Becky, twenty-one, lived and worked in Minneapolis and Josh, nineteen, was finishing his last year in a graphic arts program in St. Paul. They missed their children and worried about them, but regardless of how they felt, they both knew it was good for Becky and Josh to learn to live on their own. Lord knows, she and Will had to grow up at nineteen. They hoped their children would not marry as young as they did. Their young marriage had worked for them but statistics told another story.

Libby took her last swallow of coffee. Her attention focused on the honey bottle shaped like a bear sitting in the middle of the table. She said, as much to herself as to Will, "I think we should name her Honey Bear."

Will looked over at his wife and smiled at her. He still adored Libby for the same reasons he fell in love with her in high school. She had the biggest brown eyes, long brown hair, and just enough mystery to keep him guessing. Their personalities were so different. He, so quick thinking and quick to react; impatient and a tease more times than Libby liked. She was more the creative thinker, slow to react, sensitive and uncommunicative more times than Will liked. There were times they exasperated each other but more and more they were learning to love the other even in their incompatibility. Will had grown to appreciate Libby's quiet ways although sometimes he wished he could read her mind. She was a seeker of the unseen, a non-religious follower of Christ. Will's faith was strong, but he rarely took the time to do much meditating or soul searching. He was a man of action, and patience was a virtue he was still working to improve.

Will responded to Libby's suggestion of "Honey Bear" for a name. "Sounds cute, but maybe we won't find a puppy we like. Remember, we agreed we wouldn't take one home today because we have to go to the Cities to help Becky move into her new apartment this weekend. How could we take a puppy down there?"

Libby had remembered. She looked a little disappointed but agreed that it was best to wait.
Will was teasing her. Of course, he knew they would be bringing a puppy home today.

He thought, *How could we possibly look at little Labrador puppies and not bring one home?*

******

At the hobby farm, the little yellow pup felt a great movement from her furry cocoon. Her mother, a three-year-old Chocolate Labrador named Sienna, rose from her lying position with seemingly little regard for her suckling pups. There was an eruption of grunts and high- pitched whines from her tiny offspring. Fat wobbly bodies tried to get to their feet while others collapsed in drug-like sleepiness. Sienna stood alert hearing human footsteps. She recognized her master's heavy boots as they crunched in the hard-packed snow leading to the shed. All the dogs cocked their heads and stared expectantly at the door latch. When the footsteps stopped in front of the shed door, Sienna's tail began wagging even harder, which started her rear swaying, and the front of her body followed. Her ears perked in excitement, and she barked excitedly as the shed latch clinked and the door swung open allowing even more brittle morning air to waft in. Her master's kind face appeared in the open doorway. Sienna moaned with pleasure at seeing him.

Mona and Tom Olsen, had been raising Labrador retrievers for fifteen years. They had a small hobby farm outside of Heron Lake, both working jobs in town in order to keep their little farm going. They had a couple of horses, a large pen for a dozen fancy chickens, an undetermined number of barn cats, and three Labradors, all female, two black and one chocolate. Sienna, the chocolate lab, started into labor in the wee hours of January 1st. It had now been seven weeks since that long night.

Sienna had her first litter a year ago. She had six pups that lived; two others were still-born. She fed and groomed her little family, tenderly caring for them, and teaching them how to care for themselves. Then one by one they were taken from her. She didn't quite understand what it was she *read* in her caregiver's eyes back then. She had heard the assurance in her humans' voices but it nevertheless, was concerning to have her little offspring picked up and carried away. She was calmed by the reassuring feelings coming from Tom or Mona. When they spoke to her, she understood what they were saying most of the time. It seemed she could understand their thoughts, or some *sense* coming from them. Their words and caring alleviated her sadness.

Now again, Sienna *read* in Tom and Mona's thoughts in recent days that her puppies were going to be taken from her one by one. Trust and obedience in her pack's "Alphas" was in her genetic makeup, and she would take whatever was ahead because they were in charge.

Tom bent down and hugged her to him, talking softly," Hey, old girl, good to see you too. You have a big day ahead of you." He looked into her eyes, and she read his concern. Her joy of seeing him was momentarily interrupted by the sense of concern she felt from him. It caused only one hesitant tail wag then back to full-body wags of joy.

****

The Edwards stopped by the house on the hill to check in with the Porters. Jed met them at the door and invited them in. In the foyer sat the little woodburner, a fire roaring bright behind the glass door. It was plenty warm especially for the Edwards in their coats, hats and gloves.

"So, we are on our way to look at darling lab puppies!" she said excitedly.

"You guys haven't changed your minds about going along have you?" Will asked.

Jed and Carmen looked at each other not knowing what to say.

"Well, Jed, what have you decided?" Carmen inquired expectantly. "You know if I go, I'll break down and get one but, Jed, I want this to be your decision. You are still unsure, I can tell."

Jed let out a really deep sigh and finally said, "Maybe I'll tag along. See if I connect with one of those little buggers."

Carmen smiled at him and said, "Okay, baby. Whatever you decide is good with me."

While Jed got himself bundled up to go outside, Libby asked Carmen one more time about coming along.

Carmen assured Libby. "No. I'll be fine. I'm going to call my mom today, and I have some laundry to do. I also want to finish painting the wood plaques for the cabin numbers."

Libby hugged her friend, "Okay, I won't pressure you. Enjoy your day." She walked to the door where Will was waiting patiently-- or at least *trying* to be patient. She turned to Carmen once again and said, "I am so excited and yet nervous about seeing those puppies. It's such a big commitment, but for us, life without a dog is really hard. I guess we are just crazy dog people.

Carmen put her hand on Libby's shoulder and smiled reassuringly. "Yes, you two are crazy dog people, but that's a good thing."

The three travelers lumbered out the door in their heavy winter gear. Stepping carefully on the icy sidewalk to the driveway, they walked like tottering penguins. When they reached the car, Libby argued with Jed about taking the front seat because there was little room in the back for his longer legs. He finally acquiesced and sat in the front because Libby had already climbed in the backseat. As they headed west towards the Labrador breeder's farm, Will and Libby reminisced about their first retriever that shared their home for 13 years as Jed sat quietly listening in the front seat.

She was a mutt by breeder standards but that didn't affect the personality and intelligence of "Golda". They guessed that she was part Great Dane, Labrador and Golden Retriever. Their daughter, Becky, was eight when they brought Golda home and their son, Josh, was six. When their cat, Johnson, a stray they had taken in a few years prior, first saw Golda being put down onto her kitchen floor, she arched her back and hissed. Then, with haughty cat confidence, sauntered over to the little newcomer and in one swift motion, swung her claw-extended paw into Golda's black nose. To everyone's horror, when Johnson walked away she left a portion of her curved claw in Golda's nose as testimony as to who would rule the other. This odd relationship between a five-pound cat and an eighty-five-pound dog lasted throughout Johnson's life--the former ruling the latter.

Thirteen years later, just after their first resort season ended, they did the hardest thing they'd ever done. Out of respect for their dear companion, Libby and Will put Golda to rest. She had lost her ability to walk any distance without her back legs giving out, and then the veterinarian suspected cancer. The doctor was kind enough to come to their home to do the deed. Golda passed peacefully in their home, her head laying in Libby's lap. Her grave now held a prominent place overlooking the harbor on the south side of their home.

Jed interjected, "Yeah, I remember that painful time. Watching you two grieve the loss of Golda has been a big part of my resistance to getting a puppy. Dogs worm their way into your heart and losing them is so hard. We lost our little terrier a few years ago and it's still painful to think about her."

Will and Libby nodded. There was silence in the car as they continued their journey. It had only been a few months since losing Golda and their sadness still felt like an open sore.

Will asked Libby to check the directions given by Mona Olsen. Libby read the directions out loud to Will. "Take a left when you come to county road 5, go two miles, and you'll see their place on the left. They have a white house and a big red barn. "

She rolled her eyes and said sarcastically, "Like everyone else out in this country." Then she read on. "The mailbox post has a Labrador sign attached above the box."

The northern Minnesota countryside is varied in its breadth and beauty. There are stands of pine and aspen towering and dense. The woods might give way to an open field covered in snow. Lakes are everywhere. Little lakes, maybe a hundred acres in size and larger ones, seven-hundred acres or more, caused the roads to run serpentine through the countryside.

They saw the mailbox with the Labrador sign and as soon as they turned in, they heard barking. Three Labs were pacing and barking in a large pen just off the house, their tails wagging, which severely contradicted their barks. Mona Olsen stepped out the back door to greet them.

"Have any trouble finding us?" she asked reaching out her hand in greeting.

"No problems. Good directions," Will said, as he shook her outstretched hand.

From the distant pen, Sienna watched anxiously as the three humans chatted and walked toward the shed that held her pups. Tom had taken Sienna to the big pen near the house to feed her earlier that morning so she would be separated from her litter when the prospective adopters arrived.

As Will, Libby and Jed stepped through the doorway into the low shed they could see the lively puppies and hear their grunts and whines. Libby smiled as she peered over the side of the wooden corral that kept the pups confined. She grinned wider and thought to herself, *Oh, so many little fat, wiggly, fur-balls.*

Black faces and brown faces looked up curiously at their arrival. There, right at the front of the pack, stretching to get over the pen was the only yellow pup of the bunch. She struggled, undeterred, to get over the wooden brace holding her in. Mona picked her up and handed her to Libby "She's the first yellow we've gotten so far and she's a pistol." Libby felt a lump in her throat and her eyes began to water as she smelled the warm puppy. Libby still longed for Golda and holding this little yellow girl made her miss her old friend even more. Will looked over his wife's shoulder and chuckled at the sight of the pup in Libby's arms. The little round face looked up at him, her brown eyes searched Will's brown eyes, and in an instant, made contact with his heart.

Jed meanwhile, was crouched next to the board that barricaded the opening to the pen. He watched as all the black and brown puppies poked their heads over the board, stretching their little bodies as they leaned against the barricade, yipping and whining at him. He hesitantly picked up a black one. As he picked it up he saw that it was a male. The little guy stretched his neck out to reach Jed's face. Jed pulled him in close and let the puppy sniff his ears and lick him. He was deep in thought about whether it was a good idea to bring the little guy home. Jed wished Carmen had come along. Taking home a puppy was a ten-to-fifteen-year commitment. The decision was so hard to make without her.

******

Libby put the yellow puppy down and she wobbled around the floor, her little legs could hardly hold up her round tummy. She sniffed the straw strewn around on the floor then nibbled on a piece that stuck to her paw. Once that task was done she squatted and soon a wet puddle spread beneath her. As the Edwards and Mona Olsen talked, they failed to notice that an almost empty burlap sack of birdseed propped in the corner was moving. The yellow puppy had spied the interesting sack on the floor and had grasped an end with her teeth, dragging and spilling its contents across the wooden floor. Growls and grunts issued from her as she pulled the seed sack over to their feet. "Yup, she's a pistol," Mona said as she walked over and picked up the pup and replaced the sack.

After watching the bold antics and caressing the plump, golden-colored puppy for nearly an hour, the Edwards made up their minds to take the little girl. Jed had been very quiet during all that time. He thought through the pros and cons of bringing the little black bundle home in his arms. Finally, he looked up and told everyone that he wanted to wait; he felt he shouldn't be making this big decision without Carmen. He said goodbye to the little guy and reluctantly put him back with his wiggly littermates.

The three friends *and Honey*--it was official, she was definitely a "Honey Bear"--began their trip back to the resort. Honey burrowed into Libby's jacket grunting and howling. With each mile the cries got louder and more heartbreaking. Finally Jed volunteered to try his hand at calming Honey. He wrapped her in his jacket and zipped it up. The howling finally subsided, and she slept peacefully next to his warm belly.

"Hey, you guys didn't buy a dog, you bought a pig," Jed exclaimed as he sniffed the strong odor coming from inside his jacket. Will looked over at Jed and smiled. He was very happy to have another furry friend in their lives again. He still remembered Golda's intelligence. She wasn't professionally trained, she just plain understood them after only a few years of living with them. Her loyalty was unquestioning. She always came when he called her, unlike the Airedale they had before Golda. It was as if she could read their minds and would react to their thoughts and actions. He had found this ability of hers to be a little spooky at times.

He would never forget the time when they were visiting Libby's sister in California. The whole family made that trip, even Golda. He remembered the old Dodge van they drove, traveling all the way from Minnesota. Golda was two-years-old and already eighty-five pounds. She shared the back of the van with Becky and Josh, and they loved having her along.

When they arrived at the log home of Libby's sister, Becky Ann, they were pleasantly surprised to hear that they would have use of a pool during their stay. Becky Ann was taking care of her neighbor's pool in their absence and the two sisters' families gathered there each day for a swim. Their first day at the pool was hot and everyone was enjoying the water except Golda. She was content to watch the kids as they played, making her rounds to check on her family and elicit a pat from the adults as they chatted together along the pool. Will remembers thinking that Golda had never been introduced to water and felt it was his duty to do the introducing. When Golda made her next round for affectionate pats, he surprised her by picking her up and throwing her in. She made a huge splash as she hit the water. The big dog sunk below the surface for a few seconds and then rose with a splutter. She was scared, but instinct took over and she swam a very awkward, splashy dog paddle to the side of the pool. She struggled to climb out of the pool where Will had thrown her in, but she couldn't get out. Will remembered well his feelings of regret at that point, and he quickly bent down and pulled her out in one swift lift. She shook the pool water from her coat, twisting her body from nose to tail and slunk away into the wooded area up from the pool. Everyone chastised Will for his rash treatment of poor Golda. They all tried coaxing the wet dog from her hiding place behind a tree but she refused to leave. They soon left her alone and went back to having fun by the pool. Later, Will felt a sharp pinch on his left ear lobe. Startled, he looked around and there was Golda, facing him intently. She did not waver, looking him straight in the eye, her tail gave a slight swish. He recognized right then her intelligence--it was in her eyes. She had gone off to sulk and to contemplate the injustice done to her, and while still dripping behind the trees, she must have decided she needed to impress upon her beloved family member her great disappointment in him. So she slunk down the hill unnoticed, circled around behind him and nipped him lightly but precisely on his earlobe. Looking into her eyes, Will understood without a doubt that he had hurt her trust in him. He vowed to never break that trust again.

Now they had chosen another yellow dog. Would she be as intelligent and personable as Golda? Time would tell.

As they pulled into Safe Harbor Resort with Honey Bear, Carmen came walking out of her warm house pulling on her down jacket, excited to greet them. When they all got out of the car she looked anxiously at what each was holding in their arms and was relieved to see that there was only one yellow puppy. Jed had not brought home a puppy. In one of life's many fateful moments, after talking with her mom earlier in the day, it was clear that her mom had had enough of her six-month-old Golden Retriever. She and Jed would need to talk seriously about whether they should take her mom's dog.

As they all stood outside and talked, they watched and laughed at Honey's clumsy antics and took turns nuzzling her into their jackets. Carmen had a feeling that they too would be bringing a dog to the resort; it might not be a little puppy but maybe be a young dog in need of a good home. She picked up Honey Bear and held her close.

"Ooh-wee, this little one needs a bath!"

Jed laughed, "I told them they brought home a pig instead of a pup!"

They all laughed at the little pup who smelled so strongly of the shed she had been living in along with her brothers and sisters.

When Libby got their new charge settled into their kitchen, she gave her a bath, wrapped her in a warm towel and put her in Will's lap as he sat in his recliner. The exhausted puppy soon fell fast asleep in the crook of his arm.

Libby started the next day less rested than most mornings. The lonely pup had not been a very happy camper during the night. They had placed her in a kennel in the kitchen with warm blankets and furry stuffed animals to comfort her, but she was not fooled. She missed her mom and her brothers and sisters. Libby knew the experts would say putting her in a kennel was the right way to train a dog, but she didn't think she could go through another night like that. Her mind was already made up. Tonight Honey would be sleeping next to her side of the bed in a box, snuggly warm in a blanket. She could then put her hand down by Honey to comfort her when she cried. She thought, *experts-shmexperts.*

Now that they were all up and together again, Honey was full of investigative curiosity. She made her way out to the back hallway and found what she thought looked an awful lot like her brothers and sisters; brown and black bodies along a wall. She pranced over to them, whining and grunting and snuggled into the pile. Libby heard the ruckus and peeked around the doorway to see Honey contentedly snuggled into their many winter boots. She grabbed the camera for the twentieth time since yesterday, to capture one more cute moment.

Libby was reaching for the camera when the phone started ringing. Will walked over to answer it. The noise of the rings startled Honey in her boot-nest but Libby captured the moment with a click of the camera. When Will hung up the phone he walked over to Libby and Honey to report that the Porters were taking off for Wisconsin to bring her mother's six-month-old Golden Retriever home to live with them. Things would certainly be different around here from now on.

Chapter Two

Losing Lilly

In 1988 a Thunder Lake Ojibwe son entered into his last year of
graduate school. He had been a determined young man in high
school. He managed to be liked by everyone and was a successful
athlete, while still achieving top grades. He had the brains but, more
importantly, the drive to pursue success beyond the limits of life in
rural northern Minnesota. After Lance Timberlake passed the bar
exam, there was an entry-level position awaiting him at a large firm
on the east coast.

*****

Now, eight years later, Lance found himself unexpectedly
returning to his people's village on the northern shoreline of Thunder
Lake. It was a tragedy that brought him back and love that kept him
there longer than he ever expected.

The decision to move back had not been an easy one for Lance.
The thought of putting himself back in the depressed village of his
youth was the last thing he thought he would ever do. It all started
with a call from his sister, River, on September 15, 1995, that turned
his life upside down. River's voice was broken and tortured by sobs
as she told him that their mother had suffered a severe stroke. He
rushed back to Minnesota and met up with his family in the Grand
Rapids Hospital where his mother clung to life. They didn't know the
full extent of the damage yet but it was bad. Because it had taken
two hours before his mother received medical attention, the damage
done in those hours had been extensive. His father, Jon, thought his
wife had eaten something that didn't agree with her. He encouraged
her to rest, thinking she'd feel better after a nap. Frustration still
plagued Lance as he thought back on his father's lackadaisical
concern in taking his mother to a hospital right away. But how could
his father have known the seriousness of waiting? Lilly had always
been the one to make medical decisions; Lance's father was
dependent on his wife's guidance in such things. Being unemployed

at forty-five years of age had taken a toll on his father's self-esteem. In the last few years he had become emotionally paralyzed because of depression. Jon Timberlake had been a strong, confident lumberjack for twenty years, when an equipment malfunction caused him to take a terrible fall, shattering his leg and cracking his skull. He was left with a permanent limp and a brain injury. After months of recovery, he tried a job as a delivery man for a lumberyard, but he couldn't talk right or move fast enough for their liking--he could overhear the construction workers comments about him being a "dumb, lazy Indian." These jibes made him angry and frustrated. He quit after the summer season and tried a job at the Thunder Lake Casino, but he wasn't there for long either. He told Lance on the phone a few months ago, "I know the casino is a boon to our people, but there is something about the atmosphere that brings bile to my throat and disquiet in my heart. My spirit grows weary in such a place of dinging machines, drunks and smoke." Lance loved his father but his frustration over his dad's depression and lack of purpose had been slowly driving a wedge between them. He hadn't understood what a burden his father had to carry.

****

When Lance finally arrived at the hospital that September, he was exhausted. It had been a tragic comedy of "Train, Planes and Automobiles." He had packed a small leather bag and flagged down a cab at eight o'clock at night, allowing himself plenty of time to get to the airport and board his flight to Minneapolis/St. Paul International Airport. After the long walk down the concourse to his departure area, he checked his watch and felt good that he had twenty minutes to spare. Then he looked up and noticed a big 'DELAYED' alert for his flight. It felt like he had been struck by lightning. He went to the attendant's desk in a panic.

"What is going on with flight 9539 to Minneapolis? Why is it delayed?"

"I'm sorry, but a mechanical problem was discovered on the plane just now, and it is something that can't be quickly fixed. Another plane is being flown in from Chicago to take over this flight.

It will be a four-hour delay. I'm sorry sir...we will get you on your way as soon as possible."

The attendant had been very calm and apologetic, but Lance was not reassured nor did he believe it would only be a four-hour delay. In the end, his flight got him to Minneapolis six hours later than he expected. Thankfully, he hadn't checked a bag or that would have probably been lost in the plane shuffle. He hadn't been able to sleep on the overnight flight as his mother's dire condition was heavy on his heart. Once the plane was on the ground and after the usual waiting for people and waiting in lines he was finally walking out the sliding doors of the airport. Renting a car went smoothly once the right airport bus arrived to take him to the car rental lot. Lance breathed another sigh of relief as he sat behind the wheel of his rental car, a 1995 Acura Integra. Then he reached the intersection onto the 494 loop and his tension headache escalated. The Twin Cities' morning gridlock held him up for another hour. By the time he was north of the Cities, he was already seven hours behind when he said he would get there. When he pulled into the Grand Rapids Medical Center parking lot he was frazzled and exhausted from his cross country ordeal. Lance walked through the doors of the hospital and made his first stop the restroom, then he stopped at the front desk to get the room number for Lilly Timberlake. After his long journey from Boston to Grand Rapids, Minnesota, he would finally reach his mom in room 354.

As Lance opened the door to his mother's room the scene before him will be forever etched in his memory: the pale lavender walls, his father and sister seated next to his mother's bed, and the heavy beige curtains drawn against the late afternoon sun. He paused, fascinated by the brilliant rays of light bursting through the space between wall and window curtains. He imagined for a moment that a host of angels might be levitating just outside his mother's window. As Lance stood taking in the surreal scene, his sister turned and, sobbing his name, immediately ran to him. River, was a petite, five-foot-two, twenty-two-year-old. Her small frame and long black hair made her look sixteen. As Lance held his little sister, he smelled her fresh clean hair as her head rested against his chest. He felt her deep sobs shake her small frame as he hugged her close. Then his intense brown eyes lifted to take in the sight of his beautiful mother, tubes and needles pumping and dripping the necessary fluids to keep her body from ultimate failure. His father stood up from his chair next to her bed. It was an awkward effort, his joints stiff from his long vigil. The two men locked eyes, tears welled up and glistened as they took in the other's pain. Jon spoke softly, "I'm so glad you're here, son." Lance walked over to his mother's bedside, bent down and kissed her forehead. There was no response from Lilly at her son's touch.

So began the long vigil. For two days they waited. Tests eventually determined that Lilly's brain had been deprived of oxygen during a seizure she endured while traveling to the hospital. There was little chance of her ever waking up. A week passed, then another--finally a decision to discontinue life support was made by Jon, Lance and River. On October seventh Lilly's spirit was free.

Lilly's memorial service was held at the little community chapel in Thunder Lake. There was standing room only in the sanctuary. The ladies of the chapel served food in the basement of the church after the graveside interment. There was such an outpouring of love and remembrance of Lilly's life that it overwhelmed the family. Jon Timberlake could not talk with anyone, choosing instead to be by himself at the cemetery.

Lance deeply regretted his initial anger at his father concerning the delay in getting his mother medical attention. Jon was beyond consoling after his wife's death. Lance and River watched their father slowly pull himself out of the world of the living. For weeks, he slept through countless days and sat alone in his and Lilly's bedroom night after night, staring out the window until dawn, when he would climb back onto their bed to sleep away another day. It was no surprise to Lance when he heard the heart-stopping **bang** in the night that freed his father, Jon Timberlake, from his hellish pain.

****

River had graduated from the U of M the previous spring, so without school to occupy her days, she felt lost in her sadness that winter. Lance too, feeling the deep loss of his parents, decided to stay in Thunder Lake temporarily, to be close to River, his only

29

remaining family. So in early November, he flew back to Boston to request a leave of absence from his firm. Then he packed up his apartment, putting most of his possessions in a storage unit to be retrieved someday--he wasn't sure when. The remaining possessions--clothes, books, a box of photos and his laptop--he packed into his Toyota Camry and headed west, back to Thunder Lake. He was leaving a successful career, good friends, and an unresolved, complicated relationship with a colleague at his firm. All these relationships were left abruptly dangling with little closure and therefore little comfort on the long drive home.

River and Lance began the task of going through their parents' belongings over the remaining winter months. It was a therapeutic time for them as good memories of their childhood came flooding back, such as the many times their mother took them on special picnics far into the woods. They recalled eating peanut butter and jelly sandwiches and munching on apples. When their bellies were full, their mother had them sit very still--so still that they could hear each other breathe. Then the sounds of the forest became a cacophony. They could hear a squirrel nibbling on their tossed apple cores. The numerous birds high above them were all singing their own songs. The variety of trills, whistles and chirps sounded like an orchestra warming up for a performance.

Lilly had been a wonderful mother to Lance and River. She instilled in her children a sense of purpose and grace in everything they did in their lives. Lilly's father was a tall, sandy-haired Norwegian. He fell in love with Lilly's mother, a beautiful, raven-haired Ojibwe. He was a professional fisherman, supplying the markets, and restaurants with walleye and whitefish. When they married, Lilly's father agreed that they should live on the reservation so that his family would feel comfortable with their Ojibwe people. The only request Lilly's father made was that they belong to the little Bible Chapel in Thunder Lake. This exposure to other people helped Lilly's family feel confident and in return accepted by 'white people'. In so many ways the love they felt there encouraged them to dream beyond existence on the reservation. The chapel's young pastor presented their faith in a way parallel to the Ojibwe beliefs. When Lilly heard about God's son and his teachings, belief in a Great

Spirit and respect for others and oneself she felt it spoke of a loving, caring God. They were taught that fulfillment of all their hopes, needs, and desires came from this Great Spirit. These teachings were so close to the Ojibwe truth that she was drawn to believe in this Son of God. Lilly had settled in her heart that Jesus truly was God come to earth, and she prayed to him for everything. Now as Lance and River discussed their mother's simple, earnest faith, the loss of her rushed over them afresh.

They reminisced about their father also. Jon had been only a shadow of himself after the accident that ruined his life as a lumberjack. But before that day, their father was robust and full of fun and laughter. They remembered how he and Lilly would dance under the moonlight in their backyard when they thought the children were asleep.

Lance and River remembered their old dog, Rusty, and how their father loved that dog. Rusty was a big German shepherd/collie cross and every day before Jon went to work he would remind Rusty to keep an eye on his kids. Rusty did just that. He stayed with them as they played in the woods behind their home. If Lance would get too adventuresome, straying too far from their home, or take River too close to the lake, Rusty would get in front of him and start barking. The few times Lance tried to ignore their guardian, the consequences were immediate. The barking became annoyingly loud and soon Lilly would come upon them and scold Lance for wandering too far. When their mother's admonishing was finished, Rusty would give two more barks of agreement to what she said, as if to say, "See, I told you!"

After Jon's accident, Rusty stayed by his side; he never watched the kids again. It would seem that he was stricken with his master being broken in body and spirit. It was like the dog had taken on their father's pain and anguish. Jon was laid up for six months and then hobbled around the house for another six months. His shattered femur had been pinned together in 20 places, but it never healed right. His brain injury gave him raging headaches and frustratingly slow speech. He walked with a noticeable limp. He'd never do what he had once done when his body was whole. One day Rusty walked into the woods, never to return. They figured, after a year of watching their father suffer he just went off and died of a broken heart. The family was terribly sad over his leaving. Their father tried to put on a brave front, often complaining that the dog was a nuisance anyway, but they all knew he missed Rusty's watchful presence.

****

Lance and River were lost in their heartache and memories of their parents through the first months of the new year. They kept the old log home warm by chopping firewood for the wood burner and covering the drafty windows with clear insulating shrink-wrap. They boxed up their parents' clothes thinking that others in the community could use them. People in the Village of Thunder Lake stopped in with hot food and fresh pies. Lance and River invited them in, and they would all sit around the kitchen table and share stories about Jon and Lilly. The Porters and Edwards from Safe Harbor Resort stopped in with a gift of homemade bread and a check for River. They said it was River's and Lilly's bonus' from the summer cleaning season. She and Lilly had worked as a team cleaning cabins at Safe Harbor Resort. Every summer, while a student at the University of Minnesota, River would come home to work with her mom. With over fifty resorts in the area, an experienced and conscientious cleaning crew was worth their weight in gold, and the new owners of Safe Harbor Resort knew they had one of the best crews in Lilly and River. It was good business sense to reward the best cleaners with handsome bonuses to get them to return the following summer.

******

1996 was a long winter. As much as the love and concern of others helped, the cold void that Jon and Lilly's deaths left in the hearts of Lance and River made the winter feel even longer and colder.

Chapter Three

The Long Cold Spring

As the month of February ended, March roared in like a lion. The only joy the four friends at Safe Harbor found was in watching their young dogs. The two retrievers filled their days with boundless energy and silly antics. Sadie, only five months older than Honey, had taken to her new home with relish. When Carmen and Jed brought her to the resort in February, she thought she had been born into a new and wonderful life. The beautiful golden ran around the resort grounds releasing months of pent up energy. Carmen's mother, who was getting up in years, had been so overwhelmed with Sadie's boundless energy that she resorted to keeping the rambunctious youngster on the landing next to the back door. Clearly, the young dog was too much for Carmen's mother. Now Sadie ran with wild abandon over the hilly resort grounds and down to the large frozen harbor. The first few weeks little Honey was too small to run with Sadie, but she certainly noticed the golden streak flash by the front window of her home. The little Labrador watched in fascination, her pencil-thin tail wagging at the sight of the joyous dog outside. She wanted to play, but Sadie had yet to stop and introduce herself.

When Sadie finally settled down, life took on a routine in the still-chilly month of April. Sadie came down to visit Honey every morning as Will and Libby finished their morning coffee. She'd paw at the sliding glass door next to the table, and Honey scampered excitedly to the glass, wagging her tail and barking. Will would let Sadie in and the games began: barking, growling, rolling and chasing. Honey loved Sadie's dangling ears and great effort was made to bite at them. Sadie put up with it for only so long and then she'd place a big paw on the little imp or sometimes even lay right on her. Will and Libby watched the tussle and laughed. They totally agreed with Sadie's defensive methods. Sadie's tail would slowly wag as they all listened to the grunts from the little yellow pup under the big golden. Pretty soon Sadie would tire of playing inside and want out again where she would be off chasing a squirrel or some such fun.

Honey watched her leave through the sliding glass door. Then she would plop down for a much needed nap.

As Honey continued to grow, the play continued to get rougher. Poor Sadie's ears were almost pierced through a couple of times. Because Honey could read Sadie's patience level, she learned to run away before Sadie could sit on her. So Sadie figured out a new defense maneuver. She would let Honey run and get some distance between them, then Sadie would run full blast at the little ear-piercer. The big dog would run over the little one causing a three or four somersault spin, and that usually curtailed the ear-piercing for awhile. One day this lesson was being imposed on Honey when something went wrong. Honey immediately started yelping and holding up her back paw. She looked around for assurance and soon was being picked up by Will. He talked to her, soothing her cries and checking out her back paw. She yelped even louder. Sadie was worried too. She kept trying to reach Honey, to lick her little face, but she couldn't reach her in Will's arms.

Jed, who was with Will when it happened, looked at her injured paw, "I bet when Sadie bowled her over she accidentally stepped on her paw and twisted it."

Will and Libby took Honey to see Steve, the Veterinarian in Beaver Creek. He confirmed their fears, "Yes, she has a tiny fractured bone in her paw. She'll be fine in no time. No cast will be necessary; she'll hold it up on her own and slowly put weight on it after it's healed."

Will and Libby took Honey home, relieved that they wouldn't be getting a huge vet bill. Jed and Carmen were anxiously awaiting their return to the resort. They too were relieved there wasn't a large bill to pay. Funds were short for both couples until the resort season was up and running again.

The two dogs were separated for the next two weeks. Sadie would make her usual trek down to the Edward's house and Honey would hop to the glass door on her three good legs, so excited to see her friend, but Will wouldn't let Sadie in. Sadie would peer through the glass at him, pleading to come in and Honey would cry and bark for the door to open, but Will and Libby were determined that they not play together until Honey was using all four paws again. Soon the paw came down to rest on the ground, and in no time Honey was putting all her weight on it. It wasn't long before the two dogs were hard at play again. The two couples tried to stop the ear-piercing and puppy-bowling, but it would go on when they weren't watching. One day when Will and Jed were busy working on water pipes going into one of the cabins, they happened to see a most interesting sight. The two retrievers were playing nearby when they saw Sadie start to make her puppy-bowling run. Jed started to yell for Sadie to stop, but it was too late; she was at full speed, running right for Honey. Jed and Will observed Honey, close to five-months-old now, intently watch Sadie as she was galloping towards her. The big dog was seconds away from full body impact when, to their surprise, they watched Honey glance from side to side, and then scamper next to a fieldstone retaining wall. Sadie, veered off just before making contact, missing the little ear-piercer and the retaining wall by mere inches.

Jed looked at Will and said, "Did you see that? That little imp just figured out how to keep from being bowled over anymore." Sure enough, they watched the calculated maneuver over and over that summer--Honey would run to the nearest wall or tree and Sadie would have to swerve. If only Sadie had a similar defense with the little ear-piercer. The Porters took their turn at the veterinarian's office to get antibiotics for poor Sadie's ears.

******

Spring hadn't come early to Thunder Lake as Jed so desperately hoped it would. The snows and cold weather continued into late April. The blacktop driveway leading to their garage would cover over with a new coating of ice and snow and, every day Carmen would go out and chip away the winter's precipitation to gain back the warm blacktop. It happened to be the only pavement in the whole resort. All the other roads were a thin layer of gravel on top of sandy dirt, which created gushy, sloppy mud everywhere with the melting of each late-season snowfall.

The month of May was just around the corner and resort life shifted into high gear, becoming increasingly busy. So much needed to be done before May 12, the date of this year's Minnesota fishing opener, one of the two most 'holy days' of the year for sportsmen, with opening of hunting season being the other. You'd better not need a plumber, electrician or mechanic during those weeks as their shops are closed and their phones go unanswered.

Libby and Carmen had sixteen cabins and the big lodge to spring-clean. They had started cleaning three weeks ago and had eight cabins done. After the guest season swung into full gear they would need their hired cleaners to help with the demanding Saturday changeovers, but for now they could get by with just each other. They had lost their best cleaning crew last September when Lilly Timberlake died, and they weren't counting on River coming back without her mom. Finding reliable replacements would be almost impossible. The wonderful Ojibwa woman and her daughter had been cleaning cabins there for over ten years. Libby and Carmen had convinced the two women to continue working for them when they bought the resort a year ago. To their relief, Lilly and River stayed on and taught them all the nitty-gritty of cleaning cabins efficiently and thoroughly. When they got the news about Lilly's death both couples were devastated. It was a tremendous shock, especially for Libby and Carmen who worked right alongside their cleaners. They had lost a good friend and a good worker--Lilly would be sorely missed.

****

This Monday morning Libby and Carmen were cleaning cabin 2. Getting to the cabin was a real challenge that day as the roads were too muddy to drive their old cleaning van through the hilly resort. So they trudged down the hill in their knee high muck-boots, carrying their pails of hot water and cleaning supplies.

All of the cabins were in need of new paint, carpet and appliances. They couldn't afford to do all those things in every cabin this year but they *would* have them clean. The old cabins and lodge had been shelter from the elements for fisherman and families for over 60 years. Safe Harbor Resort had been a Carter business for half a century. The previous owners, Bud and Bev Carter, ran the place for 30 years, and Bud's parents had run it for 30 years before that. There was Carter's Reef, a mile off Safe Harbor's shoreline, named as a tribute to the family. Bud and Bev had won over many loyal resort guests during their 30 years of running the resort. People loved them, still sending them Christmas cards and pictures of their kids' graduations. The Carters didn't have a mortgage so they were able to keep the cabin rates low which all the fishermen and families liked, but low rates kept the old resort from some much needed updating. All of the buildings had peeling log siding. The roofs leaked and the cabin floors were carpeted with carpet-square samples. This embarrassing patchwork of color on the floors was almost too much for Carmen and Libby to face that spring. But if they couldn't afford to change the carpet they would make sure the carpet squares were clean. The only good thing about carpet squares is if one is really stained, you just pull it up and staple a new one down.

Libby and Carmen's first chore during spring cleaning was moving all the cabin furniture into the center of the rooms. Beds, chest of drawers, chairs, couches, and tables, all got stacked. As Libby started in on the first bedroom she saw a flat, furry mass in a corner.

"Carmen, bring the Super-Suck, there's a dead mouse where that chest of drawers sat!"

Libby looked grossed out as she waited for Carmen to come in and join her with their super-powered Sears wet/dry vac.

"Yuck!" retorted Carmen, as she turned on the huge vacuum they had nicknamed Super-Suck.

Carmen bent down, getting the vacuum nozzle closer to the dehydrated mouse and--*Whoomp*--the nozzle found the little body. Carmen turned off the vacuum and hauled it back with her to the bathroom, the only room in the cabin that had a real door; the bedroom doorways had only curtains for privacy…well semi-privacy. Libby started washing down the walls, windowsills and the four six-pane windows in the bedroom. These were a real pain to clean; plus, every time her cloth brushed against the brittle putty holding the glass to the frame, more putty broke away. She hoped the glass would stay put until the guys could re-glaze the joints. The last chore was to vacuum the carpet-squares covering the floor and put all the furniture back in its place. Then she went to the next bedroom to start all over again.

In the tiny bathroom, Carmen began to look around as she scrubbed at the dull beige walls. When Libby finally turned off the vacuum, Carmen raised her voice enough for Libby to hear her.

"Libby, do you think we should paint this bathroom before this season starts?"

Libby walked the few steps to the bathroom doorway and nodded her head at Carmen in agreement.

"Yeah, it needs it more than some of the others in the resort. It wouldn't take much paint either; it's the size of a closet in here. Maybe you could do some sponge painting. That should brighten things up."

Their work continued as they both converged into the kitchen and living room area. The morning was slipping away, and they knew the men would be checking on them soon, hungry for lunch. They usually ate their lunches together during this time of the year. It gave them time to discuss what the women had discovered during their morning in the cabins that needed fixing. There was so much to do that they always needed to prioritize what should be done immediately and what could wait.

The men's "List of Repairs" for the cabins was eight-pages long. But besides the cabin repairs, they also had the frustrating job of getting the water running to all the buildings. After a winter of freezing temperatures there were numerous waterline leaks to find and fix. They needed to finish the kitchen and bathroom plumbing in the cabin they had remodeled over the winter, but they couldn't test their work until they had water running to the cabin. The bait tank needed attention, and at least six docks needed to be repaired before any fisherman stepped foot on them. They tried not to look at the whole dilapidated picture but only do as much as they could each day, get a good night's sleep, and go at it hard the next day. Will and Jed worked well together. They were hard workers and knew that a good dose of humor went a long way in facing all the repairs this resort needed.

Sure enough as Carmen and Libby finished up cabin 2, they could hear the tramping boots and low voices of Will and Jed. From their tone it seemed that maybe something more had broken, but Carmen and Libby were able to take it in stride this year. They had learned from the year before, that that's the way it always was after the long winter months.

The women grabbed their jackets and slipped on their tall muck-boots and headed out the door to meet them.

"Hey, how are you fellas?" Carmen asked as they joined the men and two happy dogs.

Sadie was the first to greet Carmen and Libby, swishing her long feathered tail in contentment. Honey was right behind, in full body-wag. That's the difference between Labradors and Goldens--the wagging tail produces a fast speed body-wiggle in labs and a graceful swaying in Goldens. Honey and Sadie almost always stayed near the men because their work kept them outdoors, giving them plenty of room for play. The group of six made their way up the muddy hill to the Porter's house: four tired humans and two inexhaustible dogs.

Chapter Four

Muskie Run Resort

Ten miles northeast of Safe Harbor

The forest green cabin doors hung open in the bright sunshine this fine May afternoon. The radiant spring sunlight streamed through newly budding trees, striking the old buildings. The white curling paint on the cabins resembled the curling bark of the nearby birch trees. Bright green moss and dead branches covered the crumbling green shingled roofs. The air *finally* smelled of warming earth after the long, cold winter. Here and there piles of dirty snow sprung rivulets of trickling water, all dancing their way down to Thunder Lake. A robin sang its melodic greeting from a soggy patch of grass to a female sitting in a nearby lilac bush, its branches just beginning to bud. There was an eerie creaking from far above as a fallen tree, caught in the crook of another, groaned with the soft afternoon breeze. The sound gave the abandoned resort a feeling of something sinister even on this bright afternoon. Everywhere you looked it was clear that the surrounding nature was slowly taking back what mankind had constructed half a century ago.

It would seem these were the final days of this family resort. It was once a popular fishing destination in the 1950's, located on the northeast shore of Thunder Lake. Its last days, not unlike a human's last days, seemed resigned to its end. The sign at the beginning of the driveway still declared the popular fishing lodge, "Muskie Run Resort," the letters now barely legible. This place was once the object of many years of care and hard work for Herb and Jenny Grogan. They started the fishing resort and operated it until just four years ago when Jenny became very ill. Back in their beginning years, the Grogans constructed many of the buildings themselves. A huge log lodge by the waterfront had once served fishermen and families with food and fishing supplies. Now Musky Run's lodge was a blackened cavern that had burned down under questionable circumstances a few years after the Grogans sold to Charles Wiley and his wife Aggie.

The young couple had put on a good front when meeting the Grogans the first time. And when the Wileys ran the resort the first season, they seemed perfect for the job. Charlie took guests in the resort's large launch to all the hot spots he knew for walleye, northern or muskie. Charlie's good looks and charisma won over the Grogans' most loyal customers--at first. Whatever the resort guests wanted, Charlie was delighted to accommodate, while Aggie whipped up delicious meals in the lodge's kitchen to feed the hungry fishermen.

The Grogans were so pleased to find out how happy everyone was with the new owners. At first guests thought it was good to see this young couple running things. The place was starting to need some TLC, and youth is the ingredient that old resorts need as old veterans sell them to new owners.

But along with his youth, Charlie brought some *undesirable baggage*. By the second season Charlie took up with his old friend, *Mr. Windsor,* again. That was Charlie's *baggage* he brought to the resort. He stashed the whiskey bottles deep into lodge hidey-holes, where Aggie never looked: behind the minnow tank in the bait house, and even in the woods behind the house.

The guests began to notice a change in Charlie. Aggie did, too, but when she checked the level of whiskey in the bottle at the house, she had been relieved to see he was keeping his drinking under control like he promised. She was suspicious, but it was easier to put it out of her mind, she wanted to believe that everything was still okay with Charlie.

It was only two years ago that Aggie had threatened to leave Charlie, who happened to be a deputy sheriff in the town of Rockford, Illinois. It was back then he had been charged with having sexual contact with a minor. Charlie was on duty when he was called to the scene of a reported shoplifting. He had been enjoying a lunch with his friend, *Mr. Windsor,* when he got the call. It turned out instead of taking the pretty, young thief to the police station, Charlie took the very attractive seventeen-year-old-girl out to the countryside and shared a few hours of *fun* with the all too willing delinquent. On their way back to town Charlie told her he would let her go if she kept quiet about their "outing." The young girl did keep quiet. No one would have been the wiser except the store owner that reported the theft checked up on the young girl's arrest and was very surprised to find out she never made it to the police station. It all unraveled for Deputy Wiley when asked to explain what happened. He feigned innocence, but internal affairs and subsequently, a judge, did not believe his story. They did not want a man like Charles Wiley on their police force.

Charlie spent nine months in the county jail for sexual contact with a minor, lost his position in the police force, and almost lost his wife. But Charlie always had a way of breaking down Aggie's resistance with teary apologies and heartfelt promises to quit drinking and straighten out. So when Charlie mentioned the idea of buying a resort... "*get a fresh start in a new area up in God's Country,*" Aggie relented and gave him one more chance. They sold their home in Rockford to make the down payment on the resort and headed north in a U-haul truck with their car in tow.

By their third year of running Muskie Run Resort, Charlie and Aggie were hardly speaking to each other. The tender loving care that the old resort so desperately needed never happened. Aggie finally had to face the reality that Charlie was inebriated morning to night, seven days a week. She did a wide sweep of the resort and found 22 whiskey bottles in various levels of emptiness.

The few guests that showed up that season hardly talked to Charlie. They stayed away from him as much as possible because when they asked him for help, Charlie swore and slurred his words. One hapless attempt to greet new guests ended with the inebriated owner falling backwards off the step of the lodge. He got up, swore, and made some excuse under his whisky breath about the steps needing to be fixed It was an unimpressive welcome to the new arrivals.

Then the worst happened again. One of the guests came to Aggie as she was washing up the pots and pans in the lodge's kitchen. The woman was *livid*. She spit out her words in angry spasms. "Your drunken, bastard---got our sixteen-year-old-daughter drunk and who knows--", she couldn't continue because of the awkward sob in her throat that clenched any further words from escaping.

Aggie lowered her head, heaved a deep sigh, and spoke in a low, pained whisper, "I'm so sorry."

She touched the woman's arm as she walked past her out of the lodge. The woman watched, confused, "Where are you…"

But Aggie let the screen door slam hard behind her as she left the lodge. She climbed into her old Chevy Citation parked outside and drove away from the resort and out of Charlie's miserable life for good.

Later that afternoon, Charlie was relieved to see the family of the young girl drive out of the resort. Their gear was strapped to the top of their van, indicating they were not just going out for dinner. He had been hiding during the day so he didn't know that Aggie's car was also gone. He thought blissfully that he had dodged a big bullet as he watched the family drive away. But then it dawned on him slowly that something was terribly wrong as he realized their Chevy was nowhere to be seen and neither was Aggie. Charlie's blissful mood changed to fearful; he knew he was incapable of living without Aggie. She was his anchor and he feared she had just let go and set him adrift. Aggie was the one good choice he had made in his life. Without her, he was a lost soul on an angry sea.

He met Aggie when he was eighteen-years-old. He had just left his last foster home, and he was finally free of Child Protective Services and foster care. He had been in the system because his parents and little sister died in a fire when he was ten. He carried a terrible secret about their deaths. He became an angry boy, full of shame and sadness. At eighteen, he was an even angrier young man. Aggie had been working in a drug store where Charlie stopped in after school most days. Sundquist Drug Store was a favorite with the teens in town because it still had a lunch counter. He liked to order a coke and fries and watch Aggie work. He eventually got a job as a stock boy in the drug store. Aggie was three years older than Charlie, not knock-out gorgeous but pretty in her own way. He was most attracted to her good nature: honest, kind and caring. Aggie was first attracted to his intense green eyes. His heavy eyelids seemed to be weighed down by his long, dreamy eyelashes.

She found herself attracted to his dangerous and sexy persona, *something she would later greatly regret.* He put on a 'tough guy' act for others but over the months he began to show his vulnerable side to Aggie. She was drawn to his neediness as much as his good looks. Aggie always had a need to care for the hurting and she could tell there was a lot of hurt coming from Charlie the more he let her in. After a year of dating, Charlie gave her a ring and Aggie was genuinely happy to be engaged. Charles Wiley figured everything would turn out better for him now that he had someone who loved him.

Young Charlie, barely nineteen, started college that fall. It was a struggle for him as learning from books was not easy. After he graduated he pursued a career in the police force only because Aggie gave him confidence that he could do it. They married after two years and settled down in a little apartment above the drugstore. It didn't take long, once Aggie was Mrs. Wiley, to realize that alcohol was Charlie's other love. If Aggie was his angel, alcohol was his demon. After they were married he let his guard down and the verbal abuse and the affairs began. They were all symptoms of his relationship with whiskey and his own self-hatred because of his terrible secret. Aggie was grateful that she brought no children into their miserable lives.

******

It was September of his third year at Muskie Run and Charlie found himself without Aggie, and the annual mortgage payment was due in October. Charlie couldn't make his full payment on his Contract for Deed with Herb Grogan.

Jenny Grogan had passed away the previous winter so Herb was now living alone. He and Jenny had a small log cabin outside the Ojibwe Village of Thunder Lake. Jenny's family, who were members of the Thunder Lake Ojibwe, insisted that he continue to live near them even though Jenny was gone. When Charlie informed Herb of his sad state of finances, Herb tried to be helpful by accepting a quarter of the annual payment, but by November of the following year when Charlie had *no payment* of any amount, Herb threatened Charlie with taking the resort back. So in December there was a fire in the massive lodge that had once housed the restaurant and store at Muskie Run. All that remained of the old building the following morning was a blackened, smoldering shell. When the insurance check came through Charlie gave Herb most of the money, holding back just enough funds to keep the electricity on and enough food and booze to get him through the long winter. Herb was sick about the lodge burning down, but he was even more concerned about how to get rid of the drunk that was destroying his much-loved resort.

******

If the winter of '96 was long and bitterly cold for Carmen Porter across the vast frozen bay at Safe Harbor, it was even worse for Charles Wiley. The phone had been disconnected for non-payment. The only mail he pulled from his mailbox were bills and legal warnings. He was ever hopeful of seeing a letter from Aggie waiting for him but she never wrote. He rarely opened the bills after rifling through them, but used them as kindling for the fire in his wood burning stove.

Charlie did have one comforting soul enter his life that winter--a brown and white spaniel. Someone plopped the pup onto his lap as he sat at the bar located a few miles from his rotting resort. Charlie didn't remember taking the young dog home, but the next morning he awoke to the spaniel curled up next to him on the bed. He got up to take a leak and when he came back and saw the soft brown eyes of the spaniel looking up at him from his bed, he just couldn't think of a more comforting name for the dog than "Aggie" after his angel wife that he had driven away.

******

So as the rejuvenating, warm, spring sunshine streamed through the trees in the empty resort, Charlie was ready to turn over a new leaf. He had cleaned himself up which was no easy task without propane to run his hot water heater. He had to heat water on his wood-burner to fill his bathtub. He then washed his best black pants and light blue sweater in his bathwater, and hung them up to dry in the warm sunshine that brilliant afternoon. As he stood outside in his boxer shorts and rubber boots Charlie surveyed the rundown resort that lay before him; his eyes narrowed in regret. The cabins hadn't been maintained for years and the task to rescue the business was beyond Charlie's capabilities or vision. He decided he would have to get a realtor to help him sell the resort...and he needed to get a job.

*****

Northwest of Muskie Run, across the large expanse of the still frozen Thunder Lake, Lance and River had begun to accept their lives without their parents. It was on this beautiful morning that Lance was out for a run along County Road 18. He was startled when an old red Chevy pickup swerved right for him as he ran along the gravel shoulder. Deep in thought, he hadn't seen it until the truck's rattles and squeaks stopped dead in front of him, dust and pebbles spitting from the skidding tires.

"Hey there, if it isn't fancy dancin' Lance Timberlake. It's been forever my brother." The familiar voice came from the passenger's side window. Lance's shock turned to amusement, and a smile grew on his face. It was one of his high school buddies, George Bowstring.

Lance chided his old friend. "Georgie boy, what are you doing joyriding this time of day? Why aren't you at work, ya' lazy bones?"

George opened his door to get out and greet his old friend. The hinges on the door of the old red truck groaned loudly. Then the driver's door swung open creating a duet of grinding metal. A large man Lance didn't recognize dropped down from the truck seat onto the gravel and walked toward him. Lance noticed Frank LaFleur, inconveniently trapped in the back jump-seat. Frank smiled at him through the dirty backseat window. Lance smiled back.

George Bowstring introduced Lance to the driver of the red pickup, "Lance Timberlake, I'd like you to meet, Henry Ford."

"Henry, this is the impressive Lance Timberlake of Thunder Lake tribal lore. He had all the fancy moves--with the girls, on the basketball court and in track. He whupped us all in sports and, to add insult to injury, got straight A's in every class. The smartest move he made was getting the hell out of here to become an atto-r-r-ney. *Whoo-hoo, fancy Lancy, yo' the MAN!*"

Lance, embarrassed by George's introduction, offered his hand to the big Indian standing in front of him, his black hair hanging long and straight down to the middle of his back, a dark blue Minnesota Twins cap shaded his eyes.

"Henry Ford, it's interesting that you drive a Chevy, "Lance commented with a chuckle, "No relation to the founder of the Ford Company are you?"

Henry smirked, "Nah, just my parent's odd sense of humor. I think they hoped the name would inspire ingenuity. I'm mostly ingenious at creating trouble." Then he laughed so hard his beer belly shook.

George explained that his mother was related to Henry by some cousin once removed. Henry was from the Red Lake Band northwest of Thunder Lake.

After a short, uncomfortable mention about the tragedy of Lance and River losing their parents, George was anxious to talk about the newest idea they had just implemented for aggravating the heck out of the white man's fishing opener. George, Frank and Henry had just come back from hanging a long stretch of gill nets. "We hung 'um across upper Wolf Island narrows. It should infuriate those uppity sportsmen Saturday morning for fishing opener." Lance studied the face of his tribal brother and memories of their past came flooding back. The "war" between the sportsmen and the Ojibwe braves had been going on year after year as pranks and tom-foolery mostly. There had been a few bloody fights but not many. He himself had taken part in some of the lawless pranks in his youth.

The Ojibwe, exercising their treaty rights with the U.S. government, were allowed to lay their gill nets out to catch fish "in the old ways," and the sportsmen would come along in their twenty-thousand dollar bass boats and cut the nets in protest. It used to be an authentic need and desire on the part of the Ojibwe to catch fish the old way. But with the introduction of the tribe's Thunder Lake Casino, and with it, the beginnings of financial independence, the netting rites were less about the needs and traditions of the tribe and more often about bringing angst to sports fishermen who thought they owned the whole lake. Lance had no desire to get involved in something so silly anymore and he told George to have fun but count him out. They said their goodbyes. George and Henry got back in the old red Chevy truck and continued north to get some coffee and breakfast at the diner in the Village of Thunder Lake. They had a lot more scheming to do.

Lance headed down the road the direction he had been running. River would be up by now. She'll have the coffee brewing and they would have their breakfast on the front porch like they had been doing every morning for the past week.

******

Back at Safe Harbor, the Edwards and the Porters were putting the final touches on cabin seven. It had been a whirlwind of purchasing, hauling, and setting up furniture. Carmen and Libby filled the kitchen cupboards and drawers with new dishes, cookware, utensils and any other necessary housekeeping supplies. Carmen was busy hanging the curtains she had made for the three by five foot sliding windows all around the exterior walls while Libby was busy making all the beds in the three bedrooms.

Will and Jed were feeling especially celebratory as they put away their tools after a successful testing of the water lines. They all had succeeded in this big endeavor to replace one of the tiny, old original cabins with a large, open, newly remodeled version.

"I think we should plan to be the first to use the new, improved cabin 7. What do you think?" Will asked Jed with a mischievous twinkle in his eyes.

"What are you thinking Will?"

"We should make the girls dinner here and watch the sunset tonight. We can bring up some beers from the lodge along with a couple pizzas. What do you say?"

"I can do you one better." Jed said with a twinkle in *his* eyes. "I've got a case of home brew I'd contribute to the celebration."

So that evening, even though they were all dog-tired, they sat around the pine plank table that the guys had built over the winter, and celebrated their big achievements. They ate pizza and salad and enjoyed Jed's home brew. They reminisced about the previous year. There was so much they had experienced together and it all came flowing out in stories and laughter.

"Do you remember how all of us were so afraid for the first reservation call to come in the first month of owning this place?"

Will took a sip of his beer and laughed. "Yeah, I remember. It was Jed who picked up the phone and when he answered, we all gasped."

Yup, I'm the one who coined the resort's name, "*Hafe Sarbor* Resort, how can I help you?"

They all belly laughed and beer went up Libby's nose. She started coughing and laughing which made everyone else laugh even harder.

"Not to pick on you again, Jed, but there was that time when those people came a day early, arriving on a Friday, when their cabin wasn't available until Saturday. They accused you of screwing up their reservation," Will said grimacing.

Jed smiled, "Oh yeah, the bean can story. Those people were supposed to arrive on Saturday for cabin 2 but they arrived on Friday, swearing I had told them that was our changeover day. We of course do changeover on Saturdays but what could we do with these people? Where could we put them for one night? They had driven all the way from Iowa."

"That's right," Libby continued with the story, "Will's parents had that old Airstream trailer sitting in the campground area. So we offered that to the family. The parents seemed appreciative, but the teenage daughter was a little less than thrilled."

Carmen added," We brought bedding and other supplies to them. But before we knocked on the trailer door, I overheard the daughter say in disgust, "I never thought I'd be spending the night in a bean can!"

They all chuckled. Their previous year had been a real learning experience.

"Remember when we first started selling bait, we counted each minnow that went into the bait bucket," Libby said.

"Well, you might have counted each one but none of the rest of us did." Will teased Libby.

"Really? It was just me?" Libby said in a high-pitched voice.

Carmen rescued Libby. "I did it too, Libby."

Libby laughed. "Well, I was the one that called fathead minnows, flathead minnows. I even made the sign for them over the bait tank. Then one day a fisherman finally pointed it out. I was so embarrassed."

They all burst out laughing again.

After they calmed down from that story, they paused to look out the new cabin windows at the lake. They were sobered by the awesome sight of the still frozen lake and the sky set afire with the setting sun as it dipped down below the lake's surface.

"Wow, what a view from this cabin!" Libby exclaimed.

They all took a sip of beer and nodded in agreement.

Will broke the silence, "Hey, did we ever tell you about our funny experience with Kenny, the Lidke's youngest boy?"

"What was that?" Jed asked

Will told the story of young Kenny. "Well, Libby and I were on morning duty at the lodge. Libby was working on getting the cabin cleaning tubs filled for changeover and I was working on the week's invoices when little Kenny came in. He was holding a dollar bill in his hand as he walked over to the tackle bins. I let him browse for a while before going over to him. He had to crane his neck to see the bins as they are hanging at adult height. Finally I asked him what he was looking for. I'm sure you remember, he's got a little lisp. He looked over at me with all seriousness and said, "Shitsplotz." Libby walked closer to hear better, she asked Kenny what he wanted. "Shitsplotz!" he said again determinedly. We looked at each other in puzzlement. Then it came to me, he wanted Split-shots."

Jed and Carmen both groaned and then laughed.

The two couples could have gone on and on with stories from their first season with guests, but the night was coming on and there was much work left to be done tomorrow. Fishing opener was just a few days away.

Chapter Five

Frozen in On Opener

It was close to sunset the Wednesday before the '96 Fishing Opener. All the cabins were ready and now Carmen and Libby were working in the lodge cleaning and stocking shelves, and pricing the merchandise that was piling up from deliveries arriving every day. The old kitchen had been repainted, windows were washed and the wood floors polished to a shine. Jed and Will were cleaning out the bait house and getting motors on boats. When the guys finished their work in the bait house, they walked out to the front of the lodge together to look at the miles of black ice that still imprisoned the lake. Carmen and Libby saw them standing out by the shoreline and joined them. The four disheartened partners stood there searching the horizon for any open water, listening for some hint of movement. It was only a few days before the resort would be filled with anxious fishermen and there were no tumbling waves rolling onto the boulders, no loons singing their mournful song in the evening air. The silence cast a despondent mood over the four exhausted owners who had all put in twelve-hour days for the last month. The ice in the harbor was gone but no boats would get any further than the harbor entrance.

Will finally spoke in a tone of resignation, "We are going to have to call everyone renting a cabin this weekend and tell them the lake in front of the resort is still frozen as far out as we can see."

The other three partners stared out at the vast expanse of black ice and knew he was right; there was no way that the ice was going to break up in the next 24 hours. Some fishermen were scheduled to arrive tomorrow.

Fishing opener weekend brought in a large chunk of change that the resort business desperately needed after a long winter with no income and high expenses in the spring to get the resort up and running again. But it was only right that the guests be told of the situation and let them make up their minds if they still wanted to come. They all let out deep sighs of despondence and turned their backs to the frozen water and headed into the lodge to begin making calls.

"Hi, Harold, this is Jed from Safe Harbor. How are you?" Jed asked and then listened to the old guy on the other end of the phone line. Harold had been coming up for fishing opener at Safe Harbor for 40 years. He had informed them last year to be sure to have cherry nut ice cream for him next year. Carmen and Libby made sure they had it in the old-fashioned ice cream freezer. They all liked Harold and his cabin buddy, Henry. Now Jed was telling him that maybe he and Henry shouldn't come because the lake was still frozen.

When Harold heard this startling news he couldn't believe it, "That's a first. We've had snow and sleet some years but there has always been open water!"

Jed chuckled at the old guy's consternation. "Well, believe it, Harold, 'cause I'm looking out at the blasted stuff as we speak."

There was silence on the other end of the line for a few moments and then Harold responded with certainty in his voice, "We're still coming anyway--we've had years that wind and waves kept us off the lake for days in a row, what the heck's the difference if it's ice? Am I right? Don't you worry, we'll be there!"

Jed was taken aback by the adamancy in Harold's voice, but he was pleased to hear the old guy was still determined to come.

Fifteen calls later and the consensus was unanimous -- the fishermen were all still coming, ice and all. Will pulled four beers out of the fully stocked cooler as Libby and Carmen brought out two sizzling Tombstone pizzas from the lodge kitchen. They sat in front of the big fieldstone fireplace, a blazing fire spitting and popping in the hearth. The two dogs were sprawled out on the braided rug next to each other, both exhausted after putting in another great day of fun. The two couples felt dirty and exhausted but there was something else they shared, a pride of accomplishment in all they had taken on and finished. It was gratifying to hear the intoxicating excitement they heard from the voices over the phone. The opening week crowd couldn't wait to get up there. Knowing that did their weary hearts good.

The next day Libby made a run to Beaver Creek, a town 20 miles away, for some last minute grocery items: fresh eggs and milk for the lodge cooler and fresh buns and bread for the wire rack display. She also was instructed to get ten more fishing license booklets from the courthouse. As she traveled down the big hill into the beautiful little town along the lake she could see the traffic was gridlocked. Beaver Creek's local population of a thousand would grow to eight thousand over the next week.

By the time Libby returned to the resort with the supplies, she was astonished at the change that had taken place in her short two hour absence. A day earlier there had only been two guys, John and Chris, staying in cabin 10. Now she looked around to see multiple cars at every cabin and guys standing around talking and laughing with friends from the cabin next door. They all knew each other, most had been coming to this resort, this same week, every year, for at least ten years, and some much longer. The *snap*, *skirch* and *whop* sound echoed through the crowded resort as beer and pop cans were opened and cooler lids slammed shut. Libby had a sudden attack of shyness as the men watched her drive through. They all smiled and waved at her, but still she felt like she had entered into a Twilight Zone episode. She had just spent seven months with only three other people in this very place and now there had to be eighty or more people and at least thirty cars.

She pulled up next to the lodge and there in front of her was the empty harbor. A year ago there were so many boats in the harbor on Friday night that you could walk across the harbor and not get your feet wet. This year all the boats sat on their trailers like tethered horses antsy to go.

Libby hesitated getting out of the car. Maybe she could just pull out and drive up to the sanctuary of her home. But just then the car door opened next to her, startling her back to reality. Will bent down and looked at her curiously, "Is something wrong?" He sounded irritated to Libby. "We need more fishing licenses, did you get them?" Libby climbed out of the car, a little offended at Will's impatience, and handed him the license booklets. Will grabbed the booklets and two bags of groceries from the backseat and hurried into the lodge.

Jed was coming out of the bait house, a cordless phone to his ear, "We're going to need another bait run tonight or tomorrow morning--can you make it out here, Jim?"

He acknowledged Libby with a nod as he listened to the bait store owner tell him his woes of being backed up with a dozen resort deliveries before he could get a delivery to us.

Libby grabbed the last of the groceries from the car and headed into the lodge. She was greeted by John and Chris from cabin 10, and then she saw Fred and his son, Sam, getting a steaming Tombstone pizza from Carmen. Old Harold had arrived from Iowa. He was being helped by Will at the counter, filling out his non-resident fishing license. So many friendly, familiar faces. The uncomfortable shyness she was feeling was fading. These were all people she knew; there were just a lot of them all at once.

*****

As evening fell on the crowded resort, the loon clock above the tall knotty-pine counter started its mournful siren call at the top of the hour. Will looked up to see what hour it actually was--*eight o'clock already*. The day had been a blur.

As the last siren call from the loon clock ended the Edward's daughter, Becky, walked through the lodge door. Will's heart skipped a beat. He was very happy to see her and gave her a big smile. She had just arrived after the long, slow drive from the Twin Cities. Traffic had been bumper to bumper making the normal three-hour drive into five hours. She had stopped at their house to leave her car as she knew the resort would be crowded. Both of the resort homes were located off the lake and up the hill, giving the best lake views for the rental cabins. Will and Libby's home overlooked the harbor and beyond, to the lake. When Becky dropped her car off at her parent's home she also brought her overnight bag into her bedroom. Even though neither she nor her brother had ever lived up at the resort, Libby and Will had bedrooms set up for both of them. It helped give them a feeling of always being welcome. Becky missed her parents. She held a little grudge because of their desertion to live so far away but, she also admired them for taking on such a big venture.

Will walked around the counter to give Becky a hug. She was the spitting image of Libby; big brown eyes, light brown hair and a beautiful smile. "How's my Punker?"

Becky hugged her dad and winced. "Da-ad, don't call me that! I'm almost twenty-two-years- old!"

They sat down at the table next to the sliding glass door. Becky looked out at the black ice, now pocked with watery holes. The shoreline was now free of ice six feet from shore.

"Wow, I can't believe there's still ice! What are all these crazy fishermen going to do, ice-fish tomorrow morning?"

Will shook his head and muttered, "They all plan on driving to the Borden public access to put their boats in. The lake is free of ice in the narrows, open water is only about 3 miles away. They've bought out all our bait in anticipation of getting on the lake at daybreak."

It was after nine when Libby and Carmen walked into the lodge. They had gotten waylaid by one of the seasonal families that stayed in the campground area. Libby was delighted to see Becky had made it safely from the Cities. Mother and daughter hugged and then Becky turned and hugged Carmen.

Becky had known Carmen since she was a little girl. She and Josh knew Carmen's children like they were their cousins. But Carmen's children, Jessica and Mark, lived in the Chicago area. It was too far for them to see each other very often.

Carmen asked where Jed was and Will gave her a puzzled look. "I don't know. Probably got lassoed by someone who opened a beer for him--made him take it and schmooze with them for a while," he smiled at her, "it's all a part of the business, isn't it? Somebody has to do it and Jed lucked out tonight."

At nine o'clock they closed down the computer, emptied the cash register and turned off the lights in the lodge. As they stepped out into the night air, they heard a very distant call of a loon. Libby glanced back at the lake and said wistfully, "There's open water not too far away because the loons are back." Carmen heard Jed's voice in the distance saying, "Thanks for the brew, guys." He was coming from the direction of Cabin 7. So she said goodnight to the Edwards and walked over to meet up with Jed, Sadie following at her side. Honey joined Will, Libby and Becky, as they walked the path along the harbor to their home. It had been a long day and tomorrow morning would be here all too soon.

*****

Safe Harbor looked like a ghost town that Saturday morning. All the trucks with boats in tow had taken off before sunrise. There was not a soul to be seen. Will and Jed opened up the lodge at seven, started the Bunn Master coffee maker, and wondered what the day would bring. Jed looked out the window in the direction of cabin 5 and remarked,

"Harold and Henry must be sleeping in since they can't get their boat out of the harbor." The old fishermen would be stuck at the resort until the lake opened because they rented a resort boat and motor. Will gave Jed a cup of coffee and they sat down together at the lodge table.

It was around two in the afternoon when they heard a boat motor. It was such a strange sound coming from the lake, after all the months of ice. For an instant they thought their ears were playing tricks on them. Will walked to the far end of the point and looked down the lakeshore to see Brad Pullman from cabin 11 making his way through the Swiss cheese ice. Two guys in his boat were jabbing at the ice with paddles, one up front and another in the back keeping ice away from the motor. The ice was slowly breaking up as his powerful motor shoved the boat hull through the thin crust that remained. Behind Brad came his brother Phil. The two boats made a wide swath of open water as they turned into Safe Harbor. Will and Jed, on different sides of the harbor, cheered as the Pullman brothers headed into their assigned harbor slips. Brad gave Jed a big smile and said, "This is the most fun we've ever had," and opened his live-well for Jed to see. Fourteen perfect walleyes, two to three pounds each, thrashed and splashed in the water.

"We kept pulling them in, they were almost jumping in the boat on their own. I must have thrown back at least 10 others this size or larger." His brother Phil, the quieter one of the two, nodded in agreement from his boat.

The rest of the day was the same story. The other fishermen came back in a less dramatic way, arriving at the resort the way they left, in their trucks pulling their boats behind. But they all shared the same giddy excitement of the great fishing they had experienced.

The wind had picked up to twenty miles an hour in the afternoon, which eventually did its work on the last of the ice. By sunset the waves were finally crashing in along the shore. The ice had dropped out of sight and the sparkling water rose and fell with each incoming wave.

The resort was abuzz with activity. Every able hand was needed to run the lodge: work the till, write down charges, scoop bait, wrap fish, and fill gas tanks before the guests headed out onto the open lake that evening. One of the fishermen handed Will a twenty dollar bill for four dollars' worth of minnows and said to keep the change. It was a giddy, chaotic scene as Harold and Henry sat at the lodge table contentedly licking their cherry nut ice cream cones and listening to all the stories with great delight.

*****

By the following Wednesday, many of the fishermen had been down to pay their bills and were packing up their gear to head home. What the partners thought would be a long weekend of lost revenue ended up being extremely profitable. The fishermen were still beaming from ear to ear as they paid their bill and enthusiastically signed up for next year--same cabin, same week. Many hoped that the ice would go out late again next year because the fishing had been so phenomenal this year.

Out of the eighty-some fishermen who stayed at Safe Harbor, many followed the fishing regulations carefully. The others felt a little guilty for extras they had taken unlawfully, or the large female breeding fish they didn't throw back because they were sure it wouldn't really hurt the walleye population. This was one of the things the owners hated about being a fishing resort, feeling responsible for what some of their guests did, the purposeful ignorance they showed for the health of the fish population.

Will and Jed knew that the catch of walleyes over the last five days had been tremendous because they cleaned the fish cleaning houses and hauled the guts away every day. They had some misgivings about the "slaughter," but they felt helpless to do anything about it this fishing opener. They would worry about it next year.

Chapter 6

Getting in the Groove

Week two of the season had begun. Having fewer guests, the owners had their first opportunity to kick back *a little* after the hectic month of preparation and opening week frenzy. Experiencing the opening weekend of the fishing season was like drinking from a fire hose for the still rookie partners. They were learning by the seat of their pants, trying to maintain their sanity and meet the needs of all the excited fishermen. It seemed as soon as they filled gas tanks and minnow buckets for one group another group was waiting in line for the same. It had been an exhausting first week.

The second week of the season at Safe Harbor brought in another group of fishermen. All the cabins may not have been bursting at the seams like fishing opener, but this week's fishermen were just as anxious to get on the lake.

There were a few retired couples expected; most of them were old customers who knew the original owners. They had been staying at the resort since the 1950s. But there was a young couple new to Safe Harbor staying in cabin 1.

Two other memorable groups would be arriving. The *"boys,"* affectionately named by the Porters and Edwards, were three old guys from Rochester, Minnesota. Libby wasn't sure about them after their first week last spring. She was concerned about their propensity for hard drinking--*and* they seemed to draw Will and Jed into their company with purpose. It was also clear that Will and Jed, likewise, enjoyed the old *boys'* company.

"Wanna beeeer?" echoed often during that week. It was music to Jed's and Will's ears and they rarely refused the offer, as they both enjoyed the company of these fishermen. The list of resort repairs and chores was long, and it would remain so until the old boys' were gone. They came twice a year, the second week after opener and then again the second to the last week before closing the resort in late fall. Don and Jed Knutsen and Ross Peters were the core group. But they always managed to bring along some lucky fourth member to help share the cost and be a part of the fun for the week.

This week they brought along, Jerry, a retired county surveyor. Jed Knutsen and Ross Peters had a house painting business. Their high-earning clients were plentiful in Rochester, with all the medical specialists employed by Mayo Clinic. Jed's younger brother, Don, was a farmer. While at the resort, Don was the captain and also the chief cook of the group.

As Libby got to know the old boys better, her attitude towards them began to change. It took the visit in September last year for her to admit to herself that she had judged them a little too harshly in the spring. They may drink too much, but she found them also to be good-natured and good-hearted.

The old boys' first night at the resort was a bit embarrassing to watch, but by Sunday night they had gotten into a more relaxed state of mind. The boys rarely failed to share their fresh fried walleye and their stories from years past with Jed and Will. When Libby and Carmen were around, the old guys talked about their wives of thirty years with humor and affection. It came out that these weeks at the resort were their time to let loose and was really the only hard-drinking they did. They all jokingly admitted--"if it wasn't, we'd all be dead from liver disease."

The other group to arrive the second week of the season were the "firemen" from Chicago. They reserved five cabins on the north side of the harbor. They are the epitome of the brave, hunky heroes with more testosterone in their blood than your average individual. They put their lives on the line every day at work so when they come to Thunder Lake for seven days they fish hard, eat like kings, and try to let go of the stress of their dangerous jobs. They are brothers to one another. This group of 24 firemen and paramedics is organized by Harry Cunningham. Harry and his family have been coming to Safe Harbor for 25 years. Harry even met his wife at the resort 20 years ago. He personally comes three times a year: in May with the firemen, in July with his family for two weeks, and in late September with his wife, Deb, for a week.

*****

The big Saturday changeovers were not in full swing yet. Those long, hard working days were a few weeks away--once school was

63

out for the summer, is when the added cleaners would be needed. Since many of the "opener" crowd left early, Libby and Carmen had been able to clean most of the cabins over three days rather than waiting to clean them all on Saturday. Even Will and Jed had the luxury of doing their chores over three days so this Saturday, with their work done already, they were enjoying their morning coffee in front of the lodge watching the two dogs. Honey had found a pull-toy and was teasing Sadie with the loose end. Sadie took the bait and they were soon tugging and growling in play. The growling grew louder the longer they tugged. Sometimes they yanked and twisted so hard Will and Jed marveled their teeth didn't break loose.

Up on the other side of the harbor, the Chicago firemen dozed in their vehicles. They had driven into the resort hours earlier after driving through the night. Finally, one of them saw Will and Jed standing outside the lodge and woke the others in the vehicle. After a few minutes to wake up, one of the car doors opened and a tall, lean body emerged from the backseat.

"Hey, guys!" Jeff Doogan yelled at Will and Jed, as he stretched the kinks out of his back, "How's the fishing?"

Will gave the fireman the thumbs-up and then yelled back, "The fishing has been great!"

A huge smile crossed Jeff's face when he heard Will's report.

"Cool! Can't wait to get out there. I know it's really early, but are our cabins ready?"

"Yup, go ahead and settle in."

Will's words were like magic. You would think he had said "Open Sesame," as car doors opened, and tired, sore firemen emerged from their vehicles, stretched, yawned and yelled greetings from across the harbor. Soon the north side was a hub of activity. Boxes, coolers, duffel bags and miscellaneous gear were hauled into their cabins from cars, trucks and boats. After everything had been unloaded, the boats were quickly launched into the harbor. It wasn't long before Will and Jed were pumping fuel, scooping minnows and sending the firemen out onto the lake.

*****

Jed had just walked out of the lodge with the new guests who had arrived mid-afternoon. It was right about then that Jed heard the familiar "Wanna beeeer?" He looked over at cabin 7 where the voice beckoned and there stood Ross, a cooler in his arms, smiling at him. Jed gave Ross a smile and nod and then looked back at the new guests, Bobbie and Gene Sundgard.

Gene smiled but his wife's expression was uncertain; one eyebrow raised, with a hint of a smile...or was it a grimace, Jed wasn't sure.

Jed reassured her, "They grow on you."

Bobbie nodded her head and Jed pointed them to cabin 1, their resort home for the week.

"You guys will enjoy cabin 1. It should be pretty quiet around you as there is only one other couple staying next to you. They should arrive soon, the Petersons, John and Mary. You'll get along great."

Bobbie and Gene thanked Jed sincerely and headed to their small cabin tucked snug against a backdrop of towering pines at the top of the hill. They were thrilled to see that the little cabin had a screened porch that looked out on the bejeweled lake. The porch was a surprise as it was not listed in the resort brochure yet. Will and Jed had built it and three others over the winter months.

****

Sunday morning Will walked down to the lodge as Honey trotted ahead of him sniffing the ground, her hackles raised in alarm...or excitement, it was hard to say. She seemed quite interested in the invisible trail of some creature from the night before. As he walked along the harbor path, Will noticed Harry Cunningham's boat was out and so was Jerry Shramski's. He thought to himself, *"Another week of overflowing buckets of fish guts."* Since owning the resort, he had heard some guests bemoan the fact that they still had fish in their freezer back home from the previous year. The Chicago firemen were experienced fishermen and some of them kept everything they caught. He hoped they were not going to bring home coolers full of wrapped fish to already full freezers. He reminded himself to push the DNR stickers that promote 'catch and release' more this year. Will hoped the idea would eventually catch on in the years to come so that the next generation would have fish to reel in from the bountiful waters of Thunder Lake.

It was a little after nine a.m. when Libby arrived with Honey, the young lab's second arrival of the morning. Honey's daily ritual was to accompany Will as he headed down to open the lodge at seven a.m. She would hang out with him for a short time and then head back up to the house and bark at the door until Libby let her in. It would seem the lab liked her family in one place and her daily mission was to make that happen as soon as possible.

On Sunday mornings Libby often made pancakes in the lodge kitchen. It was usually difficult to sit down and eat an uninterrupted meal during the resort season. There would always be someone needing something as they took their first bite. But they would try to enjoy breakfast together although, more times than not, the hotcakes were eaten cold. Honey looked forward to their pancake breakfast too as she was a quick study in the art of catching Frisbee pancakes. It was a trick Will had started with their first lab, Golda--the queen of the pancake toss. She could catch a pancake flung from across the room, she never missed. Now Will was teaching Honey to back up further and further from him before he'd toss her a pancake. Libby didn't think Honey minded learning this trick that offered such a yummy reward.

As they sat down to a plate of hotcakes and sausage, they heard the lodge door creak open. It was Don from cabin 7. After closing the lodge last night, Will and Jed, had joined the old boys for a beer. Being asked numerous times during the day if they wanted a beer, it only seemed hospitable to finally take them up on their offer. Between the beers, the hilarious stories and the spread of food, it was very hard to leave the old guys, but Will knew duty would call on him early the next morning.

Getting up from his pancake breakfast, Will greeted his friend, "Hey Don, what can I do ya' for?"

"You should o' stayed a little longer last night, we could have used your help," Don scolded. "My brother started drinking J&B's after you left--big mistake. After more reminiscing we were all laughing...and drinking too much. Anyway, Jed needed to take a leak, so he's in the bathroom when we hear a loud thud. Yup, you guessed it, he fell over--blocked the doorway with his back end. It took us hours to get him out of there. We figured we'd have to leave him till morning but he finally woke up."

Libby grimaced thinking about the old guy falling...and...whether he peed in the toilet before he fell or later...on the floor.

"Is he okay this morning?" Will asked, concerned. He didn't think about the mess, but he did think about the liability.

"Oh, I think so. He's still in bed sawing logs. He'll be sorry all day that he drank so much. You know him."

Will and Libby nodded in affirmation, "Yes, we remember--first night's always a little rough for your brother."

*****

Because the opening season crowd had such fantastic luck fishing, the four owners were anxious to do a little fishing also. Feeling relaxed by Sunday, with the chaos subsiding and a manageable routine settling in, Jed and Carmen decided it was time to try some fishing and Will and Libby stayed back to hold down the fort. Aboard one the resort's Alumacraft eighteen-foot fishing boats, the Porters set off to try and catch some walleyes. As they fished they talked about their exhaustion and apprehension for the summer season ahead. But soon they relaxed and began to look around and appreciate the beauty of their surroundings. The sight and sound of the rippling water, the loons calling to each other just a few feet away, an eagle soaring above them. It was an amazing afternoon even if they weren't having any luck. By late afternoon Jed and Carmen slowly made their way back. They had pulled in a number of small crappies but the walleyes had been elusive.

Jed was busy on Monday morning with the daily task of cleaning out the fish-cleaning houses. He had finished the south side and had driven the lawn tractor and trailer over to the north side of the harbor. From outside the screened building he could see Jon McConnell, one of the Chicago firemen standing by the sink. He was running water into a large metal container to give the final wash to the fresh fish he had just filleted. Jon could have been 'Mr. June' in a calendar to raise money for the fire station. He was tall and handsome with a hard body like a brick wall. Jon dumped the water from the big metal dishpan and leaned against the table to visit while Jed worked. They talked about their families while Jed swept off the screens and floor, disinfected the work surfaces and carried out the buckets of fish guts to the trailer. By the time he was done there were eight overflowing buckets on the trailer from the two fish-cleaning houses. Jon stepped out of the screened building carrying the pan of fresh fish fillets and glanced over at a blackened cement slab twenty feet away.

"So Jed....*(long pause for effect)*...care to elaborate on what happened over there? Seems that there's a building missing."

Jed looked up and caught the mischievous expression on the fireman's face.

"Oh that. Yup, we had a little excitement last winter."

"Tell me all the details," Jon said, his smirk growing into a white, toothy grin. He leaned against the fish cleaning house, waiting to hear all the details.

"Well, it went like this… (Jed cleared his throat)…We decided it would be a great idea to make that empty storage building into a sauna last January. Will and I built a sauna at our lake cabin in Wisconsin and since moving up here we kinda' missed having one, especially in the winter. So we took a few hundred dollars and bought insulation and tongue and groove pine boards to finish off the inside. We found an old wood burning stove in a different shed along with some old double-walled stove pipe. We finished her up and she worked great for a couple of saunas. He smiled at Jon.

Jon, gestured with his hands, "Go on…"

The third time we planned to take a sauna it was Will's turn to start the fire in the wood-burner.   So an hour before we planned to take the sauna, he walked down and started her up. Carmen and I had our robes on over our swimsuits, snowmobile boots on our bare feet…*there was a snicker from Jon at this mental picture.*

Jed paused while Jon composed himself. We were about to head out the door of our house when I saw an inordinate amount of smoke coming from the sauna building. I called Will and told him. Then we all ran down to watch our hot sauna go up in flames. We had piles of snow everywhere but no water because it was winter and every water pipe was drained in the resort and the harbor was frozen over. It was a sad sight, my friend."

Jon's expression was serious, "Why do you think it caught fire?"

"The next day, after it had finished smoldering, we took a look at the wall where we had run the insulated pipe--that was the point of ignition. Will thought a double wall pipe would be fine but of course now we know it should have been triple insulated. We all felt terrible, Will especially."

"Well, I'm relieved you guys didn't get hurt. We see it all the time in our line of work."

Jon surveyed the resort grounds and looked back at Jed, "There's more sheds on this place, you could try again."

"I think Carmen and Libby might not agree with you," Jed said with a resigned smile.

******

Monday night it was Will and Libby's turn to try some fishing. Carmen and Jed took over lodge duty and Will headed out to a spot that several of the longtime resort guests had talked about. The most popular way to fish for walleyes is to rig up a lead-headed jig and tip it with a nice fat minnow. Then you drag the jig along the sandy bottom as the boat drifts over and around a reef or drop-off. This is where the walleyes feed and, if you are lucky, you are rewarded with a tasty dinner. It was a perfect evening, warm, with a light to moderate breeze forming a small chop on the water, allowing for a good drift. After a few passes over the submerged reef, Libby's pole bent down and she exclaimed, "Fish on!" Soon the prize was in the boat and Will and Libby were celebrating their first fish, a very nice three-pound walleye. They kept up the drift in hopes of getting a few more fish but it seemed the bite was over. Will moved the boat upwind for another drift over the bar and cut the motor. As they were getting their poles ready for one more drift, Will looked back and there, about four feet behind the boat, was another walleye swimming very slowly near the surface. He could not believe his eyes--it seemed as though the fish was maybe stunned or asleep. Not wasting any time, Will quickly started the motor and backed up towards the fish and when they were close he shut down the motor and reached over the side and grabbed the fish. It was a walleye and it was not dead. The fish seemed to wake up when Will grabbed him and it flopped madly in his grasp. But his grip was firm. Only when the fish was safely in the boat did it start to dawn on Will and Libby how odd it was to actually catch a walleye by hand. They both laughed at the absurdity. When they put the two fish side by side, the second one was a perfect twin to Libby's walleye, another three-pounder.

Will chuckled and shook his head in disbelief, "Jed and Carmen just won't believe our luck tonight."

After returning to the harbor later that night, Will and Libby had quite a fish story to share; they wondered if people would believe it, because even *they* had a hard time believing what had just happened.

******

Over the rest of the week, the old *boys* did what they did best...catch walleye. Some fishermen just had the knack, and these guys had the knick-knack and patty-wack. They rarely worked at it too long before they had their limit. Ross Peters owned the 18-foot, 1978 Blue Fin boat that they hauled up from Rochester, but for some reason Don always drove the boat. Ross just preferred it that way, positioning himself instead in the bow's swivel seat. Will and Jed asked them about this arrangement. They said, "That's just the way it is, Don drives, Ross sits up front and Jed sits in the back and hands out stuff from the coolers as we need refreshment. That's just the way we roll."

The arrangement worked well as they never came into the harbor skunked.

It was the end of a pleasant week. With only eight cabins rented, the work was easy to manage. Most of the cabins were clean and ready for the following week by Friday afternoon. That's when the Randells walked into the lodge. Being neighboring cabin owners just south of the resort, they rented a seasonal boat slip in Safe Harbor's naturally protected harbor. Many of the lake neighbors came only for the weekends, arriving from the Twin Cities mid-afternoon on Fridays. Most of these lakeshore neighbors were fishermen, so they appreciated the convenience of having such a close, safe place to keep their boats, buy their bait, and grab a tombstone pizza or pick up hot dog buns.

Libby was on duty catching up on the last minute charges for their outgoing guests using the computer program Will had put together. Libby looked up from her work as Jim Randell strode to the counter with his son and two nephews.

"Is our cabin ready?" he asked gruffly. *Jim Randell always sounded gruff.*

Libby smiled up at him and his son and nephews.

"Ahhh...hi Jim--Jerry, John, Bill."

"I called and reserved cabin 16 a month ago. We have a large group comin' this weekend and my cabin won't hold all the crew."

Libby looked at the Randells with a questioning stare. Will called it her "deer in the headlights" look as her mind clicked into a state of panic. She knew all the reservations for the following weekend and the Randell name was not one of them. She cleared her throat nervously.

"So what cabin did you say you reserved?"

"I told you already, Cabin 16! I called you last month, you or the other woman answered." he said with impatience. His fist hit the counter with a thud. "Look it up--did you forget to put it in the schedule?"

Libby was feeling panicked. She looked over the schedule, and there was no Randell entered. She looked at cabin 16--it showed that it was still open! With relief she looked up and said,

"Jim, cabin 16 *is* open for the weekend. We can have it cleaned in an hour and your extra guests can move in. Will that work for you?"

Jim puffed out his chest and took a deep breath. "Well, isn't that just dandy. How convenient that it's available even though you guys totally screwed up."

Then Libby stood up, her legs feeling a little shaky. She took a deep breath to compose herself. Her voice was strong as she responded to his rudeness, "Listen, Jim, you need to settle down. You have no right to come in here and treat me with such disrespect. I don't have an explanation for this misunderstanding at this time but the cabin is open and we can have it ready shortly."

Jim cleared his throat, not quite through with his tirade.

"You silly idiots don't know your tail end from your pie hole."

Libby's eyes started to water. No one had ever talked to her like that. She began to stammer but didn't know what to say. So she said nothing.

Jerry, Jim's son, stepped up to the counter and put an arm in front of his dad, his eyes glaring at him. He gave his dad's chest a little shove back and looked over at Libby.

"I am so sorry for his rudeness," he said with contrition.

He looked back at his dad exasperated, "WHAT is WRONG with you?"

Libby exhaled, not realizing she had been holding her breath.

"Shall we go ahead and set up the reservation then?"

This poked the bear, and Jim started in again.

What the HE-double-L...I already made the reservation! You know wha--"

Jerry interrupted, "I'll take care of this."

Then Jim's two nephews guided him towards the door. "Come on, Uncle Jim, we'll just step outside 'n' cool off."

As they turned their uncle around, John leaned towards Libby and whispered, "*We know he's a real arse sometimes!*"

Libby smiled at him and mouthed back, "*Thank you.*"

*****

Later that evening, after Carmen and Jed had taken over lodge duty, Libby started thinking about the run-in with Jim Randell. She had talked to her three partners and they all responded with blank looks and denied ever hearing from Jim Randell. There was a possibility that both parties were right, Jim had made a reservation a month ago and they were right in saying that they had not received that call, reserving cabin 16. She looked up the number for another Safe Harbor Resort only on a different lake fifteen miles away. Libby dialed the number and after a few rings Libby heard the person say, "Good evening, this is Safe Harbor Resort, Judy here. How can I help you?"

Libby had a hunch she was on the right track in solving this mystery.

"Hi Judy, this is Libby over at Safe Harbor on Thunder Lake."

"Oh hi!" Judy sounded pleasantly surprised, "What can I do for ya'?"

Libby started in. "Are you expecting a party to arrive today under the name Randell?"

"Why yes. We were just wondering what had happened to them."

"Well, mystery solved all the way around." Libby said. "We had a very surly neighbor of ours trying to argue with me that he had made a reservation for our cabin 16 a month ago but we didn't remember any such phone call. We were able to fit him in here but, *man*, was he mad! So I don't know what you want to do about him not showing up at your place. I guess that's between you and him. I will say, you can count yourself lucky that he isn't staying with you," she said, frustration in her voice.

"Sounds like I'm better off just letting it go. Thanks for the call though. We'll have to have coffee together sometime when things slow down."

"Sounds good, Judy. Have a good summer!" Libby hung up the phone with a satisfied smile. She then called down to the lodge and asked Carmen for Randell's cabin phone number.

Jim picked up the phone and answered gruffly. "Hello."

"Jim, this is Libby from Safe Harbor. Is everyone settled into cabin 16?"

Jim spat out, "They are all over here right now, making pigs of themselves and a sty out of my place. What do you want?"

"I just solved our mystery of your reservation," she said with confidence. "You mistakenly made a reservation with the Safe Harbor Resort on Big Boy Lake, not ours."

She felt vindicated by his very long pause. Then she heard a little stammer and he remarked defensively, "Well, I certainly know the difference between the two lakes, and I would never want to have my group stay on Big Boy Lake, that's fifteen miles away."

Libby replied with great pleasure, "Well, I guess you'll just have to talk to the other Safe Harbor and see what they want to do about your not showing up for your reservation there. I just spoke with them and they are waiting for your arrival." With that said, Libby said goodbye and hung up before Jim could say anything more. She put the receiver down and swiped her two hands together in a mock gesture of wiping her hands of the mess.

Next morning, Jim walked into the lodge, being pushed from behind by his son and nephews. Will was working the lodge as Saturday was cleaning day for Libby and Carmen. Will had heard the story of the rude treatment of his wife and tensed at seeing Randell come in. Will kept his anger in check but inside he was boiling. The only thing that saved him was the truth–Libby had proven Jim was in error and he had acted like a fool.

Jim stood a few feet away from the counter, unsure of Will's possible reaction to his behavior the day before. He cleared his throat and spoke to Will with deference.

I'm sorry for the accusations I made yesterday about the reservation. I realize now that it was my mistake. I remember now that I was not at home when I made the call, and when I asked for operator assistance she must have given me the number of the other Safe Harbor Resort. I failed to mention that there were two in the area only on different lakes. My bad."

Will answered him tersely, "Well, Jim, it takes a small man to talk like that to a woman. My wife is a far better person than I am. If it had been me dealing with you yesterday, your party would not have been allowed to stay. You understand what I'm getting at? Because if you do something like that again, it will be your last business at Safe Harbor. And I mean your boat will not be allowed in our harbor either."

Jim nodded that he understood. He turned to leave then turned back and said brusquely, "We'll need gas and five dozen minnows."

Will struggled to restrain his feelings. He hesitated a moment then he tucked his pocket size spiral notebook and a pen in his shirt pocket and walked out with the Randells to the bait shop. Sitting, waiting on the cement moat that surrounded the gas pumps, was a bait bucket and a gas tank. Will knew they were Randell's and went about the business of resort owner, filling the bucket with minnows and the gas tank with fuel. Jim walked out to his boat alone leaving his son and nephews to accompany Will.

*****

It had been a great week for fishing and weather. The firemen had been down to pay and reserve the same cabins for next May. Many of them had stopped by to look at the "Brag Board" in the lodge. It was a large bulletin board filled with pictures of fishermen (women and children too) holding their sizable catch way out in front them--*this always helped make the fish look even bigger in the photo*. The resort owners were more than happy to take Polaroid pictures of the proud fishermen with their catch. After the Polaroid photo quickly and miraculously developed before their eyes, they would label the lower white space with the name of who caught it, the size and type of fish and lastly, the date. The lodge had boxes of these "Brag Board" photos dating back to the 1950s. There were even black and white photos of the history-making event back in 1955 of the famous Muskie Rampage. Muskies do, from time to time, put on a frenzied 'bite,' giving thrilled fishermen something to remember, but this particular summer the muskie bite became world renowned. Anglers hauled in over fifty trophy size muskies the first three days from the lake; within a week the count was over one hundred. The old black and white photos showed long lines of muskies hung from sturdy metal pipes. The proud muskie hunters standing behind their catch were barely visible behind the large predatory fish.

As firefighter Jon McConnell walked past the bulletin board full of photos, he stopped to admire the various fish caught that week. The largest fish caught by their group was a fifteen-pound Northern pulled in by Danny Yokum. Jon was glad to see Danny pull in the top prize this year, since his year at home had been a heartbreak, with Danny's wife leaving him. Sometimes the stress of the job is too much for a marriage. The other four firemen that had come down to pay the group's bill, joined Jon to admire the pictures. There were a few back slaps of admiration given to each other for another successful week of fishing and relaxing. As they left the lodge each man had a bulging sack of souvenir sweatshirts, t-shirts and caps with the resort logo, not only for themselves but also for their children waiting for them at home.

It usually took at least an hour to settle the bill when the old boys came down to pay. So many jokes and stories were bantered about and a few beers consumed before they finally paid. Then they invited the owners to their final fish fry of the week. It was arranged that after they closed the lodge the Porters and Edwards would head to cabin 7 with their contributions of homemade cheesy potatoes and coleslaw. Their salivary glands were working overtime, anticipating the walleye supper with the old fishermen. During the course of the evening, a matter of business was brought up concerning the confusion over having two Jeds; Jed Knutson and Jed Porter. So the old boys renamed Jed Porter "Ray." Jed took it with good humor and graciously adopted his new name during the two weeks Jed Knutson was in camp. He and Will would certainly be looking forward to September and the old boys' return.

Chapter Seven

River meets her future fate

River Timberlake put on her royal blue casino uniform. The tight
skirt came up to her mid-thighs and the white sleeveless shell clung
to her breasts like a wet T-shirt. She yanked on the knit fabric
hoping to stretch it out. Then she added the royal blue jacket that
matched the short skirt and buttoned the two front buttons. She
looked in the full length mirror behind her bedroom door and gave
an exasperated sigh. "You didn't think you would end up working in
a casino dining room, did you?" she said to her mirror image. "After
four years of college, this is where you end up working!"

She was talking to herself because Lance was at the Village
council meeting with the elders today. He had been attending a
number of these meetings this spring since being hired by the
Thunder Lake Tribe. They had taken on a big legal challenge, and
Lance was hired on as the council's legal adviser.

River started working at the Thunder Lake Casino as a dining
room supervisor back in February. Even though she graduated with
a business degree, staying in the Thunder Lake area doesn't give
one much opportunity to use a college education. She had college
loans to pay off as her parents hadn't been able to help her or
Lance much financially. Even after their passing, there was not
enough inheritance to help pay off their parents' debts. She missed
working with her mom at Safe Harbor Resort cleaning cabins. They
both worked hard, but it was honest work with good people. She
always felt a sense of satisfaction when they finished each cabin.
She could see the difference her hard work made in preparing a
welcome place for families to enjoy their relaxing week together at
the lake. Now she was working in a place that never changed; night
or day, it always looked the same once she entered the windowless
building. Its only purpose was to make a game out of taking money
from fools willing to play for a chance to win big.

As River walked through the front doors of the casino at ten
minutes to three, heads turned to watch her. She was a strikingly

beautiful young woman in her size six uniform. Her long black hair glistened even in the dimly lit building. Her big brown eyes adjusted quickly to the lack of lighting on the cavernous gaming floor. She heard someone clear his throat behind her and knew it must be her friend Joe. Joe Cloudrider greeted River with a nervous nod and smile. He was head of security on the gaming floor, but he always made sure he was near the front doors when River was expected to arrive. Joe and River had known each other since they were kids. Joe was one of Lance's best friends. He was also head-over-heels for Lance's little sister, but he was afraid of showing his feelings. Joe was envious that River and Lance had been able to get away from the Rez and further their education. He and other friends weren't as ambitious; they were content to get in on the ground floor of the tribe's growing casino business. Now that Lance and River were back in their midst, it made him feel that maybe he had made a mistake staying in Thunder Lake. The Timberlakes both seemed more confident--wiser to the ways of the world--than the rest of them. He was afraid that he had nothing special to offer River and was sure that Lance would not think he was good enough for his sister. He told Lance that he would watch over River and he did just that--most importantly, making sure she got safely to her car at the end of her shift. Usually he was able to time his departure to hers in order to walk her to her car in the employee parking lot.

River had an inkling that Joe liked her, which was fine with her. She had always liked him; even as a little girl she had had a crush on him. He was a good-looking guy, tall and muscular. He wore his black hair short and his soft brown-eyes twinkled when he laughed. Most of all, it was Joe's kind heart that River found attractive, but it didn't hurt that when he looked at her and smiled, his white teeth, brilliant against his dark skin, always made her heart miss a beat.

River smiled back at Joe.

"Thanks, Joe. Working again tonight, I see. Are you getting off at midnight?"

Joe smiled and nodded his affirmative.

"I'll see you later in the dining room?" River questioned, as she continued to walk away--she was confident he would join her later. Joe just smiled as he watched her walk away. He often joined River for his dinner break. They would sit in one of the back tables, laughing about shared childhood adventures or exchanging stories about some of the strange casino guests with whom they came in contact while at work.

As River made her way to the Moosehead Dining Room, an older male customer looked up from his machine and leered at her as she walked by. He nodded his head and greeted her with a sly smile. She was nice to him because she had to be, but inside she felt dirty. She couldn't help but feel him undressing her in his mind. Sometimes, some uninhibited drunk would slide his hand down her back and bottom ever so lightly. It made her cringe in disgust.

Once she walked through the doors of the dining room, the entrance with the huge moose head mounted above the doorway, things were better. The dining room lights were set a little brighter and people seemed to respect her supervisory position. She rarely left her post, even on breaks, so she wouldn't have to enter the dark jungle of the gaming floor until she left for the night.

*****

Lance sat at the head of the table in the chief's council room. Chief Danford had been pressured into a troublesome situation by a group of individuals from the Native American Council for a United Nation (NACUN) to step up pressure on state and federal government to legislate laws enforcing stricter fishing limits on lakes where American Indians still held treaty rights. The NACUN representatives wanted to execute their power whenever and wherever they could. Chief Danford was an educated man. He had gone to college in Wisconsin to get his teaching degree and after ten years of teaching he was now the principal of the K-12 school in the village of Thunder Lake. He could understand the idea of pursuing what's right for his tribe and the lake, but he did not have an activist's heart. He just wanted his tribal children to grow up healthy and happy, feel proud of themselves, and be good people. These activists from NACUN had a knack for making him feel that his hopes and dreams fell far short of the mark for his people.

Lance Timberlake sat next to Chief Danford feverishly taking notes. This encouraged the chief; he hoped Lance might help make something good come of all this. The Tribal Fish and Game Department had documented five years of steady decline of the walleye and perch populations in Thunder Lake. A few council members, hot under the collar, vehemently blamed the greedy fishermen from the resorts on the lake for taking mass amounts of game fish. Many of the fishermen professed to practicing 'catch and release,' but many of the tribal leaders did not believe they were truthful. For the sake of open discussion, one daring council member tried to bring up the white man's argument that some of the blame should be placed on their tribal nets, often found laden with dead walleye, many large breeder size, caught and left to die. Many council members shouted out their indignation while others groaned their disapproval. As Lance listened to the commotion in the room, he thought about his old friend, George Bowstring and his buddies. He knew they often strung out nets just to irritate the white fishermen. He thought, *What a waste of a natural resource for the sake of a grudge. But humanity was not the only culprit for the falling numbers of game fish; the cormorants, an alien species of waterfowl, were gorging themselves on enormous amounts of walleye fingerlings. With no natural predators, nor anyone to hunt them, the cormorant population was exploding on the lake.* Lance was startled out of his thoughts when a NACUN representative slammed his briefcase onto the table in front of him, suggesting that maybe Chief Danford must not want to keep his position next election. Danford put his hands up to his face to cover his anger and frustration.

As Lance listened, he concluded that these situations were usually more complicated than the council was willing to see. He knew that plenty of resort owners talked about the massive amounts of fish their guests caught every year; he knew his buddies' pranks of setting nets was wasteful and the cormorants *were* out of control. Lance felt it was probably a little of everybody's doing, and each group pointing their finger at the other did nothing to solve a problem. But as the tribe's lawyer, he knew he would have to keep all these thoughts to himself. He was hired to represent his people's concerns and no one else's.

As the meeting broke up, the NACUN people gave Lance and Chief Danford a list of petitions they would bring to the attention of the County District Court in Beaver Creek. They hoped that all of this would eventually lead to hearings in the state and federal courts, which meant all the more opportunity for their concerns to be seen and heard by the public.

*****

As Lance walked out of the village's community building, he saw Herb Grogan leaning against his Camry in the parking lot. Herb and Lance were well acquainted with each other. They not only attended the same small chapel a mile out of town, but also the Timberlake family and the Cloudriders, Herb's in-laws, were close friends. Lance had not been particularly interested in anything religious now that he was an adult, but after all the love and support the church folk showed them after their parents' passing, Lance and River attended services when it was possible. They went because it was a small a gesture of respect for their mother and also because they felt closer to her and to God as they sat in the small sanctuary together.

"Lance, looks like you're putting in some long days with the council," Herb spoke as he stretched out his hand in greeting. Lance turned and smiled at Herb as he rearranged his briefcase from his right hand to his left in order to shake Herb's outstretched hand. "Herb, good to see you. How's fishing these days?" Lance inquired because Herb was a superb guide. They had taken a few trips out onto Thunder Lake over the winter months and enjoyed their time together. Herb told him about the record-breaking fishing opener, and then he changed the subject to his reason for meeting up with Lance.

"Lance, I've got a problem I need to talk to you about professionally." His look was serious. Lance searched his old friend's face and saw that worry lines deeply creased his forehead.

"Can we grab a bite to eat and talk?" Herb inquired.

Lance hesitated for a moment, thinking about River and her schedule then replied with a smile, "Sure, River is working at the casino tonight so I'm on my own. Why don't we ride together over to Charlie's Bar and Grill by the Dam. I'll drive while you talk."

On the way over to the restaurant, Herb gave Lance the details of the sorry state of his old resort, Muskie Run, and the drunk who was running the place into the ground. He told Lance about the fire and the condition of the cabins. He then had to admit that he had let this go on longer than he should have because he didn't have the heart or strength to go after Charles Wiley so soon after his wife, Jenny, died.

"But now I'm ready to fight for Muskie Run. Jenny loved that place so much," Herb said with conviction. He wiped his eyes with his handkerchief and then blew his nose with a surprisingly loud snort.

Herb and Lance talked through dinner and the drive back about what to do to get Herb's property back. Lance had a good idea how to proceed with the troublesome Mr. Wiley and told Herb he would get right on it in the next few days.

They said goodbye at the community center parking lot.

"The Lord bless you, Lance. Please greet River for me."

Herb shook Lance's hand firmly. Now there was a glint of hope in the eyes of the older man. Lance reassured his friend that things would work out as they parted ways.

******

It was finally midnight. River had tallied her worksheets, talked to her serving crew before they left, and gave the incoming supervisor the pertinent information from the evening. She then grabbed her purse from the tiny office--*more like a closet than an office*--and headed into the darkness of the gaming floor. She took the quickest route to the front doors where she was relieved to see Joe waiting for her. As they walked out the doors together, River noticed a new valet walking back up from the side parking lot, jingling keys in his left hand.

River asked Joe, "Who's the new guy?"

She watched him as he walked towards them. He was a middle-aged man, interesting looking, kind of an older, rougher-looking George Clooney-type. The slightly greying man smiled at River as he reached for her hand. "Joe, who is this beautiful young woman?"

Joe grimaced. "Charlie, this is River Timberlake. River, this is Charles Wiley."

"It's truly a pleasure to make your acquaintance," Charlie said as he brought River's hand up to his lips and kissed it softly. River blushed and Joe felt his own face get red with irritation. Charlie quickly released her hand and smiled, "See you around Joe…River."

He then turned and walked over to the next waiting car.

Joe kept his thoughts to himself, but he knew he now had one more reason to keep an eye on Lance's little sister. This new guy was going to be trouble. He could feel it.

Chapter Eight

Full tilt ahead Maties!

After Memorial Day weekend, Safe Harbor Resort switches gears and heads full swing into family mode. The Sunday night picnics were the perfect setting to encourage new children each week to meet and play together within range of the watchful eyes of their parents. The Porters and the Edwards started preparations for the picnic by setting up picnic tables on the front lawn of the lodge and preparing hamburger patties, slicing onions and pickles, and opening packages of hotdogs for the grill. The guests started arriving when they smelled the meat cooking from the two grills being manned by Will and Jed. Each family brought with them delicious side dishes and stories about their times at the resort. Often the old resort owners, Bud and Bev Carter, who lived a few miles away, joined the picnic. Bev walked in with her usual plate of deviled eggs or a homemade cobbler. The long-time guests enjoyed seeing the old resort owners again. You could always tell at which table the Carters sat because there was a circle of people around them. Everyone loved to hear Bud's stories about the old days. The sounds of laughter echoed through the resort while the sun set over the immense lake. After a spectacular sunset, the seriously stuffed guests would head back to their cabins and the Porters and Edwards would clear the tables and wash any dishes before closing the lodge for the night.

Another activity that started with the arrival of families to the resort was minnow racing. Will had gotten the idea from a fellow resort owner at the winter Minnesota Resort Conference. Dave Ottinger, from Pequot Lake Resort, had given a class on children's resort activities. Will thought minnow racing would be a blast. Dave had the plans and list of materials for anyone interested.

Will had purchased the supplies and put it together their first season. It was cheap entertainment for everyone: a five-foot piece of six-inch PVC pipe cut in half lengthwise, four end caps and scrap lumber. When put together, it made for screaming fun, and maybe a few friendly adult wagers. The exhilaration and the frustration of the race was that some minnows were raring to go and the others seemed comatose. Then, for whatever reason, the comatose minnow would fly through his trough like a Muskie was after him. It all made for great fun. This usually took place on Monday mornings. Then on Tuesday mornings, Libby and Carmen would do a craft with the kids. By that time the kids had been together enough to make friendships and the rest of their week at Safe harbor was filled with making memories that would last a lifetime.

This particular Sunday evening, the fourth picnic of the season, the resort was full and the picnic tables were overflowing with rambunctious children and friendly parents, all visiting until the mosquitoes drove them indoors at dusk. After everyone was gone and the picnic supplies were put away, Libby encouraged Carmen to go home and relax. She would finish up the few things left to do. She had been feeling this growing wall between the two of them and Libby was at a loss as to how to approach Carmen with her feelings. Maybe it was just all in her head. Will was constantly accusing her of being too sensitive.

Wednesday morning, Libby walked into the lodge a little early for her shift. She was looking for Carmen and found her working in the storage room.

"Can we try and set up a meeting sometime this week with you and Jed?" Libby asked Carmen. Her voice sounded uncertain. She and Will had decided that they needed to get things out in the open with their friends and business partners. It had been months since the two couples had sat down together to discuss problems, suggestions, or whatever was on their minds concerning the business. Ever since their spring work was done and the guest season had begun, the partners hardly spent any time together. They had worked out their lodge schedule: one couple taking the "minnow shift" and the other would take the "ice cream shift." "Minnow shift" was lodge duty from seven a.m. to two p.m.--when you scooped a lot of minnows for the fishermen. "Ice cream shift" was from two p.m. to nine p.m.--when you scooped a lot of ice cream cones. They had worked out one day off per week for each couple and then the following week they would switch shifts. The problem with this schedule was that they never had any time together anymore. Libby and Will felt the loss keenly and hoped that a meeting with their partners would bring to light any misunderstandings.

Carmen looked in the direction where Libby stood and then turned back to her work. She pulled bed sheets from stacks on the shelves and placed them in plastic tubs labeled with different cabin numbers. The two women had devised this plan to keep themselves organized and things running smoothly during the change-over on Saturdays. They filled each tub with the correct number and sizes of sheet sets, toilet paper rolls, bath soaps, kitchen towels and garbage bags for a week's stay.

"Yeah, we should," Carmen finally responded.

She gave Libby an uncomfortable smile and then handed over the schedule for next week's incoming guests and walked out of the back room. Carmen called Sadie to her side as she walked across the lodge to the front door.

"We'll see you, Libby. Jed and I are going to Duluth tomorrow for our day off so we won't be around all day."

Then she and Sadie walked out the door and up the hill to their home. Libby watched from the office window, feeling even more troubled.

Will walked into the lodge a short time later. Even though Libby was busy in the back room, she knew he was not alone as she could hear Honey's nails clicking on the old wood floor as she and Will made their way to find her in the back room. Libby turned from her chores and greeted her sweet lab first. Honey was so happy to see her, her tail wildly wagging kept thumping against the wall. Will stuck his head through the doorway next and asked Libby how her talk with Carmen had gone. Libby told him that she was even more convinced there was something going on with the Porters.

"She didn't want to talk about it, she just up and left with hardly a word. I'm so worried that we have done something to really offend them or make them mad. What do you think, Will?"

Honey leaned hard against Libby's leg and begged for her full attention. The yellow dog knew Libby was upset, and it was making her feel insecure. Libby bent down and scratched behind Honey's ears. She groaned with pleasure and looked up at Libby and smiled her goofy Labrador smile, her pink tongue lolling through white pointy teeth. Will put his work gloves down on the table, grabbed a bottle of water out of the cooler and sat down with a sigh.

"I don't know what to think, Hon. It seems obvious that there's something wrong. What do you think we should do?"

Libby walked over to the table and sat down next to Will. They both looked out at the glistening lake twenty feet away. Just then the lodge door opened and in walked three little girls who immediately called to Honey. Honey barked and wagged her tail as she went over to greet them. Will and Libby watched Honey as she wagged and snuffled the girls. They never worried about her with children. Libby got up and walked behind the counter.

"What can I do for you girls?"

The oldest girl, Maddie, said "I want an ice cream bar, please."

The middle girl, Sarah, said "I want a chocolate chip ice cream cone."

The littlest girl, Jamie, said, "I want a *banilla* ice ceam cone, pe-e-ase."

They all chuckled at Jamie's cute request. Will got up and offered to scoop the cones while Libby wrote the items down on their cabin charge-sheets. Honey wanted to follow the girls out of the lodge with their ice cream treats, but Libby called her back. The lab turned back reluctantly and gave a groan as she laid down next to Libby. Alone again, Will and Libby continued their talk concerning what to do about the Porters.

"We can't keep ignoring the fact that we never talk about anything together anymore, either as friends or about work," Will commented.

Libby remembered how last summer they hung around together at the lodge even when it wasn't their shift. They'd share a meal together on a picnic table in front of the lodge, like the friends they had always been. They hadn't done anything like that this whole summer unless Will and Libby instigated it. If Will and Libby visited the lodge while the Porters were on duty it wasn't long before Carmen would say something like "Why are you guys hanging around the lodge? Go do something before it's your shift." So they had quit visiting the lodge when they weren't on duty.

Will watched as Libby, always the quiet one, sat deep in thought across the table from him; he never quite knew what she was thinking or feeling. Finally he interrupted the silence.

"Well, all we can do is talk to them face to face. It doesn't do any good to make assumptions. We have been friends too long not to trust in them."

Meanwhile, as Carmen and Sadie walked through the kitchen door of their home, they saw Jed hunched over his desk. Sadie was quick to trot across the floor to give him a big greeting. Jed gave her head a squeeze and patted her long hair. It was their year to take care of the financial work for the resort. The Edwards had done it the year before. Carmen went over to him and hugged his neck.

"What's the matter? You look as troubled as I feel," she said as she kissed the top of his head.

"I just don't see how we're going to make our mortgage payment in October with all these business expenses," Jed told her in exasperation. He put his pencil down and leaned back in his chair. Sadie stood between them, looking up with concern, swishing her tail when one of them spoke. Carmen sighed and told Jed about Libby and Will wanting to have a meeting with them.

Carmen's voice was strained, "They know something's wrong. How can we keep it from them any longer? I hate this place, I hate this business, and I want us to get out of here, but what will that do to Will and Libby?"

Jed got up and walked to the far side of the room from Carmen. He was as frustrated as she was and as uncertain about what to do.

"There is just not enough money in this resort for the four of us. Will and Libby seem more comfortable with the financial uncertainty, but for us it's been too much of a strain."

They stood across the room from each other, both looking out different windows, hesitant as to what to say next.

Carmen looked back at Jed and admitted solemnly, "And I can't go through another winter up here, Jed," her voice trailing off to a whisper, "I can't do it."

"Then we need to tell them. They deserve to know." Jed said. "We all signed a partnership agreement that addressed this very thing. None of us knew going in if this would work, so the agreement plan covers the possibility of one couple wanting out. Remember?"

Carmen agreed, "Yes, I remember.

We need to tell them. I know they will be so disappointed, I just hope they won't be angry with us."

*****

Lance Timberlake had been researching the best way to help Herb Grogan get his resort back. He checked with the county concerning back taxes on the property and what he feared was true. The property was in arrears. He then drew up a letter to Mr. Wiley stating his breach of contract with Mr. Grogan. The non-payment of taxes as well as his delinquent contract payments should be grounds to begin the process of removing Mr.Wiley from the property. He decided he would hand-deliver the letter so he could talk to the guy face to face. Maybe they could work things out instead of proceeding through the court system.

As Lance drove down Muskie Run Resort's long, heavily wooded driveway, he was impressed with the setting. The resort cabins sat evenly spaced around a cozy little harbor, towering pines and clumps of birch shaded the grounds. Beyond the grounds the sparkling lake spread out to the horizon, inviting one and all to take in its beauty. Then his eyes focused in on the buildings themselves. The disrepair and damage was obvious even from a distance. He pulled in the driveway that led to the house and was getting out of his car as the front door opened and a dog came bounding out to greet him, his long ears flopping from side to side. Then a man, looking to be in his late forties, stepped out onto the front step.

Suspicion was written into the man's scowling features, "What do you want?"

Lance walked over to him and introduced himself, deciding to not mention the detail that he was an attorney, for now. They talked for a while about the beautiful grounds of the resort. Mr. Wiley said he was thinking about selling the place but hadn't gotten around to listing it yet. Lance paused at that admission and then told Mr.Wiley why he was there. He told him that he was an attorney representing Herb Grogan and explained that he would not be able to sell the property because the resort was legally Herb's since the terms of the contract had not been followed.

Charles Wiley stood there with a blank look on his face. Lance could tell that the man had been drinking, the smell of whiskey hung heavy on him. This explained the blank stare on Wiley's' face as his brain slowly processed the young lawyer's words.

Soon his expression hardened, and his eyes became cold and small.

"You get the hell off my property and tell that old fart he ain't gettin' this place back unless he wants to buy it back from me!"

Lance would have been amused at such a silly comment but thought better of making light of this man's illogical thinking. There was something about him that made Lance feel a little uneasy. There was a rage burning in Wiley's eyes that made Lance concerned for himself and his old friend Herb.

Lance responded in an authoritative voice.

"You'll be seeing me again, Mr. Wiley, only the next time I will be with the sheriff. If I were you, I'd start packing up your personal belongings and get ready to move out."

Lance laid an envelope containing the letter detailing the breach of contract on a nearby picnic table. He tapped it and simply said, "This is for you, Mr. Wiley. Read it and follow the advice given to you." He then turned and walked to his Camry. As he slid into the driver's seat, Lance looked out the windshield and watched the angry man walk over and pick up the envelope that held the letter. The dog peeked out from behind Charlie, his tail tucked under his belly in fear. Lance started the car and backed out of the driveway as Charlie looked up to watch him leave. As Lance drove out he looked again at the man from his rearview mirror just as the drunk pulled something out of his pocket and pointed it at the car. Lance's heart stopped as he took a harder look--it seemed that there was nothing in the man's grasp--maybe it was just a pointing finger and cocked thumb. But he couldn't be sure, and he wasn't going back for a closer look.

Charlie smirked as he realized that his little pantomime had been seen; he was sure that the cocky lawyer had flinched. As the dark blue Camry disappeared down the dusty driveway, Charlie opened the envelope containing the letter. He knew he was delinquent in the matters stated in the letter, but he felt he was being unfairly treated. He hadn't meant for this to happen; it was just bad luck. The letter also stated that he had neglected the buildings and alienated the customers, driving away the income base for the business. Charlie was indignant. He had only been going through a rough patch and people were judging him when he was most vulnerable. Now these bastards were trying to screw him out of his home and business. He crumpled up the letter and threw it to the ground. He was about to do the same with the envelope when he noticed the embossed return address on the envelope: *Lance Timberlake, Attorney.* Timberlake…Timberlake …where have I just heard that name? He sat down on the picnic table, trying desperately to clear his whiskey-soaked brain. Then it came to him, River Timberlake, the pretty young thing at the casino. It's a small world, he thought, as a look of pleasure came over his face.

The little spaniel sensed Charlie's frustration turn to pleasure, and she responded by laying her head on his leg and looking up into his face, the whites of her eyes showing, giving away her submissive nature. Charlie felt her soft head and rubbed behind her ears, not bothering to look down at her. Charlie stared out into space, contemplating. After a while he looked down at his dog and she wagged her tail in response to his gaze. "Well, old girl, it's a small world all right. I think this deserves a little drink." Charlie rose from the picnic table, the empty envelope in hand, and walked into the house. The floppy-eared spaniel romped happily at his side.

Chapter Nine

Invasion and Destruction

Jed stepped out of his house a few minutes before seven a.m. and hesitated in the open doorway. He heard something odd sounding-- a humming or buzzing in the humid morning air, but he couldn't put his finger on what it was. He started down the hill to the resort below still puzzled by the queer noise. The sun was beginning to stream through the trees behind him and a warm breeze was blowing off the lake in front of him. It would be a hot, steamy day, which meant the fishing would be lousy and the beach would be covered with sunbathers and sandcastles. As he got closer to the shoreline the humming was growing louder above his head. He looked up and saw, fifteen feet above him, swarms of flying bugs. *Fish flies! Crap! And I have the morning shift!* He muttered to himself. He started seeing them everywhere; the sides of buildings, on his sleeves, on the backs of fishermen walking towards the harbor ahead of him.

Jed remarked to the man walking in front of him. "Morning, Harry, I see our July friends are back." When Harry Cunningham turned around, Jed saw four fish-flies, on the brim of Harry's cap. The disgusting hitchhikers, also known as mayflies, have long antennae on their heads and at the tail-end the insect had two long points. At midsection, inch-long transparent wings pointed straight up as they pressed tight together when at rest. They are a non-biting insect, which helps. Their larvae begin their life cycle at the bottom of the lake. Through a sort of mystical suggestion, they all start rising to the surface, taking wing by the millions and dying 24 hours later.

Jed mused to himself, "*I wonder how many of those guys are all over me?* " He didn't even want to know.

"They always come the week we're here," Harry said with a shrug. He was back for his second visit to the resort, this time it was for a two-week stay in cabin 16 with his family.

"If this hot, muggy weather doesn't kill the fishing, these bugs will. The fish will have enough to eat for the next week with all their dead bodies floating on the lake."

As Jed and Harry rounded the cement corral that enclosed the gas tanks next to the harbor, they both groaned in disgust. The floor of the cement pen was covered, several inches deep, with dead fish flies. The live ones covered the sides of the tanks and the bait building next to the tanks. At the top of the bait building hung the old Grain Belt Beer sign still lit from the night before. It was hard to tell that it was on because it also was covered with bugs. Jed gave a deep sigh and decided he needed coffee before he could face shoveling the drifts of decaying insects. Harry joined him in the lodge. His family was still sleeping and, since fishing would be dismal, he thought maybe he'd stay and have coffee with Jed.

It was a little after eight a.m. when Will walked through the lodge door. He picked up a mug and poured himself some coffee and joined the other two men. They joked about the fish fly invasion outside, trying to make the best of a nasty situation.

After Will finished his coffee, they all went out to clean up the mess before the rest of the resort families awoke.

Will told Jed, "When Libby and I close up tonight we'll keep the Grain Belt sign off so if the wind blows our direction again we shouldn't get them so thick in the cement moat." They both put away the brooms and shovels. Jed agreed, "It won't help the beach area but it should help in the harbor and especially in the gas-pump moat."

The fish flies lasted for almost a week. The unlit Grain Belt sign did help but it also helped that the wind blew the opposite direction the last few days, sending the hoards of bugs to descend and die on the other side of the lake. The fishing was hopeless; most of the guests had given up and just enjoyed swimming and skiing. The last few nights had produced some wild thunderstorms but the days continued to be hot and muggy.

Sadie and Honey spent most of their time swimming to stay cool. Kids threw sticks into the lake and Honey would fly off the rocks into the water with wild abandon. Sadie chose her footing carefully over the rocks and walked daintily into the water for a leisurely swim as Honey chugged past her, snorting and paddling so fast she left a wake behind her. Sadie never quite understood Honey's insanity when it came to fetching sticks, but she feigned interest just to goad the little imp.

Will and Libby were kept busy in the afternoons and evenings, scooping ice cream cones and baking pizzas, as no one in the resort wanted to cook in their cabins.

*****

Five a.m. Thursday morning Will woke to the sounds of another wild storm. He figured it must be pretty bad if it woke him with the fan blowing on high in the window next to their bed. He realized Honey had joined them on the bed which meant she was scared. He reached his hand down to where he felt her soft fur. "It's ok, girl, it's just a little storm."

Just then lightning flashed and thunder cracked and rumbled like giants bowling in the black clouds above. Honey wriggled up between Libby and Will until her head rested on Libby's pillow. Libby woke up to Honey shaking next to her.

"What are *you* doing here, Honey?"

Will spoke from the other side of the shaking dog.

"There's another storm. It sounds pretty wild out there. I think this one is worse than the others....I'm getting up."

Just then he heard a powerful gust of wind and a huge tree crack in their front yard. The electric appliances in the house went silent.

"Well, there goes the electricity again. DARN."

Will tugged on his jeans and t-shirt that hung on a peg outside their closet. Honey hopped off the bed to follow but Will told her to stay. "Libby, keep her inside."

Will grabbed his cumbersome ring of resort keys and headed out the door in his yellow rain slicker. He was feeling more and more concerned as he looked around. Hopping in his truck, he headed toward the harbor. He couldn't quite make out what he was seeing through the gusting rain, but it looked to him like the harbor water level covered most of the docks and a couple of boats floated loose from the dock posts. With the rising water, the dock posts were barely showing above the surface.

"What the heck..." Will exclaimed to himself.

He pulled up alongside the lodge and hopped out onto something crunchy. In the dark of the early morning hour, with rain coming down in sheets, it was hard to tell what was underfoot so he pulled out a flashlight from behind his seat. When he switched it on, the beam of light shone on crayfish and flopping minnows all over the driveway and grassy areas. The hairs on the back of his neck tingled; his heart began to pound in his chest.

"What is going on?"

He heard voices yelling from the direction of the harbor so he headed over to see who was out in the storm. As he got closer he recognized Harry Cunningham's voice from across the harbor. He and his son had just stopped an empty boat from heading out of the harbor. It was hard to hear what Harry was yelling over the screaming wind and the roar of the six foot waves. Will could make out something about "surge" and "taking out." After a few more minutes of chaos, Will noticed the wind dying and the rain pelting down with less intensity. Then Jed appeared out of the darkness.

"Hey, Will, quite a scene, huh!"

"When I drove down I could swear the docks were all under water, now they're all showing again. What just happened? " Will asked Jed in bewilderment.

"I saw the same thing, and what's with all the fish and crawdads all over?"

Will panned his flashlight at the trees and to his horror, great basswoods and oaks had been uprooted all around them. The floating boats in the harbor were all sitting low from being filled with the driving rain.

"My God, this is bad! We've gotta' check on the guests!"

Will and Jed split up and went from cabin to cabin checking on people. Daylight was showing more of the devastation as they walked the grounds. Some of the people were starting to come out of their cabins. One cabin held two Polish brothers in their 50's and their two sons. The foursome were new to the resort. The brothers had made the long trip from Chicago to show their sons this great Minnesota lake. Now they stood outside their cabin talking excitedly in Polish about their ordeal. When Jed walked up to them, he noticed both were bare-chested and barefoot. "Are you guys all right?"

The brothers switched from Polish to broken English and told Jed, "Da vint vas blowin' and da vindows crashed open. Den da tree, two feet from our kitchen vindow, starded to groan and crack. We were so scairt that we all got under da kitchen table, hugging together and praying, Oh Got, save us!" Jed looked over at the huge basswood tree lying inches from their cabin. Its massive roots rising vertically from the ground to tower above the cabin roof.

"Looks like God answered your prayers. Is there anything I can help you with?"

"Na, na, we're fine. You go--see about da odders."

Will, meanwhile, made his way down to the two cabins closest to the shoreline. The waves were still crashing over the rocks but with less intensity. At cabin 5 he found the Merrill family from Fargo picking up their belongings scattered around the outside of the cabin. "Hey, Tom, is everyone ok?"

"Yeah, we're all fine. That was quite the storm though," Tom replied. "We woke up to the waves hitting the windows of the cabin. I thought about our lawn chairs leaning against our truck so I ran out to grab them just in time to see them both get picked up by a wave and carried out into the lake. I yelled for Marta to come and watch what was happening and just then another wave brought our chairs back to shore. So we quickly ran out and each grabbed one before the lake took them again. Crazy, huh?"

Will was incredulous. He thought, *what kind of weird storm was this?* He talked to Tom and Marta a while longer and then continued on. As he walked around to the different cabins it became clear that no one seemed to be hurt. There were some shingles off some of the roofs and a large branch had fallen on a car but no major cabin damage. The greatest loss was all the large white pine and basswood trees. So many had toppled over, their roots having surrendered under the tremendous power of the wind.

By the time Will made it back to the lodge, he found Jed and Carmen working inside cleaning up the water that had come through the windows facing the lake. Jed looked up from his mopping as Will entered.

"Hey, Will, the mystery of the high water in the harbor and fish in the driveway is solved. We just received a phone call from Verna over at Pine View Resort. *Remember she calls us when the Lake Area Emergency Call List is put into action.* She told me that the whole lake surged to our side causing our lake level to rise by four feet. I guess the resorts on the other side of the lake reported finding their boats sitting on the bottom of their harbors still hanging from their dock lines. The whole lake surged to our side! That's why Harry saw the boat leaving the harbor, the four-foot surge of lake water was rushing out of the harbor taking one of our boats with it!"

Will's face showed his bewilderment.

"You mean the lake was up past the lodge and that's why the fish ended up in the driveway?"

Jed nodded. "That would be the reason."

Carmen wrung out her towel into a large bucket. She was trying to salvage what she could of the papers and equipment on the desk.

"The adding machine is ruined and yesterday's mail was drenched and scattered all over the floor. If you are looking for Libby, she's in the bait house looking for more buckets." Carmen looked behind her and nodded to the computer, "It's a good thing the computer sits further from the windows. I think it escaped any water damage but we won't know till we get power again."

Will looked around and the reality of the ordeal began to sink in. If the whole area around the lake was affected like this, then the damage is extensive and the electricity will be out for days.

As the day progressed, the two couples alternated between feelings of great relief and sorrow. They were amazed that no one had been hurt but the loss of so many of the resort's massive trees was heartbreaking. Everyone in the resort pitched in to help clear debris from the roadways and lawns. The Polish men from cabin 9 launched into helping with the toppled trees with gusto. Jed noticed that the two tough, hard-working men were still bare-chested and barefoot as they walked around the tree roots and debris, yelling out, "Von-two-three--PULL!" as Will drove the tractor forward. And when one pull didn't do it they yelled, "Von more time!"

Boats were put back into their proper dock spaces. In areas where large chunks of soil had eroded away from the torrential rain,

Will dumped fill into the crevasses and deep holes packing it down with the tractor bucket. There were numerous calls to the power company but no promises were given as to when the power would return to their resort or anywhere else on the lake.

Jed and Will handed out five gallon buckets to every cabin so they could at least flush their toilets with lake water. People took a swim in the lake in lieu of a shower and the old oil lamps in the cabins, thought to be quaint décor, were now brought back into use as the sun set that Thursday evening.

By Friday afternoon the minnows in the bait tank had all perished. Without electricity to run oxygenated water into the tanks, the minnows suffocated. The ice cream freezer had been emptied of its half melted contents and handed out to all the guests. The children thought this might be the best week ever at Safe Harbor: all you could eat free ice cream, baths in the lake, and no water to wash dishes in their cabins. Some of the people had come down to pay their bills and head back to civilization but most stayed until Saturday morning. The Cunninghams and two other families from Chicago, would be staying for another week, as they did every year. They considered the storm's aftermath as part of the adventure of Thunder Lake. But the incoming guests for the following week would not know about the situation unless they were forewarned. So the Edwards and Porters found themselves again this season, calling incoming guests to warn them of the casualties of the unprecedented weather.

Becky Edwards arrived shortly after seven o'clock Friday evening. The drive from the Twin Cities was always long when she drove up by herself. Her brother, Josh, had plans for the weekend so she was on her own. She listened to her favorite CDs and sang along with Paul Simon, the Beatles or James Taylor, to pass the time. When she pulled into the resort, she stared in disbelief at the loss of trees. Some of the trees still standing looked like they had exploded, exposing the center of the trunk. *"What kind of power could do something like that?"* She thought as she walked down the hill to the lodge.

When Becky entered the lodge, Libby was talking to Carmen in the storeroom. She had just hung up from talking to the last guest scheduled to come tomorrow.

"Well, we certainly have some loyal guests. They've all been reached and warned about the lack of electricity and again, there wasn't one group that opted to stay away."

When Libby heard the door creak she looked over to see who was entering the lodge. Her face lit up in a big smile as she saw Becky standing in the doorway.

"I'm so glad you made it. Thank you for coming, Sweetie," she said as she crossed the lodge to hug her daughter.

The three women sat down to talk about tomorrow's cleaning. It would be a tough job without electricity or tap water, and the incoming guests would be arriving by mid-afternoon.

Libby looked at Carmen and expressed her uncertainty. "How will we do it?"

"Well, we have those 'hoky' carpet-sweepers," Carmen suggested, "They don't need electricity."

"Yeah, I guess they would work." Libby sounded a little more hopeful.

Libby and Carmen pondered their predicament further while Becky grabbed a Coke from the 'warm' cooler. When she felt the warm, dry can she replaced it and grabbed a bottle of water instead.

"We'll use lake water with bleach to wash everything down," Carmen suggested.

Libby felt more encouraged, "Yup, the bleach will sanitize everything."

Becky just listened. Soon her mind wandered into thoughts of how strange it was to see her parents through adult eyes now. As a child your parents seem invincible and always sure of themselves, but Becky was starting to see a vulnerable side as she looked at her worried mother. She was so grateful that no one had been hurt in the storm but what an ordeal they would face tomorrow to get the resort ready for the incoming guests. She looked out the window and watched as Jed and her father repaired damaged boards on docks across the harbor. A lot of the outdoor work can be done without electricity. Still, they would be dealing with damage around the resort for weeks.

*****

As the sun was sinking lower over the lake, the men came back to the lodge to relax on the deck and enjoy a warm beer before closing up. Will was happy to see Becky had made it safely from the Twin Cities. It was getting late, almost dark, so Becky said goodnight to Carmen and Jed. She wanted to unload her car before the mosquitoes carried her away.

The four owners left the lodge that night bone-weary and overwhelmed. The sun had fallen into the vast lake behind them but the magnificent sunset had been lost on the tired crew. The mellow glow of the oil lamps in the cabins dotted the darkening hillsides of the resort.

By four o'clock Saturday afternoon the two hired cleaners were done and Jed had paid them at the lodge. Libby, Becky and Carmen had their swimsuits on and were heading to the harbor. They had packed a bag of towels, sandalwood soap, shampoo, razors, a bottle of wine and three glasses. After working for eight hours straight, the last cabin was finished, and they needed a relaxing, refreshing soak. They had informed Jed and Will of their departure and were now heading out of the harbor in one of the resort rental boats to the quiet sandy beach a half-mile away. It had been a humid and exhausting day. *None of them knew that Will had gone into every cabin before them with buckets of lake water and bleach, and washed stacks of dirty dishes left by the outgoing guests. It was a very kind gesture that saved the two cleaning crews hours less work.*

The twenty-five horsepower Johnson motor putted quietly along the shoreline leading to the sandy beach. They pulled the boat up onto the shore and wasted no time diving into the clean refreshing water. After sudsing-up and shaving their legs they finally felt refreshed. The three women sat on towels on the sand, their toes touching the lapping water. Libby popped the cork on the wine bottle, Carmen pulled out three plastic glasses from her bag and Libby poured the wine. Becky stretched out for a little snooze in the sun. She could hear the familiar voices of her mom and Carmen as they talked. It was soothing to her as she relaxed next to them.

Carmen looked around at the broken and leaning trees along the shore and expressed her frustration, "Why does God allow this terrible destruction?"

Libby thought about Carmen's question and then began to speak haltingly. "It's not--God's *will*--the calamities that befall our world. The forces of nature--and, ahh--the acts of humanity bring about destruction on our world. It seems to us such a waste and, so much heartache. It's hard to see all this. We only see the loss--the hundreds of trees destroyed. So many people have been affected."

They looked down the shoreline from where they sat. The scene was littered with personal property--someone's diving raft, a half-sunken boat, and numerous dock sections bobbed in the water near shore. Some sections had secured a hold on a rock or were beached up on the sand. It was sad to see their beautiful lake in such disarray. There were trees destroyed; uprooted, split apart, broken-off tops lay beside their broken, standing trunks.

Now, Libby continued with more confidence, "Maybe we need to see through the destruction. What are the long term benefits within *us*? Our character has an opportunity to grow through adversity; to show compassion to others in need, to help repair the broken earth. How terrible is all this going to seem in time, except for the good that was shown to others and our world," Libby finished. She thought she was done but then Carmen replied with another question.

"If God is in nature, or nature is more a manifestation of God's Nature, then God *is* allowing this to happen. Right? Again, I ask, for what reason? All this disaster is to just give us character? Can't we all get character without so much destruction?"

Carmen waited to hear what Libby would say. She thought to herself how unfair it was that she voice her frustration of questioning faith in God to Libby. *Let's face it, it is an immense and complicated subject.* But she found herself drawn to Libby's thoughts on something so unexplainable. Carmen was the self-reliant type. She had a degree in biology and sought out scientific answers. Libby thought out of a different box. She was a mystic, seeing her Creator in literally *everything.*

Libby continued, "There is a passage in a book that I just love: "Without changing an outward thing, even bad things, we deliberately believe, against all appearance, that this is not the difficulty it appears to be. Instead of looking at the situation, let us look *through it* to God. He is in the very situation; He is the supplier and the solution."

Even though Libby was not known to be much of a talker, to Carmen's amazement, her friend was on a roll. "I think God is right here, wanting us to see Him and trust Him. We can be better people because of what happened this week. I think what God sees as important is so different from what we see as important. Our attitude, our trust in Him, our willingness to see others needs' over our own--that's what He sees as an opportunity to show His love. We see the destruction as a waste of time, money and effort. Time and money mean nothing to God. But, our efforts to express His love--now that's important. Our care for others and our world, are never in vain. If the experience brings us to trust God for strength, supply and understanding--to love and take care of others a little more--then, for God, it's been worth our pain."

Carmen looked around, hesitating to share her doubt in what Libby was saying. "Okay, but..." Libby interrupted her and Carmen was very surprised. She looked at Libby and listened to her friend intently. "We need to seek God with an awakened soul, mind and spirit. We are so afraid to explore God's presence with our imaginations. We have become so weak spiritually from lack of attention that we have lost the ability to deliberately see ourselves before God; to imagine Him here, leaning against our boat"--*she gestured with her hand towards the resort boat*--"listening to our conversation right now, loving us like only God can love."

Carmen looked over at the boat. Inexplicably, goose-bumps rose on her arms. Becky raised her head and looked over at the boat--a little uncertain of just what she might see.

Libby looked at the boat too and then back to her friend, "What would the Lord say about our discomfort and loss? Maybe He would say that He finds His children more caring, giving and concerned when things get a little stirred up around us, that we are much more focused on what's important, like each other and Him, when things are a little scary. "

The reality of the moment they were sharing began to sink in and after a thoughtful silence, Carmen finally spoke.

"God, if you are really *here*…right here with us now, even though my eyes can't see you…then by blind faith, *and my imagination*, I acknowledge your presence, Lord."

Libby and Carmen lifted their plastic glasses filled with wine towards the boat.

Carmen went on. "Here's to using our spiritual imaginations to seeing you, Lord, right here with us now. May we rise to your utmost purpose in the days ahead," Then they both took a sip of their wine.

They smiled at each other and then looked over at Becky who was propped up on one elbow looking at the boat and then back at them. She lifted her glass towards the boat and said, "amen."

Chapter 10

Coming Back From Ruin

Five days after the *storm of the century* the electricity was still not working around most of the lake. Everyone was at the end of their patience but complaining did nothing to hurry the overburdened power company repairmen. As Carmen and Jed closed the lodge Monday evening and headed up the hill to their home, they discussed the fact that after this mess was behind them they would sit down with the Edwards and tell them about wanting out of the business. They dreaded that meeting but felt sure they were making the right decision. They were both excited, thinking about where they might want to live. Jed had always wanted to live in Montana; they would check out numerous areas out west once the resort was closed for the year.

As they entered their darkened house on the hill, neither of them bothered to turn on a light. The first few days after the storm they continued to flip on the light switches out of habit in rooms they entered but, after five days, the habit had been broken. The afterglow from the setting sun gave off enough light through the windows facing west to walk around without stumbling. They were both tired and opted just to go to bed. There was no television to watch or music to listen to. After getting ready for bed in the dark Jed slipped between the sheets and, went right to sleep. Carmen read by flashlight for a short time before her book threatened to fall from her relaxed hands. She turned off the flashlight and sleep came instantly.

Sometime in the dark hours of the night Sadie started barking. Jed and Carmen woke with a start. "What is wrong with you, Sadie? Settle down!" Jed sounded perturbed with the Golden Retriever's barking in the darkness. Then he felt Sadie's nose touch his arm and Jed reached over to pat her head.

"Listen, Jed," Carmen murmured, "Do you hear men talking out behind the house?" Jed heard it too. It sounded like voices being broadcast from walkie-talkies.

Could it be the power company? They both hoped as they jumped out of bed and raced to the windows facing the back of the house. They could see lights flashing, hear trucks running and the sound of men working on connecting the downed power lines behind their house. Two hours later they heard the refrigerator start running and saw their digital clock start flashing. It was exhilarating to hear things humming away again. They both had a hard time falling asleep.

The Edwards slept through the momentous event. Their home was far enough away from the working crew that Honey wasn't alerted by their activities. When Will woke the following morning he was lulled by the white noise of the fan running in the bedroom window. Slowly the implication of this mundane noise dawned on him. He whooped with excitement causing Honey to jump to her feet, barking and Libby to bolt upright in bed. "The power's back!" Will exclaimed. Libby cheered and Honey kept barking at them excitedly.

The Edwards' son, Josh, came into their bedroom, a comical tangle of red hair thrust this way and that on his head. He had arrived at the resort two nights ago to help with the clean-up effort. He looked at the fan blowing in on his parents and smiled, "The electricity is back on…great." Then he turned and went back to bed.

Will got dressed and headed down to the lodge while Libby called Carmen to talk about the good news. She listened as Carmen told her about the workmen in the middle of the night behind their house. Libby was feeling so much better about their relationship now. Maybe that's one good thing about the storm; it did seem to have broken through the awkwardness between them.

By mid-afternoon the lodge services were back in full swing. The bait truck from Thompson's Bait Shop had delivered minnows, night-crawlers and leeches to the resort. Libby and Carmen made a trip to Beaver Creek for groceries for the lodge's cooler and ice cream freezer. The computer, to everyone's relief, started running when Will turned it on and all their data seemed intact.

Josh hung around until evening to make sure things were back to normal and then he made his way home to St. Paul. Libby and Will always hated to see their kids leave, and seeing Josh drive away this time was no different.

*****

The third week of July was peaceful. Jed and Will continued to clean up the resort from all the strewn branches; they cut down the many damaged trees and hauled the logs into the backwoods. Eventually they would have time to split and stack the wood for heat. The resort roads had needed grading as the storm's downpour had left great chasms along the sides of the gravel roads but, Bud Carter had come over to offer his decades of experience with grading the resort roads.

On Thursday, just as Will was heading home for the night, a favorite guest and good friend, Doug Peterson, caught up to him.

"Hey, Will, I'm so sorry to bother you just when you are ready to retire for the night but we have an electricity problem at our cabin. I looked around at the other cabins and their lights are on so it must be just us. "

Will asked him what was going on when they lost power.

"Well, we were all getting ready for bed, all five kids brushing their teeth. Nicki was picking up their discarded dirty clothes from the floor when the lights went out. I checked the fridge and that's out too. I know with a family of seven that we could easily blow a fuse, but where's the fuse box?"

"Let's take a look," Will said without a moment's hesitation. "*The fuse box for cabin 11 is in the dungeon below,*" he said in a spooky voice. Doug looked at him with a look of alarm. Will was half serious. He really did hate going down there, especially after dark.

At the cabin, Will headed to a hidden door that took them into a very low, dark, dank room under the cabin. Will felt in his pants pocket and pulled out a small flashlight and they both stepped into the darkness. The low ceiling of the room was built for a hobbit, and they both hunched over so they wouldn't bump their heads on the floor joists above.

Doug, who was a pastor at a church in the Twin Cities that Will and Libby's daughter attended, whispered, "Now this is one creepy place. I can say that if you weren't with me, I doubt I'd easily go in alone."

Will chuckled. "Yeah, I haven't had to come down here without flipping on the light switch before. It does give you an uneasy sense of a lurking bogeyman, right?"

"Yup, it does," Pastor Doug agreed.

At the far side of the room Will's flashlight beam found the fuse box. Will opened the door to the fuse box and it squeaked its resistance to move on its hinges. He bent his face in close to read the fuses for any sign of damage when all of a sudden he saw the problem and he jumped back bumping into the pastor. Then Doug took a closer look and he jumped at the sight in the box. There, fried to a crispy black, was a very dead mouse, its beady eyes bulging and its tongue sticking out between its little teeth. They both started shaking their heads in disbelief and then they began to chuckle.

"Oh my, I've seen it all," Will said. "How on earth did that little critter find his way into that box? I know they can get through anything, but a closed fuse box?" Doug just stood there, still stooped over, looking at the blackened furry mass, shaking his head and chuckling. "You know, I believe this will find its way into a sermon someday."

They both looked at the unfortunate mouse again and continued laughing. Doug had tears streaming down his face from laughing so hard.

Will cleared out the little body with a nearby paint stick, coated with paint from probably twenty years ago. Then he replaced the burned-out fuse with a new one and soon the Peterson family was back to their bedtime ablutions.

*****

Two weeks after the storm, the Porters told the Edwards they wanted to have a meeting over lunch. Carmen put up a sign in the lodge window saying they would be closed for an hour, and the four partners met at the Edward's home for a meeting. They sat at the dining room table enjoying the opportunity to talk as they ate their lunch of Libby's homemade potato salad and Italian subs. Honey and Sadie lay together on the porch, resting in the shade. They were never far from their two-legged families.

As Libby stacked the dishes and put away the leftover potato salad, Carmen began to feel butterflies in her stomach. Jed could see her nervous face and nudging her foot under the table gave her a reassuring smile. Will broke the silence by asking if they should start the meeting, a cue intended for Libby to come and sit down. The tension was noticeable around the table.

Jed began, "Carmen and I called this meeting because we have something very serious to talk over with you." He cleared his throat and continued, "We have both decided that running a resort is not for us and keeping that from you has been driving us crazy these last few months. We don't want to hurt you guys--it's not you, it's the business--the uncertainty of the money, the never-ending work to be done here--it's the bitterly cold winters that we don't think we can handle one more year."

Carmen broke in, "We've been so scared to tell you. We don't want to put you in any financial trouble, but we don't want to be co-owners of this resort after we close this fall."

Will and Libby were speechless, both looking at their partners in disbelief. They both sighed deep, long sighs, and looked to each other for ques. When Will finally spoke, his voice was strained, like the wind was knocked out of him, "Wow." He cleared his throat. "I didn't see that coming."

Libby sat quietly, allowing the news to sink in. Then her eyes brightened and a warm smile crossed her face.

"Is that all that's been wrong? That you don't want to run the resort anymore? I'm relieved! We're still friends? It's just the business that is making you unhappy? That's a relief! We were so worried that you guys didn't like being around us anymore, that you didn't want to be friends."

Will remembered, "The legal documents we had drawn up just for this eventuality! We all knew from the beginning that one couple or the other might not want to stay. Thank goodness, we thought ahead."

Will and Libby were so relieved--this was not the terrible news they feared. The friendship they had together was far more important than the business.

The Porters' demeanor noticeably changed from dread to utter relief. Will and Libby had understood and gave them their blessing to go on to do something else. Their friendship was truly important to all of them and nothing could come between them, not even a dissolving business partnership.

They got so wrapped up in talking about what the Porters' plans were that they forgot all about the lodge being closed until the dogs started barking at one of the guests walking up to the house. Jed checked his watch and realized that they had been away from the lodge for over an hour.

"Crap, the lineup must be a mile long at the lodge," Jed said with a smile as he greeted the guest at the door. "We'll be right there, Jerry. Go down and calm the masses for me, will ya'?" Jerry smiled, nodded, and turned to walk back to the lodge.

The four friends hugged and then the Porters walked down to the lodge together, Sadie by their side.

Chapter 11

Sailing the MacGregor

Last year, on his forty-second birthday, Will had purchased an old, twenty-one-foot, swing-keel MacGregor sailboat. It had been one of Will's dreams since he was a boy to own his own sailboat. When he was only ten-years-old, a neighbor on the lake recruited him to be his "first mate" on a small, 16-foot racing scow. The neighbor was a college student and Will was more than happy to hang out with the twenty-year-old and learn the basics of sailing. Now, living next to Thunder Lake gave him the perfect opportunity to relearn the skill and finesse of this graceful wind sport.

Thunder Lake could be extremely dangerous when storms kicked up. No one wants to be out twenty miles from shore when a big blow travels across such an immense body of water. When Libby's sister and her husband were visiting last year, they all headed out for an afternoon of sailing. The four adults and Honey were sitting in the cockpit enjoying the beautiful day. The breeze was light, the sun was warm, and they whiled away the hours in genial conversation. From time to time the breeze whipped up and caught Will's attention but it was still a fine, lazy sail. Later, the breeze turned gusty. The strong winds caught the sails of the twenty-one foot boat and pushed her forward at a good clip, edging her ever closer into an extreme lean. Will seemed confident that the boat was sailing fine but Libby and her sister were a little concerned. Honey, the experienced sailor dog, had learned that when the boat started leaning too far for her liking, it was best for her to snuggle onto Libby's lap. A lab is not a lap dog, but she at least got her front-end secured as Libby held her close. They continued to sail towards Gull Island, their progress taking them almost five miles from Safe Harbor Resort. As they passed Bear Island the full force of the gusty northeast wind smacked the sails with a sideways blow. Will reacted to the hard gust immediately by releasing the strain on the mainsail and turning into the wind, but not before the port side rail kissed the water. Honey dug her claws into Libby's jeans with more deliberation, trying to secure herself further into Libby's lap. Libby wrapped her arms tighter around the nervous dog. Then Libby and Honey gave Will the "deer in the headlights" look. Will didn't need any verbal persuasion; the look in their eyes told him it was time to head back, so he reluctantly turned the MacGregor back toward Safe Harbor.

As they made their way back, the wind kept building and the waves grew to four feet high, well above the sides of the low cockpit. The wind was behind them, the front sail billowed out in front pulling them forward, down one wave and up the next. The little sailboat was flying over the frothy water. It was an ominous sight if they dared to look back to watch the rolling waves a few feet off their stern, looming above them as they sat captive in the cockpit. As the waves rolled towards them, it would seem that they soon would overtake them but the little sailboat kept riding just ahead of them.

The calm water in Safe Harbor never looked so good as they entered the narrow entrance. Will and Libby had weathered other close calls over the past year, and each experience had taught them something more about the changing forces of wind and water.

*****

On a beautiful Wednesday afternoon in July, the storm's damage from a few weeks ago was fading in their memories. Will and Libby were almost done with the "minnow shift." Will could see Jed, Carmen and Sadie strolling down the hill and yelled to Libby in the kitchen.

"Hey, Libby, the Porters are on their way down, so we can get ready to go. Would you grab a few beers for me and whatever else you want to take?"

Libby filled a small Igloo cooler with an ice pack, beers and a bag of peanuts and a couple bottles of water. They talked to their soon to be ex-partners for a few minutes. The Edwards reported it being a quiet day at the lodge and the Porters seemed happy to hear that although activity around a resort could rise to craziness at any moment: a leak in the fuel line to the harbor, a toilet back-up in one of the cabins, the list is endless. Will started for the door, thinking it best to get going while the gettin's good.

Jed and Carmen settled into lodge duty for the "ice cream shift" while Will and Libby headed to the harbor. The two dogs tugged on a raggedy tug-toy outside the lodge for a while longer but soon Honey dropped her end of the toy to run after her two-legged family. Libby stopped halfway down the harbor trail and asked Will, "Do you think Carmen would want to take a sail with us? It's such a perfect day." They knew Carmen was not keen on sailing, especially after seeing the boat come in after the wild sail last year with Libby's sister.

Jed had gone out sailing a few times with Will but Carmen would always decline. Will thought about the fact that the Porters would be leaving soon. Maybe Carmen would consider taking a sail before leaving the lake. No one knew when they'd come back after they settled out west.

Will went back to the lodge. When he stuck his head through the doorway he said. "Carmen, it's a beautiful day--the wind is just right for a calm sail ride. Do you want to come for a short sail with us?"

Will looked at Jed for some help and encouragement. Jed looked at his wife, an easy smile crossed his face.

"You should go, Carmen. It's a quiet day here. Get out and try sailing. You'll love it."

Carmen hesitated, looking out the window at Libby as she waited on the dock. Finally, if a little reluctantly, she agreed to go along.

As the three friends and Honey headed out of the harbor, Jed and Sadie watched them from the front of the lodge. Libby climbed onto the upper deck to remove the ties that bound the mainsail to the boom, while Will showed Carmen how to lower the keel. Once the keel was down Will pulled the line, called the halyard, that raises the mainsail, and soon the sail was powering the boat forward. He killed the ancient motor attached to the back of the boat while Libby went to the bow and attached the front sail, called the jib, to the head-stay and pulled the jib halyard to raise the sail. Soon they were gliding through the water. The only sound the boat made as they traveled across the bay was the swish of water and the creak of the sails as they strained against the breeze. Carmen loved it! She had no idea how relaxing it could be. They all enjoyed the beautiful day. Honey hopped onto the upper deck and fell asleep in the warm sunshine under the boom.

When Carmen checked her watch she realized they had been out on the water for three hours.

"You better get me back to the lodge. Poor Jed, he's probably overwhelmed with orders for ice cream cones and pizzas by now."

"Time flies when you're having fun sailing, huh Carmen." Carmen agreed that it had been a wonderful experience.

Will swung the boat around by adjusting the sails and soon they were happily heading into the harbor. Once they entered the slip, things went very wrong. Honey leaped onto the dock at the same time Carmen stood up and leaned out to grab a dock post behind her. The rocking of the sailboat caused Carmen to lose her balance. Will and Libby were unaware of the peril about to befall Carmen as they tied off the dock lines. They both heard Carmen scream and then a huge splash. They turned around in time to see Carmen thrashing around in the mucky harbor water behind the boat.

"Auch, get me out of here!" Carmen yelled.

Her face was filled with panic as she struggled to keep her feet from touching the bottom of the harbor, which had the consistency of runny poo. Will and Libby each grabbed an arm and lifted her up and into the boat. Carmen didn't know if she wanted to laugh or cry. After it was decided that she was not hurt, Will and Libby steadied the boat as Carmen stepped onto the solid dock with relief. From across the harbor they heard claps of applause. Jed and a group of guests were smiling and clapping, one of them holding up a large tablet with a '10' written large enough for them to see. Carmen raised her arms in a victory pose to her audience. She took it in good humor, but she quickly left the embarrassing scene to run home for a long hot shower.

When Will had finished putting things away in the boat he thought maybe Jed could stand a little assistance at the lodge since Carmen might be awhile at home. When he arrived at the lodge there were lots of pats on the back and chuckles from the guests chiding him for Carmen's inadvertent spill into the harbor. Dave Johnson walked up to Will and said he wanted some shiners, if Will had time.

"Let's go," Will said, happy to get out of the lodge.

Will and Dave walked out to the bait house together and Will grabbed Dave's minnow bucket sitting on the cement wall by the bait house door.

"How many shiners do you want, Dave?"

"Oh, a couple dozen is fine."

Will filled an old pail with water and placed it on the 2x6 board laying across the bait tank. Then he took a healthy scoop of shiners from the tank with a net and dumped them into the pail. He looked to make sure there were well over two dozen minnows swimming around the pail, then he poured the contents of the pail into Dave's minnow bucket.

"Thanks, Will, put it on my tab, will ya'?" Then before he walked out the door, Dave turned back to Will, "Did you remember to mark down my gas yesterday?"

Will checked his notebook for entries from yesterday. He didn't see anything written for Dave's boat gas.

He looked sheepish, "Ya' know, Dave, looks like I didn't..."

"Well, I kinda' thought that might have happened. You were getting slammed on and I didn't see you write it down right away. It was twenty-four dollars and some cents...can't remember exactly the cents part."

"Thanks for being so honest, Dave," Will said with an appreciative smile.

Dave cocked his head and smiled, "I couldn't live with myself if I thought you were paying for my gas. You guys are great resort owners. I want to see you succeed."

*****

The next morning Libby was alone at the lodge--and probably would be for the whole day. Will, Jed, and Carmen had taken off on a shopping trip to Hermantown--the closest shopping area that had a Menards Lumber Yard and a Sam's Club. It was a two-hour drive with trailer in tow and, usually it ended up taking them all day. The resort was in need of lumber and shingles for one thing, some dock

116

boards and a few shingles needed replacing after the storm a few weeks ago. Then Will and Jed would drop Carmen off at Sam's Club and she would shop while they picked up the list of things from Menards. Carmen's long list included cleaning products for the cleaning crews, six large packs of paper plates, napkins and paper towels, fifty pounds of ground beef, ten huge packs of hot dogs for the remaining resort picnics. They also needed five cans of coffee for the lodge and, more linens, blankets, pillows and sheet sets to replace some of the worn bedding for the cabins.

Libby didn't mind staying home as shopping was not something she enjoyed, but she would miss having lunch with the crew at The Ground Round. It had been a quiet morning in the lodge after the gas and bait rush. The fishermen were quick to catch her as she opened the door to the bait house. After the rush, she opened the lodge and brewed a pot of coffee in the Bunn coffee maker. She looked out the front glass doors admiring the lake as she savored her first cup of joe. The day was warm and sunny, fluffy clouds popped up and disappeared as she lingered, watching. There was a whisper of wind, hardly enough to disturb the mirror surface of the lake. It would be a quiet day she predicted because the weather conditions were perfect for fishing and moms and kids would be off to Beaver Creek for some last-minute souvenir shopping. Thursday was always the guest's day for shopping and Friday was typically when they hung out at the lake, the last day before heading home on Saturday. Thursday for the owners meant data entry as some guests would want to see their week's invoice early on Friday. All week long, items were charged by family members and written down by the owners in their three-ring binder, under the guest's name and cabin number. These charges ranged from candy, ice cream, bait, bread, pizza, gas and so on--then these items were tallied and summarized in the resort's invoice program on the computer. On Friday, sometimes a disbelieving guest would want to take their invoice back to their family and privately 'discuss' the excesses listed: i.e., fifteen caramel-apple suckers, twenty cans of Coke, five pizzas and three of the most expensive hooded sweatshirts the resort offered. It was always nice when people 'discussed' these matters in private rather than in the lodge with two other guests waiting to pay. It was less embarrassing for all concerned.

Libby had been keeping herself busy at the computer. She and Carmen had just hired another cleaning crew that week, two young Ojibwe women, and she was entering the new employee's names into their database. When she sat at the computer desk she was almost hidden behind the chest high log-sided counter that served as their front desk. One end of the countertop held the printer, in the middle was the cash register, and on the far end was an assortment of sausage sticks, dried beef and boxes of candy. With Will, Carmen and Jed gone, Honey and Sadie felt a little lost and were keeping close to Libby. Unfortunately that meant, lying close behind her chair. After an hour of quiet, someone entered the lodge and Libby needed to stand. This started quite a ruckus behind the counter. Libby, needing to roll her chair back to stand while Sadie and Honey scrambled out of the way of the chair wheels. It made for quite a kerfluffle. Then the two retrievers were around the counter barking.

The surprised man gave a gasp and yelled at Libby. "Hey, call off your dogs."

Libby commanded the two wagging girls to come. She felt bad for the dogs' eruption. "Sorry, Brian. I guess you startled all of us. It's been a quiet day around here."

"Yeah, well, I'm very confused about where my boat is," Brian said with a distinct edge in his voice. Libby could see a muscle tick in his neck that made his head slightly shake, and his jaw muscles were pulsing, she guessed, from clenching.

"I'm not sure what you are getting at, Brian. Is your boat not where you put it--It's not in your slip?"

"No, it's not!"

Libby thought to herself, *Of all days, Will and Jed aren't around to take over this stressful situation concerning a boat.* She didn't like shopping but she was definitely even more uncomfortable when it came to boats and harbor issues.

"Okay, Brian. Let's just take a breath and settle down. There has to be a logical explanation."

Brian nodded his head in agreement. She watched him slack his tight jaw and move it side to side and then roll his head on his tight neck. There were three loud cracks as the cervical joints along his spine loosened.

Libby looked at him eye to eye and started her questioning again by first stating, "We haven't had any thefts that I'm aware of for many years. Our guests have told us that it's just not happened in their many years coming here. For some, it's been over twenty years. Now, that said, let's do a little thinking about when you last used it. Was it today--yesterday...?"

"This morning before daybreak I went out fishing along the reef out front of the resort."

"Carter's Reef?" Libby asked.

"Yeah, I think that's the place."

Brian and his wife were first-time guests at Safe Harbor Resort. Consequently, they weren't familiar with other fishermen in the resort and the overwhelming choices for fishing this vast lake's bottom structure. So for him, going to Carter's Reef was the first fishing spot that gave new guests some action.

"I came in around ten o'clock. Sidney and I had planned to go to Beaver Creek for a late breakfast at the Woodsman Cafe and then head to Reed's for some shopping. When we got back I was all excited to mount a new fishing reel on one of my old rods. So I went to the harbor to get the rod from my boat and the boat was gone!"

"How big is your boat, Brian?" She felt foolish asking this question as Will knew every boat in their fifty-six-slip harbor every week. But knowing the boats was not part of her job description. She thought, *Well, Will doesn't know all the details of the cabin interiors, but she did--from every picture on the walls to what silverware or bowls belonged in which cabin.*

"It's an eighteen-foot runabout--grey with a tan and burgundy stripe. It has all my fishing gear, a couple coolers, my Viking's poncho..."

Libby watched him as he started thinking about all his possessions he was remembering that were now missing along with his boat.

"...my lucky hat, Sidney's beach bag with her towel and stuff..."

Libby interrupted Brian, "Have you actually walked to your dock slip yet?"

Brian stopped his rambling and admitted that he had gotten close but hadn't thought to go all the way as it was easy to see from the path that the slip was empty.

"Why would I look closer?"

"Let's take a walk over there. I don't mean to alarm you but maybe your boat sunk. People don't realize sometimes that their live well water has overflowed into the boat or that their boat plug isn't seated correctly. If you have an inboard motor it can develop a leak. She was thinking to herself, with some self-satisfaction, that she knew more than she thought about boats.

Brian's face was showing signs of his previous stress returning. "I did not even think about that!"

Libby wrote a note and hung it with the old clip attached to the door trim.

THE LODGE IS CLOSED FOR 10 MINUTES.
(Should be back by 1:20)
LIBBY

Honey and Sadie followed Libby out of the lodge and as she and Brian walked the harbor path the retrievers followed behind. Soon though, Honey's nose caught the scent of a creature in the weeds behind cabin 10 and was off to investigate. Sadie, apparently not interested, decided she would mosey up the hill to where she lived. Maybe her much loved people had come home.

Brian and Libby arrived at the dock slip. They both looked down into the murky water of the harbor with curious trepidation. Brian's slip was only a few feet from where Carmen had fallen in the day before. After a brief moment of staring into the water, they both sighed with relief. There was no sign of the top of a windshield or any other part of a grey boat just below the surface.

Libby looked at Brian, "Well, that is one possibility we can check off our list."

"Now what?" Brian asked as he scanned the horizon of the enormous lake, "Call the cops?"

"Well, we could do that..."

She thought to herself--*that would be easier for me, but not so good for the reputation of the resort not to mention the peace and quiet of the resort. It might be good to think about less disruptive possibilities first. There were a few other new people in the resort this week and she had a niggling thought bouncing around her head. What it was trying to tell her she didn't know, but she felt like maybe it was worth asking around the resort first. Maybe someone saw something.*

"...let's ask around the resort a little first. You never know, maybe a child saw something but was afraid or uncertain about telling someone."

So they checked out the fish cleaning houses but no one was cleaning fish. They walked the path back to the lodge and beach area and talked to a couple of young girls playing in the water. They had nothing to report and neither did their mom sitting on a lawn chair in the shade reading a paperback book. Libby scanned the resort grounds with her hand shading her eyes. The grounds were empty around the cabins and the docks.

Brian interrupted her surveying. "What about that little boy just coming into the harbor on that paddleboat."

"Good. Let's check with him."

Brian helped the young boy tie up the boat in the harbor. Libby watched, thinking about the boy's age--older than eight but no more than ten. Always thinking of safety especially with kids, she was considering whether it was safe for him to be using the paddle boat outside of the harbor without an adult. She was relieved to see that he at least had a lifejacket with him, even if it was laying on the floor and not attached to him.

"Hey, how was your ride on the water?" Libby asked the boy. She knew he and his family were new guests this week and she couldn't recall his name.

"It was really, really nice. I saw a turtle's head pop up right next to the boat. His shell was about..." and he lifted his hands showing a distance of about eight inches. "He was really cool to look at."

"What's your name?" Libby knew he was with the Kaiser family in cabin 1.

"Ricky."

"Ricky, we were wondering if you had seen a grey boat while you were out paddling around."

"Yeah, did you see anyone take it out of this harbor?" Brian asked with a little too much edge in his voice.

"Well - e-rhh - my sister and her friend took it out. I wanted to go with them but they wouldn't let me so I took out the paddle boat instead."

Brian's voice boomed. "They wha-a-a-t?"

Libby looked up at Brian with a stern expression and then turned to talk to Ricky again. "Why would your sister and her friend think they could take a boat from the harbor that wasn't theirs?"

Ricky looked scared, "I-I guess w-we thought **all** the boats wer-r-e available to use."

Brian couldn't hold back his exasperation. "What the heck! Where did they go?"

Ricky, being afraid of Brian, looked only at Libby and answered, "They went to the beach way down there." He pointed south, his hand shaking as he held out his arm.

Libby put her arm around Ricky's shoulders and said, "Thank you Ricky. When we get back you come down to the lodge and I'll make you an ice cream cone--whatever flavor--because of all your help."

Just then the two retrievers appeared out of nowhere and walked directly up to Ricky. He smiled at the big dogs as they moved in close. He ruffled the fur on their backs. Sadie lifted her head and gave the boy a soft kiss with her tongue. Libby thought to herself how amazing it was, no matter where they had been, they both felt the emotions of a scared child and came to investigate and comfort. *What caring hearts reside within these intelligent creatures!*

Brian bent down and apologized to Ricky. "Hey, man, I'm sorry for sounding so mad. Can you forgive me?"

Ricky nodded his head but still hung onto the backs of Sadie and Honey.

Libby and Brian said goodbye to Ricky and he ran off toward his cabin. Libby told Sadie and Honey to stay while she went to the lodge and changed the note:

THE LODGE IS CLOSED FOR AN HOUR.
Should be back by 2:20--SORRY : (
Libby

She locked the door again and told Brian and the dogs to follow her. She headed to the big green pontoon docked at the end of the front row in the large slip closest to the harbor entrance.

"Hop on, gang." She swung her arm out indicating the pontoon. "Let's go get your boat."

Brian held the dock line until Libby had the engine running. She was relieved to see that the gas gauge registered full. The dogs were always happy to ride on a boat. They loved taking boat rides but especially when it was on the pontoon. Honey kept watch through the front railing, her ears flopping in the wind. Sadie eventually settled herself under the table where it was shady and cool.

As the pontoon skimmed the top of the water at twenty miles per hour, Brian sat on the front bench seat watching the beach grow larger as they approached and the dot that represented his boat came into focus. It was anchored out about a hundred feet from shore but there was no sign of anyone in the boat. Libby slowed down the pontoon boat and drifted towards Brian's boat. Just then two heads popped up from inside. Two girls watched them come towards them.

Brian shouted, "Hey, you stole my boat! What gives you the idea you can just take anyone's boat?"

The girls stood up in the boat and looked at him like he was from Mars. Libby continued to maneuver the pontoon until it was right next to Brian's boat. The girls thoughtfully threw out a couple of bumpers and grabbed onto the pontoon railing. They looked to be in their mid-teens.

One said, "What were you saying to us? We couldn't hear you with our music playing and the pontoon motor running. "

The other girl noticed Honey and Sadie who were checking them out too. "Ahhh, look at those cute puppies. Hey, Sweeties! We've seen them around the resort, right?" The girl looked at Libby questioningly.

They both smiled, not a note of shame or defensiveness in their voices."

Libby smiled. "Yes, this is Sadie and Honey. Sadie's the Golden and Honey is the lab.

Libby looked up at Brian who was searching the interior of his boat. A look of mystifying disbelief on his face.

"What's the matter, Brian? Is something missing?"

The girls looked around the boat, pleased.

Brian answered hesitantly. "I-ee don't think so-o-o." Then he looked at the two teenagers. "Did you clean my boat?" he asked, incredulous.

"Well, yeah! It was REALLY filthy in here." One said and the other followed, "we couldn't enjoy ourselves till we cleaned up all the crap and garbage. Yuk!"

Brian's one eyebrow went up and he turned to look back at Libby. "Well, I think everything is all there...and cleaned up too."

Libby explained to the girls that if boats in the harbor aren't labeled 'Safe Harbor Resort' on the side, they are other guests' personal boats and not to be taken under any circumstance. And even Safe Harbor boats need to be rented first before someone can take them out.

The girls apologized to Brian. "We're sorry. We've only stayed at a place that was all-inclusive. I guess we should have checked with someone first."

Brian shrugged his shoulders and smiled. "Well, I'll let this go only because you took such good care of it and all my stuff is here-- and organized."

The two girls boarded the pontoon and Brian stepped into his boat. Libby said goodbye to Brian and the girls waved as they headed back to the resort.

*****

Carmen, Jed and Will arrived home at four, beer o'clock for the guys. First they needed to unload the massive amount of bags and cardboard containers into the lodge storeroom then they all sat down together on the little deck in front of the lodge. Carmen had poured a glass of wine for herself and handed another to Libby.

"So, how was your day, Libby?"

Libby sighed, took a longer sip than normal from her glass. "You wouldn't believe it."

Chapter 12

Fishermen from Arkansas

The Safe Harbor crew were hard at work the following Saturday. It was already two o'clock in the afternoon as Libby and Carmen finished cleaning their last cabin. They noticed that some resort guests had already arrived for their much anticipated week-long vacation. Jed and Will were down at the lodge to greet them as the women kept scrubbing, vacuuming and making beds.

There had been an issue with the new cleaning crew they had just hired a week ago. The two young women showed up drunk at seven in the morning. The giggling women admitted to Carmen and Libby that they had been up all night partying and thought it was better to show up drunk than not at all. Carmen and Libby grudgingly had to agree that was maybe true, but not much better. They needed them if they were going to clean 16 cabins before the guests arrived. The third crew arrived a little late, but at least they were both sober. Carmen and Libby decided to split up the tipsy duo, giving the other crew one and they took the other with them. Carmen instructed the others to give the party girl only duties that weren't as important, like sweeping decks and removing cobwebs from the log siding and screens. By noon, the sleep-deprived women needed to crash so Libby told them to leave.

"Go down to the lodge and get paid, and next week--don't bother coming back. We need reliable, *sober* people."

She hated to fire them because they were experienced cleaners, but coming to work drunk is just not the kind of workers you want to depend on. That's probably why they were looking for work in the middle of the summer. Someone else had let them go. It was always hard to find good Saturday help and with Carmen leaving after this season, Libby knew she was in trouble for next year. She thought, *Oh, for another crew like Lilly and River.*

The two remaining cleaners finished the last of the cabins by 2:30 p.m. and headed over to the lodge together with Libby and Carmen to unload the dirty sheets, wet rags and cleaning supplies from the old cleaning van. Libby gave the cleaners their wages while

Carmen offered them a cold can of pop and a bag of cheese crackers. She knew they were hungry as none of them had taken a break that day.

As Libby and Carmen headed for the van they yelled to Will and Jed, "We're heading up to the house to get cleaned up before any guests catch us in these filthy clothes." Jed nodded from the bait house door and Will replied from the side deck of the lodge. "Okay, see you later."

The two women hopped into the old blue van and headed up the hill to their homes.

Jed and Will knew they wouldn't see their wives until at least seven o'clock. That had been their *modus operandi* every Saturday this summer. Even though the guys had put in a long day also, Libby and Carmen felt that they had the hardest job on Saturdays. They never saw how much work the men did around the resort. Jed usually drove the garden tractor with a trailer attached to pick up the garbage and clean the greasy grills at all the cabins, then he dropped off the trailer and started mowing the five acres of grass. Will cleaned the bait house, picked up toys and life-jackets from the beach. He stayed close to the lodge to answer the phone and take care of any last minute departing guests who came down to pay their bill. There were notices in each cabin requesting people pay their bill on Friday night but there were always a few who waited until Saturday morning to settle up and say goodbye. After all the guests were gone the men started work on the rental boats that needed to be cleaned out, motors put on or taken off depending on the needs of the guests coming in that week. The last nasty job was cleaning the fish-cleaning houses and then driving the ten large pails of fish guts to a pit in the woods. The overflowing, smelly pails rested precariously in the bucket of their old International Harvester tractor. After dumping the guts into the pit, a scoop or two of dirt was dumped from the tractor bucket over the fish guts. Once the tractor was turned around, and leaving the area, it was not unusual to look back and see two or three bears pawing through the fresh meal delivered to their backyard.

Sadie and Honey hung around the lodge on Saturdays, playing tug with each other or with one of the kids waiting for their parents in the lodge. Honey was always hopeful for one more toss of the tennis ball, and Sadie was always hopeful that the parting guests might have some leftovers for her to finish.

Carmen and Libby felt no guilt for leaving the men to run the lodge while they both got cleaned up and "wined" away what was left of the afternoon. They each downed three Advil with a wine chaser and relaxed. Usually by six o'clock they would call down to the lodge and tell the guys to throw in a pizza, and they would attempt to rise from their comfortable chairs, their seizing backs *complaining*. By seven o'clock the two couples would just be sitting down to pizza by the lakeshore when the next guests would pull up and climb out of their car. It never changed from week to week. They all expected it, Saturday dinner time was guest arrival time.

It was no different this Saturday. Just as the four hungry owners reached for their first piece of pizza, they heard the all too familiar sound of tires rolling over gravel and pull up next to the lodge. Sadie and Honey heard it also and both dogs were up and around the building to greet the newcomers.

The four men who climbed out of the large Chrysler were stiff from their long drive. Will got up from the picnic table on the front deck and walked around the building to greet the new arrivals.

"Welcome to Safe Harbor. I'm Will."

The four African American men each took turns reaching out to shake hands with Will and introduce themselves. There was Joe, Al, George and Cliff, all smiling as they made small talk with Will. After Will took them into the lodge to get signed in, he brought them out onto the deck to meet the rest of the crew. Jed, done eating by then, offered to escort the four Arkansas men to Cabin 5, the cabin with the outstanding view of the endless lake just a few steps from the door.

*****

Sunday morning Will arrived at the lodge by seven a.m. to start the minnow shift. George, one of the Arkansas fishermen, younger than the others, was waiting for him on the back step of the lodge. He greeted Will with an engaging smile, his white teeth brilliant against his black skin.

"Morning, Will." George said in his southern lilt.

Will smiled back and offered, "What can I do for you, George?"

"Well, I've been designated to drive the boat this week. None of us have had much experience with motorboats. We've mostly fished from shore or off a bridge. But old Joe always talked about his family taking him to northern Minnesota when he was just a li'l boy. That's all we've ever heard him talk about when we're fishin' togetha'. So we agreed to take our ol' buddy, Joe, back up he-ya, so he could show us this glorious state that he 'membered from his childhood."

"That's great, George. I'm glad you chose Thunder Lake. If you are going to make the trip, why not see the biggest and best lake Minnesota has to offer?"

"Yes sah', that's what we figured. We got brochures from all over the state but we picked yo' place because of this here beautiful lake and yo' prices were *so cheap.*"

Will winced about their low prices. They had been embarrassingly low when they bought the resort. They were trying to raise their rates each year without losing their repeat customers. As they continued to improve the resort their rates would become more competitive with the other resorts.

"So you want me to show you to your boat and get you set up with bait," Will responded.

"Well, that's the thang. Ya need to give me a crash course, no pun intended, on runnin' the motor before the others get out he-ya," George admitted. Will was a little surprised but more than happy to help.

"Okay. Let's get you started then. Your boat is over in slip number 35. The two men walked down the harbor path to dock 35. "Climb in and sit next to the motor," Will instructed.

George stepped in warily, catching his balance as the boat rocked under his weight. He sat on the back bench next to the motor and looked up at Will.

"Okay, start the motor by pulling the choke out and push in the start button. When the motor starts, push the choke back in."

George followed the instructions and the boat putted to life. George smiled at the simplicity of the motor's electric start.

Will said, "Great, you're a pro already. Now, just remember that you steer the boat by turning the motor opposite of the direction you want to go. You want to go left, turn the motor handle right, understand?"

George acknowledged the advice with a nod and then Will encouraged him to take it out for a spin. Will walked back to the lodge knowing it would make George less nervous without someone standing over him, watching.

As he walked away Will remembered one other important information. "When you want to turn the motor off, push the red button in until the motor dies."

George looked down, saw the red button and nodded that he understood.

Will entered the lodge confident in his pupil. But when he looked out the lodge window he saw George driving the boat out of the harbor backwards, motor running in reverse. The look on George's face was priceless--smiling and confident. Will stared in disbelief at the eighteen-foot Crestliner heading out onto the lake backwards. He hadn't been around anyone who was quite *that* much of a boating novice. Of course, it wasn't George's fault, he did try to tell Will.

George did a few passes in front of the resort as Will watched from the lodge. He should have called to George to inform him of his mistake but somehow he just didn't have the heart to embarrass him by yelling out to him. Plus the man looked so happy and proud. Will thought about the unfortunate probability, if the morning had been windy, that the waves would have splashed high over the back of the boat. But, the lake was calm and flat, enabling George to thoroughly enjoy his newly acquired skill. Will just hoped no one was paying attention from the other cabins.

When George entered the harbor, still running the boat backwards, Will went out to meet him at the boat slip. George had maneuvered the boat beautifully backwards.

"You did a great job, George. I haven't seen anyone drive a boat backwards better than you," Will said, *genuinely meaning it*.

"Really?" George was beaming, but then caught Will's words and looked confused.

"Well, George, boating on this huge lake can be very hazardous. You have to be mentally and physically prepared to survive everything this inland sea will throw at you. By driving the boat backwards, you and your friends will never survive a windy day on this lake. The waves would sink the boat and all of you in it," Will said with a measure of seriousness.

For the next hour Will and George went over all the basics of boating and all the important information about being safe on Thunder Lake. By the time the rest of George's friends arrived, carrying their gear for their first morning of fishing, Will felt confident to let them fish in the large bay out front. The Arkansas fishermen headed out of the harbor, each seated on their own bench. George, sitting on the back seat, ran the boat forward as if he had done it all his life.

*****

Two days later, the Arkansas men were finding fish. George studied the lake map with Will or Jed to make sure he knew where he should go on the lake. The weather had been perfect the first part of the week giving the fishermen a great experience. For Jed though, a very unexpected, unpleasant experience greeted him the first time he entered the fish cleaning house after the Arkansas fishermen cleaned their fish. He was puzzled by the fish scales stuck to the screens, ceiling and floor of the facility. Jed muttered to himself, "*I guess these Arkansas guys like to scale and gut their fish"* He spent the better part of an hour sweeping and hosing down the fish scales stuck to every surface in the building.

Another unexpected experience awaited Carmen later that day. Jed happened by the bait house just in time to watch Carmen standing at the fish-wrapping table, the Arkansas men standing behind her watching her every move. Jed was amused as he watched his wife try to wrap four slimy-skinned fish into the white freezer paper. He knew that she prided herself on wrapping fish fillets in an airtight package. But these slimy, scaled fish had her flustered. Just as soon as she was ready to tightly wrap the fish stacked on the freezer paper, one, then another, would shootout and fall to the floor. George, who was standing at the shooting end of the table would pick up each casualty, wash it off and put it back on the white paper and Carmen would try again. Jed made a mental note to himself not to, if at all possible, be available to wrap fish for the Arkansas fishermen.

Thursday afternoon grew gusty and the lake was choppy and grey. Will watched with some trepidation as the sky grew more ominous from the north. The Arkansas fishermen had started out onto a placid lake earlier in the day but now the lake was foaming at the edges. George had been handling the boat well during the week. Today he had decided to take his buddies on the east side of the lake. Will wondered where they were now. He wished he could call them, tell them to come back to the resort, but the resort didn't have a VHF radio, and he knew the fishermen didn't have a VHF unit either.

Many of the other guests were making their way back into the safety of the harbor, those that new Thunder Lake and knew to always watch the skies. By five o'clock Will and Jed were really getting concerned. The wind was whipping the lake into a froth.

"Should we go out looking for them?" Will asked Jed.

"There's a hundred thousand acres of water out there. Where would we begin?' Jed asked.
Both men stared out of the lodge windows at the witch's brew roiling in front of them.

Will finally sighed in resignation, "Let's call the sheriff." He already had the cordless phone in his hand when the phone rang. Will pushed the talk button, "Safe Harbor, this is Will."

"Hey, Will, this is Bob down at Stony Ridge. Are you missing some guests?"

"Yes! Do you have them?" Will asked excitedly.

"Yeah, they came walking in from the road--said they left your boat on shore a little south of here, at Borden's landing. There's three of them standing in my store, shivering and soaked to the skin."

"Three, there should be four," Will sounded worried and Jed, overhearing Will's response, swore in frustration.

Will heard Bob ask the question to the other men and then repeated their response to Will, "I guess the fourth stayed with the boat. They didn't want anyone to steal it."

Will smiled at that. "Okay, we'll be over to pick them up. I'll have to hitch up the boat trailer first."

"Nah, that's okay. My trailer's already hitched. I'll get the boat and take them all with me, to your place."

"Thanks, Bob, I'll owe ya' a beer when you get here."

A half hour later Bob pulled down the driveway of Safe Harbor Resort, the four cold, wet fishermen *sitting in the boat on the trailer*, each on their usual bench seat. Will and Jed walked over to Bob's truck window and gave him a steely glare. Will hissed through gritted teeth. "What the heck Bob, what are you thinking making them ride in the boat."

"Don't get mad at *me*. I told 'em to hop in and they all hopped into the boat. I thought about getting them to switch to the back of the truck but then thought, *what's the difference, the back of the truck or in the boat? Their still out in the elements*." Bob said with a smirk as he got out of his truck, "we only had a few miles to go." Will and Jed walked with Bob to the boat as the four fishermen jumped to the ground.

Bob reached out to shake hands. "Arkansas, must seem like a world away to you fellas. Hope this doesn't scare you away from Minnesota in the future."

George, Joe, Al and Cliff all shook hands with Bob and thanked him for bringing them back. Will and Jed helped Bob launch the boat into the harbor and then they all went back to the lodge for that promised beer.

*****

Next morning the wind was still gusting 15-20 miles per hour, keeping everyone on shore. The four fisherman from Arkansas came down to pay their bill late morning.

Will was surprised. "It's Friday. You're leaving a day early?"

"We've had the time of our lives. We'll never forget this lake, your hospitality and the great fishing, but we're quite sure we don't want to go out on that wild lake today." George said, speaking for the whole group. The other three nodded in agreement.

Joe told Will and Libby the scary details of their wild ride across the lake the day before. Joe's eyes were wide with excitement as he began, "The waves were so large that one time when we hit the crest of a wave Cliff, who always sat on the front bench, flew up into the air and landed in the back of the boat next to George's feet! *Sweet Jesus*, were we glad he landed in the boat and not in the water." Joe's eyes looked heavenward.

Cliff chimed in, "The rest of the ride I stayed on the floor next to George. We all prayed hard 'til we got to shore. It was quite the earnest prayer meeting. I never heard these guys pray so loud."

After their harrowing story was told, souvenir t-shirts were purchased for their grandkids, and then they divvied up their bill. The four fishermen shook hands with Will and Libby and headed out the door.

As the large Chrysler with the Arkansas license plates headed up the hill, four black arms waved from the open windows. The Edwards waved back.

When the car had disappeared over the hill, Will spoke, "There are some people we will never forget from our resort years and those guys are four of them." Libby nodded.

Chapter 13

Wiley Loses It

Charles Wiley sat up from the back seat of his Ford truck. His neck and back nagged him with kinks in his muscles and a crick in his spine. Since the big storm two weeks ago, his truck was the only place he had to sleep after the towering white pine crushed his home. There literally was no wall that hadn't buckled under the weight of the fallen giant. Ironically, he had a resort full of cabins he could have stayed in but, every structure had leaky roofs, rodents and insects, making them less habitable than living in his truck.

After Charlie stretched, he peered over the front seat to check on the pathetic spaniel lying on an old blanket. Aggie had been severely injured. He had rescued her from the house but that was all he dared get from his demolished home. He reached his arm over the seat to stroke her soft fur.

"How are ya', old girl? I'm so sorry this happened to you. Ga'damn storm!" He paused as his throat constricted, threatening to release a sob.

Charlie stroked her head. "Don't you leave me girl, ya' hear?"

The spaniel tried to move but only whimpered. Charlie took that as a good sign that she was still with him.

*****

It had been two weeks since Charlie left the casino before the end of his shift….his last shift. An hour earlier the floor supervisor had called him into his office and fired him for drinking on the job. Someone had complained about his stumbling and swerving as he walked back from parking a car. They had also witnessed his drinking from a flask as he got out of that car. When Joe Cloudrider was called to the head office he was more than happy to see that it was for the purpose of escorting Charlie out of the building.

When Charlie walked out of the casino to his truck on rubbery legs and swirling vision, there was little evidence of the fury that had just taken place at his home. The casino had not been hit by the worst of the storm but as Charlie drove the twenty-five mile drive east, he saw branches and leaves down everywhere. It was worse the closer he got to Muskie Run; trees blocked the roads or hung precariously over leaning utility poles. Electrical lines snaked through the grass and onto the roadways, making the drive home long and dangerous. When he entered his driveway it was blocked as far down as he could see. He climbed through the maze of fallen trees to the shocking sight of his home, crumpled under the weight of the ancient pine that once shaded his home in the front yard. The long-needled branches almost entirely hid the one-story structure. Charlie called for his dog over and over, but Aggie did not respond. He guessed he might find her where she slept every night--on his bed. He carefully made his way along the wreckage in back of the house to where the bedroom wall had been split open. Looking in through the splintery opening, he found her lying on his bed, motionless. The fallen tree had not touched the bed and luckily displaced furniture had pushed the bed over to the outside wall. Boards, branches and debris surrounded the dog's motionless body, but Charlie reached his arm through and slowly, carefully, pulled the bedspread from the bed and through the splintery opening in the wall. When Aggie felt his arms around her she gave one small whimper and a weak wag of her stubby tail. Charlie studied her condition and could see that her head was bleeding and swollen on one side, one eye was sealed shut with dried blood. A bright red trickle of blood colored her pink tongue. It should have been obvious that death was inevitable for his friend; that is, if he had been sober. But Charlie wasn't thinking clearly anymore--alcohol had eaten away too many brain cells. The skewed world of an alcoholic is unrealistic and self-absorbed. His mind refused to face reality when everything around him was a nightmare. Charlie wrapped her limp body securely in the blanket. He then began the arduous journey back out to his truck sitting at the end of the road. His arms and hands were bloodied and scratched yet he carried his dog tenderly. She was all he had left in the world.

Charlie spent the rest of the day moving branches off the resort road enough to squeeze his truck into a hidden alcove where it wouldn't be seen by passersby. It was not surprising to him that no one would care to check on him. There were not many people he could count on, except if it meant to have a good time. He had been fired from work so why would anyone check on him? He felt no one cared. Everyone was so self-serving. He felt very alone and betrayed.

That night his alcohol-deprived body rebelled, and he suffered with severe pain, retching, sweating and shaking. After days of misery, he didn't know how long, the toxins finally left his body and he began to feel better. He gathered his strength and ventured out on scouting trips into the resort to find food and whatever else might have survived the storm. On his first foraging trip he found a small crappie trapped in a large trough of water by the lakeshore. *There is a God up there watching over me*, he thought, *how else has that fish survived in there?* He found an old fillet knife in the fish cleaning shack and filleted the fish, then built a fire in one of the broken down grills and cooked it. It smelled heavenly and tasted divine. Days later he found an old fishing rod and tackle box so there was always something to eat a cast or two away.

On another gathering expedition, Charlie found one of his hidden whiskey bottles, more than half full. *Now that was another miracle but probably not from God*. He found three cans of beans in cabin cupboards and wild, fresh asparagus spears, even if a little tough, and wild blackberries. These patches must have been here for years, probably started by the Grogans. He ate everything and anything he could find. There was an artesian spring that flowed from one of the hillsides that gave him fresh water. With the taste of whiskey whetted by the first discovered bottle, Charlie soon found more. In his twisted thinking he thought maybe God had made him forget about all the half-drunk bottles from past years so that he could find them now…when he really needed them.

Every night though, he made his way back to the truck cab to tend to Aggie. He talked to her well into the night about his fears and regrets and he felt sure she understood his every word.

*****

Two weeks had passed since the destructive storm. Charlie stretched and worked the kinks from his back and neck after another fitful night of sleep in the back of his truck. He reached over the front seat and stroked his dog's fur and then felt for her heartbeat. He was certain there was none but he couldn't accept the truth. He spoke to her, as if that would drive away death's claim on her.

"I gotta' go for a while, little girl, but I'll be back with something for you to eat."

Charlie opened the creaky door of the truck, slipped out from the back seat and stepped down onto broken twigs that snapped beneath his boots. He relieved himself on the nearest tree and then headed down the hill to the decrepit resort by the lake, to scrounge whatever he could find for food or comfort.

While Charlie rummaged through the old buildings and combed the shoreline of the lake, Herb Grogan's black Suburban pulled into the driveway of his old resort. Herb sat behind the wheel taking in the destruction before him. He had to stop almost immediately after pulling onto the driveway because of the fallen trees that lay across the road, their branches intertwined together like a giant woven mat. Herb turned the key off and the low roar of the Suburban engine was silenced. He hesitated in the silence, wondering why he had come. He guessed he was worried about the place and Charlie. He didn't think anybody would bother to check except him. He was wary as he began to make his way carefully down the blocked road when he came upon a grey Ford truck, parked deep into the underbrush on the left side of the driveway. He recognized it as Wiley's and his heart skipped a beat. The old man hesitated, looking around the woods and then nervously spoke Charlie's name.

"Charlie?" Herb tentatively spoke in the direction of the truck. No answer came.

"Charlie, where are you?" This time speaking a little louder.

Again the words fell on absent ears. Herb walked over to the half hidden truck and a sickening smell wafted from an open window. He held his nose as he peered inside the cab. There, on the front seat, laying on a blanket, was a white and brown spotted Springer Spaniel, swarms of flies gathered around its eyes, nose and mouth. He quickly went around to the other door, opened it and reached in to check the poor dog for life. She was gone, of course, no question.

He spoke softly to himself, "Poor dog, she's been gone for a while." He covered her up with the blanket to keep the flies off her and shut the door quietly. His gut told him to walk back to his Suburban and get out of there, but his concern and curiosity had a firm grip on him.

But, against his better judgement, Herb continued on through the tree-woven road. When he reached the end of the driveway, what lay before him was even more alarming. The house that he and Jenny built with their own hands lay broken and almost hidden under the giant pine he had planted fifty years ago.

He yelled again.

"Charlie!"

Down in the resort below Charlie stopped in mid-gulp from his almost empty whiskey bottle--*the last of too many to count*. He listened and sure enough he heard his name yelled from the top of the hill. His heart beat fast and his fear caught in his throat like a wad of cotton choking off his breath. *Who the hell could that be,* he thought. Paranoia gripped him and his eyes darted back and forth, from looking up the hill where the voice came from to looking for a place to hide in the resort. He had been drinking nonstop for days and his disoriented mind raced. Charlie grabbed a tire iron resting against an empty gas tank and began to make his way up the hill through the low brush along the woods. As he reached the house he could see Herb Grogan poking around the branches of the fallen pine. The old man's hearing was failing, and he didn't hear Charlie approach. He was busy looking into the smashed house calling for Charlie.

Charlie worked his way noiselessly behind Herb.

"What the hell do you want, you old son of bitch?" Charlie screamed.

Spittle flew from his mouth as he yelled.

"You're trespassing, you old coot!"

Herb looked back at him in shock, his blue eyes showing his alarm. As he struggled to turn around he realized his shirt sleeve was caught in a tangle of branches. Charlie swung the tire iron at the old man's head and hit with such force that Herb's neck snapped sideways and his skull cracked. Rage ruled Charlie's mind beyond reason as he hit Herb's falling body again and again.

Chapter 14

Two Kingdoms

Charlie swung the tire iron for the third time at Herb's already broken skull. The old man's body lay still on the scattered debris of his beloved home. Facing the sky, one arm still caught in the tangle of branches, Herb's gentle blue eyes were open but unseeing. Charlie looked into the face of the man he had just killed and his rage subsided. He dropped the tire iron and backed away from the bloody body. As he retreated further back, Charlie realized that the old man's weak fingers were pointing at something in front of him, a peaceful smile graced his face in death. Charlie cried out in surprise at Herb's incongruous expression of peace in the moment of his death.

If old Herb could have talked to Charlie, he would have told him it was okay, that he forgave him. But Herb had just passed to the other side, and any communication by him in this world was done. If he could talk to Charlie though, he would have told him and everyone--that in the split second between the pain and horror that was wrought on him by a mad man, there stood instead, his beautiful Jenny. He felt no pain, just joy overflowing. The new realm he entered was brilliant in color and overflowing with love beyond expression. It was like walking through a doorway--from one room-- into the next. Herb would love to have told someone that at the end, fear and sadness was not in his heart, only joy.

Charlie turned and ran for his truck. He stopped once along the way to heave up what little was in his stomach and then he staggered on. There was no option for him now except to get away from Thunder Lake. There would be nothing for him here except prison time for murder. The fallen trees on the driveway seemed to be purposely holding him back, slowing his escape. It was as if the woods knew that he had murdered their former kindly master. A sharp branch tore at Charlie's shirt, and another scratched his cheek, almost poking his left eye. Insane with fear, Charlie was sure cops would be waiting for him at the end of the road. When he finally reached his truck, he wiped the sweat from his face with his shirtsleeve and saw there was more than sweat, there was also blood. Whether it was his blood or the old man's, he didn't know. He looked around in the woods and up the road, and saw with great relief that no one was waiting for him. His fear began to subside.

When Charlie opened the door of the truck he saw his dog had been covered up. Charlie removed the blanket from the spaniel and gagged. Aggie was dead--really dead. His murderous actions had smacked him back to reality and now he accepted that she had died days ago. Tears rolled down his face and disappeared between his parted lips. He was all alone again.

Charlie wrapped the spaniel's body in the blanket again and lifted her up into his arms. His nose was running and tears fell one after another. He looked around the woods and saw a huge hole in the ground left by one of the uprooted trees. He placed the dog in the cavernous hole and filled in Aggie's grave with loose dirt. As he sat resting by the covered grave Charlie thought he heard something behind him. He turned quickly, heart pounding, eyes still blurred by tears, and struggled to see what made the noise. Was there a face looking at him through the truck windows? It was so hard to decipher, but he thought he saw someone. Charlie struggled to his feet grabbing a large stone in his hand as he rose. He walked around the side of the truck but there was no one standing there. His fear gripped him unreasonably--*Was it Grogan? Was he alive...or was it his ghost? Maybe it was Grogan's lawyer. Maybe he had come with the old man and saw what he had done?* He let the rock fall from his hand. He felt weak in the knees. Thinking about his time years ago in an Illinois jail, Charlie knew he couldn't handle being locked up and this time it wouldn't be some county jail, it would be prison. He would have to do something about that lawyer. If that young buck saw what he had done or if he started looking for Grogan, there would certainly be an all-out manhunt. Charlie figured he'd have to find where this Timberlake lived and make sure he doesn't alert the cops. Charlie backed his truck out of the hidden spot in the woods and steered around the Suburban and onto the side of the highway. He then went back to the Suburban. He was hoping Grogan left his keys in the SUV but after a quick search he found no keys but he did find a gun under the driver's seat and bullets in the glove compartment. So he put the gear shifter into neutral, and put his strength and weight into pushing the vehicle. It finally started to roll slowly forward into the brushy woods where his truck had been. Then Charles Wiley headed northwest, to the Ojibwe Reservation.

*****

It was early evening at Safe Harbor Resort when Libby Edwards started to climb the hill behind her house. As she climbed she grabbed at the plants that dotted the steep, sandy hillside. Even though loose stones tumbled down behind her, little poplar trees and various deep rooted bushes helped keep her footing. As she reached the top she saw her private sanctuary waiting for her.

She and Will had found this spectacular setting soon after moving to the resort. It was the highest point on the property with a breathtaking view of Thunder Lake. It must have also been a favorite spot of the Carter's, the resort's former owners, as there was a rusty metal chair hidden in some brush near the overlook.

Libby soon found herself visiting this place of refuge often. She had checked the old chair for worthiness of her weight and placed it to the best vantage point of the lake view below. The metal chair had bent iron legs that curved into a C-pattern so when you sat in it, it gave you a nice springy, rocking motion. It had become Libby's version of a comfortable church pew in a perfect church sanctuary.

Libby had grown up being a P.K, a preacher's kid. Her father was retired now but she had grown up under his teaching. Both of her parents had given her a balanced understanding of faith...her mom emphasizing her freedom in Christ; her dad introducing the mysteries of God's Kingdom being here and now. They helped her understand that our purpose on this earth was to be God's love to others and to recognize His presence and live our lives accordingly.

As she sat and admired the sight before her; the sparkling lake, the cotton-puff clouds against a royal blue sky--Libby's worries and concerns of the day began to fall off her like the stones that tumbled down the hillside. Her heart and mind began to quiet and the small sounds in the woods pricked her hearing. She closed her eyes and smiled as the sun's warmth caressed her upturned face. "Here I am,

Lord." she spoke audibly as if God was present with her on the hilltop.

Libby breathed deeply. She began to think about the people in her life. She thanked God for her children and Will, the Porters; many more came to mind. She expressed her gratefulness, voicing her concerns and requesting His help. Libby sat very quietly, her eyes closed giving God opportunity to speak to her heart if He was so inclined. It came in a flash, an image that she didn't understand but there was no doubt about its origin. As she concentrated on the image that flashed through her mind, she was still at a loss for its meaning. The scene was of a small cabin with two very tall figures, giants really, standing guard. Libby opened her eyes. She thought it curious and yet a peace came over her that it was a good vision. The quiet of the moment was broken by the rapid knocking of a nearby pileated woodpecker and the rustling of the wind through the leaves of the birch trees.

Libby opened her eyes and looked out at the view before her, the sun still so bright she could barely look at the reflection off the sparkling lake. She felt so blessed to live in a place like this. She was curious about the vision. *"Angels?"* That she knew without question. She contemplated the cabin where they stood guard. Where was it? Nothing about it made sense...yet. So much of God's ways are mysterious--the unlimited heavens, invisible dimensions of eternity, where beings abide; most impressive, terrifying and ageless. There was a reason God brought this flash of mystery to her and in time she would understand. She was grateful she had opened her heart to the Lord; she never wanted to take for granted the relationship she had with Him.

She sat for a while longer enjoying the beauty around her. She looked down at the resort below and saw Will walking up from the harbor. Honey was with him, running ahead, her ears flapping, her tail straight out like an arrow. The young lab seemed to know joy in almost every ounce of her being. Libby mused. *Maybe animals see God's realm around them all the time.* She smiled at the thought and then rose from the metal chair to join them.

*****

Later that same evening, on the north end of Thunder Lake, the brilliant sun was now heavy in the orange tinted sky. Lance Timberlake sat back in his dad's old rocker on the covered front porch. He was enjoying a cold bottle of Two Hearted Ale and trying to avoid watching his sister and his best friend as they snuggled on the porch swing together. Joe Cloudrider had been spending most of his free hours with River, and that was just fine by Lance. In fact, it was Lance who encouraged the relationship as he couldn't imagine any other guy he trusted more than his old friend. Joe was honest, strong, humble and above all, madly in love with River and she with him.

Lance watched the sun fall below the thick woods that surrounded his parents' home; rays of light shot between the tree trunks. It gave Lance the impression that the Great Spirit was gazing through the trees at them. His thoughts still on River and Joe--Lance remembered the little cues he was getting from River a few weeks ago. She seemed to have a million questions about Joe: Did he ever hear Joe talk about her? Did Joe talk about any other women? What's his family like? It went on like that for days until finally the light bulb went off in his brain. *Obviously, River is interested in being more than friends with Joe!* He encouraged his sister to invite Joe over for supper and that was all the encouragement Joe needed. Lance was grateful for such a perfect solution to his worries for his little sister. He was jealous of his sister's new-found love because there was nothing he wanted more than to find someone he could love and grow old with too, but so far there had not been much chemistry with anyone special. Well, there had been someone, a colleague at the law firm, but she had made it clear to him that her career was more important than marriage. He was guilty of the same self-absorbed thinking, but now he wished he had fought harder to keep Natalie from walking out of his life.

River looked down at her hand, Joe's fingers were intertwined with hers. He gently rubbed the back of her small hand with his thumb. She looked up into his face and the butterflies in her stomach exploded into flight as she realized he was looking down at her, his eyes full of love. The corners of Joe's lips lifted ever so slightly into a smile, his eyes glistening in the afterglow of the setting sun.

"Do you need a jacket, River?" Joe asked in a low voice, never releasing his gaze.

River answered, "I'm fine. In fact, I've never felt better," she felt unable to release her gaze from Joe's soft brown eyes.

Lance pulled himself out of his thoughts and took the last swallow of beer. He looked over at River and Joe and knew his presence was not wanted on the darkening porch.

"Well, I'm off to where the wind don't blow and the snow don't snow, on the big rock candy mountain," Lance said with a smile. That was part of a many versed song that his dad used to sing as he headed to bed. It's funny how those silly things stay with you. A quick feeling of sadness washed over him afresh as he thought about his dad and how much he missed him. He still found it intolerable to think about his mother without a great ache clenching his heart. *God, how it hurt to think of what he and River had lost over this past year.* He looked over at River. It was too dark to see her face but he could see her free hand wipe away something on her face and he knew it was a tear.

"I'm sorry, River, it just slipped out." Lance apologized, realizing his reciting of the song had touched River too.

River sniffled and wiped a tear from her other eye, "It's all right, Lance, we don't ever want to forget all the wonderful memories we have of Mom and Dad. We have to remember them so we can share as much of our parents as we can with our children and grandchildren someday."

Lance got up from the low rocker, his tall, lanky body unfolding as he rose to his feet. "Goodnight, you two. Behave now and for goodness sake, no dancing in the moonlight." He crossed the old wooden planks of the porch floor and disappeared into the house. Joe immediately lifted River's chin and pressed his lips onto River's forehead, then he lightly kissed her nose and finally her lips. Hundreds of butterflies took flight in River's stomach. She reached up to draw herself as close as she could to Joe. She never thought she could feel such passion. Was this love, or lust? At this moment she really didn't care.

Joe left River's home well after two in the morning. He needed to get home to let his dog out before her bladder exploded. Joe lived on his parent's acreage but had his own home on the back of the property. It was the original home his grandfather built sixty-five years ago, an old log cabin next to a lazy stream that eventually empties into Thunder Lake. Joe's father was born in that log cabin as was his Aunt Jenny. When Joe's father got married and started a family, he built a new home closer to the road which left Grandpa Cloudrider to live out his days peacefully in his log cabin by the stream. When Joe graduated high school, he was seriously thinking of moving to the Twin Cities, but then his parents asked him to consider moving in with his grandfather. They could see that life was getting too hard for the eighty-five-year-old to handle alone. At first Joe resented the arrangement but in the end he felt only honor to have been there for his grandfather's last years. Now, the log cabin was Joe and Casey's, the black lab Joe needed to let outside.

As he drove out of the Timberlake driveway he noticed a truck sitting on the side of the road through his rearview mirror. He decided someone probably ran out of gas and walked to town. The Village of Thunder Lake was only a mile further west. He continued on to his place, giving the parked truck one more glance in the rearview mirror. Curious, and a little suspicious, Joe thought about going back to check on the truck but finally decided to shrug off his paranoia and let it go.

Five hours after Joe left the Timberlake home, River and Lance had their usual breakfast on the porch: eggs, toast and coffee. Lance watched as an eagle soared far above the treetops while three well fed chickadee's sat eating on the birdfeeder River religiously filled. Lance realized he hadn't heard his sister speak all through breakfast so he looked over at River and realized her thoughts must be anywhere but with him on the porch.

"Well, Sis, it would seem things are getting pretty serious between you and Joe. Care to elaborate?"

"Huh? Oh sorry, I was just daydreaming I guess. Things are fine. Joe wants to take me and his parents out for dinner on Saturday. I guess he wants us to meet on neutral ground. Tell me about his parents, Lance."

Lance thought for a moment and then spoke. "Joe's mom and dad haven't always had it easy. Money used to be a big problem for them, like all the families on the Rez, but they never handled the tough times as a team. His dad, Terry, is a good guy, works hard, honest, like Joe. But his mom never seemed happy or content. It's no wonder. There never was much money to be had all their years of raising kids but even now that things are better, it's still not good enough. Both Terry and Vicki work at the casino, I'm sure you've crossed paths with them when you are working."

"Yeah, I've seen them a few times but haven't had a conversation with either. They work the day shifts mostly. Vicki is a cocktail waitress in the Lone Wolf Bar and Terry works behind the cash counter. Joe's Mom is certainly a beautiful woman."

"I agree. When I was a boy I had a huge crush on her," Lance smiled. "But her sour attitude soon squelched my infatuation. Terry's older sister is Jenny Grogan--well, was Jenny. Speaking of Grogans, I haven't heard from Herb for a week. I got a notice in the mail from the county. After checking on the taxes for Herb, the clerk gave me a heads up that Herb's resort property will be put up for sale at the next real estate auction unless the back taxes are paid. The county sheriff was ready to go out to the property with us to serve Wiley eviction papers but then the storm hit and the sheriff's been too busy. I haven't heard anything since. I guess I better give Herb a call today."

River looked concerned. She liked old Herb and hoped he was all right. She stood and gathered up the dishes from the table and headed for the front door of the house. As she negotiated balancing the stacked dishes and opening the door she stopped and turned to Lance, "I have to work today at three. Just thought you'd like to know I won't be home for dinner."

"Okay. Joe working tonight too?"

"Of course. I think he's arranged for us to permanently have the same shifts. He says he worries about me unless he's working there at the same time. Crazy, huh?"

Lance gave her a smile and nod but thought to himself, "*I like his kind of crazy.*"

The phone call Lance made to Herb's house went unanswered. He called Jenny's cousin, Rose, who lived just down the street from Herb. She said she hadn't seen Herb for a day or two. Lance decided he'd head over to Herb's to check on him.

*****

The grey pick up Joe had seen parked along the side of the road in the wee hours of the night roared to life at sunrise. Charlie had been sitting in the dark through the long night arguing with himself about what to do. He had driven around Thunder Lake Indian Reservation reading the names on mailboxes into the night to find the name "Timberlake." He even snuck down the driveway in the dark and saw the lawyer's blue Toyota, and a silver Escort, he knew belonged to his sister. One more vehicle crowded the driveway, a Ford F150. He recognized it as Joe Cloudrider's truck, the security manager at the casino who escorted him out of work after they fired him. Being a casino valet, he knew the vehicles that the employees drove. *Hell, there's too many people inside to go in now,* Charlie thought to himself. So after peaking in a few windows to get the lay of the house, Charlie walked back out to his truck to wait. Soon, he fell into a light sleep.

While Libby Edwards believed there was a kingdom of God on earth, there had to be a kingdom of Darkness, and the lord of deception was well-rooted in the heart of Charlie as he sat waiting in his truck on the side of the road. The things that had been done to him, the people who had hurt him in his life, the pain he had already caused in other people's lives, were all destructive forces that brought Charlie to this dark moment.

It was close to six in the morning and the sun was about to rise above the treetops when Charlie awoke. He'd better make his move before Timberlake left for the day. He put the shifter in reverse and moved his truck further off the road, and into a field of corn. Charlie grabbed the gun lying next to him on the seat. He was glad he had had the bright idea of looking in Herb's black Suburban and that's where he found the .38 wrapped in a towel under the driver's seat and bullets for it in the glove compartment.

Charlie was relieved that the Timberlakes didn't own a dog. It made sneaking around the back of their house undetected too easy, and it took little effort to stay hidden as he walked through the thick woods to the house and hide against the back of the building. He listened to the brother and sister talking on the porch. It felt like his racing heart was going to explode from his chest as he listened to them discuss their concern for Herb. Regrettably, he would have to deal with both of them...fast.

Chapter 15

Friday--Heading to Wolf Island

River turned on the radio on a shelf over the kitchen table. It was a vintage turquoise radio from the sixties with a clear lighted dial. It would probably fetch more money at an antique store today than her mom bought it for thirty years ago, but she didn't want to change anything in the house that reminded her of her childhood. The old radio only pulled in AM stations but River remembered listening to songs by Guns and Roses, Chicago, and the Beatles old tunes when she was a teenager doing homework at the table. The station was just giving the weather forecast, "Sunny and humid today, with a thirty percent chance of showers later in the day."

"River, I'm heading over to check on Herb. Do you want to come along?"

River turned around to see Lance standing in the kitchen doorway. She gave it a moment's consideration and answered, "No, I think I'll stay here. But let me know how he's doing, OK?"

"All right." Lance turned to leave and then River heard him say in an alarmed voice, "**What the h--**" and then she heard another man's voice. He was talking too low for River to understand.

"**What the hell are you doing here?**" River heard Lance ask in the same alarmed tone. "**You think you can just barge into our home**..."

Lance saw the gun in Charlie's hand and the reality of the scene hit him as if the gun had already been fired. It felt like every movement was in slow motion--he was taking in the surreal scene as the voice of the weatherman droned on from the radio in the kitchen. Finally Lance's reactions caught up to his racing brain and he yelled,

"**River, run! Get out of the house, now.**"

Then, with a calm voice, Lance talked to the intruder.

"Just let my sister leave. You don't need to keep her here. You just want to talk to me, right?"

Charlie answered nervously. "You should have kept out of my business. Now you are a big problem to me."

Lance shook his head and again admonished his sister to leave. **"River, get in your car and go...NOW!"**

River dropped the dish rag in the soapy water she had just filled in the kitchen sink. She ran for the back door as she heard a scuffle in the living room. Then she heard the gunshot. River ran to the living room doorway to see Lance bend over in pain. She screamed, frozen where she stood. Charlie took a step closer to the wounded lawyer and said in a strained, high pitched voice, "Grogan's dead. I killed him so there's no use checking on him."

Lance fell to the floor in pain and River could see blood oozing through his fingers as he held his arms tight against his body.

"Don't you run off little sister, or you'll get a bullet too. Your brother isn't dead yet but if you run, I'll finish him."

Charlie threatened her with the wave of the gun.

"Let her go....ahhh...," Lance struggled to get the words out.

Charlie demanded, "Get over here by your brother."

River ran to Lance's side and dropped to the floor. She pulled back his bloody hands and saw the hole from the bullet. It had entered on the left side of his abdomen. She wasn't sure what organs were damaged but she knew her brother needed help fast.

"Please, just leave." River pleaded, tears filling her big brown eyes, "I don't even know you, and Lance will keep quiet if you'll leave me alone."

An absurd emotion came over Charlie when he heard River say she didn't know him. He felt hurt that she didn't remember him from the casino.

Lance struggled to talk again, "Why did you ki.." and he let out another groan. The pain in his left side was unbearable. Then Lance was suddenly quiet. His body relaxed and his eyes closed. River cradled her brother's head, kissed his forehead and cried, "Oh God, don't take my brother...please God!"

Charlie watched River as she cried over her brother and he felt only his own pain.

She didn't even remember meeting me, stupid little airhead sitting there bawling over her brother. No one ever cared about me like that.

Memories from his childhood flooded his thoughts. He was twelve-years-old when he was placed in foster care, the first of three. He remembered the deceptively kind face of the first foster dad. Charlie thought he seemed caring and his initial fears melted away--that is until the man got him alone and told him, "Young man, look at me." Charlie looked in horror as the man's kind face was replaced with the face of cruelty and Evil. His cold, green eyes bore into Charlie's scared eyes, "You are mine now, boy, and no one else's." The man's words had nothing to do with protecting or caring; this was no shelter for a lonely, messed-up child. Charlie remembered that same cold spirit of Evil in his second foster home too. This time Evil was living in one of the foster kids in the home. The fifteen-year-old boy tortured him and some of the other boys, but the foster parents turned a blind eye to the trouble because they didn't want to lose the social services income the boy brought into their overcrowded home. Sometimes the older boy locked him in the dark cellar under the old farmhouse. Charlie remembered hating the dark, musty dampness. He could hear scurrying in the darkness. It scared him so much that he would wet himself. The older boy warned him to keep his mouth shut or he'd cut his tongue out and throw him down in the cellar for good. Charlie remembered the fear and hate like it was yesterday.

Eventually Charlie told Child Protection Services and the older boy was sent to a juvenile detention facility. Charlie spent the next six months with a nice family, but they just couldn't handle all of the problems that came with him, so he was sent to a boys' home where he stayed until he turned eighteen. Now he was on his own. His hopes and dreams for love crushed…until he met his wife Aggie in that corner drug store. But now she hated him too.

River's sobbing broke through Charlie's childhood memories. Again he saw the love pouring out of River for her brother.

"Shut up!" Charlie snarled.

He grabbed her arm and yanked her to her feet. Lance's head hit the floor with a thud and then he groaned. Charlie pointed the gun at Lance and shot him again. Then he yanked River out the front door and down the wooden steps. River stumbled and fell hard, her knee hitting a rock protruding through the grass. She cried out in pain but her captor didn't stop; he just dragged her into the woods where no one would see them. When River and Charlie got to the truck, it had been close to an hour since Charlie had left it hidden in the cornfield. He unlocked the passenger door, slid the front seat forward to reach for a roll of tape on the floor and began to wrap River's hands. She screamed in terror and he frantically shoved an old rag in her mouth from the floor of the backseat. Then he taped her mouth too. River looked up into Charlie's face and for the first time, recognition was written in her eyes. *He's the new valet from the casino.* Her mind raced with so many questions. *Where is he taking me? Why? Was Lance dead?* Charlie saw the beautiful young woman's terrified eyes and only saw his own terrified eyes as a boy. *No one cared about me, no one tried to help me. We'll see if anyone cares about you,* he thought bitterly.

River struggled to break free of Charlie's grasp. He slapped her across the face so hard that her head hit the edge of the truck door. She stumbled backwards but Charlie caught her before she hit the ground. He picked her up and threw her onto the floor of the back seat, slammed the door shut and ran around to the driver's side.

As Charlie headed down the road his mind was racing. He hadn't planned on kidnapping. He just wanted to stop Timberlake, shut him up, and keep the cops from snooping around. Now that he had Timberlake's sister, he felt somehow, that he was hurting Timberlake and Cloudrider even more. He felt powerful--and then shuddered with another feeling--he felt evil. What he had once feared in others as a boy he now felt within himself.

Charlie thought hard about his next move. Go back to Muskie Run? Head for Canada? No, they'll be checking the roads. He kept driving. Then it came to him. He knew of a boat he could use and a place to hide out. Wolf Island. It was far up on the northeast end of the lake. No one was allowed on the Island because it was a wildlife sanctuary. Charlie turned the truck around and headed northeast. He pulled into an overgrown driveway and headed towards the lake. The cabin at the shoreline still looked closed up from the winter; the shades were pulled and outdoor furniture was stacked next to the cabin. This was the summer place of one of his drinking buddies, a private retreat sitting on five acres, surrounded by towering pines.

Old Jackson Potter, a retired columnist for the Tribune, hadn't been up to the lake since last year. He remembered hearing that Potter had suffered a heart attack and then a massive stroke. Jackson Potter had no family except his wife and she would never come up without her husband.

Charlie found Potter's boat in a shed and hitched it to his truck. It wasn't long and the boat was tied to the dock. He thought he might also find some needed supplies in the cabin so he broke a window on the back porch and climbed in to have a look. Charlie found crackers, Cheese Whiz, pancake mix, oil, sugar, coffee, dehydrated potato flakes and peanut butter in the pantry. On the counter he found a two-gallon container of spring water and in the freezer he found hot dogs, buns and a casserole. He packed it all in grocery sacks and headed for the liquor cabinet where he found bottles of every imaginable liquid spirit. All of these also went into grocery sacks. On his way back from delivering his bounty to the boat, he found an old mildewed canvas tarp and a Coleman stove in a shed near the lake. He put the stove in the boat, and dragged the tarp back to the truck and laid it out on the ground. When he pulled River from the backseat, the small, groggy woman fought weakly against him, but he soon had her hidden in the tarp and carried her down to the boat like a roll of carpet.

Within a short time, he was flying across the lake toward Wolf Island, River lying in the bottom of the boat, terrified for herself and her bleeding brother back home.

Chapter 16

Scattered Pieces

Joe Cloudrider arrived at work five minutes before three, Friday. He scanned the employee parking area for River's silver Escort and was happy to see she wasn't there yet. He liked getting there before her so he could greet her at the front door. An hour later, when she still had not arrived, his concern grew. He used the phone in the valet office to call River's home but there was no answer. Two hours later, during a fifteen minute break, he tried again--no answer. Joe went back to talk to River's boss and was even more alarmed when he saw his concern also. They decided to call a neighbor close to the Timberlake home and have them check on River.

An hour later a phone call came into the casino's main office from the neighbor. He informed them that there was no sign of River but he did find Lance lying on the living room floor. He had been shot several times, blood everywhere. There was no sign of River but River's purse was in the house and her car was still parked in the driveway. The neighbor said he called 911. The ambulance had taken Lance to Grand Rapids Medical Center and Tribal Law Enforcement officers were at the house now.

The casino boss, Jim Bowstring had been the one to take the call and met Joe just outside his office. Joe looked at Jim's deeply concerned face and dreaded to hear the news Jim was about to tell him. Jim took hold of Joe's shoulders.

"Jim, you look like someone just died!"

"Joe, it's Lance."

Joe interrupted, "Wh-what's happened?"

"We don't know. But Lance was found shot. He's been taken to Grand Rapids."

Joe felt numb. He couldn't accept what his ears were hearing.

"No, there must be a mistake."

"I'm so sorry, Joe, I know how close you and Lance are. You two have been friends since you were little boys," Jim Bowstring said with sadness. "My son, George, is on his way to Grand Rapids now, to be with Lance. Please go…you need to be there for Lance too.

George will be glad to have someone to wait with him. I guess Lance is in pretty bad shape. He may not pull through."

For some odd reason, Jim did not tell Joe about River being unaccounted for. Maybe he was being a chicken by not telling him; it just seemed that it was enough for him to hear about Lance. The poor guy would find out about River soon enough.

"Thanks, Jim, but what about River? Is she there with Lance? Is she okay?" Joe said in a strained voice.

Jim just shrugged his shoulders. "I don't know about River."

Joe turned and headed for the front exit. "I'll meet up with George at the hospital soon but I'm going to stop at Timberlake's first."

Jim felt awful about not telling Joe what he had heard about River. He prayed that she was okay and just hiding somewhere.

Joe brushed against people he passed in his rush to get to the front doors of the casino. People gave him dirty looks as he jostled them. He knocked one woman so hard she dropped her cup full of quarters.

"Hey, watch it," she said in an irritated whine. The cigarette hanging from the side of her mouth bobbed up and down as she talked.

Joe looked back, still moving forward, "I'm sorry!" By the time he said it she was lost in the crowd, and so he kept going. It was six-thirty p.m. as he opened the main doors of the casino into the brilliant late afternoon sunshine and seven o'clock by the time he pulled into Timberlake's driveway. Tribal officers were there to stop him as he pulled in.

"Sorry, Joe, you can't go in there."

"Is River here? Or with Lance at the hospital?" Joe asked expectantly.

"No. We don't know where River is. Her purse and car are here. Our only lead to what happened here is Lance and, so far, he's unconscious."

Joe was in shock. Who did this...where was River...why would someone want to kill Lance...all these questions flooded his confused brain.

He heard the officer's voice through his fog,

"They took him to Grand--"Joe interrupted. "I know. I'm heading over there now."

"Sorry, Joe. I wish we knew more," The officer said as he patted the door of Joe's truck.

Joe took off for Grand Rapids, stones kicking out from under his tires as he sped away.

*****

It took Charlie over an hour to drive the stolen boat to the west end of Wolf Island. It was late afternoon and the heat from the July sun was intense. He slowed down and began circling around the north side of the island. Wolf Island was three miles long and a mile wide. It was given the name because of an Ojibwe legend. Before the lake was dammed in the late 1800s, the island was even larger, and a healthy population of moose lived on the island's marsh grass and other vegetation that was so plentiful back then. A wolf pack claimed the area also, feasting on the very old and very young moose. When the five lakes were flooded by the damming up of Thunder River, Wolf Island lost half its size to the rising water level. This flooding killed off the bountiful vegetation, and the moose moved off the island. The wolves lost their largest food source, and in time they started looking for food near settlers on the mainland. It wasn't long before all but one wolf remained of the large pack. The legend claims that this lone wolf remained on the island and howled every night for his pack family to return. The mournful call was unnerving to folks and there was talk of putting it out of its misery, but no one wanted to go to the island because it was said to be haunted by the spirits of the Old Ones of the Ojibwe people who protected the wolf. Fact or myth, that was the story told through the generations.

When Charlie first took over Muskie Run Resort--when things were good between him and his wife, Aggie--he used to take people to the weed beds off Wolf Island on his launch. He would retell the wolf story to them as they fished. There was usually great fishing in the fall for jumbo perch along the island's south shore but fishing was slow during July and August. He remembered there being an Ojibwe shelter on the east side of the island where the Indians stayed while they harvested wild rice. It was abandoned since the rice beds were ruined along with other vegetation after the damming up of the five lakes. Later, the island became home to a small shore bird called the Caspian Tern. With their population dwindling, and the bird's selective choice for building nests only on the rocky shoreline of Wolf Island, it became a protected island for the little birds in hopes that their precious few numbers would improve.

So Charlie figured this would be the perfect hideout until he could decide what to do next. He had a sinking feeling that this was all going to come to a bad end but he wouldn't think about that now. He looked down at the small woman wrapped in the canvas tarp. River's scared eyes looked out through her windblown hair. She seemed to be studying the sky and treetops as the boat continued along the shoreline, listening to the cacophony of bird cries from the shoreline.

Charlie spoke to her, "I won't hurt you if you behave. You and I are going to be stuck together for a while until I figure out a plan."

River could only grunt her angry response because of the dirty rag and tape over her mouth. Charlie just smirked at her muffled outburst and kept driving the boat.

Charlie knew he had to travel the north side of the island to get to the east end. It made the trip longer, but if a boater tried to take a shortcut through the south end, the propeller would be ruined on the hidden rocks a few feet below the surface. Soon Charlie saw the landmarks he was looking for. The shelter must be close. He pulled the boat up onto a short spit of sand off the hidden, northeast end of the island. Much of the shoreline was rocky but this small sandy beach would get them safely onto the island. Charlie secured a long rope to the front of the boat, tied the other end to a tree, and then walked into the woods, leaving the boat to rock slightly in the waves. There, only one-hundred feet from the shore, was the abandoned shelter. The sides and the door were made from rough-sawn pine boards, and the roof was covered with multiple layers of tar paper. As he peered inside, he saw it had a wood floor--some boards were broken, but at least it wasn't dirt. There was a table, a long bench, and a couple of crudely constructed chairs sat near a rusty wood stove. *This will work just fine* he thought to himself, and off he went to get River and unload the supplies. Then he would do his best to hide the boat.

*****

Joe entered the Grand Rapids Hospital and asked the receptionist where he could find Lance Timberlake. She stared at her computer screen, made a call and then informed Joe that Lance was out of surgery, and he could head up to the waiting area in the intensive care unit, 2nd floor, East wing. She saw his confusion and added, "The elevators are just down the hall to your left."

Joe found the ICU waiting area and to his relief saw a forlorn George Bowstring sitting in a corner.

"George, your dad said you were here."

George rose from his chair and walked to Joe and gave him a big bear hug. "I'm so glad you came," George said as he continued to hold onto Joe.

"Lance is out of surgery. They told me to come up here to wait."

Joe asked, "Have you talked to Lance? Has he said anything about what happened?"

"Lance was almost dead when they found him. He's been unconscious so he can't help us piece things together yet. The cops don't know what to think about River. They don't think she did it, but where is she?"

Joe responded defensively, "She would never…*could* never do anything like that, especially to her own brother."

"Oh, I know that, Joe. I'm worried sick about her too but you know cops. They are suspicious of everyone until they get a good lead. These cops here are from Beaver Creek. They are county cops and don't know River like our Rez cops."

"Yeah, you're right. It's driving me crazy though," Joe said as he slumped down into a chair.

The two friends heard some soft voices in the hall and saw Lance being wheeled through the doors of the intensive care unit. They both jumped to their feet to follow but a nurse stopped them as they went through the doors, "Are you waiting for news on Lance Timberlake?"

"Yes, we want to see him," George told her.

"Are you family?" The disappointed look on the two friends' faces told her the answer. "I'm sorry, only family can be in here," she said sympathetically.

"He has no family. We're all he's got right now. His sister is missing and his parents are dead," Joe argued.

"I'm sorry, it's the rules in ICU. Mr. Timberlake is still not conscious anyway. If there is any change, I'll find you. Will you be in our waiting area or in the cafeteria?"

"We'll be waiting right here," Joe replied.

George and Joe sat through the long night waiting for any change. An officer sat on a chair just outside the door to Lance's room. It was standard procedure in a shooting.

*****

River stood in front of Charlie. He had just lifted her out of the boat, and she felt herself weave back and forth as she tried to get her bearings after being unrolled from the mildewed tarp he had her hidden in for the fast boat ride across the lake. When Charlie tried removing the tape and wadded up rag from her mouth, he was rewarded with an ear deafening scream. He quickly stuffed the rag into her open mouth again.

"What the hell are you thinking, little one?" Charlie said calmly to River. She being a good eight inches shorter than him, he felt like a giant next to her. He also knew from his years as a cop that speaking calmly, in a reassuring voice to a hysterical victim was important in de-escalating a situation.

"We are five miles from anyone. Even if a boat comes by we'll hear it way before they see us. But I tell you what, missy, there ain't no one fishing this area of the lake this time of year. The fish are in deeper waters until fall. Besides this island is off limits to people. It's a tern sanctuary. No one's gonna' bother us." Charlie chuckled which caused the ever present phlegm in his chest to bring on a coughing jag.

"Damn cigarettes. They will be the death of me, unless kidnapping you gets me killed first."

River felt a glimmer of hope at this and relished the thought of being rescued and her captor being killed. She thought about her dilemma, looking at the vast back-country that surrounded them. Then she looked at Charlie and nodded. She had to get the wadded rag sticking to her tongue and lips out of her mouth. She nodded again and looked Charlie in the eyes to indicate that she understood her hopeless situation. Charlie carefully removed the rag from her mouth again. Because her lip had been bleeding, one part of the rag refused to loosen from her lower lip. Charlie jerked it loose and her lip started bleeding again.

"Ahhhh, that hurts, you freaking *jerk*." River spat in disgust.

"Well, I don't like your name-calling, missy, but I thank you for being more quiet," Charlie said, giving her a creepy smile. "If you behave, I'll cut the tape from your hands and feet. How would that be? I bet you need to empty your bladder by now, if you haven't emptied it already."

River was repulsed by his remark but let out a long sigh of resignation. "All right, I won't cause you any trouble as I see no other choice at this time."

Charlie knelt and cut the tape binding her ankles and then stood to cut the tape around her wrists.

"You want something to eat? Need some water?"

River took the bottle of water Charlie had stashed in the duffle bag he had hauled from the boat. She guzzled it down, not caring in the least that the water was dribbling down her chin and onto her shirt. After the water was gone she decided she needed to pee. She went behind the small, rundown cabin for privacy. When she returned she told Charlie she wanted to eat.

As Charlie made sandwiches, River looked all around her. Her mind raced with any possibility of getting away. It didn't take her long to realize that escape would have to wait until Charlie was off guard. She would need to seem agreeable for a time, giving him the idea that she was going to be no trouble. Because the way she saw it, her only possible advantage would be the element of surprise.

As they sat eating, neither talked. They both ate like they were ravenous which helped to cover the fact that they were thinking about escape: River, thinking of possibilities and Charlie busy thinking on how to stop her escaping and also the possibilities of how she might attempt to disarm him. The fact that he had her on an island was reason enough to relax a little. Even if she tried to swim to Wolf Track Point, it was a mile swim and then ten miles of thick wilderness to get through. He wasn't sure if this little spark plug was capable of that kind of journey. To be totally safe, when he covered the boat later, he would bury the boat key in the woods so River wouldn't find it on him or in the cabin while he slept. She can't get far without the boat.

Later, once they had eaten, Charlie wound more duct tape around River's ankles and wrists temporarily and headed over to the boat hidden behind the island. He found dead branches to put over the top of the boat and then he covered those with hunks of tall grass, dried reeds and leaves. As for hiding the key, he looked on the ground for a marker of sorts as he walked towards the woods. He walked by a number of rocks that certainly would work but then his eyes caught sight of a very unusual rock. He was intrigued with its weird markings and decided it would make a good marker for finding the key again. On his way back to where he had left River, his thoughts took a devious turn. He began to scheme of a way to handicap her ability to run. He thought, *it was the only way to give himself a break from vigilantly watching her day and night. It's better for her than the alternative of killing her. He had already killed two people in a little over twenty-four hours. What's one more? Well, he had to face it. He liked her and just didn't want to do it.*

When he returned to her he removed the tape from her legs but left her wrists bound. He grabbed her arm and the old tarp lying nearby and walked her into the shelter of the cabin where he folded the tarp from the boat into a makeshift pillow and indicated for her to sit next to it. He stood over her for an uncomfortable minute and River's fears rose. Her heart pounded in her chest and her mouth went dry. *What is going to happen now?* Then, to her relief, Charlie turned from her, walked across the room and sat with a thud onto the dirty, rough floor. In the waning light of day, they watched each other turn to shadow figures, the details of their faces lost in the darkening cabin. It had been a long eventful day for Charlie: murder, kidnapping, breaking and entering, hauling, and let's not forget drinking. With dusk darkening the island Charlie was getting sleepy. His eyes were half closed but he struggled to keep at least one eye on his captive. River sat on the floor leaning against the wall, her hands still bound. Soon she could see Charlie's tired, inebriated brain shutting down as his face slackened and his head slumped against his chest. He was asleep. The bottle of tequila by his side slid to the floor and toppled over. Not a drop spilled as Charlie had finished it. River watched him as darkness settled into the cool damp cabin. Soon it would be pitch black. She sighed, and leaned her body over until her head rested on the smelly tarp that was folded up next to her. She fell fast asleep smelling mold, dead fish and the aromatic gastric leaks coming from Charlie's side of the room.

Charlie awoke often throughout the night to strange sounds outside the cabin. He would shine a flashlight in River's direction and always found her motionless as she slept on the tarp. He turned off the flashlight quickly so he wouldn't wake her; better she sleep, because awake, she'd be trouble. Charlie mulled over his predicament. He knew he was an idiot.

What was I thinking, taking this woman hostage? I must have been out of my mind. How will I ever get away after all I've done?

Eventually he fell asleep again and began to dream: *He was back at his resort. His dog was there with him, all fine and happy. She trotted alongside him as he sauntered down to the harbor where he picked up his fishing rod and walked to the end of one of the docks to do a little fishing. As he cast out to the middle of the harbor, Aggie barked with excitement at the dragonflies hovering over the water. The afternoon sun was warm and inviting as he enjoyed casting from the dock. Soon there was a jerk on his fishing line. Charlie gave the rod a hard yank upward to set the hook and began to slowly reel in his catch with a steady hand. When he got the catch close to the dock and began to raise it out of the water, he stared in horror at a fish with the open-eyed face of Lance Timberlake. Charlie dropped the rod but the fish hovered over the water, Charlie's fishing lure still hooked into Lance's mouth. Charlie ran from the dock and up the hill to the road. The hovering Lance-fish yelled from the harbor and his voice was magnified like rumbling thunder, "What have you done, Wiley?" Then the fish dropped back into the water and disappeared.*

Terror filled every molecule of his being as Charlie ran from the dock and headed for the artesian spring a few feet up the hill from the harbor. He needed a drink badly; his tongue was as dry as shoe leather and his lips were stuck to his clenched teeth. As he cupped his hands to carry the water to his parched mouth he saw only thick, red blood! He gasped and fell back. At the top of the hill stood Herb Grogan. Blood was flowing from Herb's gaping wounds to the ground, into the underwater aquifer and into Charlie's cupped hands.

Charlie tried to scream but nothing came out, just the tiniest of indistinguishable grunts.

"He-e-y-y...wake up!"

Charlie woke from his nightmare relieved to see that it was just that, a nightmare. He looked over at River whose voice had mercifully woke him.

"You having a nightmare?" River asked in disgust.

Charlie took a deep breath and blew it out long and drawn out. "Yeah, I guess so."

Charlie's mouth felt as dry as in the dream so he got up and poured a cup of water from the jug on the table. He drank it down thirstily until the mug was empty.

"Want some?" he asked River.

River nodded and Charlie poured some water into the same cup and held it for her to drink.

Charlie noticed sunlight shine through the cracks of the door and shuttered windows. He put the cup back on the table and stretched. His troubled mind needed numbing so with little hesitation, he retrieved the tequila bottle from the floor, but to his disappointment, there was not a drop remaining.

Chapter 17

Revealing the Madness

A woman wearing a cheerful nurse's smock stood in the doorway of the ICU waiting room.

"Are you gentlemen waiting for news on Lance Timberlake?"

"Yes," the two friends chorused, both awkwardly rising to their feet, stiff from sitting so long.

"My name is Heidi. I was sent to tell you that Lance is awake," the young woman said as she smiled warmly at Joe and George.

"How is he?" George asked.

"He's coherent but in a lot of pain. He has spoken with a detective from the Bureau of Criminal Apprehension. He gave him as much information as he could remember. He's doing well, and in time, that is, if nothing else complicates his recovery, he should survive his injuries." Then the nurse smiled and turned to leave.

Joe stopped her and asked, "Wait, Heidi, we want to see him. Is it possible?"

"I'm sorry, gentlemen, I know he's a close friend but only immediate family can be in the ICU."

"He has no other family. We are all he has right now. His sister is missing and his parents are dead."

"I'm so sorry to hear that. Maybe we can bend the rules in this situation. He's going to need some familiar faces to help him through his recovery. I'll see what I can do."

Joe said gratefully, "Thank you, Heidi.

Joe and George grabbed a cup of coffee from the coffeemaker in the waiting area. No sooner had they sat down than a hospital volunteer walked through the room carrying a tray of cookies which she left on the counter next to the coffeemaker.

She smiled at them as she was leaving and said, "These should go well with your coffee."

Joe and George scrambled to the counter and each grabbed a handful of cookies. Neither of them realized how hungry they were until they inhaled the cookies' sweet aroma.

At a few minutes past nine a.m., Heidi returned to tell Joe and George that she had pulled a few strings and they could see Lance briefly. When they walked into Lance's room they were disheartened at the sight of their buddy lying in the bed before them. His eyes, rimmed in black, were closed. His skin was so was pale he looked lifeless even though the monitors that measured his vital signs said different. They each took a side of the bed and watched Lance in silence. Then Joe laid his hand on his friend's shoulder and Lance's eyes rolled under his eyelids and a weak moan escaped his lips.

"Hey, Dancin' Lance," George said, in a quivering voice. "You're looking a little pale to be a warrior of our great people."

Lance succeeded in opening one eye a slit and gave George a weak smile, "George, my friend."

Then Lance looked to the other side of the bed and saw Joe and both his bloodshot eyes popped open.

"Joe!"

"Lance, you are a sight for my sore eyes," Joe said with concern.

"My sister--God, Joe--do you know what has happened to River?" Lance's voice was raspy and laden with emotion.

"That's what we're hoping you can tell us, Lance," Joe said as his hand went from Lance's shoulder to his forehead. He pushed a shock of Lance's black hair from his face.

"Oh God, she's been kidnapped. What if he's killed her...that crazy bastard." Lance's anxiety was written all over his tortured face. The monitors hooked up to Lance beeped and chimed alarms in the room and out at the nurses' desk.

"Who is this maniac who shot you and took River?" Joe asked.

"Charles Wiley. The drunk who bought your uncle's resort. Your Uncle Herb is dead Joe. Wiley killed him. The police--ah-h--are checking that out right now," Lance winced in pain.

"He killed my uncle? What are you saying? Herb is dead? How do you know that? Do the police know about him taking River?" Joe asked.

"Yeah, of course." Lance's words came out sounding sharp. "Oh God, I'm going crazy with wor--"

A nurse stepped in before Lance could finish," Sorry, gentlemen, but Lance needs to rest. He's getting upset. It's necessary for him to stay calm as much as possible," she said with kind authority. "You can come back this afternoon and see him again."

Lance grabbed Joe's arm and pleaded, "No, don't come back. You can help me best by finding River."

Joe looked at George and they both nodded, "We will, Lance. Just get better. We'll find her."

*****

After Lance told the police all he could remember about his confrontation with Wiley in his home, they rushed directly to Muskie Run Resort. Drivers and farmers in fields along the county road gawked at the speeding squad cars flying past them with their sirens screaming and lights flashing. It made for quite a scene through the farmland and small towns between Grand Rapids and Thunder Lake. When they arrived at the driveway for Muskie Run Resort they found Herb Grogan's Suburban parked just a few feet in from the county road. As they attempted to drive around his large Suburban it was plain to see that the driveway was impenetrable for their vehicles. For as far as they could see, the road was blocked by fallen trees. They would have to go in on foot but not before they had helicopter back-up to take a visual of the resort on the other end of the driveway. The chopper was on its way from Douglas County but until it arrived the gathering squad cars sat in front of the driveway waiting, their lights flashing and their police radios echoing through the woods and hills. Passing cars slowed down as they approached but the officers impatiently waved them on. Finally the order came through the radios. "Chopper ETA eleven-ten. Over." The sergeant looked at his watch, *five more minutes.* He spoke into his microphone, "Roger. Five minutes to ETA. Over." He barked orders to his fellow officers. "Jenkins, Reed, Johnson, Roosevelt, Ganer and Lindgren, Suit up and ready your weapons. The rest of you, keep the public moving. We don't want any looki-loos."

Soon the rumble of rotor blades could be heard in the distance. The chopper circled the resort grounds and then the pilot radioed to the sergeant on the ground. "You have permission to begin search on the ground. Be forewarned, it looks pretty grizzly down there. I'll continue to be your eye in the sky. Over."

The Sergeant responded. "Roger. We appreciate that. Over."

As the officers began to enter the wooded driveway the chopper pilot continued to circle above for a broader view of the area. The seven officers climbed their way through the tangle of trees left from the storm. Some officers had their guns drawn others kept them holstered to free their hands for negotiating through the massive trees and their seemingly impenetrable branches.   By the time the men walked out into a large open area at the end of the driveway, their uniforms were ripped and soaked in sweat, their arms scratched and bloodied. A crumpled building they assumed to be a house sat on the left side of the driveway. The men were amazed at the breathtaking view before them and the gut wrenching scene in the front yard of the house. There, strewn over the grass and cement walkway were the remains of a man's body. It had been food for a bear, wolves, coyotes, or a puma from the looks of the torn flesh. Now an army of insects marched over the corpse with determined purpose. The sergeant holstered his glock handgun and pulled out a rubber glove from his pocket and walked closer to the body. He put on the glove and carefully pulled out the wallet still in the back pocket of the dead man's blue jeans. He spoke loudly for all to hear. "Driver's license says, Herbert Jennings Grogan--what's left of him." The sound of retching could be heard in the background, and then even that was drowned out by the thumping roar and the gale-force wind of another chopper as it landed. The officers on the ground looked over in relief as three BCA officers in suits and ties jumped out seconds after the helicopter skids touched the ground.

The long day at Muskie Run turned into evening as the investigative team searched every building and wooded area for Charles Wiley and River Timberlake. The chopper had to leave and return with a coroner from Brainerd along with a K-9 unit. The dog would be invaluable in finding any missing body parts that had been dragged off by animals. There was some hope that the dog might also sniff out River Timberlake if she were badly injured or if she were in fact dead.

*****

Charles Wiley and River Timberlake spent their day on Wolf Island in awkward hours of silence and moments of cool, obligatory conversation. River kept thinking about her brother lying on the floor of their house and the man who shot him was breathing the same air she was breathing. She knew that she needed to put her hatred for the man aside for now in order to survive, but knowing and doing were two different things.

Charlie was feeling very anxious. How all of this happened to him he just couldn't figure out. *If people hadn't been so cruel to me I would not be in this mess. No one has ever really cared about me or understood my pain. Even my parents hated me, always yelling at me and blaming me for stupid things I did as a child. They deserved to die in that fire. Of course, the foster parents I was forced to live with were just as bad. Everyone in my life has been cruel to me and now is no different. That little Indian squaw would not hesitate to bash my head in if she had the chance.* He knew he would have to kill her eventually but he couldn't bring himself to pull the trigger yet.

But how can I keep her from running? Then an idea came to him…

*****

Charlie had cut the tape from around River's wrists in the morning. He wanted to give her the feeling that he trusted her. River in turn tried to seem trustworthy while she waited and watched for a break, believing her captor would slip up in time. She would be cooperative and helpful until his guard was down.

River figured it had to be late afternoon. Hunger was gnawing at her stomach since they hadn't eaten anything since morning when Charlie gave her some peanut butter and bread.

"Hey, mister *wile-e coyote*," she said mockingly. "I'm thirsty and I need to eat."

Charlie looked into her small, perfect face and his cold heart melted. He admired that this little spitfire could joke around even though her situation was so dire.

"There's food in the cooler if you want to eat. I'll start up the Coleman stove," he said with a sneer, trying to cover up his crumbling resolve to shoot her.

"You may have forgotten but my name is Charlie. Your boyfriend introduced us at work a few weeks ago. But you can call me what you want. I deserve all the hate you have for me."

"You don't deserve to know my name. You make me sick."

"I know your name is River. I didn't mean to shoot your brother. It just happened. He came at me and I panicked."

River's anger crept up her throat, constricting her airway. But she pushed the anger down and took a deep cleansing breath. She almost choked when she tried to reply so she said nothing.

As the cool of evening settled in, Charlie and River sat in the twilight talking. Charlie had offered River some whiskey and was surprised when she took it. They both had ulterior motives in getting the other drunk. River hoped Charlie would get really drunk and forget to tape up her hands and feet giving her an opportunity to escape and Charlie was working on getting River drunk enough so he could carry out his plan before he changed his mind.

"So, mister wile-e coyote, tell me about your life," River prompted as she wiped off the mouth of the bottle and took a tiny sip of the whiskey.

It didn't take too much persuasion before Charlie began to unravel the twisted version of his past. River listened, taking small swallows of the strong liquor to prompt Charlie to take long draws at his turn with the bottle. Charlie never asked River about her life. A self-absorbed person like Charlie only cared about himself. He went on for hours about the loss of his family and the mistreatment he endured as a boy. He left out the part about being caught with a teenage girl as a cop in Illinois. But he lamented about his wife's leaving him and the loss of his home and his dog from the powerful storm.

River's head began to drop in sleepy nods. Charlie had outlasted her--he had been confident that he would. Consuming alcohol was his professional pastime. He watched her sleep. Her black hair fell across her brown face and splashed over her pale yellow blouse. Her hand still held the whiskey bottle but as he watched, it slowly loosened its grip and the bottle was beginning to slip away and fall to her side. Charlie leaned forward and grabbed it before it spilled. He put the bottle down quietly, then reached into

173

his waistband and pulled out the gun. Charlie aimed it at River's foot but his hand shook so violently that he feared he would miss. He took another drink from the bottle and aimed again. She was so pretty and spunky. She had so much spirit, he hated to hurt her. But still he aimed his gun at her foot. Then he thought maybe he should just kill her and be done with this hiding-out crap. If she were dead he could head to Canada and never be found by anyone again. The Northwest Territory was immense, much of it uninhabited. No one would ever find him up there. He aimed the gun at River's skull but again, couldn't pull the trigger. In some twisted way Charlie had fallen for her. *I gotta' do something*, Charlie reasoned in his mind, *so she can't get away.*

Just then he heard something tumble from a pile of debris next to the cabin. Charlie leaped to his feet and whipped the gun around in the direction of the cabin.

"Who's there?"

Only silence answered back.

He walked quietly towards the cabin, the moonlight was bright and it was easy to see. He scanned the area, even looked in the cabin. Nothing moved. He walked back out into the bright moonlight and there, in front of the cabin, a foot away from the pile of debris was a large round rock.

H-m-m, must have rolled off the pile. That's weird.

Then it came to him that if he threw that rock on her foot, he could say it happened by accident when he was carrying boulders to make a platform for the camp-stove. If he shot her it would be hard to explain that it was an accident. Charlie began hauling small boulders from the shoreline to corroborate his story. After he had carried four large rocks and placed them in a semicircle, he then retrieved a fifth and without pausing to think about the pain he was about to inflict, slammed the large rock down onto River's sandaled foot.

"**Ah-h-h,**" River screamed and sat up. The pain was excruciating.

The blackness of the night swirled around her, the blurry dark chasing streaks of light from the stars and moon, round and round.

Charlie yelled over her screams.

"I'm so sorry, River, I tripped on a log--the rock came down on your foot."

River tried to focus in on the voice. As she got her bearings she could see Charlie kneeling on the ground and a large rock lying just off the side of her leg. Her foot was in an unnatural position.

"I was just putting rocks together to make a base for the stove--I tripped and fell, dropping the rock on your foot. I'm so sorry. Let me look at it."

Tears fell from River's cheeks as Charlie took the sandal off her foot. It was definitely broken. Charlie was pleased with his handiwork but of course did not let on to his wicked purpose.

"It's broken, River. I'm so sorry. I wish I could take back my idea of gettin' rocks in the dark. It was stupid."

River looked at his face and was convinced of his sincerity. "I've got to get to a doctor. The pain, it's unbearable."

"We'll get you to a doctor soon. But for now I'll have to make a splint and wrap your foot snug."

Charlie convinced her to drink more from the liquor bottle as he fashioned a splint for her broken ankle. She was in so much pain that every nerve in her body was electrified. River cried out as Charlie wrapped two sticks tightly against the injured leg with duct tape. He wound the tape around her leg, and instep and heel of her foot. When it was over, River's forehead was dripping sweat and her body trembled from the pain. Charlie carried her into the cabin and laid her next to the tarp. She slept fitfully the rest of the night, crying and moaning from the pain.

Chapter 18

Search Party

Business owners around Thunder Lake all participate in an emergency call program. This program allows them to get emergency information out quickly. Most often the emergency call program goes into effect because of severe weather. This time it was implemented for a far more menacing reason--murder and kidnapping.

It was just after lunch Sunday afternoon when Verna Rogers at Pine View Resort got a call from Craig Johnson at Maple Leaf Resort with news of a manhunt for one of their fellow resort owners, Charles Wiley. He was suspected of murder and kidnapping. There also was a search and rescue being organized for the kidnap victim, a young Ojibwe woman. Her name is River Timberlake from the Thunder Lake Reservation.

After hanging up with Craig Johnson, Verna immediately made her assigned call to Safe Harbor Resort.

Libby took the call at the lodge. She was shocked by the news and very distraught when she heard it was River who was missing. When Libby was off the phone with Verna, she made her assigned call to Bob at Stony Ridge Resort. Then she called Carmen who was at home. Carmen was just cleaning up her kitchen after lunch.

"Carmen, Verna from Pine View just called. She had terrible news."

"What?" Carmen asked as she put down the breadboard and dish towel she had in her hand. She could hear the panic in Libby's voice.

"There is an area-wide search for River Timberlake. She was kidnapped sometime on Friday. And get this, the kidnapper is the owner of Muskie Run Resort. There's search parties being organized. This guy killed the previous owner of Muskie Run and shot River's brother!"

"My God--River...," Carmen said, her voice showing the panic she was feeling.

"They want us to be on the lookout for anything suspicious. Will and I plan on joining the search group for River. It's being organized at the reservation. We'll go once you and Jed take over the lodge today.

"Ok, we'll be down as soon as we can." Carmen fought back tears. "That poor, dear girl. Why…" She fought back wanting to shout at God. Instead she said to Libby, "She's been through so much."

*****

Once the Porters got down to the lodge it was decided that Jed and Will would join the search for River while Carmen and Libby ran the lodge. Tourists and residents alike were on high alert. They went about their day hoping and praying no one else would be hurt or killed before the murderer could be found and stopped.

On Monday the Porters joined the search for River. They were briefed about how they should conduct themselves during the search then everyone fanned out in single file. Carmen and Jed had no idea that the young man walking beside them was so closely connected to River. Joe Cloudrider walked the trails, ditches and fields next to them throughout the morning hours, saying nothing. During a brief stop to rest, Carmen overheard the young man talking to a friend. It was obvious that he knew River well as his friend comforted him. After the friend left to get them both something to eat at the volunteer's food wagon parked on the road, Carmen introduced herself and Jed to the young man. She told him how they knew River and he told them about his relationship with River, her brother and his uncle Herb who had been murdered.

Carmen was moved by the young man's bravery in his profound pain.

"I'm so sorry for the loss of your uncle, Joe. I only hope your friend, Lance, pulls through and River is found soon. We just have to believe that River is going to be found alive. We miss her and her mom, Lilly, at Safe Harbor. We were so thankful for all their help our first year running the resort," Carmen said as she put her hand out to touch Joe's arm in reassurance.

"River spoke of you people often," Joe said. "She works at the casino now because it's full time work, but she loved working with her mom at your resort."

Jed asked, "How is her brother doing?"

"Lance is hurting in body and spirit. He was shot twice, once in the belly and the other in the chest. Amazingly, both bullets went clean through, missing vital organs but he lost a lot of blood. His spirit is heavy with worry for River; where she might be and is she even alive? He hangs between two worlds, the world of hope that the Great Spirit is watching and protecting his sister, and the world of bitterness and hatred for the man who took her and killed my uncle. My spirit also hangs between those two worlds."

He then told them how he was planning to ask River to marry him. Carmen gave Joe a hug and thought about what Libby might say to give this young man hope.

"There is only one way to look at this, Joe, and that's with hope in the Great Spirit. River is not alone, God is with her, protecting her and working out a way to bring her back to the ones she loves. Our purpose in this situation is not to be hopeless and angry but to have faith and do what we can to help."

Joe wiped away a tear from his cheek and looked at Carmen. "Thank you, Mrs. Porter. You are right. Being angry will only bring more pain. We must believe she's alive and we will find her."

The search party finished walking the ditches and woods along the county roads of the reservation but there was no sign of River or her captor after a long day of searching. The large group of searchers headed back to their vehicles, tired and disappointed.

*****

Will and Libby spent their day at the lodge thinking often about the search effort to find River. People staying at the resort all knew of the tragic events taking place during their stay at the lake. Many would stop and inquire at the lodge or talk about it as the Edwards scooped minnows for them or filled their boat with fuel.

Between waiting on lodge customers, Libby and Will sat on the front deck of the lodge, looking out at the pristine lake, the waves slapping the rocky shore in rhythmic breaths. Honey lay contentedly in the shade, a tennis ball inches from her nose.

"I remember the Saturday that River found a pair of men's underwear in one of the beds when she was pulling off the sheets," Libby reminisced. "She brought the underwear out to the kitchen with a disgusted look on her face in order to throw them in the garbage. But 'Crazy Patti' was working in the kitchen and couldn't resist teasing River. Patti laughed and told River, "That's some fine looking underwear, River. You should take them home for your pa!"

River was horrified at the suggestion which made Patti laugh even harder. After the long day of cleaning was over and River and Lilly headed to their car, River saw the dirty underwear hanging on their antenna--"

Will interrupted. "Yeah, I think I remember hearing that Patti made sure the underwear was inside out so the skid-marks showed."

"Oh, yes. But the ever-calm Lilly, used a stick and transferred the underwear from her car antenna through the open window of Patti's truck. They landed on the seat next to Patti. She just laughed and said, "Thanks, my husband's been needing another pair of underwear." Then she drove up the hill."

They both cracked up, laughing at crazy Patti's antics.

Patti was one of their fill-in cleaners. She had a horse ranch just a few miles away; that was her passion. She was as strong as most men and a hard worker, but horse shows took her away a lot of weekends. When the resort really needed her though, Patti would show up to help. It's just that you had to put aside any sensitivity to the crass humor she loved to share.

Will and Libby reminisced about a few other memories of their times with River. Will lifted his face to the sky and pleaded, "God, keep her safe and bring her home."

Libby closed her eyes and nodded.

They were still sitting on the deck talking when Jed and Carmen walked through the lodge. Sadie sauntered around the side of the building and greeted Libby and Will before joining Honey in the shady grass. Honey was quick to snatch the ball but Sadie showed no interest. Jed handed Will a beer from the lodge cooler and popped open a can for himself. He and Carmen sat down on the picnic tabletop and admired the lake for a few minutes. Jed finally spoke, "It's hard to believe something so wrong can happen in a beautiful place like this." There was a pause and then Carmen added, "We met River's boyfriend today on the search. His name is Joe Cloudrider--he said he planned on asking her to marry him."

Libby groaned and then asked, "That is heartbreaking. I suppose you heard nothing more about River?"

"Nothing. So far the search has covered over four-hundred acres north of the lake."

The phone rang from inside the lodge. Will looked down at the side pocket of his jeans in disbelief--he had forgotten to bring the portable phone with him, which he always had clipped to his jeans. Will groaned in disgust as he reluctantly left his comfortable Adirondack chair and cold beer to answer the phone inside the lodge. While he was away, Libby asked more questions about the search and about River's boyfriend.

A few minutes later Will returned to his chair, phone clipped to his pocket. "I have some surprising news. That was T.J. Watkins, the Ojibwe Rez Search and Rescue coordinator. He's spreading the news through local businesses to discourage volunteers coming tomorrow. I guess multiple busloads of people are joining in the search tomorrow from other Ojibwe tribes. He wants us to spread the news that local people should plan to show up on Wednesday if River still has not been found. So, that got me thinking that maybe Libby and I will use our day off tomorrow to take the sailboat out for the day."

Libby looked at him in surprise, "We are?"

"Yeah, I feel very strongly that we need a day on the lake, sailing. We'll join the search party on Wednesday. I mean, I pray they find her tomorrow but if not we'll be a part of the search day-after-tomorrow. Will looked at the Porters for a reaction. He smiled and added, "You guys should take a day off on Thursday. We all need time to get away and relax and we can't feel guilty about it."

Jed and Carmen looked at each other, both sighing deep sighs and then said in unison, "You're right."

The two couples ate dinner together at the lodge, sharing another "round meal" as they talked about their day. Though most of the time a round meal at the lodge was a pizza, sometimes it might be tacos--tonight it was leftover burgers from Sunday's picnic.

Chapter 19

On the Island

River awoke in the dark. She knew it must be very early morning.
It was Tuesday she reckoned--but she wasn't quite sure. As the
birds began to chirp in the darkness she smiled as she listened to
their joyous song. Even though excruciating pain was radiating
through her body from her crushed ankle, the birds still sing to her
and she still has ears to hear. It is true what her mother impressed
upon her and Lance as children. *Focus on all we've been blessed
with. No matter our circumstances, there is still a sunrise each
morning, birds that sing to us, wildflowers that brighten our day and
the assurance of God's love written deep in our hearts. We can
overcome the bad that threatens to take us down if we concentrate
on the good that surrounds us. Bad can attack our body but it
cannot touch our spirit.*

She whispered softly. "I miss you so much Mom."

Even though she had no blanket, she was not cold. It was the
beginning of August and even northern Minnesota was quite warm
and humid in mid-summer. River had been lying in the dark thinking
about what day this might be. She felt in a fog after all that had
happened to her--seeing Lance bleeding to death on the floor of
their home, being taken to this island, and now the dull, deep ache
she endured from a broken ankle. All these things added to her
feeling disoriented. She lay silent as the new day dawned. She felt a
tear run from the corner of her eye and plunge into her ear canal
where it tickled. She was about to rub her ear when she heard the
sound of scurrying little feet on the wood floor. She listened without
moving a muscle and soon she heard the small creature again this
time rustling with a cardboard box on the table where their food lay
open and in disarray. She could hear Charlie breathing on the other
side of the dark cabin. The pungent scent of the open bottle of
booze he had been sucking on the night before still lingered on the
morning air. River continued to listen to the munching critter in
silence but finally she couldn't take it anymore. She just didn't want

mouse droppings in her food so she gave out a startling "**Scat!**" This got the desired flight of the mouse from the table but it also startled Charlie to his feet, gun in hand and pointing at River in the dark.

"Don't shoot! It was a mouse--I just scared a mouse away from our food," she said, as she tried to make out Charlie's dark silhouette. "Put the gun down, you idiot, it was just a mouse I was trying scare away," she repeated.

Charlie slowly lowered the gun, putting it back on safety and sank onto the floor where he had been fast asleep only seconds ago.

"What were you thinking? You scared the crap out of me."

"I'm sorry. I just didn't want to be eating mouse poop with my crackers and Cheese Whiz later today."

"How's your ankle feeling? You were out of it all day yesterday," Charlie said from his dark corner of the room.

"It still hurts badly...I have to get to a doctor today. But this instant, I really need a drink of water, and I guess I'm finally hungry."

Charlie lay for a while longer on the sleeping bag he had taken from the lake house four days ago. The thought of River being thirsty and hungry finally stirred his conscience, what conscience he possessed, and he got up, lit an old lantern and brought her a cup of water and some crackers.

"I'll make you some hot dogs and pancakes once I start the stove. These will keep you from fainting till then."

River examined the crackers for any tiny turds before putting one in her mouth.

Their first day on the island Charlie had scrounged the cabin cupboards and closet for a few useful items and found; an old coffee pot, a couple of tin plates and cups, three wooden spoons, and an old knife with a wooden handle carved in the shape of a crude totem. There was a small cast iron wood burner in the middle of the cabin used for heat and cooking. The stove was being eaten away by rust. There was a large cast iron frying pan sitting on top of the stove, also covered in rust.

Charlie could use the cast iron skillet but did not start a fire in the old wood burner because of the rusty, holey, chimney pipe. Meal preparation was pretty convenient on the little camp stove he had taken along with all the food supplies from his friend's cabin. They had both devoured the homemade hot-dish found in his friend's freezer. The word 'hot-dish' being Minnesota-speak for casserole. It was a hamburger goulash. Its main ingredients are ground beef, chopped celery and onion, elbow macaroni, Lawry's seasoning salt, one can of tomato soup, and topped with shredded cheese. That was a delicious meal. With no oven to bake the hot-dish in, Charlie warmed it in the large frying pan. Now they were down to peanut butter, hot dogs, crackers, Cheese Whiz, a box of dehydrated potatoes and pancake mix.

As the sun began to rise above the distant shore line, Charlie was ready to serve their gourmet breakfast of blackened hot dogs and pancakes sprinkled with sugar. River gulped down the food and strong coffee hardly noticing its appearance. Charlie watched River as she ate. He was amused by how someone so delicate could devour food that quickly.

"I guess you *were* really hungry. That must mean you're feeling better. I was pretty worried about you yesterday. You slept all day and through the night. You would cry and groan sometimes but you never really woke up."

"I don't remember. In fact, I don't remember what day it is. Is it Monday or Tuesday?" River asked.

Charlie was a little uncertain himself, "It's-s--Tuesday, I think."

Later, as Charlie cleaned up the dishes at the lakeshore, River tried to get up from the cabin floor. The coffee she drank at breakfast had gone through her and she needed to relieve herself but didn't want Charlie around to watch. She braced herself against the wall and tried to stand. The pain in her ankle shot up her leg and she slumped back to the floor. Charlie heard the commotion and ran back to the cabin. As he entered he found River sobbing on the floor.

"What's wrong?" Charlie asked from the doorway.

"I have to pee and (she snuffled) I can't stand much less walk," River said as she wiped her wet face with her hands.

Charlie brought in an old coffee can that he found behind the cabin. He had remembered seeing it the day before when he was out back to relieve himself.

"Here, I'll help you"

"No! Don't you dare come near me. I'll do it myself, just leave me alone."

Charlie handed her the can. "Suit yourself."

River struggled through the day trying to do things but anything she did brought pain. She asked Charlie when he would be getting her to a doctor and he put her question off with an ambiguous, "maybe tomorrow." River could tell he was lying. She decided to spend the rest of the day in the cabin sleeping. She didn't want to look at the man anymore. Even though she knew it wasn't right, she hated him. His stale breath and his darting, beady eyes didn't help. He made her nauseous. She would keep to herself and rest. The pain was less when she lay perfectly still.

*****

Charlie watched the clouds begin to grow from the south late in the afternoon. It was obvious that a storm was heading across the lake. He decided that he'd better add two more safety lines to the boat. He made sure it couldn't slam against the rocks either way by tying a rope on each side of the back of the boat. Then each rope was secured to a tree on shore.

Charlie also brought in all the supplies he had left outside of the cabin. The additional items made the small cabin crowded and hard to walk around in but better to have everything sheltered during the storm. After he had secured everything, he sat down on the shore to watch the spectacle march across the miles of water. The terns that made the island home were nervously calling and swooping above him. He saw flocks of pelicans fly across the open water and over the island towards the protected area behind. The terns soon followed the pelicans. Some inexperienced birds tried flying through the woods but soon realized their error and headed up and over the trees to the protected area behind the island. Whitecaps, far out on the lake began to dot the tops of waves. Charlie watched them as they made their way across the lake and onto the island's shoreline.

Chapter 20

Sailing into the Storm

At the same time River Timberlake was listening to the little creature pilfer through their food, thirty miles across the lake Libby Edwards awoke to the sound of chirps and warbles also. Only instead of waking up on a moldy tarp she awoke on her comfortable bed. She lifted her head off her pillow in order to look over Will's sleeping form to see the clock on his nightstand. Only five o'clock a.m. She turned herself around to face the window which was barely a foot from her head. She looked down at the harbor, which was saved from darkness by a yard-light mounted on an old utility pole. Their sailboat, the only one in the harbor, looked graceful and impressive among all the other boats. Her tall mast and cross-stays, illuminated by the yard light, resembled a white cross glowing softly in the predawn. There was a dim grey filtering through the blackness on the lake as the sun was just beginning its journey from east to west. Libby wondered what events would shape this day before the sun set on the far side of the lake tonight? God only knows. As she lay comfy on her side of the bed, still watching out the window, she saw a shadow move in the front yard. Then it stopped. Libby focused her eyes, straining to see through the ghostly grey of early dawn. It was a deer. It had stopped, head raised and alert, listening to something in the darkness. Libby lay still and watched the graceful animal. Then in silent motion the deer continued on her way. It was heading to the harbor for a drink before day break. To Libby's delight she saw a little fawn, its small frame a silhouette against the lighted harbor. The fawn hesitated just a moment before catching up to its mother.

What a way to begin the day, Libby thought, as she lifted the covers back and quietly abandoned her comfortable nest. Will grabbed her hand as she walked by his side of the bed, "Where are you going so early in the morning?" He pulled her down to his side and she kissed his warm lips. Libby looked into the face of a man she had loved since she was a teenager. His face had changed over the years but he was still handsome. She felt so a part of him that sometimes she would look at his face and see herself looking back. It was an abstract feeling--not possible to put into words but she felt it, even if she couldn't explain it.

"It's those noisy neighbors, the birds. They wake-up sounding so happy and thrilled with the new day that it's contagious." Libby smiled as she sat next to Will.

"I saw a deer and her baby walk through our yard a few minutes ago. They were on their way down to the harbor to get a drink."

Will lifted the covers, "Can I get you to snuggle for a few minutes?"

Libby was tempted but she resisted, "My bladder is ready to burst and then I'm heading for the coffee pot. I'll see you when you get up." She kissed Will again and then left his bedside.

When Libby entered the living room she was not surprised to see Honey's body spread across the leather couch, her legs twitching in dreamy sleep. The young dog lifted her head when she sensed Libby's presence and her tail flopped a happy lab greeting. Libby sat down in her rocker, and set her mug of creamy coffee on the table next to her. Honey had opted to sleep some more and her legs began to twitch in a dream. Libby smiled and then closed her eyes and began her daily meditation. She took a deep breath to clear the cobwebs. She made a conscious effort to bring the unseen to the forefront of her thoughts. She breathed in again, deeply. She had learned to discipline her mind, to visualize what physically she could not see. She thought of the scripture verse where Jesus proclaims to his disciples, "The kingdom of God is at hand." She whispered to herself, "God is here." She had come to understand that this world and God's kingdom are separated by a mere supernatural veil. The beings of the unseen world are but a breath away, both the mighty army of angels and the minions of darkness. Because the Son of God lives within those who know Him, where He resides, all is well no matter what our earthly circumstances are. We are all a mere breath from eternity. She pondered these things bringing them into sharp focus. Then she began to pray the Lord's Prayer amplifying the text in her own words as she prayed:

My dearest Father in the heavens, holy is your name.
I am surrounded by your Kingdom of love and your mighty angels.
I boldly ask that your will be done on earth this day as it is done
throughout the heavens.
Give us this day the things that we need for survival
And forgive us our selfishness and thoughtlessness as we
forgive those that have been selfish and thoughtless towards us.
And Lord, lead us not into temptations that will hurt us or others.
Deliver and protect us from the Evil that desires to destroy us.
For your Kingdom is in us, around us and
extends to the farthest galaxy,
Your power holds the universe in place, and
your glory shines forever and ever.
In all these things, my heart believes to be true.
Amen (Let it be so)

The clink of a coffee mug broke Libby's concentration. Will was in the kitchen getting coffee.

"Are you ready for more?" Will asked

"Sure, I'll take a warm up."

Will poured a little cream in her mug and filled it up with coffee. He walked back to the kitchen to put the coffee pot back in the coffee maker and the cream back in the fridge.

"I'd like to be on the sailboat by nine this morning. No later. I know how sidetracked you can get so try to stay focused on getting packed. I was thinking we'd sail to Bass Island today."

Libby felt a prick in her heart at Will's words. She bristled at his uncalled-for impatience. *This would be strike one for Will this morning.* She let it slide though and responded. "That's a long sail! Even if the wind cooperates, it's at least four hours out there.

"I know. It's just a destination to shoot for. If the wind doesn't cooperate, we'll get as far as we can and turn back by mid-afternoon."

"Sounds good. I'll try to be ready by nine," Libby said

Will responded sharply, "Well, I would hope so."

By nine fifteen, Will was backing the McGregor out of the dock slip. He was using an old Evinrude six-horsepower motor to move the sailboat through the close quarters of the harbor. Honey lay atop the upper deck, under the boom, excited for the day's adventure. As the boat putted past the lodge, Honey saw Sadie sitting on one of the docks. She barked a greeting to her furry friend and Sadie stood up wagging her tail in graceful acknowledgement.

Libby's excitement for the day on the lake had been dampened. She sat quietly on the edge of the cockpit, stewing. Her natural tendency towards calm and peace was always sorely tested when Will expressed his impatience about her taking too long. She was a thorough, thoughtful person, always attempting to remember everything they may need for their outing. She planned a sumptuous lunch, remembered towels, lotion and jackets for them both, and food and water for Honey. But, all of her thoughtfulness was greeted with impatience as Will shouted through the screen door of their home ten minutes earlier, asking her *what the heck was taking her so long?* This was more than a prick to her heart; this felt like a stab and it was strike two for William. Strike three followed in rapid-fire succession when Will tried to defend himself by saying Libby was too sensitive and added that *she always took his comments too seriously.*

Will had now struck out with Libby. As he steered the sailboat out of the harbor and onto the lake, he looked over at his silent wife and knew he had hurt her...again. She wasn't the type to yell at him. He wished she was. No, Libby was the silent type. She would need at least twenty minutes to let go of the damage he'd done.

"I'm sorry, Lib. I'm worse than a bull in a closet, when it comes to getting going," Will finally admitted. "Forgive me?"

Libby looked at Will, no hint of a smile crossed her face.

"I'm just so weary of your impatience. Will we be dealing with this huge chasm between us until the day death do us part?"

"You don't deserve it, Libby, I know," Will said apologetically. "You know I don't mean anything by it. I'm just too intense and thoughtless."

Libby didn't respond, which of course drove Will crazy. *Why wouldn't she talk this through?* But he knew she was done talking about it. There was nothing more he could say to bring a smile to her face. It would take some time for her to smooth over her raw feelings. Twenty minutes was about how long it took. This may not seem like a long time for some men to be with a silent wife but for Will it was always an eternity.

Being married to an impatient man was the perfect sandpaper for Libby's sensitivity. She allowed someone's words to penetrate too deeply, and Will was the tool to help her cut that weakness from her character. Libby was the perfect tool to help Will become the patient, humble man he wished he could be. Their differences should have torn them apart years ago but their faith and friendship kept them going. Libby's dad often said, "My pain is my gain for the kingdom." He often taught how God loves us as we are but He loves us so much that He won't let us stay where we are. The meaning of our lives emerges in the surrender of ourselves to the adventure of becoming who we desire to be.

Libby came out of her funk, and Will was relieved his "time-out" was over. She asked him if he wanted something--a beer, some peanuts? Soon they were talking about what a great day it had turned out to be. The wind was steady from the southwest making the little sailboat sing across the open water. They calculated their speed at about five miles per hour. Both sails were taut and full of purpose.

So began the leisurely afternoon. Libby brought out a knapsack full of good food. She had prepared chicken salad sandwiches on croissants, cubed melon, potato chips and homemade oatmeal cookies for dessert. Honey got a Cool Whip dish of freshwater, and her favorite dog treats. She also mooched the last bite from each of their sandwiches.

It was mid-afternoon and they still had a mile to go to reach Bass Island.

"Well it's three o'clock, Libby. Shall we head back now or do you want to make our goal?" Will asked.

Libby looked at her watch out of reflex. Will was tempted to say that he had just told her the time, but thought better of it. He didn't have to say everything he thought. That would probably sound *'impatient'* to her. So he just smiled and waited for her to decide.

Libby responded, "You know, the day is so perfect, let's keep going. We'll make it within a half hour, won't we?"

"We should."

Libby stood up and announced, "Great. I'm going to spread a towel out up front and lay out...maybe take a little nap."

"You go right ahead." Will smiled to himself. He was proud of himself for thinking before speaking something he would regret. If only he would remember that more often.

While Libby relaxed on the upper deck of the boat, Honey sat next to Will in the cockpit. The yellow dog lay contentedly on the seat next to him, resting her head on the side of the boat, her eyes closed, and nose twitching as she sniffed the scents borne on the wind. Will noticed a bank of clouds straight ahead, far off in the distance. Even though they were dark, they were very far away. It gave him a moment of concern...but the island was so close now that he decided that it would be silly to not stop to take a swim and let Honey off the boat to relieve herself on shore.

Libby enjoyed riding on the front of the boat. It was so relaxing to look up at the tall white sails against the cobalt sky. It was unusual for her to fall asleep during the day but the warm sun and graceful motion of the boat lulled her. Soon her mind was entertained by a dream. *She was swimming to an island. Honey was swimming beside her, huffing and snorting as she always did when she swam. Then the dream jumped to them being lost in a dark woods. She felt scared, like there was something evil in the woods. She saw water birds flying in and around the woods in a bizarre behavior. Then vines grabbed at her ankles. Honey was covered in them, they were trying to choke her. Libby yanked at the vines around her ankles to free herself then she pulled the grasping, choking vines off of Honey. Her arms and legs felt like they were filled with lead, making it impossible for her to hold onto Honey as the scared dog bolted. Libby forced herself to crawl after her. When she found Honey she was frantically digging in the dirt, her tail straight out, excited about something in the ground. Libby pulled herself up to the hole to see what Honey was after. It was too dark to see down the hole but right next to the hole was an unusual, egg-shaped stone with many layers of color. In the middle of the rock was a worn indentation. It looked like an ancient tool....*

"We're here, Libby. Wake up." Will startled Libby from her dream.

"Huh? Oh, that was weird, I just had a very strange dream."

"Well, our anxious pup just jumped ship to get to the island. I need my first mate's help to get the sails down."

"Aye-aye, Captain," Libby hopped up to pull the front sail down when Will released the jib's halyard. Then Will released the main halyard and Libby quickly wrapped the falling sail with tie-downs.

They looked up when they heard Honey bark excitedly from shore. The dripping dog had already found a stick and was anxious for them to throw it for her.

"Crazy dog, she's as impatient as you," Libby said with a smile.

With the swing keel cranked up under the boat, they could glide onto the sandy beach. Honey was ecstatic at their arrival.

"You'd think she had been alone for days," Will said as he stopped to hug her wet furry head to his leg. They secured the boat by tying it to a large log on the beach. Then they all took a swim. Gulls circled above their heads and a pair of loons bobbed on the choppy waves fifty feet from them. Honey spotted the large birds on the water and started swimming towards them. Libby called her back, and Honey immediately turned around. Will and Libby watched the gulls as they rode the wind above them. All of a sudden Libby had a flash, "Will, I had such a strange dream just before we got to the island."

"You and your crazy dreams. What was it this time?"

Libby told about her dream as Will listened.

"Sounds like our sailing to Bass Island got mixed up in your dream," Will suggested.

"Yeah, I guess. It was scary though."

Will put his arms around his wife and said, "Everything's fine. It's a beautiful day. There are no evil vines coming after us."

Libby laughed and let her worries about the dream evaporate.

TWO DOMAINS

It is said, the division or distance between the physical world and the spiritual world is as thin as tissue paper. Beings with bodies and beings without, occupy the same space, just on different planes. Sometimes there's sufficient overlap, as a door being opened between worlds, offering opportunity for physical and spiritual entities to meet. Further, authors James Garlow and Keith Wall, believe there's much more two-way traffic between this world and the next than most people realize. People regularly do make a round trip from earth to heaven (or hell) and back again during near-death experiences. According to the holy scriptures of many different faiths, and supported by eyewitness testimony, angels and demons frequently leave their domains and interact with humans.

Paraphrased from Encountering Heaven and the Afterlife by James L. Garlow and Keith Wall

The Kingdom Among Us

The two figures faced each other on a high cliff, far away. They dwell in a realm unseen by mankind. A realm that surrounds us and separated from us by the thinnest veil. From a distance they look insignificant but judging from afar can be deceiving. If one were allowed a closer look they would see that the two figures were anything but insignificant--they were magnificent. These stunning beings were physically impressive with intellect far beyond our limited, human understanding. Their hearts so overflowing with their Lord's pure love as to be unbearable if borne by the human spirit.

They stood together caught up in earnest conversation.

The warrior in charge of protecting River spoke, "Even though protecting River has been my mission, I had to allow pain to be inflicted on her in order to stop the Evil One that holds her captive, from murdering her. I dislodged a stone to distract the man deceived by Evil, before he killed her with his gun. Then our Lord suggested to the man's deceived heart that the stone rather than the gun would keep her captive, and he responded. The stone brought her pain, but at least she lives. The fact that the man listened to our Lord's suggestion shows that he is not totally given over to Evil.

The magnificent warrior in charge of protecting Libby responded, "Yes, it seems there is hope for him. He may yet turn from Evil and embrace the Light. It is never too late. The trials will continue--our Lord does not want to give up on him. "Libby's faith and her human strength is about to be tested, but I will be with her every moment of her peril. I will also guide Libby's creature friend to the island where River is being held captive by Evil." Then the mighty warrior paused and smiled, "Those wonderful creatures are always ready and willing to do the Master's bidding. There was a brief pause and they both smiled as they thought about the wonderful nature of dogs.

As the Kingdom's Plans continued to unfolded, the warriors' anticipation grew. The Spirit of the Lord was on the move, searching the hearts of men and finding willing souls. As these people were chosen by God, other warriors came forth as their protectors and helpers. Will, Jed and others, were willingly, yet unwittingly, being drawn into the kingdom's mission to save River. Each warrior

194

accepted their duty to help and protect the men and women who the Lord foresaw, would join the mission.

The plans had been set and the human participants selected. The Kingdom's warriors never knew for certain how humans would respond--to serve after all, was a choice for them. But in the kingdom of Heaven, hope is never extinguished, and Evil is bound for eternal disappointment.

Chapter 21

Another Storm Descends

Will had to trick Honey into the boat by waving a stick for her to
fetch. The dripping dog paused to shake her yellow coat, water
spraying in every direction, and then she eagerly headed for the
prized stick in Will's hand. He brought it down for her to smell and
she grabbed it in her soft mouth. That's when he wrapped his arms
around her and lifted her into the boat. Libby was ready in the
cockpit with a towel to dry Honey's coat, 'dry' being a relative term.
Honey looked perfectly content even though she had been tricked.
She still had the stick in her mouth and she was getting a great rub
down.

The twenty-one-foot sailboat was easy to shove off the sandy
beach. Will hopped up into the cockpit, shedding water onto the
floor also, but a rear drain hole allowed the water to return to the
lake. He quickly leaned over the aft side of the boat to reach the
Evinrude. When he pulled the cord there was not even a cough from
the ancient motor. He pulled the cord again--and again it did not
respond. Again and again he pulled the cord but the motor hung
silent on its bracket. Libby looked a little anxious but did not say
anything. Why state the obvious? Will was certainly capable of
getting the motor going. He soon had the cover off the engine,
tinkering with the carburetor and checking the gas line. The lake off
the north end of Bass Island, where they now sat dead in the water,
was as smooth as glass. The reflection of the sky and the island's
tall trees created a liquid painting on the glassy surface. Libby
looked north and was surprised to see dark choppy water and white
caps beginning to form.

She commented to Will. "Well, if the motor won't start, Hon, it
would seem we will have plenty of wind to get us home if we just
paddle out a ways."

Will looked up to see what Libby was talking about. Sure
enough, the island was hiding the fact that a strong wind was
waiting for them two hundred feet out. They both got busy rigging
the sails and then took paddles from the storage locker and began

paddling out away from the protection of the island. Soon small ripples turned into small waves and the wind began to play with the slack sails. Will adjusted the lines and rudder to maximize the wind and soon they were off on a southeast course. The strong south-westerly wind would push them northeast so the trip home would mean 'tacking,' to keep them on course for Safe Harbor.

As they broke free of Bass Island's protection, the wind slammed into the sails and the boat heeled over with the force. Honey's claws dug into the fiberglass floor and found no hold in the hard wet surface. Libby told her to *stay*, as the dog would be safer on the floor while she climbed on to the port side, now high above the starboard side, hoping to use her weight as ballast in the severely leaning boat. Will released the main sheet, *the line that allows the boom to swing*, far to starboard. This helped release some of the force the wind had on the boat. With the hard working front sail still full, the boat sliced through the water at record speed but the five foot waves crossing their beam, *the side of the boat*, made for a rollercoaster ride. When Will finally had a chance to look to his right, his heart sank. The swirling charcoal cloudbank that he had noticed earlier was now moving menacingly over Bass Island.

Will was getting concerned. *Shoot,* he thought, *the island was hiding the growing storm from us.*

The safest way home would be to motor, but that was not an option. He tried to stay calm for Libby and Honey, "Libby, I don't dare let go of the rudder for a second so it's going to be up to you to get the mainsail down. Can you do it?"

"I can do it, Will," Libby said with confidence.

She started to climb to the upper deck when Will stopped her, "Wait! First get life jackets for both of us and then tie a line to your waist."

Libby put a lifejacket on herself and then put one on Will and buckled it for him. Then she tied a nylon rope around her waist, secured the other end to a cleat and started for the top deck, carefully holding on to whatever was in front of her. Will watched, shouting advice to her with every move. When Libby finally grabbed for the mast Will was relieved.

"Okay, when I turn the boat, just pull the sail down enough to wrap some ties around the bulk of it. Don't stay up there long," he shouted over the screaming wind and roaring waves.

Will turned the boat's bow into the wind. This maneuver kept the wind from filling the sail and would allow Libby to pull the fabric down easily. As she worked on the sail, Will was distracted by the wall of clouds that now towered above them. When he looked back at Libby again he saw her struggling with the taut sail and realized in his distraction he must have drifted off point. He adjusted the rudder and brought the boat back into a perfect point into the wind. The sail began to flop noisily allowing Libby to pull it down with little effort.

"That's a lot easier, thanks," Libby yelled.

Just then Honey took her opportunity to get off the floor and join Libby who always held her when she was scared. Will saw Honey leap onto the seat and up to the top deck but his reaction was a second too late to stop her. The scared yellow lab hit the top deck just as a five foot wave slammed the front of the boat. Water washed over the top deck and Honey was swept under the boat's safety line and into the roiling water below. Libby was horrified as she watched the place where Honey had dropped below the water's surface. She instinctively left the safety of the mast to try to rescue her Honey. Will yelled at her to get back to the mast, but Libby didn't hear him as she was already over the side of the boat and into the water, the line around her waist following after her.

Will was shocked at the sight of his wife jumping overboard. His mind screamed. *How could she do something so stupid?* He left the rudder and the boat turned and rocked as he leaped to the side where Libby went in. He was relieved to see her surface. Honey was relieved too and was swimming towards her just off the bow. Will could see that the boat was drifting fast to the northeast but to his horror, Libby was not drifting with the boat. That's when he saw the loose nylon rope floating on the water---unattached to Libby's waist.

"Libby, you've come loose from the line!" Will yelled.

Honey had reached Libby but as Libby turned to grab the rope it was well beyond her grasp. Will tried to start the motor again, pleading for divine intervention, but the motor didn't go. He looked out at the furious lake that held his wife and dog and watched them get smaller and smaller as the boat continued to take him across the lake and away from them. He yelled to them but his voice did not carry over the roar of the oncoming storm. His mind raced with indecision. He wanted nothing more than to jump into the water and be with Libby. At least no matter what happened they would be together. But better judgment ruled; the only way to save them was to sail past them in a wide figure-eight maneuver and drift back towards them. He would need both sails to make the maneuver so Will used bungee-cords to hold the rudder straight and then he began to raise the sail with the main halyard. When it was raised enough to sail he went forward and clamped the halyard so the sail would stay up. That's when the boom…something he had forgotten to clamp tight in his panic, swung around and slammed into Will's head with such force that it flung his unconscious body to the side of the boat. When the boat heaved to the side with the approach of another six foot wave, he tumbled helplessly overboard into the swirling water below.

*****

As the sailboat continued to drift further away from them, Libby fought back the panic that was gripping her chest.

"Stay calm. Will will figure out how to get us, Honey. Don't worry."

Honey swam circles around Libby, a high-pitched whine coming from her throat as she huffed and snorted in the water. They both rose and fell on the crests and troughs of the enormous waves. Libby was so grateful for the lifejacket that Will had insisted she put on. It then came to her, *If only they had thought to put one on Honey! Well, there was nothing to be done about that now.* If Honey got too tired from swimming Libby felt that she could actually hold the dog up to give her a break while they waited for Will to turn the boat around. But still, the boat kept drifting farther from them. Libby prayed for help, *"Will must be in trouble, Lord, please help him, please!"*

*****

When the metal boom struck the side of Will's head, he saw stars and then he felt nothing. When his body hit the raging lake he came to with the sudden rush of water up his nose and in his mouth. Though barely conscious he felt something travel across his face and outstretched arms and then over his left hand. Something told him to grab onto whatever it was. Conscious thought was fragile and thin, but he was aware enough to think that it might be the nylon rope that had come loose from Libby's waist--her life line was now his.

He hung onto the rope with all his strength. The boat was pulling him through the water now and causing him to bump against the hull. His brain was beginning to fire on more cylinders and he knew he needed to grab the rope with both hands. He felt woozy and weak but he kept both hands tight around the nylon rope.

*Thank you God, h*e thought, *now please help me get into the boat.*

Will realized the rope was slowly inching through his grasp. The boat side suddenly was gone and that startled him. He could see that he was now behind the boat right next to the motor shaft. He released his right hand from the rope and grabbed for the shaft. He then put the rope between his teeth and grabbed the motor shaft with his left hand also. *At least this stupid motor is good for something* he thought, as he slowly climbed the motor shaft and swung his arm over the edge of the boat. Then he rested. It took every ounce of his strength but he finally pulled himself into the cockpit where he rested again, half conscious and exhausted.

*****

Libby supported Honey's body for a few minutes so she could rest. The lifejacket held them both up as they bobbed over the frothy, rolling water. When Libby let go of Honey, the dog didn't swim circles around her this time but instead began swimming away from her. Libby yelled for Honey to return but the dog kept swimming away. Libby yelled again as she came to the top of another swell and then she saw what Honey was heading for…land!

Of course! A dog would instinctively swim towards the smell of land. She floated down into the trough of another wave and waited to be carried up to the crest in order to look for the boat and Will. The boat was now just a speck on the water. She was worried about Will and why he couldn't turn the boat around. *Did something break? Was he hurt? What should she do?* Then it was clear in her mind like a strong, calm voice within. *Get to land.* So Libby started swimming after Honey. The dog's yellow head would disappear from the horizon for long seconds and then reappear at the crest of another foamy wave.

Everything about a Labrador was made for being in the water; a thick double layered coat trapped air making the dog buoyant. Their paws, when spread during swimming, were webbed for efficiency. Libby knew Honey was a strong swimmer but she still was grateful each time she saw the dog's yellow head at the top of another wave. Libby, herself, was a strong swimmer. Her parents teased her that she could swim before she could walk. She and her two older sisters would swim across small lakes with their dad when she was young. She was confident she could get to shore. What was most troubling to her was the mystery of what had happened to Will.

*****

When Will came-to in the cockpit he had double vision. He was looking down at two swirls of red on the blue floor and four legs crossed each other below his hanging head. He lifted his eyes and saw two horizons in dizzying motion far in the distance. He was resting on something that moved with the rolling waves--back and forth, back and forth. He was nauseous and with the double vision and the boat's rolling movement his lunch soon rose up into his throat and onto his four legs and the red-streaked floor. He watched as it covered over the red stains and then he lost consciousness again.

Will revived again. He didn't know how long he had been out this time but he was thankful to see that he now had only two legs. His vomit had been diluted by heavy rain but there were fresh splotches of red on his legs and on the floor from his dripping head. He touched the aching, stinging wound on the left side of his head. There was a huge baseball size lump and an open gash about three inches long. He looked out at the horizon and could see only sheets of rain. His discombobulated mind came into focus like a discordant orchestra coming into perfect harmony. He lifted his chest off the tiller that had supported him for how long, he had no idea. He looked up at the mast and his heart sank, the main sail was in shreds. The boat was now almost useless with only the front sail still operating. The fact that he had been unconscious over the tiller had possibly kept the boat--well, he couldn't figure out all that now. He was alive and the boat still floated. That was the good news. The bad news was, he had no idea where to look for Libby.

Will tried to think rationally, which was really hard to do with his wife many miles away by now and his boat probably only a few miles from breaking up on a rocky reef. The boat was at the mercy of two forces, the swirling gale force winds and the rolling waves. The small jib was no match against this storm. Libby was at the mercy of only the waves. So, as much as he hated to face reality, the boat was most likely not heading the same direction as Libby. The slapping mainsail hanging from the mast was extremely irritating to Will but it would be too dangerous to take it down. He tried the motor again, and again there was no life in the cold metal.

I should have replaced this old piece of crap. I'm such an idiot!

The sheets of rain lightened and disappeared allowing Will to see the distant shoreline.

"It must be Wolf Track Point in the distance," he muttered aloud.

He hadn't sailed along that shore much but he knew from fishing in the area that there was a hidden reef just below the surface in front of Wolf Track Point.

"What was it called…Munger Reef."

Now, what could he do to avert this underwater collision?

As he tried to steer the boat, he had little success as the forces of nature flung him ever closer towards the cliffs of Wolf Track Point. He calculated that he was probably a minute from the reef now. The one thing he could think to do was raise the keel just before going over the hidden rocks. Will cranked up the keel like a madman. He expected to hit the reef any second.

Thud.

This is it, this is where she goes down, Will thought as he heard the first hit on the bottom of the boat. Then he realized the boat was being lifted as it rode the crest of a large wave. The boat was carried safely past the reef and into a bay.

Will yelled out in relief. "Thank God!"

Thunder rumbled from the west and lightning lit up the dark clouds in the distance. A detail that Will had been too busy to notice until now. He could see heavy rain no more than a mile away and heading in his direction again. He thought of Libby in the water and his exhilaration quickly turned to desperation again. What can he do to get to her? He looked around at the bay he was entering..."*This is Pikes Bay, I'm sure of it.*" It was one of the least populated bays on the lake, mainly high cliffs topped with thick stands of pine. The chance of meeting up with anyone was slim to none until he got to shore where a county road ran along the high bluffs above the lake.

The rain had overtaken the boat again and it was hard to see more than a few feet in front of the bow, but Will did everything he could think of to steer the boat to the far end of the large bay. After a half hour the rain had passed and Will could see that the boat would run aground on a small rocky island. He cranked up the keel again to enable the boat to get as close to shore as possible and soon he heard the welcome sound of sand scraping the bottom of the boat. He jumped out and quickly tied the tattered sailboat to a nearby boulder on shore and ran across the rocky surface of the island. The island's name was Twin Pines but Will observed that there was only one enormous pine tree that survived on the Island; the other ancient pine was just a dried up skeleton. Both trees, the surviving and the dead, stood dripping from the passing storms.

Will, breathless, struggling through the difficult terrain, finally reached the other side of the island. He looked out at his final challenge. The water between the island and the eastern shore was probably a mile wide; he could do it--no problem. Without hesitating another second, Will plunged into the lake determined to get help for Libby.

Chapter 22

Almost Swallowed Up

As another storm front descended, lightning flashed, thunder cracked and more rain cascaded down around Libby. She was thankful that she was not trying to swim against the rolling waves--it would have been impossible to have made any progress against such a force as it was driven hard across the lake. She couldn't be sure that she was even following Honey anymore as she couldn't see more than a few feet in front of her. Libby hoped that the weather would clear soon so she could get her bearings again. If the wind had switched direction, even a little, she could easily miss land in the heavy mist and rain. Libby was also very concerned about how tired Honey must be getting. Wearing a lifejacket gave Libby the opportunity to rest from time to time but Honey wouldn't be able to rest; she would have to keep swimming. She didn't know how far a swim it was yet, but she guessed it might be another mile or more. There was no use expending energy worrying about Honey or Will. She could do nothing to help either of them.

****

The yellow Labrador kept going. It took every ounce of determination to keep swimming further and further from her beloved human. She wanted to turn back to check on her; that's what good dogs do, always checking in with their humans. Libby was her security, her family, but she sensed that the force behind her determination was for both their sakes. Exhaustion was draining away the young dog's strength. Sometimes water would get into her nostrils and down her throat and she would cough and snort--still she kept swimming. Because of her buoyant coat, there were times that Honey could stop paddling for a few seconds to rest. She couldn't see the land she was heading for because of the rain but she could smell trees, grass and earth. Even above the roar of the waves she could hear the distant sound of the water crashing on the rocks and hard-packed sand.

*****

Libby didn't know the time of day but she figured it must be early evening. The rain and wind had temporarily stopped. The waves were still rolling but their size was diminishing. She had stopped to rest again, which she was having to do with more frequency now. As she laid her head back and looked up at the sky, she wondered again if Honey was safe on shore by now and if Will was all right. She had to discipline her thoughts to be strong and positive. She willed herself to kick doubt out of her mind and replace it with hope that they were protected. She talked aloud to give support to her tested faith that God was really with her.

"I'm so tired, Lord…but you have kept me alive. I trust you. My heart tells me that this predicament you have allowed me to endure is pregnant with a purpose. I don't know what your purpose is, but it's a good one or you wouldn't put me through all this. Thank you for taking care of Will and Honey. I trust you to bring about your best through this ordeal. My pain is my gain for the kingdom," she laughed and shouted, "Right, Dad?" Then she solemnly recited, "Your kingdom come, your will be done on earth--*and in this stormy lake*--as it is in Heaven."

When Libby was done resting, she looked in the direction the waves were rolling and sure enough, there were trees straight ahead, their ghostly shapes appearing as the mist began to evaporate; they were probably still a half-mile away but she knew that she could make it.

****

On shore, Honey now stood chest deep in the water, her paws firmly set on the sandy bottom. She had made it. She was so weary from the long swim that walking the few steps to dry land was too much for her trembling legs. She stood in the shallow water unfazed by the foamy waves that swirled around her. Honey's eyes closed and her head drooped closer to the swirling surface as she started to fall asleep standing in the water. She had made it, but barely. When a large wave rolled over her back, her nose sank below the foamy surface and it startled her awake. She sneezed hard three times and then took the final steps to the beach just a few feet away. The exuberant, ever playful, eight-month-old lab, looked and felt like she was ten-years-old as she lay down on the sand and fell into an unconscious sleep.

****

Libby reached the shallow water an hour after Honey. She too was too weak to walk at first so she laid back exhausted after the five-hour swim in the wild, dangerous waters of Thunder Lake. The rolling surf did not let her rest for long. She dragged herself through the foamy surf and crawled on hands and knees to the safety of the sand and rock beach. Libby lifted her head to scan the land for Honey but she didn't see any sign of her. She laid back and looked up at the sky again. Even though she couldn't feel the wind, the clouds above were still racing by, giving only brief glimpses of the twilight sky.

"Thank you, Lord. You got me here, now what?"

Nothing came to mind so she continued to rest. Exhaustion came on her like an IV sedative, and she slept.

Honey awoke to the scent of Libby. As exhausted and sore as she felt, her desire to find her human was irresistible. She struggled to her feet and began to take slow, shaky steps down the beach.

Libby lay on the sand deep in a dream about being in her bed. She was irritated with how hard the mattress felt. Then she felt someone washing her face which made no sense. Who would wash her face while she's in bed? The soft, warm cloth kept wiping her mouth, cheek and forehead over and over. It was warm and moist as it continued to wash her face. Libby woke slowly from her dream and opened one eye and saw the droopy, wrinkled muzzle of her dog hanging over her. Honey's brown nose, an inch away, sniffed at Libby's face, her drooping jowls jiggled and then her pink tongue appeared and softly licked her cheek again.

"Honey, you're all right!" Libby cried. Honey wagged her tail and whined.

Libby tried to lift her arms to touch her furry friend but she was still too weak. Honey laid down next to her and rested her head on Libby's arm. Libby felt the warmth of the dog's body on her cold skin and it felt wonderful. Together at last, they both fell asleep on the sand. Darkness had settled over the vast expanse of water that still churned and splashed a few feet away from where they slept. Both dreamed vividly of the monstrous lake that had threatened to swallow them. Libby woke numerous times to the sound of Honey whimpering, her legs in phantom motion. Libby figured she must be swimming in her dreams. She comforted the sleeping dog with a pat and then she fell back into her own fitful sleep.

*****

Will made it to the east shore well after dark. He knew checking the time on his watch would be futile. The water-resistant timepiece had been submerged for over an hour and must be shot. He estimated the time to be past ten o'clock. Jed and Carmen would be worried sick about them.

He was chilled, but even so, he could tell that the night's breeze was warm and muggy. The moon and stars gave only brief moments of illumination during his swim. It seemed to Will that the clouds were building again which was disconcerting. As he stood on the rocky shoreline to rest a minute he unbuckled his lifejacket. He was driven to keep going and began to climb the steep hillside. It didn't take long before he was sweating from the effort of the steep climb. As he neared the top he found tree roots sticking out of the hillside which were a welcome help in giving him places to hang onto as he pulled himself up and over the last few feet to the top. He knelt in the tall weeds to catch his breath. Soon he was up and heading towards the road that lay just twenty feet inland from the cliff.

Finally his feet stepped on the tarmac. He had barely started walking down the road when he saw headlights shining from behind him. He stuck out his thumb and the car stopped just past him.

"Can you take me to the nearest phone?" Will asked the driver of the sporty Toyota Celica that pulled over for him.

The driver, a young woman with blonde hair neatly held back in a high ponytail, looked at the wet, middle aged man through the open car window. In her adolescent, invincible judgment, she decided that Will looked harmless.

"Sure, hop in."

Will was surprised by her willing acceptance to let him into her car. He was thinking, he must look terrible.

"Thanks," Will said as he dropped into the low-riding sports car.

"I'm sorry, but I'm probably going to soak your car seat. My name is Will Edwards, by the way. We own a resort south of here."

"My name's Candice. And it's not a problem about the wet seat, 'cuz it's my brother's car."

The young driver ran through the gears of the manual transmission like a pro and Will was grateful she was heavy on the gas pedal. Candice looked over at Will, "What are you doing out in this god-forsaken wilderness? Looks like you've been in the lake-- have boat trouble or something?"

"You wouldn't believe it! My wife is somewhere out there on the lake, God only knows. She dove off our boat to rescue our dog during the storm earlier today. Then the storm wrecked my boat so I couldn't get back to her. I can't even believe what I'm telling you, it seems so unreal.

"Wow, that's somthin'," the young woman sympathized and pushed the gas pedal down even harder. The sporty Celica responded.

*****

Honey lifted her head from Libby's arm and looked out at the lake. From far across the fluid expanse she heard the low rumble of thunder again. She whined softly and tried to sit but every muscle in her body ached. Determined though, she rose onto her front legs, her rear still planted in the sand next to Libby. The lab whined again when she saw a lightning bolt shoot downward and strike the lake not far away. The tremendous *crack* that accompanied the strike brought Libby's head up. Honey looked back at her but Libby could see nothing of the dog's expression because of the blackness of the night. She didn't need to see Honey's frightened face; she could hear the poor dog's teeth chattering and knew she was shaking.

Libby spoke softly to Honey as much as to herself, "It's okay, girl, it's far away from us, but we'll need to find some shelter if we can. It's so dark--it may be next to impossible but we should at least try."

They both struggled to stand. Libby was so stiff she didn't think she could walk but the continued lightning display over the lake was a serious motivator. She and Honey walked slowly into the even darker blackness of the woods beyond the beach.

Chapter 23

Back at Safe Harbor

Carmen and Jed paced the lodge floor. The churning lake lay before them, the horizon indistinct from the gunmetal grey water and the dark heavy storm clouds. As the sky finally turned black, they knew the sun had abandoned the day. All hope was lost of seeing a tall mast returning to Safe Harbor.

Sadie lay near the cold fireplace, her four legs splayed out. She looked like a big bear rug. The dog's large golden head rested on the floor; only her soft brown eyes tracked Jed and Carmen as they paced from window to window. She sensed their fear. She could feel it and smell it. Fear was something any animal understands, but Sadie understood more than fear; she also had come to understand, through months of living closely with Carmen and Jed, their words and even thoughts. It is an uncanny ability that dogs possess but most humans don't give that notion any credence.

Carmen stared out the window, "Where could they be, Jed? They would never stay out this late unless something had happened."

Jed tried to calm Carmen, "We'll hear something soon. Will and Libby are good sailors and swimmers. The storm just delayed them or maybe they are tucked safely behind an island. We'll see their mast light once the storm is past"

He hoped the panic he was feeling deep down wasn't evident in his voice. The whites of Sadie's eyes showed as the miserable dog looked over at Jed. She felt his fear--it was screaming out to her. She moaned softly as she rested her head onto her front paw.

"R-Ring-g-g"

They both jumped and looked over at the phone, almost afraid to answer. Then Jed raced over and picked up the receiver. "Safe Harbor Resort--Will! Where are you?"

"I'm at the Shell Station in Battle Creek, Jed. We got caught in the storm---Libby is missing--" Will's voice broke over the phone line. "I've called 911, but I knew you guys would be going crazy. I'm on my way back to the resort now. I'll be there in fifteen minutes."

"Ok, we're at the lodge. What do you want us to do?"

"Get the "Tub" ready. I'm going out looking for her as soon as I get there."

"I'll get right on it, Will...and just so you know, I'll be going with you."

"Thanks, Jed."

The two men hung up and Jed recited, word for word to Carmen, the sketchy details he had gotten from Will.

"Libby's lost somewhere on the lake? She can't be in the lake. Is she on an island?" Carmen asked, incredulous at the thought.

"I don't know any other details, Carmen, and I don't think Will does either. She's a survivor, just hang onto that thought--we'll find her." Jed hugged his wife. Sadie had risen to her paws with the latest buzz of activity and joined their hug, squeezing between their legs for reassurance. Both Jed and Carmen reached down and caressed Sadie as she stood between them.

"I'm going to get the boat ready. You wanna' help me fill the tank with gas?

"Sure," she answered with tears streaming down her face. This latest news had intensified Carmen's fear knowing that Will was coming back without her dearest friend.

*****

The "Tub" was the name affectionately given to the large, old, white twenty-two foot deep V hull Lund, powered by an I/O, V8 Ford engine. It floated in space seven of the harbor. It was a deep-sided run-about, with four swivel seats mounted to the floor and two small bench seats in the back. The large boat may not have been pretty, but it had become an essential tool for the resort owners. It was made for the likes of Thunder Lake. The 220 horsepower I/O got them anywhere on the lake fast, and the deep, V-hull got them there and back, safely.

Jed drove the Tub up to the gas dock. The harbor yard-light made it easy to see Carmen as she hauled the fuel hose over to the big boat. Jed took the hose from her and shoved it into the gas tank. As he squeezed the nozzle on the handle he smelled the fumes as they wafted up into the humid night air.

"Carmen, would you grab my rain gear from the back room? Get Will's, too. I think we are in for more rain."

Carmen came out of the lodge holding the two yellow rain slickers. As she headed to the gas dock she saw a sports car come flying down the hill and stop in front of the harbor. Will climbed out of the low Celica and then bent down to say thanks to the driver. He shut the car door and the little Celica left the resort, the soft sound of rubber rolling over gravel as it headed up the hill. Will walked over to the gas pumps where Jed was hanging up the hose and the two men embraced. Carmen walked up to Will, her expression a mixture of bewilderment and frustration. She hugged him also but then held him at arm's length, "Where is Libby and how did this happen? I don't understand…"

"I can't explain it now, Carmen, it would take too long. I have to get out there. Believe me, I would never leave Libby unless it was the only way to save her.

"I'm sorry, Will. I just don't understand. Why does God allow…" *She kept finding herself facing this same question over and over.*

"Believe me, Carmen, I'm asking the same question….**Ahhh!**"

"What's the matter Will?"

Will had just put on the cap Carmen brought out for him. He hadn't thought about his injured head, but putting on the cap was an instant reminder. Will felt the left side of his skull. The huge bump was still there but with an additional mass of dried bloody hair. He thought to himself, *It's a good thing it's dark so Carmen can't see.* He didn't want her to examine it--he didn't have time for that. He downplayed the severity of what he felt as he fumbled with the cap's size adjustment to make it bigger.

"It's nothing, Carmen. I hurt my head--the boom got me," he said sheepishly. Admitting the cause of his bloody head was embarrassing to Will because he was constantly reminding people to watch out for the boom.

"I'll be fine. It's just a little goose egg."

Carmen didn't insist to have a look. She could tell he wouldn't take the time. He wanted to get out on the lake without anymore delay.

Will and Jed talked over the plan for finding Libby and Honey as they continued to get the Tub supplied. Carmen kept hauling out things from the lodge: numerous flashlights, a thermos of hot coffee, candy and crackers…whatever they might need and more, during their search. She ran in one more time and brought out blankets to keep Libby warm once they found her.

One of the sheriff's patrol boats was docked in the resort's harbor, and Will knew most likely the boat would be brought into the search as would other patrol boats from around the large lake. Will looked at Carmen, "Carmen, I have no idea what Sheriff Sandstrom is going to do, but I'm sure he'll be calling or coming out to the resort soon. Tell him we are heading out to Bass Island and then we'll crisscross our way to Wolf Island and Wolf Point. Ok?"

"Just go--I'll take care of the phones." Carmen sounded in control even though she was filled with anxiety.

Will hugged Carmen and patted Sadie's soft head as she stood next to Carmen on the dock. "Thanks, Carmen. We'll find both of them. Wherever Libby is I'm sure Honey is with her. Just keep praying, faith is all we have to keep our hopes alive. I know it's tempting to ask "why," but it's a strength-stealer. Just put all your energy into hope. "

Carmen nodded and started to walk away then turned back. "So Honey went into the water with Libby?"

"Yes," Will replied. "She is the reason Libby ended up in the water. Honey slid overboard and Libby went in after her."

Now it all made sense. Knowing her friend the way she did, Carmen understood how this could happen. Libby would put her own life in danger to save her dog.

*****

Will and Jed hung onto the windshield as the big boat bucked and kicked its way through the froth-tipped black water. They both stood in front of their swivel seats in order to see the lake surface over the rain spattered windshield of the speeding boat. A high beam spotlight lit up the rolling waves ahead of them.

"Looks like there's lightning just ahead, Will," Jed shouted.

"I see it. I was hoping we would get to Libby before another storm hits us. It was so humid and calm when I got to the resort, but now the wind is picking up and the temperature is dropping. It feels like the next storm front is minutes away."

For a long while both men rode in silence. It was too hard to hear each other over the roar of wind and waves. The thought of Libby out in the water as another storm front passed was unbearable. Within minutes the rough ride got rougher. Will tried to keep his speed up but the waves were starting to splash over the windshield, drenching them as they hung on. They would need to slow down. Jed looked behind him to see their flashlights rolling from side to side and the thermos clunk against the seat pedestals. He had tried numerous times to put the stray items back in the side pockets but soon they were jarred loose and rolling helter-skelter again.

*****

Sheriff Sandstrom and Deputy Theis arrived at the resort twenty minutes after the Tub disappeared on the black lake. The officers got out of the squad car as Carmen ran out to meet them in back of the lodge.

"Jeff, any news?"

"No. I was hoping *you* might have some good news. Have you talked to Will yet?"

"Will and Jed are out in our resort boat. They have no radio so I can't talk to them."

Carmen admitted that last bit of information with a pang of guilt. It was one of those expenses that they had discussed last year but all of them agreed to wait. Now, she would pay five times the price for a two-way radio to be in touch with the men.

"Oh, that's not good. They should never have gone out in this. There's another bad storm heading over the lake, coming from the northwest, heading southeast at thirty miles an hour. Jed and Will won't be able to make any headway when it hits. I hope they aren't going to be more victims for us to find." Then he looked at Carmen's frightened face and quickly added, "They'll probably wait it out behind Bear Island, Carmen. What time did they leave?"

Just then the radio hanging from the sheriff's jacket crackled to life.

"Sheriff Sandstrom, this is Junior. Over."

"This is Sandstrom. What's up, Junior? Over."

"We aren't going to get out onto the lake until the storm passes. Over."

"I agree. Sit tight and tell me when your weather clears. Over."

"Will do. Over."

Because Thunder Lake was forty miles across, weather on one end of the lake may not affect the other. But it seemed that this large storm front was, unfortunately, going to affect the whole lake.

"I'm not going to be able get out on the lake either, until this front has passed, Carmen. I'm sorry."

"What about Libby? She's out there somewhere. If she's in the water she's been there for hours already."

"She could have made it to land. We have to consider everyone's safety. It would be impossible to find her in the dark in this advancing storm. We'll head out as soon as it passes."

*****

Rain pelted Will and Jed while the waves knocked them off their feet in the rocking and rolling boat. They would continue north through the narrows between the island and Red Cliff Point where it's more sheltered and wait out the remainder of the storm at the north end of Bear Island. When the storm had passed the Lund's V8 screamed across the open water, past Gull Island and on towards Bass Island.

The universe waits in anticipation for the Creator's divine whisper. His Kingdom's mission would soon be in motion and nothing would be in play that wasn't in the plan.

Chapter 24

The Lost Are Found

Libby had been barefoot on the sailboat, so she had no shoes for protection against the sharp stones and sand burs hiding in the tall grass as she and Honey ventured warily into the thick, dark woods. In the blackness of the stormy night, every few steps her foot landed on something sharp, or she was hit in the face by low hanging branches. Her legs were scratched and bleeding from thorny bushes. Even Honey was a hazard for Libby because the wary, exhausted dog walked too close to Libby's legs causing her to stumble.

Libby heard the powerful wind of the descending storm. The trees creaked and groaned above them but she felt no drops of rain under the thick canopy of branches above. She hated to stand under any one tree just in case lightning struck it and traveled to the ground, electrocuting them. Libby cried out as she stumbled on, *"Lord, we need shelter!"*

They continued into the woods when Honey abruptly stopped and turned deliberately in front of Libby. Libby, caught off balance by the dog's body, stumbled and fell to the side.

"Listen Honey," she said angrily, "I know you're scared but you can't stop right in front of me!"

Honey stood over Libby and whined. Libby felt bad for her outburst, "I'm sorry, baby--I know you're scared. I'm scared too….and tired….and I hurt all over."

Honey hurt all over too--especially her tail. She felt searing pain every time she moved it or bumped against something.

Libby pulled herself up and squinted into the darkness. Rain began falling through the water-laden branches now and the wind blew twigs and leaves down around them. She maneuvered around Honey and took a step forward in the dark and her foot came down onto….*n-o-t-h-i-n-g*. Her forward motion propelled Libby down into a void.

Her knees hit, then her hands, and she collapsed in a heap onto a surface that gave under her weight. It felt like she had landed onto a bed of straw. Honey barked wildly from above and then finally decided to look for a different way down. She sniffed her way here and there and found a way around the drop off.

Libby lay still, her face buried in the soft pile. It smelled like dried, decaying leaves and grass, a nice earthy scent in the pouring rain. She mentally assessed her aching body for any injury. *Nope. No broken bones.*

Honey scampered down rocky steps she found a few yards away. When she reached Libby she was stopped by a slatted fence that encircled the soft pile Libby was on. With Honey desperate to get to her, Libby slowly began to make her way off the pile. That's when she realized how close she had come to being impaled.

"Whoa--amazing aim, Lord!" Then she climbed over the wooden slats with much effort onto the ground where Honey anxiously waited.

"And you're amazing too, Honey," Libby said as she hugged the lab's wet, furry neck. "You tried to stop me from going over the edge, didn't you?" She scratched her ears and kissed her. "You somehow knew there was a drop off, didn't you, and you stood in the path to stop me. Such a smart, good girl." Libby gave her another big hug. Then Honey did her little happy dance. She yipped and whined and groaned out of happiness and pain.

Libby began exploring the area around them. She held her hands out in search of something…a tree, a rock, or a structure of some sort. Her fingers touched a vertical wall of splintering boards. She felt further--a latch--it's a door! She lifted the latch and old hinges creaked as the door swung out. Libby opened the door wide and smelled inside, then listened as best she could over the wind and driving rain. It seemed alright inside. She called Honey and let her check it out. Honey hesitated in the doorway then walked in. The young lab showed no fear of the dark room so they both entered the dry, musty, space. It seemed quiet and safe as the two wet, tired castaways settled onto the dry dirt floor to rest and wait out the remainder of the dark, stormy night.

*****

The rescue boats were out on the lake at first light. Will and Jed had been running a cross pattern over the wide open area at the center of the monstrous bay. The sheriff and his deputies had just begun their own patterns, crisscrossing the choppy water. Other boats had also joined the search, each driver taking a square mile section of the lake and slowly covering every inch of the surface looking for any clue or hopeful sign of Libby or her dog. Will and Jed were told that a helicopter had been called into service and would be arriving soon.

The sun had been rising over the lake for over an hour when Jed saw a boat coming towards them. It was coming fast, cutting through their search area at an angle. He wondered what this could be about. It wasn't a sheriff's boat or any of the other search boats.

"What do you think this guy wants?" Jed asked as he put the binoculars up to his eyes.

"I hope it's not bad news," Will answered, his heart felt as cold and hard as a rock.

Jed's back became rigid with excitement as he looked harder into the binoculars, straining to be certain. Yes, his eyes were not deceiving him--he took the binoculars away from his face and handed them to Will.

"Look. It's Libby, Will. She's the one driving that boat."

Will grabbed the binoculars and looked for himself. His knees gave out and he collapsed into the seat behind him. It really was Libby.

Will threw the throttle of the V8 into high and raced the half mile to meet the boat. Jed had just finished tying two bumpers to the right side of the Tub when the two boats came alongside each other. Will leaped from the Tub into Libby's boat and grabbed his wife in his arms. They cried and laughed as they held each other. In the seat next to Libby was River Timberlake. She sat quietly in her seat watching the Edwards hug each other with joy and relief. Only minutes ago she and Libby had used the stolen boat to get away from Wolf Island. She smiled at the sight of the happy reunion, but the pain in her foot and ankle kept her subdued. Honey, on the other hand, was so excited that she jumped up on Will and Libby, scooted from one seat to another, then jumped into the Tub to greet Jed who was holding the two boats together. She scooted around the Tub's large open floor and then jumped up and gave Jed a sloppy kiss. The happy lab had lost any semblance of control. Her joy was too much for her to bear modestly. She leaped and scooted, from one boat to the other while poor Jed tried his best to keep the two boats from separating.

The reunion of Will and Libby was so touching that Jed didn't want to say anything. He had a thousand questions running through his head at seeing River. He felt overwhelming relief that all the lost had been found safe. All his questions could wait for another time.

One of the nearby deputies saw and heard the commotion from the Safe Harbor boat and arrived on the scene. The deputy then radioed the good news to the sheriff and the other rescuers. When the sheriff and five other water patrol units joined them, Libby told them of the location of Charles Wiley. Sheriff Sandstrom radioed the approaching helicopter and instructed him to head for Wolf Island where the suspect was last seen.

The Sheriff and his water posse, whose mission had been search and rescue, had new orders: Apprehend the monster who had killed and kidnapped in their jurisdiction. They headed for Wolf Island to find their suspect.

Chapter 25

The Rest of the Story

Back at Safe Harbor Resort, Carmen was confused at the sight of Jed driving a strange boat into the harbor, but when she saw River resting in the boat with him, she was in shock.

She ran down the length of the dock and caught their boat. "Whose boat is this, Jed? How did you end up finding River when you went out looking for Libby? Where's Will?"

Jed smiled as he jumped out of the boat and tied it to a post.

"Libby found us. She had River and Honey with her. She is on her way in the Tub with Will. She ended up finding River this morning and they got away in this boat--I don't know much more than that. River is in bad shape and needs medical attention. Libby stayed to fill the sheriff in on her side of the story before heading back here."

Carmen looked down at River and was concerned about her injuries and obvious state of shock. Jed told her that EMT's had already been dispatched by the sheriff and should be arriving any minute. As if on cue, they heard distant sirens approaching.

As Carmen watched River being tended, she thought about River's boyfriend. *What was his name? Joe--Joe Cloudrider!* When the ambulance left she ran into the lodge and looked for Joe's number in the telephone book and called him. When Joe heard her news he dropped the phone he was so excited and relieved. He grabbed it off the floor and said, "Sorry, I dropped the phone! Thank you so much for calling me to let me know she's finally safe. I'll call her brother right now." He thanked her profusely again and they said good-bye. Joe immediately dialed Lance's hospital room and told his friend the good news. Carmen had told Joe that River was being sent to the same hospital where Lance was recovering.

As Will and Libby motored back to the resort, Honey sat contentedly on the padded platform over the Tub's large engine, her tongue lolling through her smiling mouth. *No dog could look happier than that little lab,* Will thought as he glanced back at the dog, *What kind of ordeal had she gone through, tossed overboard in a storm, having to swim for miles in six-foot waves?* He looked over at Libby--she had her head back, resting in her seat, exhausted but safe. He was feeling overwhelming gratefulness. What an ordeal for all of them, but they had all survived.

*****

Joe Cloudrider arrived at the hospital shortly after River arrived by ambulance, but Joe had to wait to see her. In the emergency room, doctors assessed her condition and ordered her sent up to surgery. X-rays revealed multiple fractures in her right ankle and foot. Surgery would be needed to repair the extensive damage. Before River was wheeled away the doctors allowed Joe to see her briefly. River stared at Joe's face; she didn't seem to know him at first. She was hooked up to an IV, dripping Dilaudid to help her pain. Her blank stare broke his heart, but slowly a spark lit up her beautiful brown eyes and she was brought back to reality at the sight of Joe's face. She smiled at him and Joe kissed her lips. He never wanted to be apart from her again.

After the long surgery, River lay quietly sleeping in her bed. The hospital arranged for River to share a room with her brother. They felt the trauma brother and sister had been through could be helped by their being together.

Lance still couldn't believe his eyes. Lying in the bed across from him was his little sister. He dared not blink for fear it would break the glorious spell he must be under. He had feared the worst after hearing nothing for days. Then he got the call from Joe that River had been found. His spirit soared and his health began to improve immediately with the good news.

Joe was slumped over onto the side of River's bed. He sat in a chair between the two beds, but his head rested next to River. His deep nasal breathing indicated he was heavy into sleep. River's breathing was almost imperceptible to Lance, and he had to tell himself often, that she was fine. Lance had been living in a nightmare--stuck in the hospital while River was kidnapped or possibly dead. He wondered what had happened with the arrest of Wiley. He also was going crazy thinking about what River must have gone through. *She had certainly been beaten but had she been molested by her captor?* Those questions would have to wait. River would talk when she was ready. All that mattered now was that she was alive and recovering. Lance wanted to sleep, but his eyes refused to shut.

*****

Safe Harbor was a beehive of curiosity. Most of the guests at the resort had no idea what had happened the night before, but word of the rescue traveled through the little resort community like wildfire the following morning. Soon people stood watching outside their cabins or along the far side of the harbor. A few had been bold enough to gather in small groups near the lodge, getting tidbits of information from each other.

Libby had been in the lodge with two BCA agents for close to an hour. She hadn't had a chance to clean up before the two black sedans drove into the resort. Will had to wait outside like everyone else. He sat on the cement wall that contained the large gas tanks and two pumps. He was exhausted but there was too much to take care of before he could relax. He would need to get Libby home and into bed and then go after the sailboat still over on Twin Pines Island--with the two pine trees, one live, one dead. He wasn't sure how--maybe Jed would come with him in the Tub and help with dragging the sailboat back. He was sure the Tub's large motor would handle it just fine--that is, unless the sailboat hadn't survived the second storm. That thought made him sad. He loved that boat, but then he was mad at himself for being concerned about a boat. He had just had his wife safely returned to him. Anything else is inconsequential. He looked down at their little lab. Honey slept in the warm sunshine next to his feet. She looked fine except for her tail looking kinked half way down. He had noticed how stiff both Libby and Honey seemed. The long, difficult swim had put quite a strain on their muscles. He hoped that a few days of recuperation would bring them around.

It was mid-afternoon, and the local law officers had also taken their turn questioning Libby one more time about the odd *coincidence* of finding River and escaping with her. Once they finally left the resort, Carmen served Libby a tuna sandwich and some chips. Then the four friends sat down together to each eat a bowl of ice cream while Libby tried to tell her story one more time for them. But, soon she was nodding off so they decided to wait for more details until she got some sleep. She was so grateful to take a long hot shower and finally slide between the sheets of her bed instead of laying on the hard sand. Honey lay beside her on the bed, she seemed to be in pain, whimpering as she slept fitfully. Libby wondered if the dog's restlessness would keep her awake. It didn't.

When things settled down at the lodge, Carmen removed Will's cap to take a look at his head wound. It was an unpleasant task but after soaking and shaving the area, she could see that it was a small deep gash on top of a very large goose egg. She decided that telling Will to get stitches would fall on deaf ears so she pulled the sides of the gash together with small strips of tape from the first-aid kit and decided it would have to do. Will thanked her as he put the old dirty cap back on his head. Carmen cringed but thought, *it'll probably do more good than harm.*

A short time later, Will and Jed took off in the Tub to tow the sailboat back. As they entered Pike's Bay they could just make out the tiny boat and mast in the distance. As they pulled up on shore of the island with the two pines, they found the boat still tied securely to the boulder where Will left her. She was looking a little tattered and forlorn, but she was still floating after being hit by the second storm-front. An hour later and the two men were heading into Safe Harbor; the Tub had handily towed the sailboat home. Once that worry was over, Will decided to call Steve, the veterinarian in Beaver Creek, and explain to the vet about Honey's kinked tail. When Steve heard of the young dog's long swim the night before he was quite sure he knew what her problem was. "She has strained her tail. Dogs use their tail as a rudder, and when they swim too long it puts a strain on the tail joints and muscles. She'll be fine in a few days but keep in mind, it's very painful. You can give her buffered aspirin."

"Okay, that's a relief and it makes perfect sense. I was afraid she somehow broke it."

"I'm sure glad you found Libby, Will. And what an amazing rescue of River Timberlake." Steve added before he said goodbye.

The sun was making its slow, daily drop into the lake by the time Will finally entered the dark bedroom of his home. He hadn't slept in 40 hours. As he quietly undressed in the dark and climbed under the covers, he heard Honey's tail thump once and then a whimper. He touched her soft fur and talked to her in the darkness, "I know you're happy that I'm here, girl, no need to wag your feelings."

Chapter 26

The Unseen

At the Grand Rapids Medical Center, two extra chairs were brought into room 311. It had been two days since the big rescue and River had been awake for very short periods of time. Her ankle had been healing nicely after surgeons screwed five pins into her ankle and foot to repair the splintered bones. This morning though, with daylight streaming through the hospital windows she finally felt renewed and ready to talk, and Libby Edwards was the one she needed to see face to face.

In their hospital room chairs had been arranged so that all present could be included in the conversation. Will and Joe sat on chairs next to Lance's bed and Libby sat beside River's bed. The two women held hands and smiled at each other. They were ready to finally unravel the mystery of how Libby found River and how they escaped together.

River spoke first. "Thank you for saving me, Libby. If it weren't for you I'd still be stuck there. But...I'm so confused about how you and your amazing dog ended up on the island. How did you get there without a boat?"

"*Getting* to the island is an unbelievable story in itself...." Libby began telling her side of the stormy night, of jumping off the sailboat to save Honey and of their long swim in the heavy rains and rolling waves that took them to Wolf Island.

Then Will chimed in with his harrowing experience on the sailboat trying to get back to Libby: the dead motor, the boom knocking him off the boat, the sails being torn in the sixty-mile-per-hour wind gusts. "It felt like fate was orchestrating failure to my every attempt to get back to Libby. I know that's a terrible thing to say but that's the way it felt."

Joe and Lance sat listening to Will, their heads nodding in agreement. They understood all too well his exasperation. When Will was finished, both men expressed their own anger and frustration brought on by the murderous, drunk, Charles Wiley.

River and Libby sat quietly listening to the three men as they vented. Libby was struck by Will's comment. She thought to herself, *it was fate, or actually it was God, orchestrating failure to Will's every attempt to rescue me.*

When there was a pause in the conversation Libby expressed her thoughts. "Will, I think God *was* orchestrating your failure to get back to rescue me. I was supposed to get to that island to find River. Through every six-foot wave I never felt alone, God was with me. And Honey swimming away from me and heading to land, I know seems natural, but I can't help but feel that there was more than "doggy nature," at work. Will, you may not have chosen to be helplessly stranded on our boat, being blown across the lake, but you did make it safely to shore. It may not have been the way you wanted things to go but River needed rescuing. The storm and our mishaps made it possible to get to her. If you had been able to sail back to pick me up then River might still be suffering with her broken bones alone on an island with Wiley.

Then, Libby continued on with her side of the story. "Honey and I woke up that morning in a shelter we found during the night." She laughed a little and continued, "I literally fell from the roof of that shelter built into the hill. It was so dark and rainy that night…and Honey tried to warn me by blocking my way…but I went right over the edge." Everyone gasped.

"Thankfully, my fall was softened by a pile of dead leaves and grass.

Everyone nodded, "Oh-h-h."

"The shelter's door was just a few steps from where I fell! It was really just an alcove in a rocky cliff but it was such a relief to find some place out of the rain and wind. That's where we stayed the rest of the night. In the morning I woke up feeling something jerking me. I was grateful to see it was only Honey. I watched her, fascinated, she was sniffing so hard that her whole body was jerking. It seemed to me that she was seeing and smelling something in the open doorway. This really freaked me out, you know? *What was she smelling? What was out there?* I couldn't see anything but she sure was interested. Then it occurred to me that she wasn't growling or cowering--she was curious and that made me feel better. I patted her head and she looked back at me. Then she got up and walked through the opening, sniffed the air--looked back at me once more and then headed out. She was leaving me again, something she never normally does. So I got up with a lot of effort and followed her. I must have followed her for five minutes before I saw her sitting in front of a cabin--looking back at me, waiting."

"Yes, that must have been when I heard some whining outside," River interjected.

Libby smiled, "Right. It was Honey. I could see her stand up when she saw me finally coming. She was so excited that she was doing her happy dance and whining. Then she turned to look at the cabin door expectantly.

"Where was Wiley?" Will asked, "Didn't he hear Honey whine?"

River jumped in at that point. She looked at Will and then looked at her brother sitting in the bed next to hers. She could see that his strength was returning. When she was taken from Lance a week ago, he lay bleeding to death on the floor of their home. Now he was sitting up in his hospital bed anxious for her to continue. Then she looked over at Joe, his facial expression brimming with anticipation. She smiled at him and he responded in turn. He breathed out a long-held breath and the furrows in his brow relaxed just a little.

River continued, "This is the weirdest part. When I opened my eyes that morning, I was expecting just another day stuck in that cabin on some God forsaken island with a crazy, murdering drunk. But instead I was shocked to see this huge guy kneeling next to me. His gaze was so intense and full of compassion that I could hardly bear to look up at him. I looked over at Wiley and saw that there was another huge guy kneeling over him--he was using his massive hands to cover Charlie's eyes and ears. The guy next to me told me to not be afraid, that Charlie could not hear or see or harm me anymore. At one point, Charlie stirred, but he didn't seem to know about the visitors in the cabin. I was so afraid of what Wiley would do. After all, his gun was laying right next to him. But the big guy just smiled over at me. He seemed unaffected by the puny man or his gun."

River's mouth felt like a desert and she asked for a drink of water. Libby gave her the Styrofoam cup from the bedside table and River took a few sips.

River continued with her story. "These guys reminded me of the elves in the book series, *Lord of the Rings*, only bigger and their ears weren't pointed. It was like they were from another world--they were real--but a different real, there was an aura about them. Then the one kneeling next to me stood and looked at the door as if he were expecting it to open. That's when your sweet Honey, bounded in followed by you, Libby. I thought I must be in the middle of a dream, but you were really there. I couldn't believe what I was seeing. Your dog was all over me, wagging and giving me sloppy kisses." Everyone laughed at that. River did too and then she continued. "Wiley never uttered a word as you helped me out the door: he just lay there with those big guys blocking him with their massive bodies. After we were outside I looked back one more time and saw that they had moved and now stood in front of the cabin doorway. They watched us go as they stood guard. They looked impenetrable.

Libby sighed, "I couldn't believe my eyes either. I could not see the men you are talking about River, but just seeing **you** was so awesome! People had been searching for you for days, and there you were, lying in that cabin. It was very strange, creepy really, how Wiley just lay there while I helped you get up. Libby thought about that and then continued, "Once we were out the door..." She stopped talking, her mind was racing. She was remembering something else, her prayer time just days before this happened. She remembered the brief glimpse she had of angels standing guard in front of a cabin doorway. She burst into tears at the realization that she had seen the unseen...angels sent from heaven's realm. God had given her a glimpse of what was going to happen. She kept the vision to herself. She didn't feel right sharing something so personal from the Lord.

She repeated her words, "Once we were out the door we slowly made our way into the woods. We hadn't gotten far; River was really hurting badly so we rested on a fallen log together just a short distance from the back of the cabin. That's when we really hugged

231

each other and cried. We didn't notice Honey at first as she started to sniff the air in excitement. She started her happy dance again, stamping her front paws and bouncing up and down like she was expecting a dog treat. Her strange behavior really caught our attention. She walked away from us then, not sniffing the ground but sniffing in front of her, like maybe she was following someone. Do you think she was seeing those beings? Neither River nor I could see anything, but Honey seemed to be following something *again*."

River's left eyebrow went up in a questioning expression, "Maybe it was more angels, like the big guys from the cabin, who else could it be? Anyway, Honey saw something, or someone, that really excited her."

Libby smiled, now confident that it was true. Dogs really do see things we don't see. She kept this thought to herself also.

"We hobbled through the woods following Honey as best we could. When we caught up to her, she was busy digging a hole in the ground. Then I saw the rock--the same rock that was also in my dream on the boat, Will. In the dream Honey was digging a hole and this large egg-shaped stone with many layers of different colors and grooves indented in the middle--like an ancient tool--was lying next to the hole. Do you remember me telling you that, Will?"

Will nodded his head to the affirmative.

Libby continued, "This same rock with the worn indentation in the middle, like in the dream, was lying next to Honey. Then we heard a jingle of metal as Honey furiously dug, the dirt and rocks flying from her paws. Something metal had been unearthed and landed behind her. I picked it up and showed it to River and she recognized it as the floatable key-ring from the stolen boat. River remembered the way to the boat, which was well hidden with branches and tall grass. River rested on a rock while I pulled off all the debris. I helped River and Honey into the boat and pushed it out to deeper water. A short time later we were heading across the lake. That's when we saw all the search boats crisscrossing the water. It dawned on me that they were looking for me, so we headed towards the search party. Then I saw the Tub, our wonderful, ugly resort boat. I was so happy to see Will and Jed and so was Honey."

There was silence in the room. Each person was deep in thought and emotionally exhausted from the crazy story they had just heard.

Joe was the first to speak,"I can't begin to understand what happened out there but something--or someone--came to River's rescue besides Libby and Honey. All I know is that Lance survived, River is back with us, Libby didn't drown, and Will didn't crash the sailboat on Munger Reef. We did lose my Uncle Herb, and I will miss him, but I will live the rest of my life with these memories of anguish ending in overwhelming joy. I will be eternally grateful to the Great Spirit--for all that was accomplished in getting River back to me.

Chapter 27

Saying Goodbye

This first Saturday of August, the sun rose unobstructed from the east, its dazzling brilliance magnified against the pale blue sky. The first week of August is generally known to be the best weather week of the summer in northern Minnesota, and the week ahead was forecast to be gorgeous.

Libby was rested and ready to get back to work--every cabin needed to be cleaned by three o'clock. After that she and Carmen would be popping Advil and relaxing with a well-deserved glass of wine--or two. Will and Jed were busy with the outside tasks of the lodge and harbor, and the bears would be waiting patiently for their daily haul of fish guts delivered to their woodsy neighborhood by tractor bucket.

Honey and Sadie enjoyed their usual Saturday routine. Both loved the attention they got from the children leaving after their week at the resort and from the arriving families later in the day. Honey's sad, crooked tail was improving. She still didn't wag it with much enthusiasm, but if you watched closely you could see a slow, awkward swish when people came up to give her some attention. Her sad looking tail was eliciting more attention from people than normal, which she didn't mind a bit.

This was another of those "special" weeks anticipated by the four owners: The arrival of the Bergman group. The multi-family group occupied seven cabins. All the couples were 30-something, three of the men were brothers, the rest were friends. Their career fields ranged from education, law enforcement and firefighter/first responders.

Their children, eighteen of them at last count, ranged in age from fourteen down to three. They had been vacationing together for many years at other resorts, but last year they tried Safe Harbor Resort and none of them had any thoughts of looking elsewhere. The big group felt an instant connection with the Edwards and Porters. The women especially loved the clean cabins. They didn't feel the need to bring cleaning supplies and re-clean their cabin after their positive experience last year.

When the Bergman group arrived, the resort went into high gear. The swim raft rarely sat without a gaggle of kids climbing up and jumping off, and every inch of the beach was covered with a patchwork of brilliantly colored towels, and swimsuits; and bronzed bodies oiled and glistening. The aroma of cocoa butter was rich and pleasant in the air. If there was a week that the resort ran out of ice cream, it would be the week of the Bergman group. It was fun to watch the families make the most of their time together. Parents and children played croquet, volleyball or badminton and every night they all ate together. The four resort owners were always welcome to eat with them and many evenings they accepted the invitation.

*****

The first Bergman group vehicle to drive down the resort driveway that Saturday was a silver Chrysler minivan. It pulled into the parking area for cabin 11 and a tall gangly boy got out first, a towel around his neck, followed shortly by a small girl, already buckled into her lifejacket--both made a beeline for the beach. After a short pause, the two front doors opened, and a tall thin woman stepped out of the driver's side and a big, round-bellied man with sandy hair climbed out of the passenger seat. These were the Mickelsons, Colleen and Chris. The big man stretched his arms high above his head, his raised t-shirt exposing his rotund belly. As he stretched he looked around for any activity and spotted Will and Jed working down by the harbor. He told his wife he'd be right back to help unload the van, then headed down to greet the owners.

When Chris got to the harbor he yelled, "Quit working so hard, guys."

Jed had just climbed into one of the rental boats in order to drive it to the launch where Will waited on the tractor. They were hauling out resort boats in order to make room in the harbor for the seven Bergman boats--sleek, open bow runabouts that could zip from one end of the lake to the other in search of largemouth bass and walleye pike.

Jed looked up to see Chris and his ever-present beaming smile. He yelled to Will across the harbor to wait a minute, and then climbed out of the boat to shake hands.

"Chris, good to see you." Jed greeted the big guy as he looked up at the cabins expecting to see more of the Bergman group.

Chris, still smiling, nodded. "Lookin' for the Bergmans? They are probably all grumbling in their church pews right now. Some cousin of theirs had the audacity to get married this weekend. They'll probably sneak out of the reception early and be up here to get out on the lake by sunset."

Jed chuckled, "Wow, that's some pretty bold relatives, huh? Planning their wedding on this week, knowing this is John, Mike and Greg's "big chill" week at the lake.

The two men laughed and chatted for a few minutes and then Jed got back to the task at hand, and Chris headed up to the van where his wife was busy hauling supplies into the cabin.

It was late afternoon. Libby and Carmen sat peacefully in Libby's living room; the two recliners they sat in looked out at the stunning view of the harbor and the sparkling lake. They sipped their wine and watched in amusement as newcomers arrived to put in their boats. Some people could probably get their boat into the water blindfolded and others backed their trailers in every direction except straight down the cement landing. They watched as Will made his way to the launch area to help one of their guests, Jerry Kotchevar. Jerry had actually jackknifed his boat trailer almost into a tree. The old guy's shoulders visibly relaxed in relief when Will offered to back the trailer in for him.

Then there were the antics of the two dogs as they played with the arriving children while the mothers headed out of the resort to buy more groceries now that their cars were unloaded. From Libby's living room window they could see a panoramic view of the activities.

"We should probably head down and help those guys," Libby said, ending the statement with a big sigh.

"Yeah, we should," Carmen also let out a sigh.

Carmen lifted the wine bottle and gave Libby that questioning look. There was no need to ask the question. The gesture was perfectly clear.

"Ah...okay, half a glass more. The Advil is just starting to kick in,"

Carmen poured a half a glass each and they took a sip.

Libby looked over at Carmen, "It's hard to believe that your new adventure with Jed is less than a month away. Don't get me wrong, I know it's what you two need to do but it doesn't seem real that I won't have you close. Do you know where you will start looking for a place to live? Colorado--Arizona?"

"Moving has not been in my thoughts, Libby. I'm still trying to get over almost losing you. I was so scared that you had drowned that stormy night last week."

The two friends talked and sipped their wine for another hour and then headed down to the lodge to see what they could do to help. Plus, they were starting to feel hungry and they were thinking it might be about time for another round meal at the lodge, ala Tombstone.

*****

At the county jail in Beaver Creek, Charles Wiley sat at the side of his bed. His face bore an expression of bewilderment, one eyebrow pulled up in a silent question, the other furrowed in confusion. Both his eyes held a faraway gaze, seeing nothing in his eight-by-eight foot cell, his mind's eye fervently attempting to recall the events of the last few weeks.

After he was taken into custody at Wolf Island he spent two days in detox after he was arrested. It was a miserable 48 hours of shaking, sweating, and horrible nightmares. Every night he was startled awake by the sound of a gun firing. He would sit up and in the darkness see Lance laying on the floor bleeding, River's screams so real he thought she was in the cell with him. Another nightmare played over and over: the smiling face of Herb Grogan as he lay bloodied and broken, the tire iron he used to kill Herb still in his hand, dripping blood on his boots and jeans. Charlie would wake from the nightmare, feeling sticky and wet with blood. He would scream and look down at his drenched body and realize it was just sweat--not blood--that soaked through his clothing. He remembered other nightmares also. One was of River laying on the floor of the cabin, two rats resting on her shoulder whispering in her ear. The rats then turned in his direction and River nodded her head. In an instant the rats grew to human-sized men in uniform, cuffing his wrists and taking him away. All these nightmares centered on his unbelievable crime spree. Each nightmare was a reminder of what he had done--the inspired behavior of an insane mind.

*****

Back at Safe Harbor Resort, the Bergmans finally arrived late Saturday night. Not wanting to cause a ruckus in the resort after ten, they waited to put their boats in until morning. But John, Greg and Mike were up and out the doors of their cabins at sunrise. Their wives and kids were happy to stay in bed until a more reasonable hour.

Kate Bergman climbed out of bed a couple hours later. She looked out the front bay window at the beautiful scene. The lake lay flat as an enormous sheet of glass. She looked through the bay window at the trees next to the cabin; there was no movement of the leaves. She thought to herself, *Oh dear, not very good weather for walleye fishing, but a gorgeous day for me and the kids at the beach.* She smiled and walked over to the kitchen cupboard to get down a mug for some coffee. She knew John had made it hours ago so it was probably old and bitter by now. But it would get her going anyway and then she'd make a fresh pot. She opened the door to the bedroom where their two teenage daughters slept. Emily, fifteen, and Jessica, thirteen, were sleeping soundly; their pajamas, sheets and blankets were a twisted tangle around them. She closed their door quietly and returned to the kitchen to make fresh coffee. While the coffee dripped into the carafe below, Kate started the water for a hot shower. She looked into the small mirror over the sink in the bathroom and sighed at what she saw in the reflection. Age was beginning to show on her face but she kind of liked what she saw. The wrinkles made her look mature, but she also saw warmth and wisdom looking back at her. She took her brush and ran it through her shoulder length hair then disrobed and climbed into the steaming shower. Warm water plastered her dark brown hair to her scalp and face. It felt wonderful. She backed away from the flow of water and began to suds up when something above her made a tiny noise, like a click or chirp. She stood still as a statue and then she heard it again. Alarmed now, she shut off the water and listened. Then to her horror something small and black began flying in circles around the steamy bathroom. She screamed, clearly in a panic. She backed as far as she could into the corner of the shower stall still screaming but now adding a few swear words for good measure.

Half a minute later the girls jumped out of bed to check on their mom. Emily opened the door to the bathroom, young Jess peeking over her shoulder. Confused and still half asleep, an edge of alarm and irritation in her voice, Emily yelled in at her mom through the swirl of steam escaping through the open door. "What's wrong, Mom?"

Kate screamed and swore with even more intensity as she witnessed the black flying thing soar just over her daughters' heads and into the kitchen. Somehow, Emily was unaware of her close encounter, but Jessica's eyes popped open in alarm as she watched the alien thing fly just above their heads. She let out a piercing scream.

Emily screamed. "What IS wrong with you two?"

Kate hastily grabbed a towel from the shelf next to the shower. She was so upset she dropped it on the floor. She swore again as she bent down to grab it. She screamed at Emily, "There's a bat in the cabin!"

Then, covered in only her towel, she brushed past her now screaming daughters, making a beeline for the door.

"Come on, let's get out of here!"

She ran toward the lodge screaming "Bat! Help us PLEASE!" Following on her heels were Emily and Jessica also screaming "bat...bat...bat!"

Jed was lost in thought as he swept the floor of the bait house when he heard the commotion outside. He threw the broom aside carelessly and ran out to see what was happening. To his surprise Kate was running towards him, her not-so-large bath towel falling precariously low as she struggled to keep hold of it. Emily and Jessica had passed her and had already reached Jed before he had a chance to even react to the unexpected sight.

"We have a bat in our cabin!" Emily and Jessica chorused.

Jed said in a calm voice, "Well, I hope you are taking good care of him for us."

"It's not funny," Emily said in disgust.

Jed smiled, "I know. I'm sorry." He began walking towards Kate, who was more in control of her towel by now. She was no longer screaming but she was out of breath.

"I'm sorry for being a total freak about this Jed," pausing to catch her breath. "I was taking a shower"--*she paused to catch her breath*-"and this bat started chirping above me"--*another pause*--"I just lost my mind, I guess," she said in embarrassment, tugging at the towel around her chest.

Jed tried to keep his eyes looking above her neck as he listened.

By this time Colleen Mickelson came running from her cabin towards them. "What's going on, Kate?" She put her arm around Kate's shoulders, concerned for her friend.

"You take Kate and the girls to your cabin, Colleen, and I'll take care of the bat in their cabin."

Colleen readily agreed. "Of course. Come with me girls. We'll find something for you to wear Kate, but first let's get the shampoo out of your hair."

Kate looked up. She couldn't see her plastered hair but she groaned at the thought of it. As they walked away, Jed could hear Colleen comforting Kate, "Poor dear."

Jed went back into the bait house and grabbed a large fish net and headed over to cabin 5. He propped the door open just in case he got lucky and the bat flew out on its own. He walked around inside the cabin looking in corners. Then he remembered when the Edwards had trouble with bats getting in their home, Will kept finding them hiding in the folds of curtains. So he started lifting up and extending the curtains in the living room. As much as he knew that bats didn't hurt you or get tangled in your hair, they still gave him the creeps. He lifted the second curtain, extending the material and--*holy crap!*--there it was. Just this tiny little black lump clinging in the fold of the curtain. He didn't know what to do next. He didn't want to hurt it, but how should he get it?

When he shook the curtain the bat flew up and started circling the room. Jed swung the net carefully at it but missed. It landed on a picture frame and faster than he could blink, the bat disappeared. He thought; *It must be behind the frame.* He put the net's metal frame solidly against the wall, enclosing the picture-frame, then slowly lifted the net until it started to lift the frame off the nail. In the instant the frame started coming off the nail, the bat flew out and into the net. Its wings caught in the holes of the net and Jed hoped that's where it would stay until he could release it outdoors. When he backed away the picture dropped with a crash to the floor but the little bat was still in the net. Jed turned and ran through the open door and flipped the net inside out allowing the bat to hang from the net. Soon it gathered itself together and took flight. Jed sighed with relief and went back in the cabin to clean up the broken frame. He examined the photo as he pulled it from the wreckage. It was an old aerial picture of Safe Harbor, probably taken by Bud Carter back in the 1960s. He remembered Bud was a pilot and used to take his guests up in his seaplane to look at the enormous lake from above. He threw the frame and broken glass away and carried the photo back to the lodge. He was relieved the old photo had not been damaged.

Jed walked up to cabin 11, which sat on a higher level from cabin 5. He knocked on the door and Kate came to let him in. He smiled at Kate, who was now wearing sweatpants and a *Safe Harbor* hoody sweatshirt.

"Your little bat friend is hanging out elsewhere now. I'm sure he's happy to be outside again."

Kate's left hand went up to her chest and with her right hand squeezed Jed's arm. "Thank you so much, Jed." She blushed then and said,"I'm so sorry for being such a freaking lunatic, running outside with just a towel."

Jed just kept smiling, cocked his head, and told her, "No worries. I would have done the same thing if I saw a bat while I was showering. By the way, did you guys get in after dark last night?"

Kate nodded, "Yes, it must have been eleven o'clock."

"I bet you had the door propped open while you carried all your stuff in from your truck."

"Yup, we did." Kate nodded again.

Jed hesitated before telling her, "Well, that's probably when the little guy got in." He gave her a small one-sided smile.

"Ah, that's probably right," Kate said. "I'm so sorry--and believe me we will never do that again!"

****

The weather so far that week had been perfect. The Bergman group had been out horseback riding at Beaver Creek Riding Stables on Sunday afternoon. On Monday they headed to Itasca State Park, the headwaters of the great Mississippi River. Tuesday they all participated in their annual water skiing event in front of the resort. A few dads and kids rode in the boats pulling the skiers, while the rest of the families cheered them on from shore--giving the biggest encouragement to the newest member to get up out of the water and stay on their skis. Some of the adults even showed off that they could still barefoot ski behind the boat. Will Edwards was one of those who still could speed across the lake with just tennis shoes between him and the water's surface. He had learned at a young age that being literally barefoot was very dangerous if you hit a floating board or log going forty miles an hour.

Even though many of the Bergmans were die-hard fishermen, they still enjoyed being with their friends and family for these group activities. Leaving time for fishing in the early mornings and after their dinners together in the evening.

It was Wednesday morning and two of the Bergman brothers, John and Mike, stopped by the lodge after they finished cleaning their morning catch. They had a hand written invitation to give to the Edwards and the Porters.

You are invited to attend our
2nd annual Safe Harbor Progressive Dinner
The festivities will begin at 5:00 p.m.
Cabin 11--Chris and Colleen Mickelson
cocktails and appetizers
Cabin 3--Greg and Sandy Bergman
salad and soup.
Cabin 1--Mike and Brenda Bergman
Fresh Walleye and fabulous side dishes.
Cabin 5--John and Kate Bergman
dessert at the water's edge to watch the sunset.

Carmen and Jed had the "minnow shift" that morning so they were the ones to accept the invitation. They assured the Bergmans that they and the Edwards would be happy to come. Will and Libby would have to put a note on the lodge door directing other guests to ring the large bell outside the lodge if they needed something. One of them would head to the lodge to attend to their needs.

An hour before the dinner was to begin, the Bergman men retrieved extra picnic tables from the lodge area and carried them to their cabins for the progressive dinner. The children then laid table cloths and anchored them with stones on the table's corners. The large propane cooker for frying the fish was set up at cabin 1.

At five o'clock sharp, the Mickelsons 'opened the bar' for cocktails. On their countertop was a spread of appetizers: Chips and dip, crackers for cheese and smoked white fish, veggie squares and more. The families all sampled and mingled but soon everyone was gathered around the resort owners as they told the group about Libby and Will's sailing misadventure and the horrible news that a lawyer had been shot, a resort owner murdered and a young woman kidnapped. There was a group sigh of relief when they heard that the young woman had been rescued and her brother, the young lawyer, was going to recover. The story was shocking to hear--it all seemed so out of place in this beautiful, tranquil setting.

At five-thirty, the group moved on to cabin 3 where Greg and Sandy had cups of wild rice soup, a mixed green salad and freshly baked Italian garlic bread. Then everyone headed to Mike and Brenda's cabin for the main course. While the men cooked the fish, the side dishes began to multiply on the serving table: cheesy potatoes, ramen cabbage salad, homegrown tomatoes and fresh green beans.

After Greg had fried up a large batch of fish he announced, "Let's eat!"

After an hour to digest and continue on with their conversations, they realized the sun had begun to sink precariously low in the sky. So they headed to cabin 5 for dessert at the lakeshore. While everyone was gathering, John and Mike left for a few minutes and returned with a big birthday cake. One of the little girls trailed behind carrying a gift. They walked over to Will and placed it in front of him and everyone broke out in song,

"Happy Birthday to you…happy birthday to you…"

Will was surprised they remembered it was his birthday. They had been at the resort the same week last year so it shouldn't have surprised him that they were such a thoughtful group of guests. As the sun fell into the lake, he blew out the candles and everyone cheered. Then they handed him his gift. When he opened it he was touched again by their thoughtfulness. It was an apron for grilling all those hamburgers and hotdogs each week for the resort picnics. It had signatures from the whole group and smiley faces from the littlest kids.

"Thank you, everyone. This gift is great--I will get a lot of use out of it and always be reminded of you each time I put it on. We look forward to your group every August--that is, if you decide you want to keep coming back," he said with one raised eyebrow and a questioning smile.

The group all laughed and said in unison, "We'll be back!"

Then John said, "Our kids will be bringing their kids someday!"

****

Friday was another perfect lake day. It was hot by nine in the morning. By noon it was 95 degrees and the beach was covered with wet, sandy kids building sand castles and parents slathering them with sun-block. In the lodge, Jed had just scraped the last of the mint chip ice cream from the three-gallon container. The empty Rocky Road container had been pulled out of the freezer two days ago. The truck that delivered their food supplies wouldn't be there until the following Monday; it would be slim pickins' for incoming guests this weekend, if this ice cream raid kept up.

When Will walked into the lodge to start the second shift of the day, Jed remarked about the ice cream run.

"Shoot. We'll have to buy some of the smaller tubs at the grocery store to get us by until Monday."

As Jed left the lodge, Libby met him in the doorway.

"Have a good rest of your day, Jed."

"You too, Libby. I think Carmen and I will take the boat over the Butterfly Beach and enjoy some solitude."

Libby smiled, "Sounds great, I wish we could join you."

Libby walked into the stifling lodge. Even with two fans blowing air around, it was like an oven.

"Do we still have that water balloon slingshot somewhere?" Will asked Libby when she found him rummaging through shelves and drawers in the storage area.

"Yeah, I think it's in the far right drawer behind the front counter."

Will went over to the counter and pulled out the drawer. A big smile grew across his face. "Yup, it's here and so is a bag of balloons. We are going to have a little excitement at the beach this afternoon."

After talking with the parents and kids at the beach about having a balloon shooting contest, they all were on board to play. The kids formed a line, filling the balloons with water and the parents tied the open ends and placed the water bombs in a big metal tub. As they worked, Will told them how the contest would work.

Soon there was a reluctant "volunteer" riding out with Will on one of the resort paddle boats. Jamie Bergman, the seventeen-year-old son of Greg and Sandy Bergman, climbed onto the raft and stood in the middle, feeling self-conscious at being the center of everyone's attention. Meanwhile, on shore, the slingshot release technique was being perfected by Carly Bergman, Jamie's fifteen-year-old sister.

When Will had paddled out of the way, he shouted, "Are you ready, Jamie?"

Jamie nodded, firming his stance on the raft, which bobbed and tossed in the waves heading for shore.

Carly picked up a water balloon from the stack and placed it in the sling. Her Uncle Greg and her cousin Jack held the stretchy ends of the slingshot for her as she took three steps back. She released the sling and the balloon sailed straight out and dropped into the lake ten feet shy of the raft. Her relieved brother gave a great hoot and laughed loudly at her short volley. Carly would have two more tries to hit her brother. She reloaded, stepped back a little further and aimed. **Whop**, the slingshot vibrated with the hard release. This time the balloon hit the corner of the raft and exploded.

Jamie was still cocky. "One more try, Sis. You'll never hit me."

Carly was already aiming her shot by the time Jamie finished his taunt. She released the sling with just a little higher angle. The balloon sailed high into the air and descended right over Jamie. Jamie backed up and the balloon missed him. He gave a little victory dance and jumped into the lake. When he reached shore he announced that it was now his turn to shoot at Carly.

Carly too was able to escape any balloon hits. Her brother over shot the raft twice and then his last soaring water balloon splatted on the raft just to the left of his sister. Carly was relieved, and gave a victory shout as she waited for Will to pick her up with the paddle boat.

And so it went, the teenagers each took their turn on the raft and with the slingshot. It was a wild, hilarious time. A few balloons connected and exploded but many landed far flung from the raft. Will and Jennifer, one of the Bergman daughters, maneuvered the paddleboat around the raft to retrieve the dozens of floating water balloons.

When Will returned to the dock with Jennifer and the balloons he asked who was going to be next. Everyone was quiet for a moment then they started volunteering each other. Finally Will made the choice. "I think John should volunteer to be the target and Kate should be the shooter."

There was an uproar of cheers and laughter as John and Kate Bergman stood up. Kate, who is five-foot four-inches, to John's muscular, six-foot frame, flexed her arm muscle for the crowd. They all cheered louder. John hugged his wife and said for all to hear, "Be kind, sweetie. Remember, I'm the one you love." He bent down and kissed her cheek. Kate gave a shy smile and kissed him on the lips. There was cheering from the adults and groans from the kids.

Kate's first volley landed in the water. Everyone moaned in disappointment while John laughed and taunted his wife from the raft. Kate's next shot got close enough that John reached out and caught it. The balloon exploded in his hand. The crowd laughed as he waggled his hands next to his ears and stuck out his tongue. Then Kate loosened her tight shoulders with a couple of shrugs, placed her last balloon in the slingshot and pulled back hard, aimed and released. The crowd held their breath as she released the slingshot -- THWANG. Kate had pulled so hard that she fell to her butt when she let go. The red balloon hurtled through the air as straight as an arrow. When it hit its target, the impact was hard and true. John dropped to his knees in pain. The balloon had made contact right between his legs. Kate looked surprised and then horrified. She called out to John, "Are you alright, Honey?"

John raised one hand in response and the whole audience of friends gave a cheer. Then they all started chanting. "Kate, Kate, Kate…"

John dove into the lake and swam slowly to shore. The cold water probably felt good on his sore privates.

*****

As the Bergman week drew to a close, so ended another highlight of the resort season. The Edwards would look forward to the next year and seeing them all again. The Porters knew this would be the last time they would spend with these special people. Groups like this made it hard to leave the life of resort ownership.

Chapter 28

September's Beauty

Nature's finest artistry is reserved for autumn. It's true of most
northern states. Minnesotans may be a little prejudiced but they
firmly hold to their conviction that here is where the Creator's nature
shows off his best work. The shimmering silver-green leaves of
birch trees turn a bright yellow-gold above their vivid white trunks.
Sunlight hitting on the brilliant splashes of orange and red of the
maple leaves, make one's heart beat faster, while the mighty oaks'
russet leaves add depth against the rich greens and blues of pine
and spruce. It is the perfect composition. As if that scene isn't
splendid enough, a mirror image duplicates the artistry on
Minnesota's ten-thousand glassy lakes. Each morning heavy mist
rises from the warmer lake water meeting the chilly autumn air and
then dissipates as the day's temperature rises with the sun.

It's at this time that adult loons take flight for warmer climate.
They leave their surviving offspring to fend for themselves on the
steaming lakes. Watching this parental abandonment seemed rather
cruel to Libby; she had witnessed their exodus over the years, but
understood that is nature's way. The adults need to hurry south to
claim their territory, and their offspring need more time to mature
before they can make such a journey. The true mystery is the young
loon's ability to find their way their very first flight south. Migrating
loons fly at speeds as high as forty miles-per-hour, amazingly fast
for a large heavy bird. The loons from the Great Lakes states
migrate to the Gulf of Mexico. Meanwhile back in Minnesota, many
of the juvenile loons use this time to socialize, making short flights
from nearby smaller lakes to rendezvous with other juveniles on
large lakes like Thunder Lake. Some of these groups can get very
large. It was once reported that as many as a thousand birds
gathered on Mille Lacs Lake. Libby had not seen anything quite that
amazing, but she had seen a flock of loons thirty or more strong.
She and Will were out sailing one early October when they came
upon a large group. They decided to sail through this rendezvous of

loons...the birds seemed hardly affected by the tall, silent, ghostly boat gliding through their midst.

Winter was just around the corner and waterfowl must abandon the lake before freezing temperatures solidify the water's surface. Eventually the ice will be over two feet thick--enough to hold the weight of a city of fish houses and trucks. There are a few aerated ponds and harbors in the town of Beaver Creek that lure some geese and ducks to stay all winter. A few caring souls in town take on the job of feeding the fowl through the winter until the lake is free of ice again.

*****

After closing the lodge Saturday night, the four owners headed to a burger joint in the little Village of Moose Junction. With the shortening daylight, they had started closing the lodge at seven o'clock. They wanted this time to just enjoy a night out together before Jed and Carmen headed out on their expedition in the morning. They all knew that the Porters would be moving on, but to where? They really didn't know where they wanted to live. They had narrowed it down to somewhere out West...but the west is a very big area.

Libby and Will were trying to be brave and not show how much they were feeling the impending loss of their partners and friends. They both still fought with their feelings of uncertainty that they were the reason for their friends leaving. The Porters had reassured them that they were not the reason, but still the doubts persisted. Tonight though, the Edwards put aside their sadness and enjoyed this time together.

"We think we have an itinerary for our trip," Carmen announced after they had ordered food and drinks.

"Let's hear it," Will responded.

Jed pulled out a folded piece of paper from his shirt pocket. As he unfolded it and placed it in front of Libby and Will, he verbally recited what was written on the paper:

"We'll head to the Dakotas and then go south until I-90. We'll travel I-90 across southern South Dakota and into Wyoming then head south again and go through Colorado and into New Mexico. You remember Carmen having friends in Albuquerque? They would love for us to check out that area, so we'll make that our destination. I've always wanted to check out Montana, but after experiencing the cold winters of the north I think both of us are wanting some place a little warmer. "

Will and Libby knew the route across southern South Dakota very well, traveling I-90 from Minnesota to Wyoming almost every year to visit Libby's parents who lived in Wyoming. They enjoyed their visits out West. The big sky, open prairie and mountain ranges were such a contrast, a relief from Minnesota's lake country where the roads meandered through thick woods and wound incessantly around lakes. The trips were pleasant reprieves, but the west was not where their hearts felt at home.

"Are you sure you want to bring Sadie?" Libby asked.

"Yes, she's a part of our family, and we want her to be with us. But thanks for offering to keep her while we're gone. We hope to be back within a week, maybe two at the longest. If we find where we want to live we will want to come back and get packed before the snow flies."

"Let's not think about that yet--I'm not ready to see your stuff packed in a truck heading out of the resort for the last time," Will said with a sigh.

Jed thought about the fact that in a week the old boys from Rochester would be returning. He had a twinge of doubt about what they were doing--moving away from their friends, the business, and some really good times at the resort.

"You'll make something up to tell the *boys* about where we are-- like we're just taking a trip, not that we're moving. Maybe it will become clear to us that we are supposed to stay here--and then we won't have to explain ourselves if we stay."

"Okay. That's fine. It's nice to think that maybe there's some hope of your deciding to stay," Will said.

It was a bittersweet evening. Laughter would flow into awkward moments of sadness. They could talk freely with these friends they knew so well, but there were some things that each of them held back, not wanting to hurt or discourage the other.

The next morning, the Porters were on their way--westward bound.

*****

Will and Libby had been working the resort on their own almost a week, but with just a few cabins being rented, it had been easy for them to handle. As Will walked along the harbor entrance he watched the frothy waves from the big lake race into the channel and quickly dissipate. Then, to his amazement, from around the point, came two large, white pelicans, riding in on an incoming wave and gliding effortlessly into the calm harbor.

These birds rarely are seen in shallow water, preferring to nest on rocky islands far offshore where they soar above deep water, miles out, to find their food. It was the first time Will had seen any fowl in the harbor except geese or ducks.

He talked softly to the strange looking birds as they glided around the harbor.

"What are you two crazy pelicans doing so close to shore? "

They seemed uninterested in stopping to talk; instead their attention was focused on looking down into the harbor's murky water. One of them dove and quickly surfaced holding a small perch. The fish flipped and flopped in the pelican's beak, but before it could wriggle free it disappeared down the bird's expanding throat. Will thought about the fish guts in the fish cleaning house that he was on his way to remove. He told the pelicans, "Hang on, I'll be right back."

When he entered the cleaning house he was surprised to see Danny Enga cleaning his day's catch. Catie, his five-year-old daughter, was standing on an overturned bucket next to him. Will was amused as he watched her little finger gently touch the eye of one of the fish on the table in front of her.

"Catie, do you want to help me feed some pelicans? Come on…there's two of them swimming in the harbor. We could feed them a little of the fish dinner we usually bring to the bears."

Catie's eyes were wide with excitement, "Okay!"

As Will walked slowly out to the end of the dock, Catie followed with her dad close behind. The pelicans swam away a short distance from them. Then Will pulled out a carcass from the bucket. The only parts missing from the fish were the meaty sides--the head, skin, fins and bones were still intact. He held the fish over the water and waited patiently. After a few minutes the pelicans began to glide slowly towards them, pausing from time to time to assess any danger. Soon one of them got close enough and Will tossed the carcass. Both pelicans surged forward to snatch the offering. Catie, jumped back in surprise and grabbed her dad's leg. As the partial fish slid down the bird's odd, expanding throat, Catie burst out laughing. Will smiled down at her and then took out another fish and flung it at the other pelican. The meal was down the bird's pouch in a few gulps and it was ready for more.

Soon other guests arrived, cameras swinging from their necks, interested in the strange spectacle. When the bucket of fish was gone, the large, white birds swam silently out of the harbor and onto the choppy lake.

Will was mystified by their visit, but pleased they had stopped by his humble harbor. He turned to Catie and recited a poem from his childhood.

A wonderful bird is the pelican
His bill can hold more than his belly can.
He can take in his beak, enough food for a week
But I'm puzzled to see how in the heck he can.

Catie looked at Will quizzically, cocked her little head and giggled. "You're funny."

*****

Will and Libby had heard from their partners by phone six days ago. Jed and Carmen were in New Mexico after traveling through the Dakotas, Wyoming and Colorado. They had much to share with their friends but saved any news until they returned at the end of the week. Jed (aka Ray), wanted to see the 'boys' before their week at the resort was over. He was sorry that he would not be there to greet the old fellas when they arrived.

******

It was Saturday, changeover day for the third week in September. The boys from Rochester had arrived for their second visit of the resort season.

"Wanna beeer?" echoed through the resort that Saturday afternoon. Up the hill at cabin 7, the old guys were moving their weeks' worth of gear, food and cases of beer into their cabin. Will was glad to see them back, but without his cohort, Jed, it was bittersweet.

Will yelled up to Cabin 7, "Hey Ross, I'll join you in a little while. I have to clean out a few boats and pull their motors first."

Ross quipped, "Don't fall in! We don't want our new carpet getting soaked."

Will smiled to himself as he turned towards the harbor.

Late that afternoon, while Don Knutsen maneuvered Ross's trailer holding the 1978 Blue Fin fishing boat into the harbor, Honey watched intently from the gas dock. She liked the old guys and she was confident the feelings were mutual. The old boys from cabin 7 had become very popular with both Honey and Sadie as the dogs would often find a big plate of leftover eggs and bacon on cabin 7's deck in the morning. Whichever dog got to it first never left a scrap for the other. Winner take all is a dog's opinion on all things delectable from a human's plate. With Sadie gone, every day would be an unchallenged breakfast for Honey.

With the boat floating in the harbor, Don's brother, Jed, hopped into the van and pulled the empty trailer up the ramp and parked it on the nearby lawn. Don tried the outboard on the Blue Fin; it sputtered once and started. He and Ross putted over to the gas dock where Honey was waiting to greet them, her whole body wagging with happiness. Don cradled Honey's furry head in greeting and then climbed out of the old boat. Will was ready at the gas pump, flipping the lever up in order to fill their boat with fuel. While Don was busy talking to Will, Ross stayed in the boat and organized the fishing gear. Then Jed Knutsen, smelling of bourbon already and walking a little tipsy, arrived with a bag of snacks and a cooler of beer from their cabin. There was a bustle of activity in the boat with Ross up front detangling fish line from hooks and poles and Jed busy in the back of the boat putting sandwiches and snacks in the boat's hidey-holes for safe keeping. From time to time, he would look away and tip back a flask he had hidden in his jacket. He knew this would not bode well for himself later, but he wouldn't think about that now. It was time to celebrate. After all, they were back on their beloved Thunder Lake. Don and Will stood on the gas dock lost in conversation about the summer and, to Will's dismay, the awkward topic of "Ray's" absence. He did his best to say as little as possible about the subject and finally succeeded in changing the subject as he topped off their gas tank and clicked the nozzle off.

"Well, it sure is great to see you guys again. I can smell the fish frying from your cabin already," Will said with a warm smile. It did his heart good to see these old friends heading out onto the lake for fall fishing.

"We will be frying fish by seven o'clock tonight...I guarantee it," Don boasted, "We will return with a meal of walleyes and jumbo perch--enough for us all, so you and Libby join us, okay? I only wish Ray and his lovely bride were here too." Don's voice sounded a little disappointed.

Will saw the look on Don's face and felt his own disappointment. "I know," he said with a sigh, "but maybe they'll be back in time for your last night here."

Don looked hopeful at the possibility. "That would be great. I have a big surprise planned for our last night."

"Thanks for the invite for later tonight, guys. Libby and I will look forward to joining you after we close the lodge. I just can't believe the season is coming to an end already. With your arrival, it means we are just a week away from being an empty resort for seven long months!" Will said as he looked down to see that he hadn't pulled the gas nozzle out of the boat tank yet. "I guess I'll leave you to your mission then," and pulled out the nozzle from the tank, put the gas cap on, and turned it tight.

With everyone busy and excited to get out onto the lake, no one had noticed when Honey made her move.

Then the fourth member of their party came running down the hill, "Wait for me!"

He was a much younger man, 40ish maybe, donning a purple and white Vikings jacket and purple Vikings cap.

"And who's the "fourth" in your party this week?" Will asked.

Don introduced Will to the younger man. "Will, this is Lenny Bingham. Lenny, this is Will Edwards."

The two men shook hands and then Will said, "Well guys, good luck. It's a little chilly so keep reeling in those fish just to keep yourselves warm."

When Don turned to climb into the boat he burst out laughing... Lenny too, let out a big guffaw. Then Jed and Ross looked around and joined in. Will had turned to walk away but when he heard the outburst he turned back. There, sitting expectantly in Don's seat behind the steering wheel, was Honey. She looked around and then straight ahead, ready to pilot the old green and white boat out of the harbor.

Lenny got a picture of their uninvited furry captain and then Will called her to his side. Honey, was a little reluctant to abandon her adventure with the boys--she knew they had snacks--but she obeyed and hopped out of the boat and Don and Lenny climbed in.

*****

Around four o'clock that afternoon, an old Buick drove in and headed to cabin 5. The car was packed to the ceiling hauling a new Lund fishing boat. The old man opened the driver's side door and peeked his head out with open-mouthed amusement. He was happy to be back at Safe Harbor...and very relieved that their three-hour trip from western Minnesota was over. His stiff joints still held him in the driver's seat, so he looked around the resort contentedly through the open car door. He looked back at his wife, also still sitting in her seat.

"Well, my dear. We have arrived in one piece. Praise the Lord."

The old couple had come the previous year when they found out Libby and Will had bought the resort with another couple. Clayton Olsen and his wife Ruth were excited to have their same cabin from the year before. They loved the cabin's close proximity to the rocky shore. The old couple were family friends of Libby's from way back. They had been members of her father's church and eventually, in-laws of a sort when Libby's sister married their son.

Ruth climbed out of the car. She was a little bit of a woman, a much frailer version of the woman Libby knew forty-some years ago. She pulled a heavy winter jacket tight around her body when the chilly lake breeze buffeted her thin frame. Ruth's vision was so poor that the old woman's hazel eyes were magnified and distorted behind her coke-bottle glasses.

"Ruth, it's wonderful to see you again," Libby said as she hugged her parent's old friend.

Clayton had finally gotten his long legs out of the car and planted them firmly on the ground when Will walked around the car to greet him.

Will put his hand out, "Clayton, let me give you a lift."

After Will had him up and steadied, Clayton gave Will a big bear hug. Will had grown to admire this tall, good-natured man since getting to know him last year. Clayton had a way about him; he seemed ready to share a smile along with some good-natured kidding. He had a love for God that oozed out of him like warm honey and a passion for fishing that Will found endearing.

Will and Libby offered their help in unloading the Olsen's overloaded car but the old couple refused.

"We like to put things away slowly. We'll unpack, rest, and unpack some more later. I'll get everything unloaded by early evening and then I'd like your assistance in putting my new boat in, if that works for you…" Clayton said, with his eyes a-twinkle and his ever-present smile showing off a gold tooth.

"It would be good if we could take care of your boat before we close for the night, Clayton. We are invited to a fish fry at cabin 7," Will explained.

Clayton smiled. "Ah, the boys from Rochester... glad they are here too. I'll be sure to get you before then."

Two hours passed and Will saw Clayton backing away from his cabin, his new boat, *his* pride and joy, leading the way as he backed the Buick towards the lodge.

"That was fast, Clayton."

"Well...Ruth fell asleep in a chair, and I thought it best that she rest without my clambering in and out of the cabin. Might as well get this beauty launched."

Will hopped in the passenger side and they headed to the ramp together. The new sixteen-foot Lund slid easily off the trailer bunks and Will drove it over to a covered slip closest to the lodge, the most convenient location for the old couple.

After Clayton dropped off his trailer and drove his Buick to his cabin, he made his way back to the harbor. While Will waited for Clayton's return, he busied himself with adjusting bumpers and dock lines so the new boat would sit secure next to the dock. He was amused to see the quickness of Clayton's steps as the old guy headed towards his boat. Will thought he looked like a man twenty years younger. It's a strange phenomenon he'd seen over and over again with the resort's aging clientele; often, their love of fishing trumped their age for a week.

Will listened with great interest as Clayton showed off his new boat. The experienced fisherman explained that after last year's experience on Thunder Lake, he and Ruth felt that their old fourteen-foot aluminum boat was just a little too small for a huge body of water like Thunder Lake. He gave a wink, and Will understood the old guy's gesture. It was the best reason they could think of to finally buy themselves a bigger boat.

Will smiled and looked around, "But, Clayton, it looks to me like there's a lot of aftermarket and beautifully hand-crafted additions in this boat."

Clayton beamed, "Ruth and I have been fishing together for fifty years. We know what works for us and all the things we need especially as we get older, so I've worked on it all summer getting it ready for this week."

There were lockers for every conceivable gear and gadget for fishing. A high pole with a large hook was securely fastened to the side of the boat for a lantern because they only fished in the waning hours after sunset. Clayton had also secured a propane heater close to where Ruth liked to sit and fish, "because she suffers so from the cold now."

Before he climbed out, Will thanked Clayton for showing him all his thoughtful additions to the boat. And Clayton thanked Will for giving them the covered slip close to the lodge. Will left Clayton to putter in his boat as darkness descended on the resort. He joined Libby and together they closed down the lodge. Libby closed out the cash register and turned off the computer while Will turned off the gas pumps and locked up the bait house. They met in the doorway of the lodge as Libby was locking the door.

"Where's Honey?" Will asked. They both looked at each other, puzzled. It was rare that Honey wasn't with one of them--how long had she been missing? Will had, from time to time, locked Honey in the bait house not realizing that she had followed him in when he went in to shut off lights and the gas pumps. They both looked in the direction of the bait house and Will shrugged, "Well, I better go check."

There was no anxious lab in the dark bait house.

"H-m-m, where could she be?" Libby asked when Will returned.

"She'll find us. Let's head up to cabin 7. I can smell the fish from here!" Will said as he rubbed his belly.

"Okay, you're right. She'll know where to go."

To their surprise--and really once they thought about it, should have been no surprise--Honey had already been invited into cabin 7 and was making herself as attentive and cute as any hungry dog.

*****

Tuesday evening after dark, Will was waiting anxiously for the lantern's glow from Clayton's boat to make its way into the safety of the harbor. Even though Clayton had promised Will he would not go far from shore and stay in front of the resort, Will and Libby still watched and worried until the old couple entered the harbor. It had been three hours since the Olsens had gone out. Will had watched

Clayton, earlier in the evening, as he helped his frail wife into the boat and covered her legs with an old quilt. Even though Will and Libby closed the lodge and headed home, they still were on duty watching the lantern light travel back and forth in front of the resort as they relaxed in their living room. Will could always tell when the old couple got another fish because the light would stop traveling. This time, the light had stopped moving and then went out. Will and Libby wanted to go to bed but knew that it would be impossible until they knew the Olsens were safe. Will was just about to leave the comfort of his recliner when he saw the light come back on and head slowly into the harbor.

"Whew, it's tough worrying about kids being out late, but it's just as nerve-wracking to worry about seniors!" Libby said with a sigh.

The next morning Clayton arrived at the lodge bright and early to show off Ruth's prize catch from the night before. He explained how the lantern had gone out just as Ruth's line went down with the whir from her reel. As frail as Ruth looked, she was a determined fisherwoman. She hung on and played the line expertly as the unseen lunker fought hard beneath the water's surface. Clayton was so proud of her.

"She's always been the better fisherperson," he said with a big grin. "She kept that northern on the line till I could light the lantern again. When I got it lit and saw her struggle, feet braced against the boat, her gripping fingers white from holding tight, her glasses hanging cockeyed from her nose, I could hardly contain my pride. She was a glorious sight. I love that spunky little woman!"

Clayton held up the northern for Will, "Well, I'm gonna' clean this baby. What do you think he weighs, over twelve pounds? Let's check."

So Will and Clayton went out to the scale in the bait house. Will hooked the lip of the northern and Clayton read the scale, "Ooh-wee, twenty pounds!"

"I'm surprised you didn't weigh it last night, Clayton. You must have a scale in one of those nifty storage compartments."

"Oh yeah, we've got one, but Ruth and I were so spent from landing the big guy that we just had to head home. So he spent the night in the live-well. Thanks for helping me weigh him, Will. Ruth will be delighted to hear."

Will watched as Clayton headed to the fish cleaning house. He was thinking that, possibly, Clayton was walking like he was another ten years younger this morning.

*****

Carmen and Jed arrived back at the resort on Thursday night. Will was relieved that Jed would have one more night to enjoy the hilarity and fun with the old boys from Rochester. Friday nights were usually the coup de gras of fish dinners at cabin 7. When the four resort owners and two dogs arrived for the boys' last fish fry, they were greeted at the door by Ross wearing a waiter's uniform--a dish towel hung neatly over his left arm.

"Welcome, honored guests. The famous Chef Donamichi has been preparing your meal for this evening."

The two couples looked at each other and smiled. Carmen said, "M-m-m, oh boy--we're all salivating."

As they entered the smoky cabin, *smokey from cigarettes and fried fish*, they burst out laughing at the sight of Don--*Chef Donamichi* wearing a tuxedo, starched white shirt, bowtie and a tall puffy white chef's hat.

Everyone in the cabin started laughing until tears rolled down their cheeks.

The night was filled with laughter, stories--some new, some old-- and food enough to serve an army: fish, stuffed mushrooms, onion rings. Chef Donamichi had batter-fried everything.

Chapter 29

Second Chances

The glory of autumn was just as picturesque at Muskie Run Resort. The resort buildings were still rundown except for the old owner's home, which had been bulldozed and hauled away. Nature's beauty still trumped man's neglect as River Timberlake and Joe Cloudrider surveyed the panorama of the old resort resting next to the shimmering lakeshore.

River, still in a cast, rested her slight figure on her wooden crutches. She surveyed the beauty and the decay with giddy excitement. Joe stood beside her, his arm resting on her shoulders.

"Well, River, what do you think of our future resort?"

River's smile was so big it made her high cheekbones stand out, and Joe bent down and kissed each side. With Herb Grogan's passing, the resort would become the inheritance of Herb's brother-in-law, Terry Cloudrider. Terry had no interest in fixing up his deceased sister's rundown resort so he offered it to Joe. Before Joe accepted the responsibility, he first talked it over with River. She would be his wife in a few months, and he would only take the resort if she wanted to be a part of building it back up.

River was thrilled. The idea of building a life together with Joe in such a beautiful setting was more than she ever hoped would happen in her life. She remembered with fondness cleaning cabins with her mother, Lilly, at Safe Harbor Resort. Someday she would be proud to welcome families to this place, only this time she would be the resort owner.

*****

Lance was making arrangements to go back to his life in Boston. His firm had fully expected his return and said they would have him back as soon as he was settled. There was a tug-of-war going on with his emotions. Leaving Thunder Lake, his childhood home, was easy but leaving River was almost too much to bear. But he knew it was exactly what he needed to do. River and Joe might not agree, but having a big brother and best friend interfering in their lives could be difficult. It takes a lifetime to become knit together as a couple, and family interference can do some unintentional unraveling. No, he didn't want to mess with such a good thing as his most trusted friend marrying his beloved sister.

He was ready to throw himself back into work. That's what he needed now. Maybe in time he would meet the right person to spend his life with, but that could wait. There was always a chance that he could make things right with Heather Brown, the colleague he dated a few years ago. He and Heather were both on the fast track at his law firm, but really one must come to one's senses eventually and realize there is more to life than money, status and power. He had just experienced the power of love to overcome great heartbreak. Joe's and River's love was growing roots and blossoming. Someday it would happen for him too, and he wanted that more than he ever realized.

Before Lance could go though, he had some loose ends to tie together. With the murderer, Charles Wiley, in jail awaiting trial, the transfer of ownership of Muskie Run Resort had been easy to accomplish. What with Wiley's delinquent contract payments and back taxes, the resort was legally Herb's again. Thank goodness that before Herb was killed, Lance had insisted that they get an heir in place if something happened to Herb. Since Herb had no living relatives besides his wife's family, he felt it best to name Jenny's brother, Terry, as inheritor of the old rundown resort. With Terry's less than enthusiastic response and his wife being emphatically against taking over such a disastrous place, Lance mentioned their son, Joe, as a good choice to take on the task. Lance couldn't help but feel it was a stroke of genius on his part. With Joe and River's youth, hard work and great personalities, they would have that place hopping once again.

Another matter still to be set in place was getting a reputable, local attorney to assist him with the pretrial evidence gathering and statements concerning their ordeal with Charles Wiley. When the trial date was set, he would return to assist council and of course be a witness to the nightmare they had all been through because of Charles Wiley's rampage.

*****

Charles Wiley had been in jail for seven weeks. His mind, once poisoned by his alcoholism, was now clear and sharp; barbs of shame and regret, wounded and cut into every wakeful hour. Sleep was also a torture of nightmares. He had called for a minister, someone--anyone--who could help him over this mountain of guilt. A few days later when he awoke in the morning, there stood a man outside his cell, hands folded together, head bent, praying softly. The man's name was Paul Johnson, the minister from Beaver Bay Christian Fellowship. The pastor made a weekly visit to the jail to bring the message of mercy to any hurting soul wanting God's love. The jailors had informed Rev. Johnson of Charlie's request and so he stood that morning, praying, ready to deliver God's message of Grace.

Paul and Charlie spent hours together. Paul listened as Charlie sobbed and blew his nose through his life's story. The loss of his family, and his part in their deaths; the abuse he endured in the welfare system; his terrible regret over neglecting the only person he ever loved, his wife Aggie. Paul knew of the reason for Charlie's incarceration and yet Charlie had not brought up regret over his recent acts of murder, attempted murder, and kidnapping. The mind is a curious thing; so much recent anguish to deal with, yet Charlie's brain had walled off that carnage until the past could be unknotted and released.

The fourth week after being arrested, Charlie began to talk about his recent guilt in taking the life of Herb Grogan. He was obsessed with the last second of Herb's life. The look in his eyes, how they twinkled with joy. The peaceful smile that barely curved the corners of his mouth confounded Charlie.

"Why was Herb at peace at that moment?" Charlie asked the minister.

Paul, being a believer in God's kingdom, found the description of that moment priceless. It would stay with him through any future loss…a man being bludgeoned to death seemingly at peace a second before death. What an illumination of what awaits us all who believe in a life with our Creator after this earthly life.

He spoke to Charlie's question. "There may be pain and fear in such a horrific attack, but Charlie, it proves that death is impotent after all. It holds no power over us who have faith."

Charlie was silent. Then a small smile crossed his lips. "You mean to tell me that I don't have to be eaten up with guilt? I mean I know I did a terrible thing and I deserve to die, but Herb is in a better place?"

"Yes, Charlie, and that is true for you too. We all fall short of God's desires for us but His Son paid the price so that we can escape death's finality. All we need is faith that He really did die to set us free."

Charlie put his face in his hands and shook his head. "I find that too hard to accept, Pastor. I don't deserve to be set free, even if it is only in my heart."

Paul Johnson nodded and spoke softly. "It's really true, Charlie."

*****

On another visit Paul Johnson listened to another mystery Charlie struggled to understand:
The time at Wolf Island when Charlie woke to find police standing over him, guns cocked and pointed at him in the cabin. How had River gotten away, hurt as she was by his cruelty? It didn't make sense. "It's not that I'm not relieved that it ended that way. I had to be stopped. I am so relieved that I hadn't time to hurt her any worse. Who knows, I might have decided to kill her too." His eyes and nose were running. Paul reached for a napkin lying on Charlie's table and gave it to Charlie who blew his nose with a great honk.

Charlie wiped his eyes and then began to breakdown and cry harder. He cried like his heart was broken in pieces. He finally stopped and blew his nose again. Another honk echoed off the cement block walls.

Charlie spoke with a broken voice. "I want so desperately to see her and tell her how sorry I am, but that will have to wait for my trial. I will face her then and tell her."

Chapter 30

Peace in Chains

Ten weeks into Charlie's incarceration, Rev. Paul Johnson had been granted permission to take Charlie out into the courtyard in back of the county jail. It was a rare request and even rarer to have the request granted. The pleasant courtyard was surrounded by a three-foot-high serpentine brick wall, planters atop were filled with yellow and rust colored mums. Nestled in the wall's graceful curves were clumps of young birch trees. Even though their branches were now bare, their white papery bark was striking against the dark brown brick. Most of their yellow leaves that rested on the patio had gathered into small piles around benches, tables and the building's east wall.

It was a crisp day. Fifty degrees according to the thermometer-- but the warm sun at noon made it feel like seventy. Paul made the request a week ago and it was finally granted yesterday. The powers that be, reluctant at first, finally agreed after Paul's persistence. He pleaded for his friend, a changed man, to be given an opportunity to feel the wind on his face, see the clouds and autumn's blue sky without looking through the bars on the windows. He won the battle, or maybe *his* "Power that be" had the final say.

Charlie sat with his back to the building, his face to the sun; an officer of the jail sat behind him a few yards away, keeping watch over his prisoner. Charlie's eyes were closed but his ears were aware of every rustling leaf as it skittered across the patio and the incessant whoosh of traffic going by on the front side of the building. He focused on a dog barking in the distance. It sounded to him like the bark of a dog on a chain: that persistent, frustrated, annoying bark of the locked up and lonely. His heart broke a little as he considered the dog's plight. He loved dogs and knew how very cruel it was to relegate such a social animal to an isolated tether.

Paul spoke and jarred Charlie's obsessing thoughts over the dog. "You haven't touched your lunch, Charlie."

Charlie sat up straight and looked over at Paul with a grateful smile, "Oh yeah, I forgot. Thank you so much for doing this for me-- getting the food and arranging for this outing."

He reached for the McDonald's bag on the table in front of him. His reach was abruptly blocked by the metal handcuff around his wrist. The buoyant mood of being out of his stuffy cell and into the fresh clean autumn air was pricked and deflated. There were no words spoken between the two men. Charlie struggled to move his heavy metal chair a little closer to the table and felt the restriction of the cuff on his left ankle. He adjusted his footing, lifted the chair by the arm rests and shuffled forward. The effort enabled him to reach his food.

"I haven't had a McDonalds Double Cheese for a long time. I've been looking forward to this ever since you told me you were bringing it." Charlie unwrapped the sandwich and took a big bite.

"I haven't either--and my wife better not hear about it," Paul said with a chuckle. "She's pretty particular about what I put in my stomach these days. Now that I've crossed the half century mark, getting rid of excess weight is harder than ever."

The men relished their forbidden meal. When they were done Paul gathered up the trash and delivered it to a nearby receptacle. When he returned, they began to talk. It was something that had become very comfortable and familiar to them both.

"God has been speaking to me, Paul. I have these *thoughtful feelings*--I don't know how else to describe them--reassuring thoughts, full of love, no guilt. That's why I know they are not my thoughts. What is next? I feel the need to do something, but what?"

Paul smiled at his captive friend. He loved this man because God loved him, but he actually liked Charlie too. He was a good man. It took weeks of soul-searching talks, but eventually the effort revealed someone precious. Charlie had come a long way in freeing himself from his past. He had so much guilt and fear from his childhood. He had struggled with anger towards his parents as a young boy, feeling they loved and respected his older brother more than him and spoiled his little sister, letting her do things he never got to do. They seemed never to be happy or proud of him. So the night that the house caught fire it was because he had set it. In reality it wasn't on purpose but it was his fault. He had used the wood burner in the living room to burn their family photo books--an act of revenge after his mother had screamed at him for some infraction of her rules. The fire got so hot that it started a chimney fire. The roar in the chimney was terrifying and young Charlie ran from the house, leaving his sleeping family unaware. He didn't know it as he ran out of the house but the roaring flames in the wood burner sparked and caught the picture albums on the floor creating a blaze that mushroomed and grew into the death trap that killed his family.

Anger. It's a devastating and destructive emotion. Paul knew that Charlie had been possessed with a spirit of anger from childhood into manhood. It had been festering and slowly possessing him all his life. The disease had wrapped its tentacles into every aspect of Charlie's body, soul and spirit. The alcohol was a mere attempt to deaden the anger that possessed him. Anger and bitterness began to choke any happiness in his childhood and ruined his life with Aggie as an adult. It blurred his perspective and distorted his memories. Those who hold resentments and anger cannot see straight, mentally, spiritually and even physically. The phrase, *so angry that you can't see straight* is so true. Charlie had become nearly blind from all the anger locked up in his soul.

Anger had taken away much of this man's life, but Grace was rescuing what was left. Paul was confident that the Christ who died to set us all free from our self-destruction had the very soul of Charles Wiley in mind when he journeyed to the cross. All Charlie needed to do now was believe that God loved him so much that he came to rescue even him.

"Charlie, it's time that you accept the gift of Christ. Take Him into your heart and accept His forgiveness and live for Him."

Charlie sat in silence, contemplating the pastor's words. He again heard the disembodied barking from the chained dog. An anger began to burn from deep in his soul. The cruelty to this poor creature, was a distraction heading to a full-blown fit. Then Charlie heard God speak to his heart in an inexplicable way calming him, persuading him to stop the burning anger, release it, and God would throw it into the deepest ocean. Charlie could see that he had to release the anger in order to possess the Love.

"I get it, Pastor...I want this source of Love. I want God."

When they were done praying there were glistening tear tracks on both men's faces. Paul got up and hugged Charlie as he sat imprisoned in his chair. He knew his friend would never be physically free in this life, but he hoped Charlie's spirit would soar with the eagles.

Charlie realized, to his relief, that the barking dog was now quiet.

Chapter 31

Coming to an End

The old Chicago love song, "You're the Inspiration" came on the radio and Libby turned up the volume. It was a distraction she desperately needed. She sang along in an attempt to assuage her overwhelming sadness.

She was working in Cabin 11...*alone*. The resort was closed for the season and she had decided to begin the arduous process of closing up cabins, but she was without her partner and friend. Carmen was probably somewhere along interstate 90 driving west again in their pickup with Sadie in the backseat. She was following Jed who was driving their U-Haul truck. They had taken off this morning, when darkness gave way to dawn. It would be a long, cross-country journey for them in separate vehicles, heading from, interestingly, MN to NM, Minnesota to New Mexico.

Before going into business together, the four friends had been advised to have a financial contingency plan for dissolving their partnership if one of the couples wanted out. If within five years their business partnership fell apart, the partners leaving would get their initial investment. If it was five or more years, the partners leaving would get a portion of the appreciated value of the business at the time they left. The Porters were driving away with their initial investment from the resort, money they would need to get started in their new life.

When Carmen and Jed returned from their initial trip out west they were very excited about their future. They had both fallen in love with Albuquerque with the rugged Sandia mountain range rising dramatically above the warm, picturesque valley. It was a beautiful city that combined a very old past and a progressive vision of the future. So when they returned to Thunder Lake and the weather was already dipping close to freezing some nights, it was all the push they needed to quickly pack up their household and head for the warm sunshine of the southwest. It was probably easier on everyone, if they were really leaving, to do it quickly, like ripping off a bandage. It's best to get it over with.

Knowing how hard it would be to leave their friends, the Porters wanted to say goodbye the night before. They didn't want to see Will and Libby as they drove away. So the Edwards watched from their dining room window as the two trucks left at dawn. There was no mistaking the empty feeling in the large resort. The guests were gone for the season and their partners had moved on. Honey had barked as the vehicles rumbled to life, and she continued her alarm well after they were gone. She could feel such sadness in the house and voicing her concern seemed to be her only outlet.

*****

As Libby continued to work in the kitchen of Cabin 11, she was filled with regret and sadness. *What had we done to push our friends away? Were we too bossy...too opinionated...thoughtless, what did we do wrong?* She was lost in her misery when she happened to look out the kitchen window and saw Honey traipsing down the hill from the Porter's empty house. This was not the look of a happy dog, her tail down, her head low, heading someplace with purpose. Libby realized that she was heading for the cleaning van. Honey was looking for some love and comfort. The yellow lab also sensed the emptiness of the resort. She climbed the steps of cabin 11 and lay down on the front stoop. Libby noticed she had something in her mouth...it was one of Sadie's toys. She must have visited their house and found it in their yard.

She went outside to join Honey on the stoop and they sat together in the chilly October afternoon. Honey continued to hold the old ripped toy in her mouth and let Libby hold her and cry into her warm, golden fur.

Will was having a tough afternoon also. He was shutting down the water supply lines for the cabins. He was under a time crunch to get the resort buildings ready for winter. He and Jed had used an air-compressor to force the water out of the pipes in the cabins and from underground pipes between the buildings after their first season. Now he was doing the job alone. There were three wells that supplied water to the resort buildings and all the water lines needed to be totally drained before they froze. It rarely ever happened that all the lines were successfully drained in the fall.

Stubborn pockets of water, sitting in a low point in a cabin or underground were always frustrating surprises waiting for them in the spring. Will paused on that thought; it wouldn't be *them,* meaning him and Jed, but just him next spring. How would he ever get all that work done alone? For that matter how was he going to get all the closing work done before this winter? *How had this happened? Why? God, it just isn't going to be the same without those guys.*

Libby was ready to go back to work in the cabin after a good cry. It's what she needed and she felt better after releasing some of her inner turmoil. Honey stayed on the cabin stoop for a while longer, her front paws crossed and Sadie's toy still in her mouth. When Libby looked out a short time later, she was gone. Libby turned up the radio again and sang along as she worked washing down all the surfaces in the kitchen, especially the stove burners and oven. She didn't want any crumbs to lure in mice or squirrels over the long winter. Then she bagged all the linens: The sheets, bedspreads, blankets and curtains. All these would be laundered and ready to put back in the cabin next spring. Lastly, she vacuumed all the floors to make sure there were no crumbs.

As she lugged the last load of cleaning supplies out of the cabin and into the cleaning van, she realized that her intense sadness had lessened. She looked around at her surroundings, the empty resort always felt so different from the busy days of summer, filled with people having fun. She felt an overwhelming sense of love for this place and their life here.

Libby was coming to terms with the change in their lives and she spoke aloud, her eyes open as if seeing the unseen standing alongside her.

"I'll miss Carmen and Jed, but I'm happy for them. They are doing something they have always wanted to do, experience living out west...living where it's warm...hiking and exploring the mountains. I love them too much not to be happy for their new adventure. This resort was **our** adventure; it had always felt that way. The Porters came along almost reluctantly to this crazy life. I'm so thankful that we had their help for the first two years. What would we have done without them? It would have been too overwhelming.

But now that we have run this business for two years I'm sure we can do it on our own, of course, with your blessing."

Libby pulled out a tissue from her pocket, wiped her tears, blew her nose and then finished loading the van. As she drove past the Porter's empty house she saw a little yellow dog curled up on their front step. Libby was startled, thinking it was Sadie. But then she realized that it was Honey. When Honey saw the van she sprang from the step and followed alongside to their home just down the next hill.

Honey continued to lay on the Porters' front step every day for weeks. She probably wanted to be sure to give them a proper greeting when they returned. Eventually, her vigil on their doorstep happened less often and then not at all. She did pilfer every toy she could find of Sadie's and carried them down the hill to her own yard. The collection of toys eventually disappeared for five long months under three feet of snow. But as April's warm sun melted away winter's blanket, they appeared once again, a little dirtier and more decrepit.

******

After Will and Libby finished winterizing the sixteen cabins, lodge, fish-cleaning huts and bait house, they started thinking about what they should do with the Porters' empty house. They couldn't just let it sit empty, but they also couldn't afford to hire full time help and give them the place as living quarters. Plus they were a little hesitant to work with anyone else after the failed partnership with their friends. The failure and the persistent questions of 'why' and 'what they could have done differently, still lay heavy on their hearts. They finally made the brave effort to walk through the Porters' empty house. It was a task they had been putting off long enough. They walked through the rooms of the small, three bedroom home with Honey. Her powerful olfactory sense went into hyper mode, as it conjured up all sorts of familiar scents of Sadie, Carmen and Jed. She wagged her tail expectantly as she searched each room.

Will and Libby walked around in silence; it was too hard to communicate what they were feeling. They left the empty house with heavy hearts and more questions. Could they make it into another rental unit? Who would want to stay in a cabin way up on a hill, away from the shoreline? A few days later they decided to test their idea and called longtime resort guests, school teachers from Indiana, who liked staying for two to three weeks each summer. Sure enough, the school teachers loved the idea of having the house, and they wanted it for the whole month of July! That was all the encouragement the Edwards needed. The home on the hill would now be the new Cabin 12. The old Cabin 12 had burned down twenty years ago and had never been replaced. When Will and Libby sent out their mass mailing in January to all their guests, they added Cabin 12 to the brochure and website. Large families started calling to reserve the new addition. Over the remainder of the winter, Libby and Will started adding dishes, cookware and furniture to the house.

The last item added in the spring was a wooden plaque, with Cabin 12 painted on it. She attached it next to the front door where an old "Welcome to the Porters" sign had hung only six months ago. Libby thought of Carmen as she hung it on the siding. It was Carmen who made number plaques for all the cabins during the long record-breaking winter of 1996. Libby had used Carmen's simple stencil of three pine trees and then painted number 12 on the plaque.

Chapter 32

Twenty-two years after the Porters left

Retirement at Last

The first week in February 2018 Libby and Will were on their winter trip with their fifth-wheel RV following behind their truck. They were on their third day of travel since leaving the sub-zero temps of Minnesota. It was mid-day when they pulled to the curb of Jed and Carmen's house, their first stop along their journey west to California. The Porter's lived in a beautiful stucco home, sitting on a small hill with a breathtaking view of the Sandia Mountains and the Rio Grande below.

The warm New Mexico sun was shining bright and not a cloud to be seen. The temperature was a balmy sixty-five degrees as Will put the gear shift into PARK and looked over at Libby. "We're finally here, dear." Libby looked over at him, smiled and nodded her head. "I am very ready to be out of this truck for a while." She said this with emphasis on *very*.

As they slid from the high seats of the Ford truck, Will's and Libby's shoes hit the ground with a less than graceful thud. They both groaned a little at their resistant, painful joints as they tried to stand straight after sitting for so long. While they stretched their kinks out, leaning from side to side, there was an eruption of whining and barking from the backseat. A big beautiful golden-blonde with long eyelashes and soft curly hair was crazy to get out. The messy back windows indicated her nose had had numerous contact with the glass surface since leaving Minnesota. There was no denying her. She wanted immediate freedom from the confines of the backseat. Lucy, their eight-year-old Golden-doodle, was their latest furry family member. She knew the Edwards' place well and couldn't wait to greet her friends.

Ten years ago Will and Libby both felt the heart-wrenching void after putting Honey down at the age of twelve. Will had resisted getting another dog. He didn't want to face going through the inevitable pain of losing yet another retriever. Dogs just don't live long enough for those who love them like family. In time Libby realized the void would never be filled for either of them until they brought home another puppy. She started working on Will and soon he also was looking up pictures of doodles online, and it wasn't long before they were welcoming Lucy into their home.

Libby opened the door for Lucy and she flew through the opening and up the steps to the Porter's front door. She barked three times before the front door opened. As Libby shut the truck door, she watched with amusement as Carmen bent over and talked to the wiggling dog lovingly, giving her hugs and squeezes as Lucy gently mouthed Carmen's wrist, snorting and whining with pleasure. Jed had joined them, and Lucy wagged and wiggled her way to him. Carmen met Will and Libby as they walked up the flagstone steps. There was much hugging and greeting, it always felt like coming home to be back together again with their friends.

After hauling in suitcases, coolers and bags, they all made their way to the backyard. Jed had passed around glasses and filled them with his latest home-brew. It had been twenty-two years since they enjoyed his first batch of homebrew when they celebrated the finishing of the remodeled cabin 7. Though, Jed had taken this pastime to a whole new level, studying the chemistry of yeasts, syrups and grains to create perfect hops harmony. Will took a sip and nodded his head with approval. Then he took another and complemented Jed. "This has to be your best yet, Jed. What are you calling it?"

Carmen interrupted before Jed could answer. "A toast to your safe arrival."

They all clinked their glasses and sipped.

Then Jed answered Will in his humble demeanor. "This one I'm calling, Nut-n'Do-n' Ale."

They all chuckled at the name.

Libby raised her glass and the others waited for her toast. "To friendship all these years. We are so grateful for you guys. Thank you for sharing your home with us...again."

They joined glasses once more. 'Clink-clink-clink-clink' and all took another sip of Nut-n'Do-n'.

Will shared their experiences traveling south; the horrible hours driving on icy roads in Iowa, to the temperature finally moderating into Kansas. "We spent our first night in Paxico, Kansas, and our second night in Guymon, Oklahoma." Just then Lucy interrupted him with a very bedraggled, dirty...*something*. She proudly showed it to all, as her whole body swayed with happiness and pride at finding something special.

Carmen looked at it closely. She thought to herself, *what is it?* Then recognition hit and a wave of sadness washed over her face. "Where did you get this?" She asked Lucy as she bent over and cradled her head in her hands. Lucy released the 'thing' into Carmen's hands.

Jed looked at it and said, "Huh...it's one of Sadie's old tug-toys. Lucy must have dug it up or pulled it out of some obscure place in the yard."

Will was incredulous. "That's crazy. Sadie's been gone for over 10 years. But there's no other explanation; the back yard is completely walled off. She couldn't have gotten it from anywhere else."

Jed agreed. "I know it seems crazy that it hadn't disintegrated much after ten years, but in a state with very little rain it's not that unusual."

Carmen hugged Lucy hard. "I miss Sadie so much, but when I hug you I feel better."

Carmen and Libby went into the house and came back with a plate of crackers and cheese, two more beers for the guys and two glasses of wine for themselves.

Jed and Will accepted the beers. As Jed poured his beer slowly into his glass he admitted, "We always felt bad for Sadie, taking her away from 'puppy heaven' at the resort. When we moved out here she was deprived of swimming and big sticks. New Mexico is not noted for either lakes or large trees."

Carmen chimed in. "When we would hike in the mountains and she found a puddle, she would belly flop into the shallow water and just lay there with contentment on her face. If she found a stick she wouldn't drop it but carried it in her mouth like it was a treasure."

They all laughed and Libby said, "Poor Sadie. But she got in a lot of hiking. You guys took her everywhere. She walked alongside you through rain, snow and heat. She was always by your side. I'm surprised she didn't wear off her little pads." Will added "Sadie always remembered us. After so many years she still greeted us with whines, wiggles and even a little trickle of pee to let us know we still *really* mattered to her.

There was more chuckling and sipping from their glasses. Carmen popped a slice of cheese and a cracker in her mouth and remarked, "Sadie and Honey never forgot each other either as they got older. Do you remember how they would play together, even when they rested they'd still touch paws as they slept on the floor, exhausted after playing so hard. I remember that we lost them both the same year."

Lucy could feel their emotions and came over to check on them. She went to every person to illicit a pet on the head and make sure they were okay. After she felt all was well with her humans she returned to her new-found treasure and laid down, confident that everyone was all right.

As the hour was getting late and the cool of the evening settled into the backyard, they moved into the house for dinner. Carmen had made a pork roast. It had been slow-cooking all day. She and Libby got dinner on the table and Jed picked out some music from his phone. They sat down together and Carmen asked Libby to pray. Jed, caught unaware; not being used to praying before meals, had picked up the platter of meat to pass. He said a quiet *"whoops"* and set the platter down. They all snickered and then Libby proceeded to briefly give thanks for safe travels and the food before them.

As the dinner progressed, their conversation returned to their lives together at Safe Harbor and the antics of their dogs.

"Libby, do you remember that time--it was about a week after you brought Honey home. You called my house frantic that your little girl had been taken by an eagle or owl or wild cat?"

"Yes, I remember. Then you had to sheepishly admit that my little imp was visiting you guys."

Carmen responded. "I just thought it was so cute when I heard these little yips at our front door. When I looked out my kitchen window there was your little girl sitting on our doorstep. So I let her in and forgot about the time, until you called me crying."

"I was so scared," Libby admitted. "I had let her out just as the phone rang. I ran in to answer it but a few minutes later when I came out she was nowhere to be found. I called and called for her but she didn't come waddling back to me. Then, of course, my mind went to my worst nightmare--that a large creature took her away. It never dawned on me that she would take that long trek up the hill to your place. The only world she knew so far had been our plowed driveway bordered by six foot high snow banks. How did she know to leave our driveway and head up the resort road to your house?"

Carmen just shrugged her shoulders.

Libby continued, "Well, it was a huge relief to know that she was safe and a very good lesson to me that our little fur-ball was going to be a challenge. No more letting her out alone until she was too big to be eagle meat."

With dinner finished and everyone groaning from full stomachs, they all helped to rid the table and clean up the kitchen. Will fed Lucy, sneaking a few table scraps into her dish. When all was washed, put away and counters sanitized with bleach, Carmen felt ready to leave the kitchen, turning off the lights as she left.

It wasn't long before all of them were ready for bed. Jed stayed up long enough to grind coffee beans and set the coffee-maker to brew at seven o'clock the next morning. He locked the doors and turned out the lights. It had been a big day and sleep came on fast for all of them.

*****

Next morning, with the smell of coffee wafting through the house they were all soon up and clutching mugs of fresh brewed coffee. They sipped in silence for a while as they each checked their devices for texts, news and emails.

Carmen broke the technical spell they were all lost in. "What do you want to do today?"

282

"Well, I know one doodle that is ready for a good long walk," Libby volunteered.

Will piped in, "We all need a good long walk."

"Let's grab a little breakfast and then head across the street to walk the bosque."

An hour later they headed across the street to hike along the Rio Grande River on trails that wound through an area called the *bosque.* Lucy had walked ten miles to their three. Her tongue lolled from her mouth as they crossed the street back to the house. She was in need of water.

Back in the house, Lucy lapped up a dish of water and flopped on the cool ceramic floor in the kitchen. Carmen used a paper towel to wipe up the drool on the floor near her dish and then picked it up to fill it again.

Libby watched her friend care for Lucy and brought up the subject that had been brought up many times in the past. "So, my dear, have you and Jed thought any more about getting another dog?"

"We have. We talk about it often now that we are both retired. We never felt right about getting a puppy when we still worked. We always felt bad for Sadie being alone all day. Now that we are retired we would love to bring a furry friend into our lives, but now is the time that we can do more traveling and it's hard to do with a dog. You guys have talked about traveling with Lucy being difficult, not all the time of course, but *sometimes* you wish you didn't have her along."

"Yes. We end up missing many opportunities when we travel because she's our responsibility. When we want to see a museum or a gallery, we can't leave Lucy in the RV alone. What if she started barking and bothered others in the campground? It's not fair to the people around us."

Jed and Will interrupted their conversation as they walked into the kitchen, racquets in hand and announced they were going to play pickleball.

"Great. Have a wonderful time. Libby and I will just relax in the backyard with Lucy."

After the men left and the two friends headed for the back door carrying glasses of water for themselves. Lucy's head popped up from the kitchen floor and scrambled to her feet to join them.

"Speaking of traveling with dogs," Libby declared with a laugh. "Do you remember the dachshund people that stayed in cabin 6?"

"No. Remind me."

"Well, these people arrived in the latter part of the season, maybe September. I think it was the season after you left. They pulled up to the lodge in this big Cadillac. Will walked out to greet them and noticed in the backseat, some kind of structure was built up to the height of the windows. Sitting on top of the structure were four little wiener dogs. When the woman opened the backdoor, Will watched as she flipped down this carpeted ramp which went all the way to the ground and the wiener dogs scampered down. I was at the beach area raking weeds when I heard them barking. I knew right away it was dachsies. You remember, I grew up with dachshunds so I have a soft spot for them.

Carmen nodded, "Yeah, I remember."

"Well anyway, I walked over to the car to check them out. They were so darling, four miniature dachsies, two black, two brown. The two people, an older couple, were very friendly and happy to see how much I loved their little dogs. So we had started out on the right foot, but things changed in a hurry.

We got them set up in cabin 6--remember, it was the little one bedroom with the huge windows looking out at the lake. A short time later, while I was still raking the beach area I heard one of the little dogs yelp. I looked up at their cabin and the woman was standing on their deck holding her little dog, jumping and screaming by now. The other little dogs were barking and snapping in the air. As I ran over, there was another yelp from one of the dogs on the deck. I was close enough finally to see that they were in the middle of a swarm of angry hornets. I ran up the steps to their cabin and grabbed two dogs while she grabbed two dogs, and we all raced into the cabin. I checked them over for bee stings. The dogs must have bitten at the hornets when they swarmed them because two had fat lips. I was more concerned for the woman as she was having trouble settling down. She had a stinger in her arm that I pulled out. I thought she might be allergic or having a heart attack but she said no to both. She was very upset and worried about her little dachsies, but other than their fat lips they seemed to be calm once they were in the cabin. I left them to find Will and he followed me back to investigate the deck, looking for their nest. Sure enough he found a very incognito nest tucked up high between two railing supports. He said the hornets were still very mad and frantically flying around so he would have to wait for them to settle down and go back to their nest, probably after the sun went down, and the temperature cooled.

When the hornets settled-in for the night Will came back with a ladder and a pail filled with gas. He put the pail under the nest and as the fumes raised up into the nest all the hornets died in seconds. They all fell into the bucket of gas and the job was done.

Unfortunately, those people left the next day. They packed up their little dachsies and headed back home. I felt bad. The woman seemed very traumatized."

They sat in silence for a while then Libby added, "You know, Carmen, that incident sticks in my memory because it still bothers me that someone left our resort so unhappy. It was just one of very few upset guests in all the years we owned resorts. Most were happy to be by the lake and enjoy time with family and friends. All we needed to do was treat them kindly and honestly and they were excited to come back year after year. Owning two resort was mostly a wonderful experience and a privilege to have known so many great people over ten years of resort life, both at Safe Harbor and at the smaller resort we had near Pine River."

Carmen was petting Lucy's head as she rested it in her lap. Carmen admitted with a smile. "It was a great experience for Jed and I too, even if it was only two years."

*****

Their time together was coming to a close. It was their last day and Carmen insisted on doing all the Edward's laundry while Libby packed their things back into their 5th-wheel trailer parked at the curb. Jed and Will hauled out suitcases, bags and boxes for Libby to put away. Lucy's job was to pace nervously between house and RV, watching every move, showing great concern about being left.

After all the packing was done, everyone showered and dressed for going out for dinner. Watching everyone get ready made Lucy very worried; she had a feeling she would be left behind. It was a dead giveaway when they all took turns petting her curly coat with "we'll be back soon" assurances. She got her treat from Libby and then the door was shut. She watched at the front window for a while and then curled up on Will and Libby's bed to wait for their return.

Once the two couples were settled in a booth at the Mexican restaurant in Albuquerque's Old Town district, the server arrived to drop off menus and take drink orders.

"I'll have the Albuquerque Brown Ale," Jed said and Will nodded, "Me too."

Libby and Carmen decided on two margaritas on the rocks."

The server left and they looked at the menus until she returned. She left their drinks, chips and salsa and took their order.

While they waited for their meal, the four friends ate chips and salsa and soon their conversation returned to more resort stories.

Will took a sip of his beer and began to laugh, almost spitting out his beer. "Do you guys remember those crazy Polish guys that came to the resort?"

Jed asked, "You mean the guys that were there for the storm?"

"No. Not those Polish guys. These guys were younger. They came later in the season, August I think. They stayed on the north side of the harbor. They had a huge motor mounted on their small speedboat. Do you remember them?

"Oh-h-h my gosh, I remember them," Carmen said as she wiped her napkin over her mouth. "They were characters all right."

Jed laughed and said. "Yeah, I remember them. I was a little taken aback when they pulled up to the gas dock wearing nothing but speedos. You don't see many guys wearing speedos at a fishing resort. I noticed they had two buckets full of crawdads in water. Weren't they the ones who had so much trouble with their motor? Their first three days were spent tinkering with their motor out in front of the lodge. Smoke billowing out as they adjusted the carburetor and gas lines, trying to get the darn thing running further than a few feet from the harbor."

Will chuckled, "Nope. That was the Polish guys from the storm. They were quite entertaining too, but these guys dove for crawdads. Jed, it seems like at the end of the week you had to go to their cabin for something and they invited you to have a bowl of their crawdad boil."

"Yes, one of their girlfriends called from back home needing to talk to one of them. So I hiked over to the other side of the harbor, to cabin 15 I think, and as I got close the aroma was amazing. So while one of them went to the lodge to call his girlfriend, the other invited me in for a taste of their crawdad boil. It was very good. While I ate, the guy with a very heavy Polish accent I will add, told me they don't like to fish. Instead they like to dive for crawdads, and Thunder Lake has some very large ones. He said they found the best area off Red Cliff Point."

Libby laughed and said, "We have certainly met a lot of characters and made many good friends through our years owning resorts."

Will nodded in agreement with Libby and said, "Well, what about some of our crazy experiences with animals? Do you guys remember when we first bought the resort and we lived together in your home the first season? Libby and I--and Golda--lived in the basement and all the months we lived in the basement we heard a creature running very fast in the ceiling tiles above us.

"Oh yeah, I kinda' remember something about that," Carmen said thoughtfully, still trying to bring back any memory of those first days together at the resort.

Will expressed more of what he could remember. "Libby and I would lie in bed at night listening to the race going on above us. It was too loud to be a mouse. We hoped it wasn't a rat! It didn't seem like a rat though. Rats don't race around. They are stealthy, I think."

Libby chimed in, "I think at one time we thought it might be a woodrat but we really had no idea."

"It's so weird that we didn't hear it upstairs," Carmen commented.

Jed agreed. "Yeah, we never really did hear it. We were even there all that following winter and summer. Maybe it finally got out after you moved out."

"Well, after you guys left we eventually made your home into a large rental. The first big group of fishermen who stayed there in the spring had enough people that they used the basement bedroom. The guys sleeping in the basement started hearing the racing feet their first night. When they told me about it I was incredulous. How could something be in that ceiling for two years and you not hear it and we not hear it as we worked on getting the place ready to be a rental? I didn't admit to them about our past experience with the mysterious critter, but I said I'd take care of it while they were out fishing for the day. I only hoped I could. It was such a mystery.

Anyway, later that morning I entered the basement of your old house and listened. Not a sound came from the ceiling. I walked into the bedroom, still no racing overhead. On a whim, I opened the closet door, and there sitting on the upper shelf was a startled little squirrel-sized creature only with big, bulging eyes. It looked at me intently. I think he was in a quandary about what to do. I quickly reached for a blanket off the bed and used it to grab for the little guy. It sprang off the shelf, flew over my shoulder and onto the bed. I quickly shut the bedroom and closet doors so he couldn't get out of the bedroom. Then the race was on. I kept throwing the blanket over him, but he was so fast that he was halfway around the room before the blanket landed. We did this routine numerous times until finally I got smart and threw the blanket ahead of the direction he was running and *BINGO,* I got him. I carefully picked him up in the blanket and held him close to me. Then I cautiously pulled the blanket away to find his head. He was so scared, I could feel his little heart beating like a drum through the blanket. I knew what kind of creature it was finally because when it was running like a streak around the room, I could see that it had wing-like skin attached between the front and back legs. He was a flying squirrel. The mystery was finally solved. They are nocturnal so he was only active at night. That's why we only heard him when we were in bed. You guys never heard him because you weren't down in the basement at night. You were upstairs sleeping. Well anyway, I put him in a box

288

and took him in my truck down the road a few miles. I let him go in the woods at the end of White Ash Road."

Jed shook his head and chuckled. He thought about it for a minute and then said, "So when we lived there, we didn't hear him because we were upstairs at night but also I suppose he hibernated over the winter. He must have had a secret way into the house between the top of the foundation and the base of the house. Crazy."

Will said with amusement, "He was so cute and so-o-o fast! He was just a blur as he ran around that room!"

*****

Will asked their server for the bill and after arguing with the Porters for a few minutes about who should pay, he finally laid down a tip and got up to pay at the till. Once they were all outside together they took a moment to enjoy the starry night sky.

Libby exclaimed, "What a gorgeous night. It's always so fun to be with you guys and reminisce. It was quite the adventure we thought up sitting around the campfire twenty-five years ago." Her eyes sparkled with welling tears.

Carmen chimed in, "We wouldn't have missed such an incredible adventure for anything."

Will teased, "Now that we are all retired--I just read about a small resort for sale up on Thunder Lake..."

Carmen and Libby both chimed together, "No way!"

Jed just laughed and said, "Well, Willy, I think that's not going to happen this time.

Author's Note

I felt called to write this book for many reasons.

Reason one for writing this story is to share my unashamed, crazy about, love of dogs. We have had three lovable, intelligent retrievers in the last thirty-five years. There have been many a time we have been dumbfounded by their understanding and their deliberate planning to outsmart us or other animals. They have added so much love and depth to our lives.

Reason two for writing this book was to remember many of our memories from running a resort with our good friends back in the 1990s. Life was so different back then. Cell phones were not yet available to the masses. GPS had just been introduced to the market. Computer programs for small businesses were in their infancy. We had email but no social media. Businesses still used the yellow pages (what are yellow pages?) for advertising. We were in the resort business on the cusp of many changes, but those technical changes hadn't made it north yet.

We were exposed rather quickly to the ill-will some locals had for the native people, the Ojibwe. Coming from the Twin Cities area, we were surprised by the tensions between the Ojibwe and the sportsmen when we moved up to northern Minnesota lake country. Some of our guests bragged to us and others in the lodge of their cutting through the Ojibwe nets laid out across sections of the lake. We were not sure how to handle the hostile attitudes of these few. Most of our guests came from different states so they were unaware of the tension, but the Minnesota fishing clientele had it out for the Ojibwe netters. The fact that Minnesota laws gave the Ojibwe people special lake privileges didn't help soothe their hard feelings.

The early history of the people in northern Minnesota has been one of tragedy, tough grit and determination--dealing with the vast wilderness and little money, especially for many native families. It was a great honor to get to know the old resort owners that started resorts around the lake back in the 1930s. I wish so much I could recall with clarity, some of the stories of their parent's boldness and tenacity in carving out a family business so far north. There were stories told of Indians traveling across the frozen lake in the winter to get to better hunting grounds on the other side of the lake, and white families having experienced the fear of these traveling Indians walk through their doors without knocking, and expect to be fed. *The Ojibwe felt differently about their food and possessions. They did not feel the need to ask permission, it was meant for any and all to partake.* As neither understood the other's language, the settlers and their visitors spoke no words but just fed the travelers, watching them eat with some suspicion and curiosity. Then without a word the Indians would leave. These two cultures, for the most part, learned to put up with each other in the vast wilderness they shared. For the first resort owners, winter's isolation was usually six months of going nowhere. The snow was so deep that travel, many times, was impossible except by snowshoes. Now so many of those brave, hearty people are gone and their stories along with them. I am sad that I didn't make more of an effort to record their experiences.

Even though this novel was about a resort on Thunder Lake, the many incidents and stories I used came from our real life experiences on beautiful Leech Lake. This is a terrible name for a supremely gorgeous lake so I chose a more fitting name. In order to save embarrassment or upset from persons I chose to use in my story, I changed their names. Even the name of our resort was not Safe Harbor, but Chippewa Lodge. Bud Campbell was a young boy when his parents built and ran Campbell's Chippewa Lodge back in the 1930s. Bud related stories to us of his dad cutting big blocks of ice from the lake and storing them in the bait house, covering them with thick straw in order to keep them from melting too fast come spring. When the resort guests caught fish in the summer, Bud's dad could then keep them from spoiling by putting them "on ice" for their guests. Bud was quite the mechanic as a boy and built himself a fan-driven snow vehicle. He said one time he fell out of the vehicle (admittedly going too fast,) on the ice and had to watch helplessly as it went round and round on the frozen, snow covered lake. As he continued, in vain, to catch the vehicle he grew tired and collapsed on the snow, to watch the incongruous sight. He said he became fearful when he felt a presence off to his right. He knew he was vulnerable, a boy out alone on the ice. He felt this fact keenly as he remembered many times seeing packs of wolves cross over the ice in the past. When he warily turned his head he was relieved to see it was only a small red fox. The fox was also watching the circling machine intently. Bud was very relieved. They both sat on the ice, a comfortable fifty feet apart, and watched until the gas ran dry and the vehicle finally stopped spinning. Then, bored with watching young Bud as he struggled to pull the machine back to shore, the fox headed off across the ice. Those years must have been quite an adventure for him and all the other resort families back in the 1930's and 40's.

Reason three for writing the book was to express my insatiable desire to understand the spiritual realm that surrounds me (and you.) There are characters in this novel who are fictitious. I used their lives in the story to share the idea that there is another dimension, God's dimension that intervenes for us. I call that dimension, the "kingdom of God among us." God's angels are warriors, comforters, messengers and protectors. Who of us knows if the stranger who encouraged us when we needed a supportive word or hug, or saved us in the nick of time, or stayed with us after a terrible accident just to comfort us until help arrived, was a caring human or an angel sent from their dimension to intervene in your time of distress. Many of you will not agree, casting these spiritual ideas aside. Everyone must come to their own conclusions in matters of the heart and spirit.

Author
Mary Ernst
If you are interested in writing to me, I would love to hear from you.
ernstmaryk@gmail.com

"The Kingdom of God is emerging as the only solid foundation for human society. We have hid this kingdom light under the bushel basket of church forms and structures. We must now put it on top of the bushel as a shining beacon."

Back cover of 'Victorious Living'
Written by E. Stanley Jones

54612472R00176

Made in the USA
Columbia, SC
02 April 2019